THE BOOK
OF
INVASIONS

THE BOOK
OF
INVASIONS

BY

ROD VICK

www.penmorepress.com

ISBN:-13: 978-1-957851-02-0(Paperback)
ISBN:-13: 978-1-957851-01-3(e-book)

BISAC Subject Headings:

FIC028010/FICTION / Science Fiction / Action & Adventure
FIC028140/FICTION / Science Fiction / Crime & Mystery
FIC028090/FICTION / Science Fiction / Alien Contact

The Book Cover Whisperer:
ProfessionalBookCoverDesign.com

Address all correspondence to:
Penmore Press LLC
920 N Javelina Pl
Tucson AZ 85748

DEDICATION

To My Lovely Wife Marsha

To Dr. Richard Nelson and Al Young, superb teachers
and my most beloved mentors

ACKNOWLEDGEMENTS

I would like to thank Niels Martin Schmidt, scientific leader, Zackenberg Research Station; and Soren Kyed, logistics, for their willingness to share a wealth of details about the amazing facility, ZERO Station, in northeast Greenland, for this novel. Their kindness in answering questions and even emailing floor plans brought an increased sense of realism to this book's opening chapter.

I would like to thank Liz Hacker-Hadad for her assistance in researching overland travel from Egypt to Israel.

Thanks also to Michael Fox of boynvalleytours.com (web site www.newgrange.com) and Clare Tuffy from the Boyne Valley Visitor Center for their help with details about public access to the Newgrange Passage Tomb. Thanks also to Michael for allowing me to use his photograph of the Newgrange Passage Tomb in the novel.

In addition, I would like to thank the following amazing individuals for their editorial assistance and advice, which I relied upon extensively in completing rewrites: Jared Drahanovsky, Becky Grotelueschen, Becky Hanson, Tom Kornkven, Chris Maxfield Ponder, Becky Roehl, and Kevin Wilcox.

My thanks to Michael James, and to the editors and production team of Penmore Press for their invaluable assistance in bringing this project to life.

Finally, I wish to gratefully acknowledge the following:

"Gimme Three Steps"
Words and Music by Allen Collins and Ronnie Van Zant
Copyright © 1973, 1976 SONGS OF UNIVERSAL, INC.
Copyrights Renewed
All Rights Reserved Used by Permission
Reprinted by Permission of Hal Leonard LLC

CHAPTER 1

The plane appeared without warning, sweeping in low over the steel-gray waters of Young Sund and gliding onto the clay runway just north of ZERO Station. Sasha dimly registered the buzz, since her real focus was on counting out points and moving pegs along the wooden cribbage board resting on the small table in front of her.

Hell, who was she kidding? Her real focus was on the Danish hunk seated on the far side of the cribbage board.

Despite the small part of her consciousness the buzz occupied, after thirty-four days in this far-north outpost, even Sasha Crowe—whose ears were more accustomed to the Chicago horns, sirens, and rumbling trains that had provided an incessant background cacophony for two-thirds of her life—could easily recognize the familiar snarl of the Twin Otter plane. Her science team's study of ice recession at Greenland's Zackenberg Ecological Research Operations Station—or ZERO Station for short—was supposed to have lasted twenty-eight days and yielded predictably distressing results. But something extraordinary had happened, a remarkable discovery in the ice, and her stay had been extended.

Sasha was glad for the extended stay for multiple reasons, and one of them was Mathias Schmidt, who sat across from her now, considering his own cards with exaggerated seriousness. The 29-year-old from Taastrup was part of the seasonal logistics staff that kept Zackenberg running from May through early September. Typically, the staff kept to itself after supper hours, but Mathias had begun to spend increasing amounts of his down time in the common area of House 9, where the research teams relaxed and bunked. Sasha told herself that he was simply being friendly, but now, after weeks of card games and quiet conversation, she wondered whether something else was happening.

"Must be a new pilot," said Felix Mogensen, a gaunt 24-year-old grad student from Copenhagen, peering out of House 9's wide windows even though the Twin Otter had now disappeared behind the building. "They're supposed to fly at least 500 feet above Young Sund, you know, to avoid disturbing the wildlife. That *roevuhl* almost nicked the rooftops!"

This was not the first time visitors had arrived in Zackenberg, Sasha noted, but the red Twin Otters that carried passengers and supplies had never flown in from Constable Point at this hour.

"Bet they'll get an earful from Aksel," Felix added with barely suppressed glee.

Aksel Hermensen was the director of operations at Zackenberg, and at 21:00 hours, was probably in his office in House 5, one of ten bright blue buildings that stood out from the greens and browns of the surrounding tundra. He generally kept things running smoothly at the research site, welcoming new teams of scientists and grad students, making sure they went through orientation in order to remain safe in this remote region and to have as little impact as possible on its fragile environment.

"Do you feel guilty?" asked Mathias, smiling coyly over his cards.

"Guilty?" Sasha squinted at him. "About what?"

"First, *you* upset Aksel's finely tuned little world by staying on, and now, airplanes are dropping in at all hours!" he said playfully.

"It's complete chaos! Nothing like the well-oiled machine we had before you arrived!"

Sasha stuck out her tongue. *I'll oil your machine*, she thought, and then blushed, grateful that she had not blurted *that* aloud.

"Maybe he's landed here by mistake, you know?" continued Felix, always a bit more anxious than circumstances warranted, always compelled to share his thoughts with the world. He had now been joined at the window by Anke Sorensen, 30, a teaching assistant from Denmark's Aarhus University who had become Sasha's closest friend over the past six weeks. "Maybe the pilot thinks he's at Daneborg," Felix added, referring to the military base just 25 kilometers to the southeast. He now moved toward one of the side windows to try and get a better look.

Mathias set his cards face-down. "No peeking," he said. Shoulder-length blond hair, strong chin with a stubble of beard, and sky-blue eyes. Sasha decided she could definitely get used to that view. He rose from his chair. "I'd better see if Aksel needs help. Who knows? Perhaps there is some mechanical trouble. Or a medical issue." He shrugged.

Returning his smile, she lay down her cards. Sasha Crowe, 26, athletic, and gifted with waves of stunning auburn hair, was one of five Americans at Zackenberg. They had come to study the density and composition of the rapidly shrinking ice sheet that rested upon much of Greenland. Zackenberg, over the past decade, had become an increasingly important player in the game of climate study. Sasha guessed that most people had no idea of the volume of ice covering the island nation—or that, if it were to melt, the level of the world's oceans would rise by twenty-three feet. This was partly due to Greenland's rather quiet stature, the least densely populated country on the planet. Legend stated that Erik the Red, exiled from Iceland, had discovered a habitable region, settled, and named it

Greenland in the justifiable though ultimately forlorn hope that the name would attract more settlers.

However, scientific ignorance also relegated discussion concerning the island to background noise. While most people thought of the world's nuclear superpowers as holding the probable key to mankind's fate, more of the scientific community was beginning to consider the role of Greenland and other ecologically fragile regions in predicting—and possibly heading off—the extinction of the human race.

"Ah!" said Felix, stroking his unkempt beard in satisfaction as he pressed his nose against the side window. "There goes Aksel! Now they're in for it!" The three others lounging around the common area, listening to music over headphones or reading, did not react to Felix's narration. The six remaining researchers had already retired to their dorm-style rooms down the hallway and probably would have cared little if the Snoopy Thanksgiving Day parade balloon had just tethered itself to Zackenberg's fuel depot. Indeed, their recent discovery in the field made Sasha wonder whether *anything* could surprise them anymore.

No one had arrived at ZERO Station looking to stagger the scientific community and add a new chapter to history and science textbooks. The first few weeks of their stay at the research outpost had been uneventful for the American team. Then, only a week ago, Haldon and Bernard had discovered something in the ice.

Artifacts.

Which, of course, was impossible. Everything they knew— everything that historians and archaeologists or anyone had written up to this point—suggested that humans had arrived in Greenland long *after* the ice. So now the detective work would begin. Sasha's team had carefully worked to remove the remaining ice encasing the artifacts without damaging them, had taken photographs of everything and had journaled extensively. Most of their research and observations were stored on their laptops and would be downloaded in Chicago when they returned. For now, it was their "little secret". And their edge-of-the-world location made it a bit easier to keep.

One drawback of spending time at Zackenberg was communication with the outside world. In that respect, ZERO Station was aptly named. The outpost was one of the planet's northernmost research facilities, located in the National Park of North and East Greenland. Cell phones did not work. House 5 held satellite phones, but those were not used for casual conversations, nor to transmit data. One could send an email from House 5—the major buildings, whether living quarters, administrative, or work areas were referred to as "houses"—but the process was tedious and involved writing one's message onto a sheet of paper for Jayson, the assistant, to send. Replies, when they arrived, would be printed out and hand-delivered. And because of the low baud strength, no photos or attachments were allowed.

For the most part, during a research stint, what happened at ZERO Station stayed at ZERO Station.

Upon returning to their schools or think tanks, however, they would all write papers about their discovery, publish them, and become famous. Or more accurately, become as famous as research scientists can become in a world that worships reality TV stars and supermodels. They would get a few speaking engagements, if they had an aptitude for that sort of thing. They would have a leg up on the crowd when applying for grants. Some would write books—most of which would sell dozens of copies. And just maybe they would become part of a historical footnote. Or perhaps more than a footnote, considering the strangeness of their find.

If the artifacts were genuine.

Discovered in the valley to the northwest where ice cover had recently receded, the artifacts consisted of three items. The first seemed to be a boat, or more accurately, part of one, made of rough-hewn wood, no larger than a common rowboat, but far older and primitive in construction. The second was a pouch that had survived its journey as a consequence of being lashed to the boat. These items alone, considering where they were discovered, had the potential to dramatically alter the narrative about Greenland's human history.

But it was the third item that defied logic.

Inside the pouch was a sleeve of parchment, amazingly well-preserved beneath the ice. While later testing would tell for sure, it appeared to have been made from the skin of a sheep or goat. Anke, who had considerable training in ancient history, suggested that the parchment resembled some of the earliest-known world maps. They had not been able to read what was written on it, for none of them had studied the language. Yet, they had agreed that the symbols, with one striking exception, were likely Egyptian hieroglyphs.

That was what made it all so bizarre, so impossible.

Egypt was 4,000 miles away.

No human remains had been found with the wreckage, suggesting that the boat's original occupant may have been lost at sea. Yet, even if someone had been aboard to pilot it for part of its journey, there were no currents that explained how the craft had come to rest in this place, if it had indeed originated in the land of the pharaohs.

Of course, the researchers knew there might be a host of possible explanations that would assert themselves over time. For now, however, it was a most unusual and tantalizing mystery.

And because of its potential to reshuffle the cards of history, one that was being handled with caution.

They had been advised not to post photos to social media or to release information to outside sources of any kind—not that this was possible for those still at ZERO Station. Still, there was no margin for error. Should the artifacts turn out to be part of a hoax, for instance, irreparable damage might be done to the reputation of Zackenberg and the HARP Foundation, for which Sasha worked. The four other Americans represented other U.S. think tanks and research centers. Since cell phones were useless and all communications in or out of ZERO Station had to go through House 5, the compliance of students and researchers was easy to monitor. In truth, there was little need to worry. As serious scientists, they realized that the artifacts could impact their future credibility and, more importantly, their ability to attract grants.

Anke had summed up their cautious attitudes. "No one wants to be that scientist who endorses the next Cardiff Giant."

Sasha had not understood the reference.

According to Anke, in the mid-1800s, a couple of rural New York farmers had carved a statue of a man, seemingly in agony, out of an eleven-foot block of gypsum stone, and then had buried it for a year on the farm property. When they "discovered" it a year later, they claimed that it was the petrified body of a giant from Biblical times and charged viewing fees to thousands of people who believed their story. Newspaper reports trumpeting the amazing find swept the world, and many so-called experts examined the giant and swore by its authenticity—until P.T. Barnum challenged its veracity in a lawsuit. When the truth was revealed, those who had championed the giant, some of them scholars and archaeologists, were humiliated.

For Sasha and the others, the message was clear: Once you

were labeled a sucker in the scientific community, it was difficult to recover.

Mathias had grabbed his coat, exited House 9 through the boot room, and now strode purposefully toward the airstrip, disappearing out of view of the front windows. Sasha joined Felix and Anke at the side window. The Twin Otter had taxied back toward the fuel depot, out of sight from their angle.

"After Aksel's done with him, that young pilot will probably drop off future passengers at Daneborg, you know, and make them walk cross-country!" said Felix, laughing then at his own joke. Sasha turned away from the nothing-to-see view and took only a single step before a sharp crack sounded outside.

Anke inclined her head, startled. "Did the plane make that sound?"

"That sounded like a gunshot," said Felix, his face now radiating concern.

Of course Felix's suggestion, born of his natural anxiety, was ridiculous. Guns were not allowed at Zackenberg, Sasha knew. A couple of rifles were locked in a gun safe in House 5, and these were often issued to the leaders of research parties that might be expected to encounter polar bears on their treks into the valley or beyond. However, no teams were out at this hour.

Before any of them had a chance to give the matter much thought, Mathias burst into view, racing around the corner, past the window, onto the deck and finally through the door. "They shot Aksel!" he cried, his face a twisted mask of grief and terror.

Anke gasped and attempted to steady him by grasping his forearm. "What? No!" The others who had been lounging about the living room stood, uttering various exclamations of disbelief.

Mathias spoke between deep, rasping breaths. "Four! Four of them got out of the plane! Get in your rooms! Lock yourselves in!"

Terror squeezed her so that she could hardly breathe, yet, Sasha felt tightness in her throat that she knew was because of Aksel. Despite his rigidness, he had displayed a wry sense of humor and had watched over them all like a mother hen.

The others moved down the narrow hall, but Sasha hesitated when she saw Mathias turn toward the door.

"What are you doing?"

"I have to get to the rifles!" said Mathias hoarsely. "They've got assault weapons! We've got nothing!"

He bolted out the door before she could beg him to stay. Rushing out onto the deck after him and leaping down onto the hard ground, she was torn between the impulse to follow Mathias, and the natural instinct to barricade herself inside House 9. The sound of close voices, just around the corner forced Sasha to abandon either choice and instead scramble beneath the building.

"Follow him!" said a male voice, the accent vaguely Germanic. "Take care of him and any other staff."

All of the habitable structures at Zackenberg were raised a foot or two off the ground so that air could circulate underneath, discouraging mold and rot. Sasha dragged herself far enough into this crawlspace so that she was directly beneath the common area of House 9. Moments later, she heard the clout of boots on the vinyl-covered floor and then the click of the door separating the common room from the bedroom hallway being opened.

This can't be happening!

She struggled to control her breathing as the man who had spoken earlier called out, his voice muffled only slightly by the wooden sub-floor. "Listen to me! Come out! We can come and get you if we have to! We have keys to all of your rooms!"

Aksel's keys!

Not a sound.

"We have keys!" repeated the man. "If we have to come and get you, it will be less pleasant!"

Silence at first. Then, the sound of two voices, low but arguing. A few seconds later, the click of a lock mechanism releasing, and one of the doors down the hall opened.

"What do you want?"

She recognized the tremulous voice as belonging to Dr. Haldon. She heard the shuffling sound of his shoes against the smooth floor, moving down the hallway and into the living room.

"Please," Haldon continued, "don't hurt any of these young people. If you're looking for money or equipment, take it and go. We'll offer no resistance. But please, don't harm anyone." Sasha heard a hoarse grunt of agreement and realized that Haldon's roommate, Dr. Bernard, had followed him into the room.

"That's very reasonable of you," said the intruder. "What we want is for the others to come out here and bring their electronic equipment. Laptops, tablets, cell phones, all of it."

To Sasha, this seemed an odd request. Ripping off a Best Buy in Cleveland would be far easier and more lucrative than flying to Greenland to rob a small group of college students and scientists. However, she heard the muffled sounds of what she assumed was Haldon and Bernard moving back down the hallway, going door-to-door.

Outside, in the distance, three more gunshots sounded.

Sasha prayed that Mathias had reached the rifles and that the shots had been fired by him.

Five minutes later, she could tell that all of her colleagues had been assembled in the living room. All seemed to have come quietly, if not enthusiastically, except for Felix, who had needed to be dragged out by his roommate, Erik, another grad student. She could hear him sobbing quietly.

Sasha began to shiver, for she had left House 9 without a jacket. Then she stiffened as the leader went through roll call, which he must have been reading from a document. "Erik Andersen. Kale Arendt. Sasha Crowe."

She held her breath

"Sasha Crowe," the leader repeated. After waiting several moments, he addressed the group tersely.

"Where is she?"

"I don't know," said Haldon.

"She said something about walking out to the ice recessions in the valley to confirm her earlier measurements." Sasha recognized the voice as belonging to Anke. She had to stifle a sob. It was complete bullshit, of course, which Sasha realized—with heartfelt gratitude—as an attempt to get at least some of the intruders far enough away to give her a chance to escape.

The leader continued with the roll call. "Felix Mogensen. Hans Mundt…"

Sasha heard the sounds of restrained crying and of Aksel's name being spoken quietly.

"What is the purpose of all this?" asked Haldon, who seemed to have, by default, assumed the mantle of spokesperson. "Why did you…" His voice trailed off.

No one said anything for a few moments, and Sasha could not tell whether the question had been ignored or whether the leader was deliberating over the answer. Then: "Haven't you ever dreamed of changing the world, Doctor?" asked the leader. "Isn't that why you're here at Zackenberg?"

Without waiting for an answer, the leader asked, "The artifacts you retrieved from the ice, did any of you photograph them?"

No one said anything for a moment. Then Haldon said, "What do you mean?"

"No games please, Doctor," replied the leader. "Do you think we would come all this way if we did not know?"

Haldon took a beat to consider this before answering. "Because there's no reception, many of us didn't carry our cell phones into the field. We used a digital camera in the dry lab to document the pieces."

"And where are these digital images?"

"The camera and storage devices are still in House 3, the dry lab," explained Haldon.

This did not make any sense, thought Sasha. Four men fly to a remote research station, shoot a man, and hold researchers at gunpoint over some photographs of a 5,000-year-old boat and artifacts with possible Egyptian origins. The value of the artifacts, of course, was beyond calculation, if they were genuine. However, they were not the sort of things one could sell on eBay, or, for that matter, on the black market. Their value was scientific, historical, not monetary in a practical sense. At least not enough to justify a military-style assault on a remote outpost like Zackenberg. On top of it all, it was incomprehensible—considering the difficulty inherent in sending messages from ZERO Station—that these men even knew of the existence of the artifacts.

"Actually," said the leader, as if reading Shasha's mind, "one of you did take a cell phone photo. Isn't that right Dr. Bernard?"

A bit of shuffling about, a mumbled protest, but then Bernard's voice: "Maybe three or four. That's all."

"And," continued the leader, "who knows? Maybe you are all lying. No? Maybe you all have photos on your phones and tablets and memory chips. Plus, you've certainly written about your discovery. For the books and papers that will make you famous."

A murmur of apprehensive confusion.

"What can it matter?" asked Haldon. "Please, take our laptops if you wish. Anything you want, it's yours. But don't hurt these good people. They've come here to try and do things to help the planet."

A bit of a chuckle. "How very noble. But let me explain how dangerous a single photograph can be. Dr. Bernard's photograph. He got sick a week ago, yes? Food poisoning, though they thought, at first, it might be something worse. So they flew you to Queen Ingid's Hospital in Nuuk—really the only decent hospital on this block of ice. While you were there, Dr. Bernard, you used the rare luxury of satellite service to send messages to Frannie."

"My wife," said Bernard, sounding as though he might cry. "Please—"

"And you sent a photo you had taken!"

"Please..."

"A photo of the parchment that had been recovered with the boat. Not a very good photo. It only showed a portion of the amazing find. But your wife—your Frannie—decided to post it to social media. To show what her *amazing* husband was doing. And to make a little joke. What did she write, Dr. Haldon, to go along with the photo? '*Egyptian writing in Greenland? Maybe next they'll find a pyramid made of snow!*' A very humorous woman. And that's when the world became a more dangerous place."

"I..." Bernard began, and then had to stop to compose himself. "She normally doesn't. I just assumed she wouldn't. My own excitement must have..." His voice trailed off.

The leader continued. "Hundreds of people saw the photo. Most of them probably forgot it within minutes. But one remembered it. Recognized something in it. I won't bore you with the details, but that one person was part of a group. Small, only a few thousand worldwide, but possessing a vast reach. The parchment you photographed is a primitive map to the location of something we have been searching for a long time. You only photographed a section of it. But it showed enough to set the wheels in motion. So now, we are here to see the whole map!"

"If it's money you want," said Haldon, "our foundations and sponsors have very deep pockets. I'm sure they would gladly pay in return for our safe—"

The leader's laughter stopped Haldon short.

"I'm afraid you do not understand. It is not money we seek. It is something that makes money irrelevant!"

Haldon's silence prompted the leader to continue. "Imagine having no fear, Doctor. Not even of God!"

Sasha shuddered, partly because of the cold, partly because it was clear that this man was insane, part of a calculating organization of fanatics. He was not interested in money. He wanted the parchment. And he wanted to destroy any record the researchers had created of it so that there was no danger of others following the trail. History was filled with cruel and vicious narratives of such extremists, made drunk by their quest for what they hoped would give them absolute power, impossible to reason with.

Footsteps thumped across the outer deck. *Matthias!* thought Sasha, but the door opened and closed without incident or comment. Sasha bit her forearm to keep from crying out, tears spilling onto the cold soil, her whole frame shuddering in grief.

"Now," continued the leader, "I would like you all to lie down on the floor, on your stomachs, and clasp your hands behind your heads."

They had already killed four people, if the three more recent gunshots meant what she feared. Sasha bit back another sob thinking about it. But the pain of her teeth in her own flesh cleared her mind, too. She had to do something. Perhaps *she* could get to the guns now that the attention of the fanatics was diverted away from House 5. Crawling to the other side of the building, she scrambled from beneath it. Standing, she noticed that cans of petrol intended for the generator had been carried up from the fuel depot near the runway. A stab of horror slashed through her.

They're going to burn down House 9! They're going to kill everyone, destroy the evidence!

She took the caps off the three largest containers and laid them on their sides, letting the petrol gush out onto the frozen ground. The act caused her an almost palpable pain, for she knew how cautious they were supposed to be with respect to ZERO Station's eco-system. However, this was life or death. And the petrol had given her an idea. She grabbed the remaining smaller canister and raced through the chill, dusky evening toward House 3.

Sasha knew what she had to do. She only prayed that there would be time. At some point, the leader would determine that Sasha Crowe needed to be found, that she was not out in the valley. And then they would search. Her heart pounded wildly and tears streamed down her face.

She thought again of Mathias.

Can't let them win!

A few minutes later, her grim deeds were finished. She had sloshed petrol onto the boat and the entire insides of House 3 before setting the building ablaze. Then she had sprinted to House 5. Now, as flames and black smoke lapped at the dull evening sky, she crept outside once more. The guns were still locked away and, unfortunately, she had no key, but she at least had the satisfaction of knowing that the murderers would never find their "prize".

However, she had discovered the bodies of Mathias, Jayson and Anna, the cook. It had taken all of her self-control to not scream or spend precious minutes weeping over them as she had finished her tasks. Now, standing beneath a fuliginous parody of the Milky Way, she hesitated.

What do I do now?

The intruders had disabled the satellite phones and the computers. She had no weapons. It occurred to Sasha that her best bet might be to head cross-country toward Daneborg. It would be cold, but if she kept a brisk pace, she might avoid hypothermia and make it to the military base in three or four hours.

But if the fanatics searched ZERO Station—and they would—and found no trace of her, would they come after her on the ATV? If they had Aksel's keys, they had the keys for those, too. And if they caught up to her out there, with nowhere to hide, she was done for.

Think! There has to be a way out of this!

A sound like thunder rolled across the station and Sasha cautiously peered around the corner of House 5 to see that the intruders had carried more petrol from the fuel depot and set House 9 ablaze.

No! She fought back a scream. If she cried out, then they would find her for sure. *Can't let them win!* she repeated to herself. But the thought of her friends in the house... It was maddening. All gone! People she had come to know closely in the past weeks. She noted that there had been no additional gunshots. Had her friends been alive when the fire was ignited? She could hardly bear it.

There was nothing you could do.

But there was no time to lose in guilt or weeping or memories. Now, two of the men rushed toward the dry lab, cursing.

They'll find me if I hide here. They'll anticipate that I'll try to make a break for Daneborg. And if I try to hide outside instead, I'll die. I've got no warm weather gear to survive a night in the valley.

Then, an idea occurred to her, so bold that it frightened her to think about it. On the other hand, they would never expect it.

The plane!

The Twin Otter carried up to 19 passengers, but there was a baggage compartment at the back that could be accessed through the cabin. If she stowed away in there, she might be overlooked. The Twin Otter had probably been stolen, for it bore the markings of the company that typically shuttled passengers and supplies to Zackenberg. When the killers returned to Constable Point and abandoned it, she would be safe. And then she could tell what she knew to the authorities.

The fiends would pay, she would see to that.

The distance from House 5 to the fuel depot was short, yet she moved carefully, crouched low, kept a structure between herself and the men as often as she could. Suddenly, she wondered whether a fifth man might have been assigned to guard the plane. She canvassed the depot for anything that might give her an advantage against the killers. Then she crouched, squinting toward the Twin Otter, which was now only one hundred feet away. Seeing no movement, she darted out from the cover of the building and ducked behind the plane. Opening the right rear cabin door, Sasha climbed inside.

Empty.

She breathed a relieved sigh.

Unlatching the small door between the two back passenger seats, Sasha faced a dark, empty space too low to stand in. If the murderers opened this door, she would have no place to hide. On the plus side, they had brought only their guns, which meant they had no equipment to stash. As she pulled the latched door shut behind her, the darkness was overwhelming, except for a couple of inconsequentially small slivers at the base of the door and where the wall met the curved ceiling. Sasha's cell phone had been packed away in her duffel—which she was reminded, with a dull ache in her chest, was now ashes—and she wished she had it now to provide comforting light.

She waited. But not for as long as she would have guessed. After only a few minutes, she heard hurried footsteps, which paused abruptly just outside the plane. It seemed just a single individual. After a few moments, the footsteps resumed and then sounded on the steps, and the rear cabin door clicked open. Sasha held her breath, afraid even the tiniest of sounds in the empty plane might alert him. Whoever it was seemed not to have noticed anything amiss, for he stayed only a moment before slamming the cabin door and running off again toward the base.

How long would they search for her? she wondered. It seemed that they wanted to get rid of all witnesses, but there had to be a limit on how long they would stay and chance being discovered by those who would come looking when Zackenburg failed to keep up its regular contacts with the outside world.

Or perhaps she had overestimated her importance to them, for barely five minutes later, she heard muffled voices, presumably the whole group, and then the click of the rear cabin door again. Their voices quieted, and then Sasha felt the vibration of boots on the floor. After that, silence as the men strapped themselves in.

Sasha's mouth went dry. Why are they so quiet?

As if in response, the leader's voice boomed out. "Let's go. Follow the shore, Clavering side, until you reach the open sea. Then take us out about a mile."

Then the only sounds were the engines humming to life. Sasha had flown in the cabin of a Twin Otter during her arrival at Zackenberg. Now she held tightly to cargo straps as the plane jounced down the runway and veered skyward. She wondered why the leader had instructed their pilot to head out to sea. Could they be meeting a boat? The thought horrified her, yet she could think of no way such a rendezvous would be possible, since this Twin Otter was not equipped with pontoons for sea landings. They climbed for at least five minutes, and then the craft began to level out.

The temperature in the cargo area was frigid, and Sasha wondered whether she should chance moving about or attempt to find a tarp with which to cover herself. A moment later, she heard a sound that chilled her even more.

"Miss Crowe!" said the leader, speaking loudly in order to be heard over the buzz of the engines. "I assume it is you, since you were the only one missing at roll call! Congratulations on a superb plan. However, when you come in off the tundra, make sure to wipe your feet. When Max returned to the plane to get an extra torch while the rest of us searched for you, he could not help noticing. Wet clay leaves just enough of a calling card to betray you."

Sasha said nothing. Silence was one of the only cards she had left to play.

"Why don't you come out and join us?" continued the leader. "You may as well ride comfortably, at least for a while. I'm afraid you won't be with us for long, however. You've been quite the troublemaker. Our employer is not going to be happy that you destroyed the parchment. Although we have half of it, thanks to Dr. Bernard's intolerance of spicy food and irresponsible social media habits. It may take many years before we figure out the rest of the puzzle. So we are closer, but not there quite yet."

She continued to say nothing. Anything that she might utter at this point would simply be shrill, vulgar and hateful. He was a madman who deserved to burn in hell. They all were. She had no desire to converse with murderers.

"Still not talking?" When she continued her silence, he laughed softly. "Well, I should really thank you. It was important that we silence everyone who might have seen the parchment. When you turned up missing, I thought we might be in for a long night. I mean, we couldn't just leave you. But then, as I said before, you unintentionally announced yourself and gave us a little gift. An early night. So yes, thank you. We will be back in Constable Point before too long."

Hatred coursed through her. She wanted to cry out, wanted to hurt him with words, but instead bit her lip so hard that it bled. Yet, beneath the hatred was something else, perhaps a mix of confusion and dread. If their destination really was Constable Point, why were they heading out to sea?

"You probably have many questions, no? Let us just say that some secrets must be dearly protected. The authorities will discover your unfortunate friends, but no one to tell the tale. Lots of bullets. Two buildings burned to the ground. But no clue who did it. No reason for it. No evidence that an ancient map had been found or ever existed. All electronic evidence gone. The map and artifacts themselves just ash. The only irregularity? One of the researchers is missing. It may take them awhile to discover which one. Perhaps they will even think you were in on it, eh?" He chuckled quietly.

Sasha was far beyond tears. What she wanted was to make these men pay. For her colleagues. She thought of Matthias.

"Of course, you must already realize that you will not be around to proclaim your innocence. You will simply disappear! We are now about a mile up and more than that from shore. It's a long way down, and the sea is frigid at this latitude! In a minute or two, we will pull you out of the cargo hold and send you out the rear door. You needn't worry about drowning. The fall will be sufficient. And your demise will give us some measure of satisfaction after your thoughtless and unfortunate destruction of the parchment map. So, Miss Crowe, what do you think of that?"

In response, Sasha removed the cap from the item she had brought with her from the fuel depot—her *advantage*, a five-litre container of petrol—and emptied its contents onto the floor. The liquid seeped under the door, creating a growing dark spot on the aisle carpet.

The leader squinted at the wet area, and then the smell of the fuel reached his nostrils.

"No!"

At the same moment, Sasha flicked the butane lighter she had brought with her from the dry lab.

A brilliant fireball lit the sky south-east of Daneborg, and then plunged earthward in a steep arc where, half a minute later, it was swallowed by the cold sea.

CHAPTER 2

It was dangerous for Ricky to be in a bar with a vodka gimlet sitting in front of her. Dangerous for any recovering alcoholic.

But, she told herself, it's only one. After six years of sobriety, she had earned the right, hadn't she? And it wasn't as if she didn't have a good reason.

Goddamn Bricker.

David Gates, her boss and the owner of Gates Cultural Heritage Management, Inc., or GCHMI, had hired Bricker seven months earlier to dig, sometimes operating the heavy excavating equipment, other times hoisting a pick or shovel. About thirty, six-foot-three, red bearded and well-muscled, he boasted relentlessly about his never-miss-a-day lifting schedule, and—as far as Ricky was concerned—he never missed an opportunity to be a world-class prick.

For the first couple of weeks of his employment, it had been fine. She had noticed him joking around with some of the guys, who seemed to tolerate—if not actually like—him, an occupational hazard borne by the coworkers of self-absorbed bullshitters. Only an occasional glance in her direction. Sometimes lingering a little longer than she found comfortable. Curiosity, maybe, like everyone else. Then one morning, he had asked, loudly and without preamble:

"So what's your story? The scar and all."

Just beautiful. No 'Hi, I'm Jordan Bricker. Thought it was about time we met.' Just elbow your way to the front row of the freak show, point, shout out anything that comes to mind. No class.

She had noticed that he spoke with a slight southern accent. Ricky had nothing against the south per se, but she suspected the accent was an affectation, for Gates had mentioned that Bricker had formerly worked in Wisconsin, where he was born and raised. Not exactly a state teetering on the Mason-Dixon line. This suggested to Ricky that Bricker was a phony. It also triggered memories of Alabama, when she was thirteen. Just one night half a lifetime ago, but a game-changer.

Fucking Alabama.

She ran her finger along the cool glass, trying to force away the memories, to imagine the ecstasy that would accompany even a single sip of the gimlet.

She hated talking to people. To anyone. And being an arrogant phony didn't sweeten the deal. So her reply to Bricker had been concise.

"It's nothing."

This simple rebuff, which most would have shrugged off and forgotten, had seemed to set off something dark inside Bricker, almost as if she'd tripped a fine wire hidden in the sand. Something that resented not being favored with a real answer, even though the subject matter was probably highly intimate and unpleasant. There followed taunts and inappropriate comments, almost always delivered gracelessly and without warning, when no one else was within earshot, often days or weeks apart. In her opinion, they bordered on obsessive, suggesting that he entertained not only an unwholesome fascination regarding her disfigurement, but felt entitled to share its intimate details.

Three days later: "So what are you embarrassed about? You do that to yourself? Are you one of *those*?"

She had walked away without responding.

The following week: "Why don't you have plastic surgery or something? Are you some sort of lesbo who don't care how she looks?"

She had kept on working, ignoring him.

After two weeks, an interval that had convinced her that Bricker had lost interest: "Hey, next time you give a lumberjack a blowjob, remind him to put down the chainsaw first!"

No response.

And so it went: "Y'know, it's really fuckin' disrespectful not to answer someone when he talks to you. Do you understand what I'm sayin', or are you some kind o' retard?"

She closed her eyes against the memories. Tucked into a booth now for privacy, Ricky imagined the wooden table in front of her upon which the gimlet continued to wait: four nefarious gin scoundrels lurking behind a single, innocuous lime frontman who sang the sort of sweet promises that might allow him to tease his cool melody between lip and tongue. She enjoyed this image alone. Most restaurants and bars were more than happy to grant a little privacy to the girl with the eight-inch facial scar.

Goddamn Alabama.

Going to Gates over the harassment seemed futile. Though a few co-workers might have overheard a shred or two, she suspected there was nothing to establish the sort of pattern that would get the bastard fired. Having experienced Bricker's obsessive tendency toward retribution for even a minor slight, she knew that in the aftermath of any unsuccessful charges against him, things would only get worse.

So she continued to meet his gibes and assaults with silence. After awhile, she had wondered whether her instinct to ignore Bricker had proved correct, for it had gotten better at work. Not that Bricker had become a candidate for sainthood. He just went about his job, maybe growing tired of or bored with the taunts. She still ran into him at lunch. A picnic table was normally set up just outside of the portable site office where members of the team could eat, weather permitting. The men usually occupied the table, although there was room for her if she had wanted. She opted, instead, to sit on the ground, her back against the outside of the office, her lunch a protein bar and water from a refillable bottle.

Bricker always arrived like a warrior returning from battle, slamming his lunch bucket down loudly on the table and shouting, "Semper fi!" This never failed to elicit tight smiles or a couple of patriotic fist pumps from the others, though to Ricky, it was just another example of what a lowlife poser the man was.

"I know, he's obnoxious, but he's a hard worker," Gates had said surreptitiously to Ricky, after she had settled against the shed for lunch one day, just as Bricker's latest booming *Semper fi* rang out. Then Gates had leaned closer and dropped his voice to a whisper. "But between you and me, he's got no record of military service. Zippo."

Thankfully, there were intervals, days or even weeks, where Bricker would be working a different site or a remote portion of the same site, and she would not see him at all.

She now let her eyes roam the bar, attempting to distract herself. She always noticed ceilings. This one had those twelve-inch tiles that looked like Swiss cheese, a number of them stained with coppery splotches. Ceilings told you a lot about a place.

GCHMI was currently working a federally funded project

south of Chicago's Little Village, a geographic area of huge importance to the Potawatomi and Algonquin tribes prior to the treaties that required they vacate the land after 1833. For centuries before the arrival of European explorers, it had been a portage point between two rivers, the Chicago, which connected to Lake Michigan and thus to the rest of the Great Lakes, and the Des Plaines, which ran to the Mississippi River and, ultimately, the Gulf of Mexico. French explorer Robert de La Salle, recognizing the immense importance of this converging of waterways, is reported to have stood in the marsh and proclaimed, "This will be the gate of empire; this the seat of commerce."

Initial project excavations had uncovered fragments of human bones, not particularly unexpected, given the area's history. And so GCHMI had moved in to conduct an archaeological review and assure compliance with historic preservation laws.

Ricky opened her eyes to the dim lights of the bar, shuddered, closed them to the cold tempter again, unwillingly reliving the events of the afternoon.

She had sat against the shed at lunch, half listening to the table conversations about sports and money and—in Bricker's case—the hot chick that he had allegedly banged the previous evening—a recurring theme in his lunchtime discussions, though Ricky suspected a vivid imagination and a lot of online porn. Whatever.

It had rained yesterday, and Mickle had urged her to sit at the table. "You sit down there on the ground and you're gonna be all mud. Come on. Besides, it's Gino's birthday and he brought cake." Reluctantly, she had taken a seat next to Mickle on the end of the bench with Bolan beyond. Both possessed some kind of archaeology credentials or degree. Opposite her had sat Gino Pinkowski, with Bricker next to him and Hernandez at the end. Pinkowski was another digger and Hernandez seemed a sort of jack-of-all-trades who handled just about anything Gates threw at him. Gates himself usually ate in the portable office with his wife, Cyd, who was also the company's office manager.

"Here." Mickle had slid a thick slab of cake in front of her.

"Thanks."

Bricker's eyes had widened in mock horror. "Jesus, the Bride of Frankenstein actually speaks!"

Mickle had shot him a look. "Christ, Bricker, lay off."

"What?" Bricker had responded to the group with an endearing smile, pretending to be wounded. "It's just a fucking nickname. If I had a scar and you guys called me Hellboy or something like that, I'd consider it a badge of honor and laugh right along with you. I swear, people nowadays got no sense of humor."

He was full of shit, she knew. The nickname with which he had christened her had hardly been intended as a "badge of honor." His weeks-earlier comments had clearly been aimed to belittle her, to make her hurt. Still, after a few minutes, Hernandez had the paper open to the sports page, and conversation had centered around the upcoming Bears season. Things settled into an innocuous cacophony. The cake—made by Pinkowski's wife—was good, and Mickle and the others had always treated her well. Sitting by herself was safe, but it was good to be *At the Table* for a change.

"Jesus, who the fuck is this?" Bricker had shouted suddenly, tapping the front page of the newspaper that Hernandez held open. Ricky had looked up and immediately had felt herself go rigid. On the front page was a follow-up story about the massacre at Zackenberg, including pictures of the slain researchers with local ties. Bricker's finger had rested on the photo of a beautiful young woman, smiling and fair-haired. "If I'd been one of those terrorists, I'd have done her before I'd killed her! And maybe after, too!"

Bricker had giggled stupidly and looked around the table for the laughter he typically expected in response to his boys-will-be-boys, sexually explicit banter, but this time, had received only stunned silence. An instant later, Ricky, whose face had clouded in hurt, embarrassment and anger, spat in Bricker's face. Almost as a reflex, Bricker's hand had shot out and delivered a hard slap across her face, knocking her off the bench and onto the ground.

Mickle had immediately stood to help her up. "Jesus, Bricker, that's her sister!"

Bricker had sneered. "Yeah, fuck you, Mickle. And my sister's Khloe Kardashian!"

Then Pinkowski had stood. "It's true, you moron. How can you not know that?"

Ricky figured it was because Bricker had been working off-site when the news had first broke, because he wasn't the type to surf the news sites, had mistaken her grief over her sister for just another cloudy manifestation of her personality, or he had simply been too dumb to connect the dots. None of that made him any less a fetid pile of steaming human garbage.

Then everyone had stood up from the table.

"Fuck all you guys!" Bricker had shouted threateningly, gesturing toward the crumpled paper resting atop the table. "No way Bride of Frankenstein is related to her!" Then, as Ricky had been helped off the ground by Mickle, Bricker had seemed to grow worried. "And you all saw! She fucking spit! I coulda clocked her good!" He had raised his huge arms meaningfully. "I woulda been justified! But I gave her an open palm! You saw! A slap! Not to hurt her! Just teach a little lesson!"

The door of the office shed behind her had burst open at this point and Gates—perhaps hearing the shouting, perhaps seeing the commotion from his window—had come across the muddy ground to the table at a trot. "What the hell is going on?"

Bricker had rounded the table to meet him. "We were having lunch, just like every day, and they start fucking with me!"

Ricky had glared at him, massaging her red cheek. "He said he wanted to fuck my dead sister!"

Bricker had seemed to find this impossible to process. "No way that's... are you kidding me? Shit, then she spit on me!"

"And then Bricker hit her," Mickle had added quickly.

Gates, a small man, had taken another step toward Bricker. "You hit this young woman?"

"A little slap! And fuck, she spit in my face!"

"You laid a hand on one of my employees?" Gates had said evenly but more forcefully. "You're done! You're fired! I want you out of here now!"

Bricker's hand had shot out again, viper-like, delivering a vicious slap that had knocked off Gates's glasses. The others had quickly moved beside their boss. After a tense moment, Mickle had picked his boss's glasses out of the mud while Hernandez pushed Bricker back a step.

"It was a slap! *A slap!* Look at these!" He had held up his barrel-shaped arms. "I coulda hurt him if I'd wanted! But it was all open hand!" Then, seeing that no one was going to blink or back down, he had given them the finger, uttered a series of vulgarities punctuated by "Semper fuck you all!" and headed toward the site gate.

Ricky pinched her eyes tighter, but she could smell the lime of the gimlet. *Just a sip*, the tempter seemed to be singing. *That first sip will feel so good, so right.* And she knew this was true. It was also perhaps true that, if she had controlled her own emotions she might not be sitting in The Edsel, a dive bar whose walls were lined with black-and-white photographs of old cars. Or if she had just sat in her usual spot at lunch. Out of sight, out of mind. She hated it when people noticed her. Lost in the background was where she preferred to be.

Gates had examined his broken glasses. "Looks like I should have gone with the buy-one, get-one free deal." Then he had turned to Ricky. "You okay? Maybe I should have Cyd take a look."

Ricky had shaken her head. "I'm fine. The guy's an asshole."

Gates had regarded her silently for a moment. "This is my fault. I looked the other way on a lot of the crap he said. He was toxic... and I look the easy path. I... I let it slide. I'm sorry."

She looked at the ground. "I... I shouldn't have spit."

Gates had sighed heavily. "No. You should have kicked him square in the balls. I *would* have looked the other way on *that*! On the other hand, that loose cannon probably would have killed you, and then I'd be out one of my best workers."

Ricky had felt the gazes of the others and wished she could disappear, wished she had decided to work through lunch.

Her eyes snapped open to the dim bar. The gimlet still sat there angelically on its napkin. She reached out again, tested the feel of the stem in her fingers.

Gates had rested a steadying hand on her forearm. "Hey? Really? Are you all right?"

In truth, she had felt cold, unable to keep herself from trembling. On a typical day, she interacted with almost no one. Her comfort zone was working in the dirt between the strings on a three-meter-square plot and whatever artifacts were buried within.

Artifacts. The word hit her like a jab to the stomach. That was part of it too, the reason she now sat staring down a gimlet. Maybe a reason even bigger than the roid-raging, soldier-wannabe, charm-school dropout's manners. It had been more than a month, and still no word about Sasha.

"You sure you're okay?" Gates had asked, noticing her

discomfort.

Ricky had nodded.

"Well," he had continued, not buying it but not wishing to cross a line, "why don't you take off the rest of the day? My guess is you're not going to be able to concentrate much on working. Or feel like it."

Ricky had mumbled an agreement. She needed to get out of there.

"Need a ride home?"

"Bus is right at the corner," Ricky had replied, pointing. "Thanks anyway."

Gates had regarded her for a moment. "I know it's hard for you right now." His eyes, perhaps involuntarily, traveled to the newspaper fluttering on the ground next to them. "Any time you need a day, you feel free to take it. Or more than a day. Okay?"

She had nodded again. Then she had gathered her things and set off on the short walk to the bus stop. When she was out of sight of Gates, she had changed direction, walked three blocks, and plunged into The Edsel.

They say that when something happens to one twin, the other feels it as well. Perhaps only a subtle sensation that something is amiss. Perhaps a sudden feeling of alarm for no apparent reason. She had even heard a few individuals describe instances of acute physical pain felt simultaneously.

Yet, Ricky Crowe had felt nothing when her twin sister had died. No ominous dream. No catch in her breathing. No telepathic warnings. Zilch.

In fact, the news out of Zackenberg's ZERO Station had been confusing, slow in coming, and often contradictory.

The day after what was being referred to as the Zackenberg

31

Massacre, she had received a telephone call from Dr. Leo Brenner of the HARP Foundation, who informed her with effusive sympathy that it appeared her sister had died in a tragedy at the research station. Details, he had said, were still sketchy.

About the same time, the news channels and online sites began their saturation coverage. Then Ricky had received a telephone call from the FBI, indicating that it could not positively confirm that Sasha Crowe had been among those killed. The victims had been badly burned by a fire fed by accelerants, and so it could be days or weeks before the identities were established. Somehow, this information was almost immediately leaked to the media:

"Startling new information tonight on the mass killing at Greenland's Zackenberg research station. According to a source close to the investigation, officials are now considering the possibility that one of the researchers may have played a role in the tragedy."

Thankfully, no name had been leaked. But it was merely a matter of time. Speculation was already rampant on the Internet.

Yet, it made no sense. Ricky knew that Sasha was incapable of such a thing.

And then there was the plane crash.

Ricky refocused on the untouched gimlet. Perhaps this would be enough, she thought. Perhaps merely having it there in front of her would help her to get through this hell of loss and anger heaped upon a really shitty day at work. She closed her eyes again, let out a long breath, tried to ignore the part of her that seemed to be screaming for the sweet relief of gin and lime.

A Twin Otter aircraft had been reported stolen the same day as the killings at Zackenberg. Scraps of fuselage that matched the missing plane had washed ashore near Daneborg, but nothing else had been found. The singed condition of the scraps suggested a mid-air explosion.

The FBI released a statement saying that it was working with the National Police of Denmark, which provided law enforcement to Greenland, to investigate a possible link between the missing plane and the Zackenberg tragedy. What this might have to do with her sister—if anything—Ricky was at a loss to say.

Two weeks after the killings, the medical examiners had finished identifying the victims from House 9.

Sasha Crowe had not been among them. There had followed a lengthy interview with FBI Agent Scott, who had visited her at the job site.

Did your sister have any history of mental illness?

Did she communicate regularly online with any individuals in foreign countries?

Did your sister own a gun?

Did Sasha Crowe, to your knowledge, ever mention or communicate with any militant or anti-government organizations?

Did she have a boyfriend?

Did she ever become violent in response to events that occurred at work?

And dozens more.

She had no idea whether her answers—mostly no, although she was aware that Sasha *had* communicated with researchers from Greenland and Denmark—had helped Agent Scott. For her part, they simply seemed to muddy the issue. She began to wonder how well she had really known her twin. Did Sasha have secrets about which Ricky knew nothing? Was she still alive somewhere in the world? Or was her fate linked to the mystery of the crashed plane?

Two men in grungy factory blues entered The Edsel, laughing loudly, and seated themselves at the bar, ordering after-work beers. She now realized that she had been staring at the gimlet for hours.

Their conversation quieted once their own drinks arrived, and Ricky thought again of her sister.

In some respects, it was hard to believe she and Sasha were twins. At least in recent years. With identical explosions of curly, rust-colored hair, sprinkles of freckles across the nose bridge, a predilection for dressing alike, and jewel-green eyes, their primary school teachers had often mistaken one for the other.

That was then. Ricky estimated that no one had mistaken them for family in the past decade.

They were still both 5'7" with green eyes and freckles, but that was where the comparison ended. Where Sasha's vibrant red curls played upon her shoulders, Ricky's hair was now straight, dyed nightmare-black, and hung like a funeral shroud, often obscuring a portion of her face. Where Sasha wore soft blushes or liners that projected warmth and blended well with her naturally striking eyes and lips, Ricky wore no makeup.

And there was the scar. Her Alabama souvenir.

Three more people entered the bar, distracting her. Only one sat anywhere near Ricky. He appeared to be stoned.

As the newcomers were absorbed into brown shadows, malty smells and the subdued conversations of the establishment, Ricky's eyes returned to her table, although her fingers gently traced the irregular, pinkish line extending from just outside and above her left eye and down along her cheek to half an inch below her lip. While it did not render her grotesque, it was not something that one could miss—like a key gouge along the length of a Mercedes. Would he have cut her if she had not resisted a decade ago? She would never know. She might be dead. No regrets.

Well… perhaps one.

Leaving Ireland.

That had been seventeen years ago, when she and her sister

were nine. Their father had died in an industrial accident the year before, and the settlement had been enough to convince Rose Crowe, their mother, to join her sister in Chicago. Even in Chicago, the twins had played the same games, read the same books, done well in school.

Until Alabama.

She did not like to talk about it. Or even think about it. But it had changed her profoundly, as violations of trust often do. She knew some people were able to internalize such things, shrug them off and carry on as if the world had not been forever fractured.

Ricky was not one of those people.

Sirens sounded outside. A few heads turned automatically, returned to their conversations even before the wailing began to dim. The stoned guy at the nearby table seemed to be asleep.

You should go, she told herself. *Just get up right now and walk out of here. You've been strong for six years. Five and a half. Go to the gym and punch the goddamn bag!*

But she could not go. The memories flowed like muddy water through the breach in an earth dam. That was when the grades had slipped, after Alabama. When she had stopped looking forward to the parties. Then she had begun to spend more time in her room playing fantasy games like *Clandestia* with faceless online "friends". She had stopped watching television completely, replacing it with books, usually dark fantasies, historical mysteries, or tomes of mythology, particularly anything of Celtic origin. Trying to cling to her heritage, she supposed.

And she had grown away from Sasha, who in high school, became the party girl, the popular one. The cheerleader. Yet, in college, her sister had settled down. Naturally bright, she had discovered an interest in science and, to both of their surprises, found herself majoring in climatology.

Ricky had been drawn to archaeology—the strangeness of ancient civilizations, the mysteries beneath one's feet. The dead. As a result of her poor grades, Ricky was unable to follow Sasha to Northwestern. Instead, she took general education credits at a community college, as well as science, history, and archaeology classes that would prepare her for transfer to a four-year school, at which she could pursue her major. She applied for an internship of sorts with Gates during her second year and proved herself a reliable worker who picked up the nuances of the business quickly. She had continued to work for GCHMI part-time after her internship ended. Even after her grades had tanked, Gates had gradually increased her hours until she was nearly full time.

He was a good man, David Gates, who in his mid-fifties seemed to regard her as kind of a wayward daughter who, with a bit of nudging and kindness, might ultimately land on her feet. Yes, he had screwed up with Bricker, but Ricky knew he felt awful and would do whatever he could to make it up to her.

Where the hell had the tears come from?

They surprised her, and although she endeavored to wipe them away with a sleeve, they kept coming. She tried to catch her breath. Instead, a wretched sob escaped, and she pounded her fist on the table, sending ripples across the surface of the friendly gimlet. All the death and the violence and the loss and the unfairness—and after all of it, the kindness and flawed decency of Dave Gates had been the thing that destroyed her, had made her blubber like an idiot. What the hell kind of world was it anyway?

She grasped the gimlet and, without hesitation, downed it. She knew that it was mostly psychological, but it seemed to calm her immediately—an old friend, promising warmth and smiles and more friends to come.

She ordered another.

CHAPTER 3

She woke in stages, slowly, feeling less inclined to continue the journey toward consciousness at each checkpoint. Her head ached behind the eyes and above the brow, and her limbs felt as if they had been hollowed out and refilled with sand.

Eventually she opened her eyes to a narrow, dingy, shelf-lined back room. A single fluorescent tube provided grudging yellow light, revealing silver kegs stashed beneath the lowest shelves, cases of beer, bottles of hard liquor, jars of olives, loose sheaves of papers and ledgers, a microwave oven, and a small, liberally dented refrigerator. The place had a dusty, yeasty smell that made her stomach roll.

Ricky realized that someone had folded a faded, patchwork comforter and placed her upon it on the unswept floor, its cracked linoleum littered with grit, scraps of paper, a few shards of brown glass, and mouse droppings. Fragments of muddy conversation drifted in from elsewhere, and, feeling alarmed by the unfamiliarity of it all and her lack of memory regarding how she had gotten there, Ricky struggled to stand. As she reached a sitting position, a man she recognized as the bartender from The Edsel stepped into the room to pluck something from a shelf. He was probably mid-sixties with white hair and the wide, mashed face of a boxer.

"You okay?" he asked in a voice like a wooden hinge.

"Why am I here?" She tried to take stock of herself. Had she been touched? Or worse?

"You passed out. Been back here for three hours. Gimme a sec. We're kinda busy."

He stepped carefully around her, moving out of the room and back behind the bar. She sat, gathering her strength, angry with herself, not certain whether she cared that she was angry. A few minutes later, the bartender returned.

"You fell asleep at your table," said the bartender, continuing the narrative, jabbing a thumb back in the general direction of the bar. "Too many gimlets, I guess."

"How many?"

"Too many. Junkie at the next table woke up, started going through your pockets."

Ricky patted her pockets, thrust her hands inside to take inventory.

"He didn't get anything," said the bartender with a modest smile. "You woke up and clocked him."

"I what?"

"Slugged him. I mean, it was a hell of a punch. Broke the little fucker's nose, I bet. I had Teddy toss him out. You passed out again right after that and Teddy and I brought you back here. Excuse me."

He headed out to the bar again. Ricky slowly stood. She had no recollection at all of punching the junkie. Right now, she doubted she could punch a hole through a sheet of newspaper. A minute later, the bartender reappeared.

"Here," he said, offering her a glass containing clear liquid.

"Seven-up."

She sipped. Then took a larger gulp. It felt good. Not gimlet good, but welcome cold on her cottony throat.

"Three hours?"

He nodded. "Sorry we didn't have a cot or nothing. S'pose we coulda sent you home in a cab. But I didn't want to go poking around in your pockets to find an address."

"Afraid I'd 'clock' you?" she asked.

The bartender seemed surprised by this question. "No. It's just that, well, it wouldn't be proper, you being a young girl."

Ricky stared at him for a few moments and then said, "Thank you. For being decent."

The bartender seemed grateful for the compliment as well as a bit embarrassed. "Well, I dunno. Do you need me to call you a cab? Or... what do they call 'em? Oobers?"

Ricky shook her head and took another sip from the glass before answering. "I'll be all right. The bus."

The bartender nodded, picked up the blanket and shoved it into a random cubby on the shelf. "Well, I'd stay away from those gimlets, if I was you."

As she exited the bus half an hour later, the night breeze brought the warm, alive smell of Lake Michigan, hidden in the darkness beyond the last of the streetlights. For reasons she could not articulate, Ricky was not yet ready to return to the silent apartment, and so she walked toward the lakeshore bike path, two blocks to the east.

What was I thinking? she asked herself. She had passed out in a public place, had nearly been robbed. Yet, as much as she hated herself for having given in, she knew how easy it would be to cross that line again.

The second time was always easier.

A few minutes later, she paused beneath the stars reaching far out over the lake, trying to draw something from them to strengthen her. For thousands of years, people had found answers to their most profound and daunting questions in the stars, hadn't they? Where, she wondered, were the answers *she* sought?

Where are you, Sasha?

But there was no answer forthcoming. Sasha, who had taken Ricky in off the streets, had shamed and threatened and ultimately begged her toward sobriety. This, Ricky knew, had literally saved her life. Knowing that, on most nights, someone else was nearby, *that* in itself had been enough to keep her from giving in or going to pieces.

And today had confirmed what Ricky had already suspected. Without her sister's steadying presence, Ricky was too weak to avoid being pulled back into the abyss.

Everything was so immaculately ruined. She longed for the days of their youth in Ireland. It was as if Death, in taking her father, had carried away the family's compass, leaving them to stumble ahead into an uncertain and malignant darkness.

Finally, Ricky turned and headed back to their building. She used her key to let herself through the security door and was halfway across the marble floor of the lobby before she remembered her mailbox. She turned and stepped into the niche on the right that contained the locked boxes for each apartment. Using her key again, she opened hers, removing two business-sized letters and a larger padded envelope. She took a few steps out of the niche and toward the elevator before skidding to a stop.

The two letters were clearly bills. But the padded envelope was addressed by hand, and she would have recognized that handwriting anywhere.

It was from her sister.

CHAPTER 4

The older, remodeled, four-story brick building that housed the HARP Foundation was less than a mile from Ricky's apartment. An easy walk. And she hoped that the morning's cool air would rally the sort of clarity she needed. As muddled as she had felt after waking in the back room of The Edsel, her thoughts were even more disarrayed now.

She had slept fitfully for perhaps two or three hours after discovering and opening the padded envelope. The elevator ride to her eleventh-floor apartment had seemed to take forever, but once she had locked herself inside, she had hesitated.

What would she find when she opened it?

The envelope had been addressed to Ricky, the handwriting of its sender unmistakable. Would it be Sasha telling Ricky that she was alive, and that she was not responsible for the horrors at Zackenberg? That scenario had seemed far too good to be possible.

Or would it, more likely, be Sasha simply checking in, narrating the dry, scientific details of her stay at the frigid outpost in a note that she had placed in Zackenberg's outgoing mail prior to the horrors of the massacre? After the authorities had finished examining the crime scene, operations at ZERO Station would almost certainly have resumed, at least on a limited basis, and that would mean sending along any mail that had been languishing in the facility's out box. By the feel of it, however, the envelope contained something more substantial than a single sheet of stationery.

Opening the envelope as if she were unwrapping a bandaged wound, she had discovered a folded leathery scrap of tattered parchment, half again larger than standard typing paper. Ricky could only guess how old the parchment might be, and she felt an acute sense of intimidation at having such a fragile item in her possession outside of a research setting.

It seemed to depict a map. Her sister had scrawled a message near an edge in black marker.

GET TO HARP – MASON CROCKETT

MARE DESIDERII

KEEP FROM CULT!

Her heart had beaten wildly as she stared at the words. If Sasha were dead, they were the last words her sister would ever write. And those last words implored Ricky to get this parchment to people where Sasha had worked, to two individuals, Mason Crockett and Mare Desiderii. And then the final plea.

KEEP FROM CULT!

Despite the chilling tone of the message and its grave importance, Ricky felt something lift away, one of many stones pressing upon her soul.

Sasha is innocent!

On one hand, Ricky felt relief. This seemed to prove her sister was no murderer. Yet, her heart ached for her twin, imagining Sasha desperately scribbling this message to her after the killers had arrived at Zackenberg. The tears had streamed down her cheeks as Ricky realized this was also likely proof that Sasha was no longer alive. She would not have sent the parchment map to her except as a last resort. Her sister's desperation was evident in the fact that she had scribbled her message directly onto what was presumably a valuable historical artifact, partially obscuring some of the document's original symbols, something Sasha would never have done except under extreme circumstances.

Another realization quickly came to her: She now possessed significant information that authorities investigating the massacre did not have. While the various investigating bodies had largely given up on the idea of the massacre being a one-woman show orchestrated somehow by the missing Sasha, they had determined no clear motive for the murders. However, reporters had discovered a social media post from a researcher who had been briefly hospitalized. The post suggested manmade items, including the remains of a boat, had been discovered in 5000-year-old ice. Why these might interest thieves, zealots, or terrorists—if the artifacts were indeed their target—no one seemed to know. And while Sasha's message still didn't provide the answer to why the terrorists had killed the researchers, it seemed strong evidence that the artifacts had drawn them to Zackenberg.

Ricky had opened her laptop and brought up one of the news stories that mentioned the online post made by the wife of a Dr. Bernard. She felt her pulse quicken as she realized Bernard's posted picture precisely matched a section of the parchment she now held. There was little doubt. Bernard's post had lured the killers to Zackenberg in search of the full map.

Ricky had brought up more stories about the massacre on her laptop. A plane had been stolen, which authorities believed the outside group had used to reach Zackenberg. A bunkhouse had been burned with researchers inside—but not Sasha. Her remains had not been found. They had also burned a lab, which was probably where the items discovered in the ice had been kept. Then they had gone, but a plane—theirs, presumably—had exploded and crashed.

But why had they burned the lab? If they had come for the map but were unable to find it, why did the lab matter? Had they simply torched it out of anger? Or was there something in the lab that the killers didn't want the authorities to find?

And where was Sasha? She had not been in either of the burned buildings. Was her body lying frozen behind a heap of rocks miles from ZERO Station where she had tried to hide from the killers? Had she been taken hostage and gone down with the plane?

Trying to make sense of it all made her head throb.

Ricky had looked again at the parchment in her hand.

KEEP FROM CULT!

Her sister had somehow dropped this into the compound's outgoing mail during the siege. She must have been unimaginably frightened, convinced that she had mere seconds to act. Again she attempted to reconstruct the state of mind that would have compelled her sister to deface a 5,000-year-old artifact.

Sasha had mailed the map to her to keep it away from the killers.

But why? Why not just hide it at Zackenberg? Unless Sasha had been convinced that there was no place she could hide it that the killers would not look. To Ricky, that seemed likely. Men who had traveled so far and who had killed so many innocent people would have been relentless in their search.

But they hadn't searched the outgoing mail slot. Perhaps it was some sort of secure, locked contraption and they had no key. But that would not have stopped them. They would have just broken the lock.

So they *hadn't* searched everything. Why? What had compelled them to leave without checking every nook and cranny? And why had they set the lab on fire? Had their real goal been not to possess the map, but to burn it? No, they would have made certain the map was inside the lab before setting the building ablaze.

Unless...

She had tried to twist her perspective, come at it from another angle, imagine a less obvious scenario.

Why did they burn the lab if that was where the artifacts were kept? She had stared at the ceiling, the question gnawing at her for hours.

The lab caught fire accidentally.

No. She had looked at the site maps. The lab was a good distance from House 9, which they *had* burned. The lab had been burned purposely.

They couldn't find the map, but assumed it was hidden in the lab. They burned the lab, thinking they had destroyed the map, rather than risk it falling into the wrong hands.

No. They would have tortured the researchers until someone had given up the location. The fact that Ricky had the map confirmed that there was no secret hiding spot to reveal.

The only thing that made sense was that the killers had left because they thought the map could not be recovered, that it had burned in the lab. And if one of them had not started the fire, and Sasha's fellow researchers had been hostages or corpses, then the only one who could have started the fire was Sasha herself.

And the more Ricky thought about it, the more it made perfect sense. Brilliant, in fact. If the cult had been convinced that the map had been destroyed, there would have been no reason to keep searching.

Had the Greenland police checked the outgoing mail after the attack, or had the investigation centered on the kill sites? The fact that Ricky now held the parchment rendered that question moot. And why *would* they have checked? If a man had been mugged and murdered on a street in Chicago, the police would have checked the corpse, but nobody would have said, "Hey, let's check all the nearby mailboxes to see if he dropped off a letter!"

Even if Greenland authorities had finally examined the outgoing mail, no one other than Ricky would have recognized Sasha's handwriting and grown curious. And eventually, once investigators had allowed Danish officials to begin the process of returning the base to operational status, the mail would have been flown out and delivered.

So Sasha had mailed the letter, and then...

And then the rest of her story, including where she was now—dead or alive—was a mystery.

Ricky had refocused on the first part of the message. GET TO HARP. That part was no puzzle, at least. The HARP Foundation—the Habitat and Atmosphere Research Project Foundation—was where Sasha worked. Then there were two names: Mason Crockett and Mare Desiderii, the second name obscuring a portion of a spiral symbol. Sasha's desperate efforts showed she trusted the two individuals named and believed they would understand the map's significance. Ricky had heard her sister talk about Crockett, with whom she apparently had worked closely on a number of projects. The other name was unfamiliar to her.

Once the map and its message had made the case that Sasha was probably more hero than accomplice, Ricky immediately felt an urge to take her discovery to Agent Scott at the FBI. Not only was this the logical action, but safer than putting the parchment into the hands of people she did not know—especially if the map was valuable enough to inspire the great evils that had been done in Greenland. Yet, her sister had asked her to take it to her two coworkers at the HARP Foundation, had been so adamant about this that she had made the message her last act of defiance against the cult killers. The least Ricky could do was honor the request.

Just what is it I'm supposed to be delivering to HARP?

Carefully, Ricky had smoothed the parchment for a better look, revealing what seemed to be depictions of land masses and the kinds of markings she had seen in books and museums on Egyptian relics.

What the hell? What was this doing in Greenland?

She had found a desk lamp with which to illuminate the map and then snapped a photo with her cell, noticing, as she did so, an oddity. While most of the artifact's edges were irregular, the edge along the spiral figure appeared to have the unworn feathering and coloration of a newer tear. However, a search of the envelope yielded no missing piece. According to reporters and the social media post, this artifact was a very recent find. She could hardly imagine that someone had cut away a piece of original document for analysis, yet it was certain that some small piece had been removed since its discovery. Whether by accident or on purpose, she could not guess.

Finally, replacing the map in the envelope, Ricky had tried, without great success, to sleep. Too many questions.

Had Sasha really been on the plane?

Why was a cult willing to kill for this thing?

What did the symbols on the map mean?

If they had traveled all the way to Zackenberg to try and get the parchment, would the cult members come after her here in Chicago?

While Ricky was sure that Sasha had sent off the envelope secretly, there was no way of knowing with certainty just what the killers knew or how intuitive they were. Did they really think the map had been destroyed, or would they search out the family members of all the Zackenberg researchers just to cover their bases?

Or was she simply being paranoid?

Although morning had found her insufficiently rested, Ricky was more resolved than ever to honor her sister's request and take the map to Sasha's HARP coworkers. If they understood the symbol language, they could perhaps shed some light on what had really happened at Zackenberg. After that, Ricky would take it to the FBI.

She finally gave up on sleep and got out of bed at 5:00, which was her typical rising hour. She dressed in an ancient pair of black warm-up pants and a gray t-shirt, walk-jogged three blocks to the Bel-Aire Gym, which had once trained boxers, but which was now home to a handful of well-used treadmills, exercise bikes, and free weights stations. The Bel-Aire was cheap and never crowded. Ricky had been coming here since she had moved in with Sasha six years earlier. Her routine was always the same: ten minutes of jumping rope, twenty minutes of yoga, and thirty minutes of beating the hell out of an old sand-filled punching bag that hung from the ceiling, a relic left over from the boxing days. For the first month, she had kicked and flailed recklessly. An old boxer with bad knees who came to do bicycle workouts three times a week had eventually spent an hour instructing her in proper technique. Now, almost six years later, Ricky harbored no delusions that her jabs met the pro standard, but she felt more effective, less likely to injure herself by repeating dangerous wrong motions.

And it felt goddamn good to hit something.

She was sure the old boxer had looked at her scar, felt pity for her, and had assumed she wanted to learn how to defend herself. In truth, she just wanted to beat something. Anything. Really beat it, angrily, savagely, as if by doing so, she could somehow modify, if only slightly, the darkness in the world. She never failed to leave the Bel-Aire feeling spent. Sometimes, she even felt content.

Returning to her apartment, she showered, dressed in brown khakis and a black t-shirt from a heap of laundered but unfolded clothes in her closet, fixed herself a cup of tea and a yogurt. She glanced wistfully at her gaming system and the large flat screen monitor in front of it. Then she slipped the mystery envelope into a backpack and walked to the HARP Foundation.

Ricky stood outside for almost half an hour, thinking that she might simply turn around and head back to the apartment. She could already feel the eyes of the people inside, staring at her. She could feel the questions they would ask and the ones they would leave unspoken. Maybe they would believe she was lying or even call the police. If she returned to her apartment, she could still mail the envelope to the Foundation or the FBI. She became even more reluctant to venture inside when she realized that the t-shirt she had grabbed from the heap featured Cinderella and the pumpkin coach on the front—a shirt that Sasha had picked up at a thrift shop. She rolled her eyes. Yeah, she was a *real* Cinderella, she told herself. At least most of the glitter had long ago worn off.

But no. She had to do this for Sasha.

Inside was a modest, marble-floored foyer that led to a glassed-in reception booth. A blonde woman with a neat bob cut behind the glass greeted Ricky with a warm smile and asked if she could help.

"I'm Sasha Crowe's sister," Ricky explained. "I'd like to see Mason Crockett or Mare Desiderii."

Since Sasha had worked here, Ricky had expected the pause that usually came after she introduced herself, a mere extra second during which her lack of resemblance to her sister would be assessed and the eyes would narrow doubtfully, wondering whether Ricky was either joking or adopted. It was a look she had gotten used to. However, the receptionist, who appeared to be about 30 and whose name badge read "Betty," merely smiled kindly and asked if she could spell Mare Desiderii's last name, entering Ricky's response with mechanical efficiency.

"I don't believe we have anyone with that name on staff."

Ricky thought this odd, though it was possible that the person no longer worked at Harp. After all, it had been more than two months since her sister had departed for Zackenberg.

"Mason Crockett then."

"Is Mr. Crockett expecting you?"

Ricky rolled her eyes. "No. But I have something for him."

"I can give it to him, if you'd like," said Betty.

"No. It's too important."

Betty nodded. "Could I see your driver's license?"

"I don't have one," Ricky replied testily.

"Do you have any photo ID?"

Her decision to come to the HARP Foundation in the first place had been difficult enough. Now, standing here, facing what seemed to be unnecessary questions and delays, holding a secret document that had gotten more than a dozen people killed, she felt her anxiety and anger spiking.

"What the hell! You act like this is Fort-fucking-Knox! I just want to deliver an envelope in person!"

Betty's smile disappeared, replaced by a wounded expression. "I-I'm sorry for the procedures. I'm still just getting used to them myself. We use your license to make a temporary photo ID. It's part of our commitment to a secure campus. Perhaps you have something other than a driver's license?"

Ricky, who now felt embarrassed by the abruptness of her response—which made her angrier still—produced her Gates ID.

In addition to the delay it created, she just generally hated using official identification, for it meant revealing her real name. Their mother had been a care-free, club-hopping twenty-something whose liberal and indiscriminate use of illegal drugs had eventually worn her down into a prematurely withered and aloof middle-ager. However, the girls had been born during her free-wheeling days. Sasha had been the more fortunate, receiving the fairly common Irish name Saoirse. This had posed few problems until they had moved to the United States, where no one could pronounce it, the proper pronunciation being SEER-sha. To make her life easier in The States, Saoirse simply began using the name Sasha, which sounded similar.

Their mother had opted for a more whimsical approach with the other twin: Limerick, after the county in which the twins had been conceived. Of course, all of Rose's friends had thought this adorable, which was understandable, frequently high or drunk as they were. But to other children, the name was merely an invitation for cruelty, and so by the age of eight she had begun to go by "Ricky."

The receptionist copied the ID to make a sticker badge, and while Ricky had expected a smirk when Betty glanced at the name, all she received was a polite apology. "I'm so sorry for the delay," she said while tapping at her keyboard. She spoke into her headset briefly before turning her attention back to Ricky. "And... and I just wanted to say... everyone here is hoping for positive news about your sister." There was an awkward pause and then: "You can drop your badge with me on your way out." Then she buzzed Ricky through the security door, telling her to take the elevator to the third floor.

Arriving there, anxiousness had returned to displace most of her anger, and Ricky found Mason Crockett's office at the end of the hall. A nearly empty, blond-wood, platform-style desk sat at the center of the room, looking as if someone had set off a bomb that had blown all of the clutter to the walls, which were almost completely covered in shelves bulging with books, stacks of papers, and rolled charts. From one open spot on the light-green wall hung a poster of Albert Einstein with the caption, "If we knew what it was we were doing, it would not be called research, would it?"

From behind the two computer monitors that were the only items on the desk, a man's head rose, its unruly tangle of beer-colored curls looking like they had been styled by the same explosion that had cleared the desktop. He stood immediately, came around his desk, swayed awkwardly for an instant in indecision. He was thin, early thirties, about 5'11", with blue eyes and a nose that looked like it had been broken at least once. He wore jeans and a white shirt, sleeves rolled up, no tie. Ricky assumed his indecision suggested that he, like everyone who knew Sasha, was pondering the lack of resemblance. After the typical interval of assessment, he extended a hand.

"Y'all must be Ricky?" he inquired, tentatively. It occurred to her that Sasha must have talked about her, using Ricky's preferred name. When she nodded he continued, still holding her hand. "None of us here knows what to think about it all. We're sure there must be more to it than…"

He left the sentence unfinished. Ricky withdrew her hand, felt her fingers clench and her stomach begin to roil. With a name like Mason Crockett, she might have guessed that he would have a Dixie accent as thick as a NASCAR driver. An image of Alabama flashed through her mind and, for the good of her mission, she did her best to suppress it.

"My sister wouldn't hurt innocent people," said Ricky softly, settling into a chair Crockett directed her to in front of his desk while he returned to the seat behind it.

"Sasha was a good friend," said Crockett. "This has been difficult for everyone who knows her."

"Yeah," said Ricky dully, feeling more out of her element by the moment. She could be home in the cool darkness of her apartment playing online games with people who would never see the scar on her face or silently pass judgment about the sort of life a person must lead in order to acquire such a souvenir. People with whom there was no need to share anything personal or important or real.

They sat in uncomfortable silence for a bit.

"Can I get you something?" asked Crockett suddenly. "Coffee? Water? Actually, that's about all we have. Oh, and tea, I think, in the break room."

It occurred to her that if she had not already left, she was probably going to stay until she had delivered the envelope and seen to its safety. She noticed how dry her mouth was and decided that she really could use a cup of tea. Crockett hurried off to fetch it. Once he had left, she again considered leaving the envelope on his desk and beating a hasty retreat before he could return, but her loyalty to her sister just kept her in her chair. For some reason, Sasha had trusted this guy. Perhaps she should, too.

Her eyes traveled around the room. More books, binders, stacks of loose papers.

Slob.

She considered her own wrinkled Cinderella t-shirt, pulled from a pile on the closet floor, and moved past this observation.

Then, on the wall in back of her, she noticed more posters. One showed the Charlotte city skyline with the words, "The Queen City". Two more were music posters, one featuring the band

Lynyrd Skynyrd and another of Shania Twain.

Thank God he works in silence.

Crockett returned with the tea, set it on the corner of the desk nearest her. "I hope this is all right."

She said nothing, took a sip.

Crockett cleared his throat as he resumed his chair. "Miss Crowe, how can I help you? Have you heard… anything?"

She took another sip of the tea. *Dammit, Sasha, you'd better be right about this guy!*

"Yesterday, I received this letter in the mail." She handed him the envelope. "The handwriting is Sasha's. It was mailed from Zackenberg."

Crockett's mouth fell open slightly as he took the envelope, staring at it for a moment as if it were an original draft of the Declaration of Independence. Then he carefully slid out the contents onto his work area. As he read Sasha's message, he cleared his throat in a way that seemed to indicate a wave of emotion. After a long assessment, he fully unfolded the parchment, turning wide-eyed toward Ricky.

"The news reports said something about artifacts in the ice! Is this one of them?"

Ricky nodded. "Has to be. I think Sasha sent it to me to keep the sickos from getting it."

Crockett considered the matter for a few moments.

"They found pieces of a plane near Daneborg."

They let this hang in the air, and Crockett continued.

"This is amazing!"

"Sasha wanted me to contact you. Or Mare. But I think the FBI has to see it, too. All of this."

"Naturally," said Crockett, nodding. "Who's Mare?"

Ricky pointed. "Sasha wrote the name right next to yours on

the map. I thought she worked with you."

Crockett squinted at the writing, seeming to notice now exactly what it said, which generated a sliver of smile. "I'm afraid that's not a person's name. It's the name of a landmark on the dark side of the moon."

Ricky felt her ears burn with embarrassment. She suppressed the all-too-familiar feelings of inferiority and pressed ahead. "Why would she write that on the map?"

Crockett shook his head. "No clue." His eyes traveled again over the Egyptian symbols. "Would you allow me to keep the map for a day or two? I don't know what to make of this, and I can't read these symbols, but I have a friend at Clark who might be able to translate."

Ricky stiffened. She had met this person barely ten minutes ago, and now, he was asking her to trust him with information that might prove Sasha's innocence and answer so many other questions. Every molecule in her frame screamed in protest. Yet, Sasha had asked her to trust Crockett.

Dammit, dammit, dammit, Sasha, you'd better be right about this guy!

She hesitated.

Crockett sensed her reluctance. "Sasha and I worked very closely together on quite a few projects," he explained. "After awhile, it got to the point where we almost knew what the other one was thinking. We had this amazing complementary research relationship. Though, I could never quite parlay that into anything else." Seeing the confusion on Ricky's face, he smiled grimly and explained. "Couldn't get her to go on a date with me. Not for lack of trying. We were like an old married couple in the lab or in the field, but she felt no personal chemistry." He looked at his feet for a moment. "But she was a good friend." Then he corrected himself.

"IS a good friend."

Ricky tried to process this. While she had heard Crockett's name mentioned on occasion, it had always been in relationship to a project. There had never been anything of a confidential nature, the way siblings sometimes talk about romantic interests. She guessed that the attraction truly had been one-sided, and to her surprise, it elicited a very tiny sliver of sympathy.

Very tiny.

"What do you think is really going on? I don't know anything about this Zackenberg place. Except it's cold, a lot of researchers go there, and they live in blue buildings. Do you have any ideas?"

Crockett leaned back in his chair and thought for a moment before responding. "Most of what I know is what I've read in the newspapers or online. And you more than tripled that with what you brought here today. Sasha's message," he pointed to the map for emphasis, "leaves little doubt that this is what the killers were after and that they were willing to do whatever was necessary to get it. But I think this parchment is also evidence that your sister tried to stop them, which makes her kind of a hero."

This acknowledgement of Sasha which echoed her own feelings seemed to lift more stones from her soul.

"But no one knows you have the parchment, right?" continued Crockett. When she nodded, he continued. "No one. Just you and me. Whoever this cult is, they don't know you have it, either. And we want to keep it that way. Don't tell anyone. Don't send any e-mails or texts. Nothing. If these fanatics will fly to Greenland and kill more than a dozen people, they're certainly not going to be intimidated by a trip to Chicago. But…"

Ricky watched him silently turning something over in his mind. "But what?"

"Your sister wanted me to see this." He indicated the

parchment upon which his name had been scrawled. "She also knew that I couldn't interpret it by myself—but that I knew someone who could."

He held up an index finger as if to put the conversation on pause, then pulled out his cell and tapped it a couple of times. After a few seconds, his face became animated.

"Bash? Yeah, well, you've got diapers to change now! Ha-ha! Sure, maybe for a beer later this week. I know. Up to your eyeballs. But hey, I have something I think might interest you. Uh-huh. No. No, this is some serious shit. I'll let that remark slide! I'm going to text you a picture. Just part of it to whet your appetite. Ha-ha, well, I'm a better cook than you think! Take care, buddy!"

Ringing off, Crockett smoothed the map on his desktop and photographed a section with his phone. A few more taps sent the image on its way to his friend. Ricky's eyes widened and her entire body stiffened.

"But you said not to—"

He waved a hand dismissively as he sat down again and endeavored to explain.

"Bash—his full name is Samir Bishara—is a freakin' genius when it comes to this stuff. We roomed together as undergrads. And I'd trust the man with my life!"

"It's not *your* life I'm worried about."

Crockett let it slide. "Teaches a couple of classes in Egyptian history at Clark. Got his hands full. Little girl, three months old. So now he just took a part-time job at Target to pay the bills. Is that crazy or what? A freakin' genius with a doctorate, and he's got to stock shelves! We've got to be the most effed-up country in the western world! But like I said, Sasha knew I couldn't read this stuff. I think she intended it to end up in front of Bash. I'm just a link in the delivery chain."

"Sweet Home Alabama" interrupted him. Crockett tapped his phone.

"Uh-huh. Uh-huh. Slow down. Uh-huh. Yeah, from Zackenberg. Uh-huh. Wow. Where? All right."

Crockett tapped the screen again and let a beat pass before speaking. "Bash. He was impressed." Crockett chewed on his lip for a moment. "Do you have a bit of free time?"

"What? Me?" She felt her back muscles tighten again.

He nodded. "Bash wants to meet for lunch, take a look at the whole thing. Thought you might want to stick around, see what it says."

CHAPTER 5

Bash's office at Clark University was on the third floor of Main Hall, a building that had reached the "needs renovation" stage at least two decades earlier. The wooden floors were uneven and warped. Cracks webbed the plaster on most walls, and brownish water marks discolored at least a third of the sagging panels on the suspended ceiling.

They climbed a wide central staircase to the uppermost floor, where a long hallway stretched in either direction. To their right, a scaffold was positioned far down the hall, as well as a ladder, stacks of ceiling panels, rolls of insulation, wire coils and toolboxes, though the way was still passable. However, Crockett directed her to the left.

Window air conditioning units struggled to cool the offices on the third floor which, being directly under the roof, seemed to collect the bulk of the heat rising from street level. At best, the shuddering, condensation-shedding window units succeeded in transforming a blast furnace into a mere electric blanket.

On one hand, Ricky wished that she had refused Crockett's invitation. Now she was stuck in this nauseatingly humid dump attic of a dump building at a dump college with the rejected southern-fried suitor and the "freakin' genius" who worked part-time at Target.

On the other hand, curiosity.

If something on that 5,000-year-old rag was worth the lives of her sister and the other Zackenberg researchers, she wanted to know what it was. Particularly if the information would make those responsible pay.

Ricky observed that the "freakin' genius's" office was furnished with a battered and defeated desk and little else. A single wall shelf was crammed with academic texts, most lying on their sides in piles of five or six. In addition to the wheezing window air conditioning unit, a more modern air cleaner stood in a corner, purring efficiently between half a dozen stacked cardboard packing boxes. There were no pictures on the yellowish, cracked walls, but several sepia blueprints of what appeared to be Main Hall were thumbtacked into the plaster and marked with pencil and hi-lighter. A photograph of a dark-skinned woman, presumably Bash's wife, rested on a corner of the desk next to an open box of twenty disposable hospital face masks.

On the calendar pad in the center rested a printed enlargement of the section of the map that Crockett had texted. This startled Ricky at first, for she was afraid that others might see the image if it was displayed so prominently. Then she relaxed a bit as she realized the lonely upper floor of Main Hall was as quiet as a desert tomb—and about the same temperature.

After introductions, Crockett noticed Ricky's gaze lingering on the blueprints tacked to the walls. "Bash is kind of phobic about asbestos in old buildings."

Bash smiled awkwardly. "Every time they fix something in this salute to obsolescence, there's a chance they'll release carcinogens. And they're always fixing something. You probably noticed the repairs going on in the east wing."

"It's pretty quiet over there today, Bash," said Crockett.

Bash shook his head and waved a hand in the general direction of the construction. "My actual office is in the east wing. This rat hole is temporary, and I can't wait until the work is done. Unfortunately, they always seem to be working in a different part of the building. They're not resuming on this floor until next Tuesday."

As if reminded of the quantity of microscopic toxins released by the renovation, Bash stepped to the heavy-duty air cleaner and clicked the dial up a notch.

Their host ushered them toward mismatched wooden chairs that faced his desk and invited them to sit. Crockett's friend wore tan dress pants, a short-sleeve navy blue dress shirt, and a tattered brown tie. Ricky noticed a tan jacket that matched the pants hanging from a hook on the wall. Slim with Rosewood skin, wavy raven hair, and a neatly trimmed moustache, Bash seemed anxious, as if he feared the object Ricky carried might suddenly explode. He moved behind the desk and sat, offering an awkward apology for the temperature on the third floor and for the increased risk of lung cancer that their visit might bring them.

Crockett jabbed a thumb toward the door. "Aren't we going to lunch?"

Bash ignored the question. Instead, he leaned back in his chair —a proper office chair—then shifted forward again uneasily, unable to get comfortable, letting out a long breath as if considering where or how to begin.

"Do you know what you have here?" he asked, a slight tremble in his voice.

"If we knew, buddy, we wouldn't be here!" said Crockett brightly.

Bash nodded nervously, shifted again in his seat, then attempted to compose himself, lifting his elbows off the print-out he had created from Crockett's text and rotating it toward his visitors.

"This is really from Zackenberg?"

Ricky nodded.

Bash shook his head and opened his mouth to speak, but it took several seconds for him to articulate what was on his mind.

"If it's genuine, if it was really found in the ice like they said on the news, this is incredible! I don't understand it all, but it's incredible! Do you have the whole thing?"

Ricky nodded, pulled the map carefully from the envelope. Bash spread it out on his desk as if he were caressing a sleeping crocodile. After a minute, he shook his head again, his eyes wide and riveted on the image.

"Even more incredible! Amazing!"

"Okay, I can see that this thing has your attention," said Crockett patiently. "Can you give us a clue as to what it is?"

Bash nodded, massaging a spot between his eyes. "I'm sorry. It's just...do you mind if I take a moment?"

Crockett nodded and Bash focused even more intently on the map.

Several minutes ticked away. They remained quiet in order to give Bash an opportunity to study the document. Then, without warning, Bash began to tremble uncontrollably.

Crockett stood and moved to his side. "Bash, old buddy, what's up?"

For a long moment, he did not answer. Then: "It's been such a shitty, shitty year," said Bash, his eyes on the desktop. "We've been buried. Student loans, upper-five figures! How do they ever expect anyone to get out from under that?"

Ricky wondered what this had to do with anything. *Who gives a fuck about your loans?*

"And then when the baby came, there were complications," Bash continued. "Chione's all right now. But there were more bills. Medical. And even with the second job, we're having trouble paying the rent on a shit-hole efficiency with a two-burner stove! It wears on you! All I think about is how to keep us off the streets, how to keep from dragging Chione and Anisa into some shelter!"

Tears streamed down Bash's cheeks. When he spoke again, his voice was low, hoarse. "But this..." He gestured toward the map. "This could turn everything around!"

"What do you mean?"

"If I can be part of this, doing the translation, bringing it to the scientific community, publishing articles explaining it, why, it could mean everything!" said Bash, his eyes gleaming. "Credibility! My name in the journals for something important! Something that rewrites history! And that means better job opportunities! A better *paying* job! This is huge! This is Howard Carter discovering Tutankhamun's tomb huge! And... and I just hope you'll trust me to help."

"Calm down, buddy," said Crockett, patting the air with his hands. "First, you have to tell us what this thing is. Then, we have to decide the best way to proceed. But of course you're going to be a part of it."

This seemed to settle Bash some.

"Sorry," he said. "You—you can't know how major this is."

Crockett nodded. "That's sort of the point of our visit. What do we have?"

Bash seemed about to reply, but then he leaned toward them and spoke in a lower voice. "You didn't tell anyone else about this?"

Both Ricky and Crockett shook their heads.

"I mean, after what happened at Zackenberg, you can't be too careful," said Bash. Then he steadied himself again and turned the parchment sideways so that he could address its features to the others. "Of course it's a map. And the writing is definitely Egyptian. It tells of four—"

He was interrupted by the sound of three distant raps on a door and a man's voice calling out, "Dr. Bishara?"

Startled, Bash instantly rose from the desk and cautiously poked his head out the open doorway. Instinctively, Ricky quickly folded the map and replaced it in the envelope along with Bash's printout in case someone else should come into the office. A moment later, Bash ducked back inside and spoke in an anxious whisper.

"You're sure you told no one you were coming here?"

Crockett shook his head, rose, peeked around the corner of the door frame. "No one." Then, a moment later he corrected himself. "Only Betty, the Harp receptionist. But not *why* I was coming."

"Shit!"

Crockett peeked, observed two large men in polo shirts, facing away, leaning toward Bash's former office door about a hundred feet away in the east wing. One had a GI Joe haircut. The other, Crockett observed from his profile, wore a porn-star moustache. Receiving no response to his knock, Porn Star took a couple of thin tools from a pocket and seemed to be considering the lock. Crockett whispered a report to the others.

"They must have checked the lobby directory for my office," hissed Bash. "It hasn't been updated to reflect the construction."

Ricky swore under her breath, cursing her decision to bring the map to Harp. She could have mailed it. Taken a bus to the Chicago FBI branch. Now she had wasted her sister's sacrifice and perhaps her own life as well.

"What do we do?" whispered Bash.

Crockett watched the two men from around the door edge. Porn Star now reached out a hand to test the door, and a moment later, lunged forward, throwing his shoulder into it. They heard the distant clatter of splintered wood. Then the two men disappeared inside.

"We've got to go now!" said Crockett. Bash grabbed his laptop off the desk and followed Crockett and Ricky into the hallway. Instead of heading back toward the main staircase and the east wing, they raced toward the scarlet exit sign at the other end of the hallway.

As they arrived at the fire door, they heard rapid footsteps on the hardwood floor. Without looking back, Ricky could tell that the two thugs had finished with Bash's empty office and had spotted their prey. Wasting no time, Crockett, Ricky and Bash pushed into the narrow stairwell and raced to the ground floor exit. However, when Crockett swung open the door to the outside, he immediately saw, fewer than fifty yards away, two men in jackets, one with a cell phone to his ear, striding purposefully toward the building. When they saw Crockett, the men broke into a run.

"No good!" He ducked back inside, pulled the door shut. "They're covering the exits!" Footsteps now sounded on the stairs two floors above them.

"I'll call the police!" cried Ricky.

"No time!" said Crockett. "Not by a long shot! In about ten seconds, those doors are going to open and it's game over!"

CHAPTER 6

I should have gone straight to the FBI, thought Ricky, stifling the urge to scream. *I could have handed off the envelope, and I'd be back at the apartment by now.* A cup of tea and an afternoon of *Clandestia* among people with whom she did not have to make eye contact and whose problems with her were entirely virtual.

Instead, she was going to die at the hands of the same evil that had probably killed her sister—who had sacrificed everything to get the parchment to Ricky. *Sure*, Ricky would take care of it, get it to the right people, see that justice was done.

Yeah, right.

They could not exit the building or retreat up the stairs, and in moments, their pursuers would burst through the doors. If these were indeed part of the same coven that had mercilessly slaughtered scientists at Zackenberg, it would be over quickly. There was nowhere to go.

"Wait!" cried Bash, as if struck equally by inspiration and panic. "Keep going down the stairs! To the basement!"

They descended frantically. Emerging in a dimly lit hallway that snaked beneath the building, they raced past locked storage rooms, doors marked ELECTRICAL and MAINTENANCE, around a corner to the right, another to the left, through what appeared to be an unused cafeteria, and then skidded to a stop on the concrete floor in front of restroom doors.

"In here!" said Bash, pushing open the door marked WOMEN.

"This seems like a bad idea on so many levels!" said Crockett.

Bash crashed inside. The restroom was windowless, its floor covered with thousands of inch-square black-and-white tiles forming art-deco patterns. The sinks were thick porcelain, stained yellow over the years. Half a dozen wood-partitioned stalls showed white toilets with black seats. The only door was the one through which they had entered.

Ricky's eyes fixed on the entrance. The gunmen would be covering both ends of the hallway, realize there was no way out. They would close the noose slowly, inspecting rooms along the way, proceeding cautiously in case one of the pursued had a gun. It was not a race anymore. Eventually, the gunmen would have them.

"So how are we not trapped?" whispered Crockett, his eyes darting around anxiously.

"I'm really paranoid about stuff like asbestos in old buildings," said Bash, moving toward the far wall.

"Old news. But I'm listening."

"When they moved me into the temporary office on the third floor, I dug up a copy of the building plans, after the latest remodel. Wanted to figure out where the worst of the stuff was."

"Still listening."

"When Clark opened a century ago, the only buildings on campus were Main Hall and the old gymnasium just to the south. When women's sports were added, they built the locker room in the Main Hall basement and a short tunnel connected it to the gym. Years later, when the new fitness center was built, the tunnel was sealed off, but part of the locker room remained as a bathroom.

This bathroom."

"Okay," said Crockett, his eyes scanning the room. "And this helps us how?"

Bash rapped his knuckles on the back wall. "Plasterboard! If we bust through, we might be able to take the tunnel to the old gym! I think it might be right behind this wall!"

Ricky's eyes widened angrily. "Might?"

"Unless they filled it in with dirt," said Bash. "Or put up a brick wall on the other end. I don't know what we're going to find. But it's better than staying here!"

Without waiting for an invitation, Crockett kicked at the drywall a foot above the floor, easily making a small hole which, with additional kicks, he enlarged.

"Go!" said Crockett, motioning them to crawl through. Bash went first, followed by Ricky. After squeezing himself through the narrow opening, Crockett reached back out and pulled the garbage can against it. "Maybe it'll keep them from noticing for a few minutes."

They stood and immediately lit the space with their phones.

The floor matched that of the bathroom, though it was covered with a layer of dust, mouse droppings, and broken tile chips. A couple of wooden benches rested on pipes bolted to the floor. Some dingy wire-mesh lockers leaned against a wall, and straight ahead a short distance was a doorway, though the door had long ago been removed from its hinges. They passed through this opening quickly and found the tunnel, dark and dusty, white-painted block walls, thick pipes running horizontally along the left side, electrical conduit fastened to the ceiling. Overhead fixtures that had once held bare bulbs were now empty sockets. As they moved, Bash called his wife, instructing her to pack a night bag and telling her where to meet.

After about a hundred and fifty feet, they came to a second doorway. Piled near this were a dozen broken student desks, boxes of obsolete textbooks, several tarnished trophies, and a worn-out faculty desk that, nonetheless, looked to be in somewhat better condition than the one in Bash's office. The second doorway had a door, and it was locked, but, fortunately, could be released from their side. They opened it, found stairs leading up, raced across the slightly warped parquet floor of a basketball court without disrupting the pick-up game being played, and finally peered out into the sunlight half a block from Main Hall.

"Let's get a cab, make sure Chione and your little one are safe," said Crockett.

"Go wherever the hell you want," shouted Ricky, heading for the street. "I'm going to the FBI! Which I fucking should have done in the first place! So stupid, so fucking stupid!"

"We can go to the FBI after we drop Bash," said Crockett, following.

Ricky whirled about to face him. "There is no *we*! This is *my* problem! *My* sister mailed the letter to *me*!"

"When you stopped at the HARP Foundation, you made it our problem," said Crockett. "Your sister had to know we'd get in touch with Bash. And she wouldn't want you to just leave him hanging. She and Bash were friends. And admit it. You're curious about what the map says."

Ricky stood seething while Crockett hailed a cab. Twenty minutes later, it deposited them in front of the Delray Hotel, four floors and one star worth of grimy brick and smeared windows slumped between a restaurant that smelled of spices and cabbage, and a tattoo parlor. They connected with Chione in a third-floor room that radiated austerity, but which seemed clean, had a table, a plug-in electric burner, a can opener, and a painting of a circa

1950s Chevy sedan parked on a beach with gulls sailing by in the background. It also had a shoulder-high air cleaner that—somehow—Chione had lugged to the hotel along with the baby and their bags. They waited for Bash to conduct a mattress check for bedbugs, a bathroom mold check, and an examination of the ceiling panels to satisfy himself that they contained no asbestos. Then he held little Anisa while addressing their situation.

"We should be safe after Ricky and Crockett take the letter to the FBI," said Bash hopefully to his wife. "At that point, the psychopaths can't keep the contents a secret simply by silencing a few people. Of course, the psychos might not realize this for a few days. So it will be better if we stay here for a while. A little undercover vacation."

Chione glanced around at the room. "This is not the vacation I was dreaming of. Oh, Samir, what have you gotten yourself into?" She said this so lovingly that Ricky felt a renewed surge of anger at herself. If she had not gone to HARP to begin with, Bash's family would not have been forced into a cabbage-scented safe house.

"I still don't understand how they knew where we were," said Ricky.

"You only told the receptionist?" asked Bash.

Crockett nodded, his expression suggesting that he could make no sense of it. "Betty."

Ricky recalled her encounter with the woman. "Wait! She said something like the office procedures were new to her!"

The three took a moment to consider this.

"Could she have been a mole?" asked Bash. "You know, for the cult?"

"I told her I was Sasha's sister," said Ricky.

Crockett considered the evidence. "You had a package for me.

Ten minutes later, I tell her we're going to see Dr. Bishara at Clark. A quick online search reveals that Bash is a noted professor of Egyptian studies. She connects the dots."

"But Betty worked for HARP," said Bash.

"Only for a couple weeks," added Crockett. Then his face suddenly drained of color. "Jesus!"

Bash put a hand on his friend's shoulder. "What is it?"

Crockett shook his head slowly. "Betty was hired right after the Zackenberg incident. Right after Barb, who had been the receptionist ever since I've been there, died. Forty. No family history of heart disease."

"And then thugs show up at Clark," said Bash.

Ricky tried to wrap her head around it. "Are you saying that Barb was murdered so this cult could plant a mole? But as far as they knew, the map was destroyed in the fire at Zackenberg."

"Maybe they were suspicious or hopeful because Sasha was never found," suggested Crockett, his unfocused eyes gazing out the grime-streaked window. "Maybe they hoped that some information about the map had been—or would be—relayed to the HARP Foundation. Maybe they even suspected Sasha would try to communicate with you and that this would lead you to the Foundation. It's pretty clear that these bastards are ruthless and damned well connected."

Ricky shivered. She wanted to drop the f-bomb, but there was little Anisa. However, she considered that little Anisa probably understood nothing at this stage of her life, and so dropped a string of them.

"We'll be safe here, I'm certain," said Chione, although her eyes suggested that she was saying this mostly for Bash's benefit. "And I don't really understand any of it! But the killings in Greenland…horrible. These people must be brought to justice."

71

Crockett nodded agreement and then turned to his friend. "Bash, before we go, what's the story with this map?"

Bash handed Anisa to Chione, who pulled a bottle from a bag and slid the nipple into the baby's greedy mouth. Ricky licked her own lips. *God, I want a drink.* She imagined how perfect a gimlet from The Edsel would taste right now.

"I still don't understand," said Bash, taking the parchment from Ricky and spreading it out atop the table, "why people are willing to kill each other over this thing."

"You mean the map doesn't say?" asked Ricky, the disappointment on her face obvious. "But isn't it like super valuable just because of its age and where it was found?"

"Not in an instant 'you won the lottery' sense," said Bash. "I mean, as an academic game-changer, it will ultimately make a number of researchers and universities and museums a boat load of money. Which, because of my prominent role here, will hopefully include me." He smiled sheepishly. "Let's face it, wow! Egyptians in Greenland? That's going to get people talking! But it's not the sort of thing that crooks typically go after, because no one is going to want to pay millions to have it hanging in their living room. It's knowledge, not art. A stolen Picasso? Yeah, you could get a pretty penny on the black market. This? Not so much."

"What did you learn, Bash?" asked Crockett, trying to move it along.

Bash leaned forward conspiratorially. "Okay, this is the best I can do on short notice." Then he turned toward Ricky and pointed toward Sasha's message. "Did your sister write this?"

Ricky bristled at what sounded like an accusation. "She was in a hurry."

Bash nodded. "Did your sister have any experience with ancient Egyptian languages?"

"She learned some Klingon for a *Star Trek*-themed party once," said Ricky, deadpan. When Bash frowned, she added, "Not that I was aware. Probably had no idea what the map said. Just knew it was important to the shitheads."

Bash twirled his index finger at the scrawl. "What's the deal with *Mare Desiderii*? One of the so-called *seas* of the moon, right?"

"Not a clue," replied Crockett. "Tell us about the rest of it."

Bash refocused. "Okay, the first part of the thing is in a form of Archaic Egyptian."

"I thought Egyptians spoke Arabic," said Crockett.

"Today they do," nodded Bash. "Most speak Egyptian Arabic, though there are other dialects, depending on the region, such as Saudi Arabic."

"But not Egyptian?"

"Not since about the 17th century."

Chione had placed the baby on the center of the bed and now brought three cans of beer to the table from a small cooler. Crockett and Bash thanked her and popped theirs open. Ricky stared at hers.

Oh, God, I need this. Damn it, I need this!

Then she pushed it away.

"Water, maybe?" Chione prompted. Ricky nodded and Chione brought a filmy glass smelling strongly of chlorine.

Bash continued. "As I was saying, before the 17th century, most Egyptians spoke Coptic—which is, by the way, still used in Coptic Christian religious services. That goes back to about the second century. Then—" Bash paused, looked up from his beer, smiled sheepishly. "Too much, right? It's the professor in me. I'm not comfortable unless I'm boring my audience to death with an avalanche of minutia."

Crockett shook his head. "No, of course not, go on."

"Wait!" interrupted Ricky. "Why are we even here? Couldn't we have looked up all these hieroglyphics online and saved ourselves all this freakin' trouble?"

"The old languages are very complex," Crockett replied. "They can take years of study, right Bash?"

"Well, you're both right to some extent." Bash smiled tightly. "I mean, you can find the basic deities and alphabet online. So with some writings, yes, that could get you into the ballpark, so to speak. But the online guides and tutorials wouldn't account for all the variables and subtleties. Hell, a hundred years is the blink of an eye in human history, yet language can make huge leaps in a century. Symbols, words, pictures are created, evolve, disappear."

Crockett nodded. "All right. Lead on, my friend."

"Well, to try and keep it simple, the language changed over time," Bash continued, lapsing again into teacher mode. "Roughly every 700 to 1000 years, there are distinct differences that allow us to classify it as Late, Middle, or Old Egyptian. You can tell how old something is by the variety of Egyptian demonstrated in the writing. The variety shown in Ricky's map would be classified as Archaic Egyptian, one of the oldest written forms. Only Sumerian is older. The writing on our little treasure could be more than 5,000 years old."

He paused to allow the enormity of this to register.

"And translation can be challenging," continued Bash. "The written language 5,000 years ago was truly a work in progress. In some respects, the priests and scribes were making it up as they went. Not so difficult to understand. Even today, we add hundreds of words to the English language each year. And even though the English language is about 1,600 years old, we've only standardized spellings of words in the last couple of centuries. So in many respects, the evolution of any language is always a bit of a free-for-all. Muddying the waters a bit more with Archaic Egyptian is the fact that they sometimes wrote things out phonetically, and other times, they would use a logograph—kind of a ready-made symbol to represent words, sounds, or ideas. And at times, they would use both, one right after the other, just to make sure you got the idea. And did I mention that there are dozens of symbols whose meanings are still a mystery to us even after all this time?"

"So what are you trying to say here?" Ricky scowled, seemingly frustrated by Bash's vagueness. "That you haven't figured out jack shit?" Suddenly, her ears warmed, remembering Chione, how she must feel, hearing her husband addressed in this manner.

Bash seemed gobsmacked for a moment, then forged on. "Well, no. I mean, I haven't figured out *everything*. And with the ancient glyphs, there are typically a few guessing games. You know, does it mean *this* or does it mean *that*? But... it looks like a map to find a hidden scroll."

"That's it?" asked Crockett.

"Well, it's a scroll associated with symbols for life and death,"

"A scroll of life and death," said Chione ominously. "Sounds like something to be avoided."

"What was it doing in Greenland?" asked Crockett.

"I'll get to that," said Bash, sneaking a peek over his right shoulder at the baby, who still held tightly to the bottle, Chione sitting beside her, watching. "There's also a reference to four travelers. Their leader was a woman. It's hard to translate her name exactly. That's the trouble with an abjad language."

When the angry look on Ricky's face grew angrier still, Bash endeavored to explain.

"It means no vowels."

Ricky grunted. "How is that even possible?"

Bash helicoptered his left hand, searching for an appropriate response. "It's… funky. A little guess work involved. Think of writing Crockett as KRKT. Or… or how we abbreviate airports on boarding passes and travel schedules. We include enough so you get the idea. Similar principle."

"I get it," said Crockett. "Using my name, again, as an example, we'd spell it KRKT, and infer some sort of vowel sounds. Whether you guessed KROKOT, KRAKAT or KREKET, you'd get the basic idea of how it sounded."

Bash nodded. "I wish all my students were so quick. But, again, the leader's name was only mentioned once phonetically. By phonetically, I mean using the Egyptian glyph alphabet."

Seeing their uncomprehending gazes, he sighed, started again. "Let me explain. If we saw the Egyptian symbols for KRKT, we'd know sort of how it was supposed to sound. That's phonetics. Sound. On the other hand, if we created a symbol for Crockett using an illustration of a baseball, the outline of North Carolina, and a bottle of beer, we would learn to associate that with him, too, even though it didn't represent the *sound* of his name."

"Someone knows me pretty damn well!"

Bash moved on with only a slight smile. "And if we were ancient Egyptians, sometimes we might use KRKT, and other times we might use the baseball-North Carolina-beer symbol, even in the same document. That sort of inconsistency—or randomness, if you want to call it that—isn't unusual in Egyptian writings. But it can create some translation headaches."

"So who's this woman?" asked Crockett, anxious to steer Bash back on point.

"The leader's name translates phonetically to something like SSR. Or maybe CCR."

"Creedence Clearwater Revival!" said Crockett brightly. "Those Egyptians had good taste in music!"

This got a chuckle from Bash. "And I certainly heard plenty of them when we roomed together. It's funny, though, the things we free-associate when we see these glyphs. First thing I thought of was Caesar, but, you know, it was just a silly, momentary thought because of the phonetics. I mean, Julius Caesar didn't show up for another two and a half millennia. And, of course, he was male."

Crockett smiled. "Yeah, those are deal breakers."

"In other places, her name appears in a cartouche, which is interesting because—"

"Whoa, whoa," interrupted Crockett. "Cartouche?"

Bash smiled impishly. "Sorry. Sometimes for their leaders or gods, the Egyptians would combine several symbols inside a set of brackets or a vertical oval. A cartouche. SSR's cartouche is…how can I put this? Kind of disturbing."

Ricky frowned, impatient. "What do you mean? This is *all* kind of disturbing."

"This is worse. It indicates she was associated with Ammit."

Crockett looked from the map to Bash. "Which is uber-disturbing because…?"

"Because no one was a follower of Ammit," replied Bash. "And I mean *no one*. She frightened the hell out of the Egyptians. She was a demoness with the head of a crocodile, the embodiment of all their most horrifying fears and nightmares. The Egyptians believed that when you died, a woman named Ma'at weighed your heart against her divine feather. If your heart was lighter than the feather, you were welcomed into the afterlife. If it was heavier, Ammit devoured your soul."

CHAPTER 7

Crockett was the first to break the silence. "Devourer of souls. Yeah, I'd say that if you're playing for that team, you're probably someone to be feared. What else can you tell us about this Sasser?"

Bash raised an eyebrow. "Sasser?"

Crockett smiled. "Well, you said the leader was represented with the letters SSR. I just added a couple of vowel sounds, like you said the Egyptians would do."

Bash's mouth curled into the ghost of a smile, reluctantly it seemed. Then he resumed. "She was apparently very much feared. Whoever made the map associated... *Sasser*... with the worst evil imaginable. But there's lots more here." He gestured toward the parchment with both hands. "It's a map of the world. Now this is really cool. It—"

"Wait a minute!" interrupted Crockett. "Doesn't it say anything more about the Scroll of Life and Death? Like what the hell it is?"

Bash sighed, frustrated. "If it had said what it was, I would have told you! Now listen, this is amazing! This thing may have the oldest map of the world in existence! That alone would make it one of the great finds of all time!"

"How old are we talking?" asked Crockett.

"I don't know, exactly," admitted Bash. "But let me explain." He rotated the map away from himself and directed them to an incomprehensible amalgam of shapes and figures.

"What makes this so fascinating is that it incorporates features of both the Anaximander and the Imago Mundi, yet it appears to pre-date them!"

"English, please," said Crockett.

Bash swallowed, took a deep breath, and attempted to explain slowly.

"The Anaximander is one of the earliest world maps, probably created a little less than 3,000 years ago. It's really pretty simple:

the Aegean Sea is at the center, surrounded by Europe, Libya and Asia. The Ocean completely surrounds them."

Noticing their uncomprehending stares, Bash removed his tablet from its case, tapped on it for a moment and then rotated it on the table for them to see.

Afterburner

Science, History, Big Ideas

featured Celebrating Anaximand
continues to spark disci

Although surprisingly littl
his life, Anaximander con
scientific thought in a var
perhaps the most well-kn
his iconic map of the wor
during roughly the 7th cer
Anaximander was said to
attended school with Pytl
contributed ideas in mete
cosmology, mathematics,
fields. With respect to th
Anaximander differed fro
his contemporaries in mo

"This isn't the original, of course," Bash explained. "It's a drawing based on the work of Anaximander, a philosopher who lived about 600 B.C. Carl Sagan called him the first real scientist. The map's obviously missing a lot of detail, but it was pretty good for people who rarely traveled fifty miles from the place of their birth."

Bash rotated the tablet, tapped away, and a few moments later, presented another graphic.

"What is that supposed to be?" asked Ricky.

"It's a sketch of the Imago Mundi, which was created roughly the same time as the Anaximandar, but this time, with Babylonia as the center of the world. Babylonia is the horizontal rectangle just above the center of the map. Each of those shapes represents a different location in the world. As with the first map, Ocean encircles everything. It also is believed to show our here-and-now world connecting with strange, mysterious worlds beyond Ocean. Maybe heaven? Or at least the realms of their contemporary myths. That's what the triangular wedges extending outward may represent. This sketch is quite similar to the original, which is inscribed on a clay tablet."

The sounds of a dog barking in a room down the hall broke Bash's spell momentarily. The barking ceased abruptly, and Bash resumed.

"As you can see, *our* map has some of the same landforms as the other two, although its center appears to be Memphis."

"Why Memphis?" asked Crockett.

Bash tapped the parchment carefully. "This little glyph in the center essentially means 'city'. *The* city in ancient Egypt was

Memphis, its capital until the Romans came and threw a monkey wrench in the works."

"What are these markings that encircle the land?" asked Ricky, finding herself drawn into the mystery of the artifact despite her misgivings.

"They represent gods and goddesses," replied Bash. "In that respect, it's similar to the Imago Mundi, which had spikes reaching out toward the gods in the realm beyond Ocean. And here's something different." He pointed to the upper left portion of the map. "It's an island that neither of the other two maps has. It's the only other item labeled on the map, which suggests that it's important."

"What does the label say?" asked Crockett.

Bash shrugged. "Just 'island'."

"Maybe the British Isles?" suggested Crockett.

Bash nodded. "That's what I was thinking. Of course, the scale on these ancient maps is way off. They had no way of accurately measuring distances and often made assumptions about areas that had not been extensively explored. But they did the best they could. That's why the Anaximander has only three misshapen continents, the Imago Mundi looks like a Tetris game, and our map is cats."

Ricky and Crockett exchanged a concerned glance. Crockett broke the silence.

"For a moment there I thought you said our map was cats."

Bash smiled, pointing to the map. "It's *three* cats actually. The first cat is pretty much the top half of the map."

"I'll be darned," said Crockett, smiling. "And it looks like he's playing with a ball."

Bash nodded. "If I'm seeing this the right way, that ball is Sicily. If you rotate the map 180 degrees, you can see cat number two, which looks like it's pouncing. And the third cat is just a face. Kind of where Asia is on the Anaximander map. Like I said, geographically, the maps weren't always that accurate. But many cultures incorporated animals into their maps of the world, like Native Americans with the turtle or the Hindus and the four elephants. And cats as part of an Egyptian map is not particularly surprising. Cats were worshipped by the ancient Egyptians, were hugely important to their culture. And now that I'm looking at the map a little closer, here's something else. They divided the world into seven land masses. Not to represent our modern continents, but likely because seven was symbolic of perfection, completeness. In their lore, Isis was guarded by seven Scorpions, gold is pictured with seven spikes, and so forth. So naturally if the world was a perfect thing, it would reflect the significance of the number seven."

"Hold on," said Crockett, narrowing his gaze on the map. "That seems a little far-fetched if I get what you're thinking! People traveling from Egypt to Britain thousands of years ago?"

"It's already been proved," Bash replied. Back in the 1930s, they found the remains of a couple of Egyptian sailing ships in a Yorkshire estuary. Those were dated to around 1400 B.C., but it's conceivable that others came before them."

"Bash, your students must be just riveted," said Crockett.

Bash grunted. "Try bored to tears."

"What about all of the hieroglyphics above the map?" asked Ricky, pointing to four columns of symbols.

"This is where it gets pretty funky," said Bash. "The first— wait, let me get my notes. I jotted down a few things before you arrived at my office." He dug in a pocket and unfolded a sheet of paper. "Here it is. The first says 'book—or scroll—of life and death.' Then next we have roughly 'tomb in the shape of an X' and the sun showing the way. The third column talks about a 'river of milk'. And then in the fourth we have 'great river' and the reference to the four travelers, and this…" Bash glanced at Crockett before continuing, "this *Sasser* person, or whatever the name is. Plus there's some sort of spiral symbol that could be a symbol of power. Or a mehen. Or…" He moved closer, squinting. "Did one of you do this?"

"What, Bash?"

"There's a corner of the map that's been torn off. The lighter color on the edge indicates it was done recently."

"That's how it arrived," explained Ricky. "There was nothing else in the envelope."

Bash sighed. "Maybe it's nothing. The removal of the corner left most of the spiral intact, which is good. But there's no way of knowing whether the missing fragment held anything important. Then again, if your sister sent this, I can't imagine *she* would have deliberately removed anything important."

"Connect the dots for us, Bash," said Crockett. "Using what you already know."

Bash nodded. "Mind you, I've had only a very short time to examine it. But here's what I'm thinking. There's something called the Scroll of Life and Death. It's hidden in a tomb with an X-shaped passage, what's commonly called a cruciform tomb. I'm not sure what the 'river of milk' is. Maybe a landmark near the tomb. But it seems to be separate from the 'great river' that's mentioned."

Crockett sighed. "Calling Sherlock Holmes! So, long story short, it's a map to find the Scroll of Life and Death. Whatever that is."

"Long story short," repeated Bash.

"That's what the bastards are after?" asked Ricky. "Some

fucking scroll? But… why the hell…?" Now her eyes grew moist. "All those people… my sister… for some 5,000-year-old curiosity that they'll never be able to sell!"

With a glance at the baby in the middle of the bed, Chione moved beside Ricky to offer comfort, settling a hand on her shoulder, at which Ricky, without intending to, bristled.

Bash shrugged. "Again, we can't expect fanatics or cultists to act rationally. Look at Hitler. He spent years trying to steal the Ghent Altarpiece, an oil painting on twelve oak panels done by Jan van Eyck. He was convinced it contained a coded message that would lead him to a hidden treasure, the Arma Christi, which allegedly included the crown of thorns worn by Christ during his crucifixion, the so-called Spear of Destiny that pierced Christ's side, and the Holy Grail, among other items. Hitler believed the Arma Christi would endow him with supernatural powers that would help his Nazis conquer. We can only guess at what value— real or imagined—the cultists who attacked Zackenberg believe this map might have, or what they think it might lead them to."

"Bastards!"

"Whatever they're hoping to find with this map, I'd like to know a little more about it. *Great river*." Crockett rubbed his chin. "Gotta be the Nile, right?"

Bash nodded. "That'd be my guess, considering that this is Egyptian in origin."

"And the map starts in England," said Crockett. "So how did whoever was following it 5,000 years ago end up in the ice in Greenland? Somebody's GPS was not getting four bars that day!"

"Not England, *Ireland*!" cried Ricky unexpectedly. Then she looked toward the baby and lowered her voice. "It's been bugging me ever since you mentioned Caesar or Sasser!"

"What has?" asked Bash.

"I grew up in Ireland," said Ricky. "Until I was nine. Then when I moved to Chicago I..." She had no desire to reveal too much to either of these relative strangers. "...I started reading a lot about Celtic legends and myths. Some of it's pretty twisted. There was a woman with a name that sounded similar to Sasser. Cessair, I think it was." She spelled it out for them.

Bash looked to Crockett. "That could be it. It would make more sense than Julius Caesar. Do you remember any more?"

"She supposedly came to Ireland to escape the flood," said Ricky.

Crockett squinted at her. "What flood?"

"You know," said Ricky. "Noah? The ark?"

"THE Noah?" Crockett could not suppress an amused expression. "I've never heard Ireland mentioned in the ark story before. How does that work?"

"Let me think." Ricky rubbed the area between her eyes. Suddenly, after weeks and months of feeling her world spinning out of control, she felt herself on firm ground, traversing territory *she* knew. As much as she hated volunteering anything, there was a certain satisfaction with being not only the one who controlled the moment, but with being able to help out her sister in bringing this nightmare to an end.

"Cessair was Noah's step-granddaughter, or however you would say it." She looked up, saw that they were listening raptly. "She spent much of her life in Egypt where she came under the influence of one of the high priests. A sorcerer. However, when word came that Noah was building an ark, Cessair traveled to her grandfather to ask to come aboard. Noah refused."

"That's harsh," said Crockett, grimacing. "You'd think he could find an extra bunk for a granddaughter."

"It's not clear why he refused her," said Ricky, "but she

apparently returned to Egypt, where the high priest advised her to go to Ireland."

"Wait a minute," said Crockett. "Noah's Ark... Egyptian mystics... Ireland... where is all of this coming from? The Bible?"

Ricky shook her head. "Hold on a second." She grabbed Bash's tablet and tapped it a few times. "Here it is. From *Lebor Gabála Érenn*." When this simply evoked a look of even greater confusion, she elaborated. "In English, it's called *The Book of Invasions*. It's supposed to be a history, of Ireland. But most of it is regarded as myth."

"Fascinating," said Bash.

"Okay," said Crockett slowly. "Big flood coming. Grandpa says tough luck, no room on the ark. Magic man sends her to Ireland. Why Ireland? Why not Madagascar or Australia?"

"There were no people in Ireland," said Ricky. "According to *The Book of Invasions*, anyway. As a result, there was no sin in Ireland. The theory was that because of this, it was the one place in the entire world that God would not cleanse by flooding."

"Okay, I'm following," said Crockett, though the creases in his brow suggested more than a modest degree of confusion.

"She went to Ireland with three ships. Two were lost on the way. The survivors included Cessair, three men—Fintan, Bith and Ladra—and forty-nine women."

"Why am I never marooned on an island with those odds?" asked Crockett, which got a chuckle from Bash and a frown from Chione. Ricky ignored him and continued.

"Things sort of fell apart after that. Most myths say Bith and Ladra died and Fintan swam off."

"Whoa, slow down," said Crockett, marveling at how telling this story had transformed Ricky. Instead of sullenness and anger, he had, for the first time, seen something almost resembling Sasha in her face. "Bith? Ladra? Fintan?"

Ricky paused, stared down at the tablet, ran a hand through her hair, thinking. "Bith was supposedly a stepson of Noah. He and his wife—Birren, I think—were Cessair's parents. When Cessair went to Ireland, her father, Bith, came with her, as did Fintan, who became Cessair's husband. Ladra was the pilot of her ship. Everyone died in Ireland except for Fintan, the only true believer among them. He turned himself into a salmon and swam away."

Crockett glanced sideways at Bash and cleared his throat.

"There's something fishy about that story. But I don't know what all of that has to do with our mystery boat or the Scroll of Life and Death. Or the guys who are after this thing. Here's what we've got: A map that supposedly shows how to get from Ireland to Egypt thousands of years ago somehow ends up in Greenland. When word gets out, people come after it, and they want it so bad, they're willing to commit mass murder. It's clear they've got some pretty heavy financing for all of this nefarious activity, not to mention a pretty broad reach. So whatever they think is at X marks the spot must be some pretty bad-ass stuff."

"Not an X," Ricky corrected him. "I think Bash called it a mehen. A spiral."

Bash nodded.

"Whatever," said Crockett. "So where's this *mehen* located?"

Bash shrugged awkwardly. "Somewhere near the Great River. Again, probably the Nile. And… somehow those other directions help point the way."

Crockett grimaced. "We're in way over our heads here. We need to get that map to the FBI. Then you should be safe."

"I don't need a chaperone," said Ricky, noticing his use of the word "we".

"Maybe not," said Crockett. "But until this thing's in the right hands, I'm not sure I feel safe going back to *my* apartment. And if I stayed here, it would just get awkward after a while."

"It would get messy after a while!" said Chione, feigning anger, hardly able to suppress a smile. "Samir has described your apartment to me!"

Bash chuckled, nodded. "It's a disaster area."

Now Crockett smiled. "But it's my little disaster area. And right now, I'm missing it terribly. It'll be nice when this is all over."

"Yeah," said Bash with a sigh. "Then we can get out of this one-room shit-hole and go back to our other one-room shit-hole."

Ricky retrieved the map and slid it back into the envelope. Then she and Crockett made their way to the sidewalk.

CHAPTER 8

The Chicago branch of the FBI was an easy bus trip to the southern extremity of downtown, and then a mile west on Roosevelt Road. Unfortunately, Agent Scott was in the field. They waited for an hour. Then Ricky left a message, but not the envelope.

"I'm not leaving something as important as this with a receptionist," said Ricky. Especially, she added to herself, not after her experience with the HARP receptionist. They vowed to try back in another hour.

"Let's get out of here."

"Why?" asked Ricky, hugging her backpack to her chest as she stood in the center of the lobby.

"Because it's a beautiful day outside and this place has all the charm of a public restroom," replied Crockett.

"Aren't you afraid someone might come looking for us?"

"A little," said Crockett. "But if we hang around this building, I think we'd be in greater danger of being spotted. Those creeps might guess we'd come here. Until Agent Scott comes back, probably best to keep moving. And frankly, I'm kind of jazzed up. Antsy. I'm not used to being at the center of something... well, something dangerous."

Ricky grunted. "You think I am? I feel like everyone is watching me!"

Crockett nodded. "We won't go far. Keep our eyes peeled for anyone who gives us a sideways glance."

Eyes toward the floor, she darted ahead of him heading for the door, slipping on her pack with swift, violent motions as she walked. "I just want this to be over with!" The solitude and security of her apartment had never seemed so inviting—or so unattainable.

"Come on," said Crockett as they reached the sidewalk, and he directed her across the street and toward the University of Illinois-Chicago campus to the north. He lifted a hand toward the low buildings. "I'll give you a tour of my alma mater. Even if someone comes looking for us at the Fibbie building, they won't have any reason to suspect that we'd wander over there."

She flashed him a look of disbelief.

Crockett laughed. "I get it. You were thinking, 'Why, a hayseed like this with his Dixie accent probably went to some unaccredited, backwater Bible Belt diploma factory.'"

"As a matter of fact, yeah."

He turned toward her and smirked. "Not particularly fair, you know. Not any more than me assuming that, just because you have a hint of an Irish accent, you're a drunk who starts fights with everyone!"

Ricky kept her eyes on the sidewalk ahead as she walked. "I'm a goddamn alcoholic. Last night, I broke some sonofabitch's nose in a bar and then woke up three hours later on the floor of a back room, not remembering anything or knowing how I got there."

Crockett skidded to a halt. "Jesus! For real?"

She said nothing, continued to walk.

"I—I'm sorry," said Crockett, jogging to catch up as they crossed over to the campus.

"Why are *you* sorry?"

"Because I kind of feel like a heel for what I said."

They both walked silently for a minute, until Ricky could almost palpably feel his remorse and embarrassment. She knew she would never see the poor bastard again after they got rid of the envelope, so she decided to cut him a break.

"So you really went to college here?"

Crockett smiled weakly but seemed grateful for the question. "Well, I didn't spend much time in this part of the campus. The baseball stadium is over on the eastern edge, near I-94."

"Baseball stadium?"

"I was recruited to play college ball. Tough to say no. Free tuition, books. Then I blew my arm out during winter training. Never played a single game. Suddenly I was a little fish in a really big pond where I didn't know much of anyone. Started a rehab program late in the spring, but never got the ol' wing back to where it had been. Was going to head back home in the fall, but then I sublet a room in an apartment that summer and met Bash, who was already living there. He sort of took me under *his* wing, and then one day I realized I wasn't thinking about going back anymore. This was home. What about you?"

"Didn't Sasha tell you anything? I thought you two were friends."

"Sure," said Crockett. "But she never talked about Ireland. What was it like?"

Ricky's eyes dropped to the sidewalk again. "Better than here."

"Okay."

"And it was a long time ago. Ever since we came here, things have been shit. Someday I'm going back. Maybe then I—"

She stopped. She had been going to say, *Maybe then I won't be afraid*. But that was not right. She wanted to go back because people here were loud, arrogant, insufferable, perverse. In Ireland, her life had been in stasis, had possessed a kind of balance. Sure, her father had worked way too hard and her mother had smoked way too much weed. Yet, during those first nine years of her life, she had felt—

The first word that popped into her mind was *safe*, but that was weak tea. *Hope* was tea with a shot of whiskey.

"Maybe then you...?" prompted Crockett.

She recalled her unfinished sentence, but shook her head. "Nothing."

An hour later, they retraced their steps to FBI headquarters, but the woman at the reception desk informed them that Agent Scott had still not returned.

They exited the building again and paused on the sidewalk.

"Now what?" asked Crockett.

"I don't know," said Ricky, "but I really want to get rid of this thing." She held up the envelope, which she had removed from her backpack in preparation for delivering it to Agent Scott. "I keep expecting shit-heads with Uzis to appear out of nowhere."

"Relax," said Crockett. "Bash is the only one that knows you and I brought the map here."

"*You* didn't bring the map anywhere," said Ricky gruffly.

Crocket shook his head. "I'm just shit on your boots, aren't I?"

"Your words. Not mine."

A voice from behind surprised them. "Miss Crowe?"

They turned and saw a man in a dark suit wearing a photo I.D. striding toward them from the direction of the FBI building entrance. He extended his hand to Ricky.

"I'm Agent Sloane. I was passing through the lobby when I

overheard you inquire about Agent Scott. I'm actually assisting him on your case."

Ricky breathed a sigh of relief. "Thank God! Since I talked with Agent Scott, a lot has happened."

Agent Sloane nodded. "Look, Miss Crowe and Mr....?"

"Mason Crockett," said Crockett, shaking the agent's hand.

"We're afraid there might be some activity in relation to your sister's case," said Agent Sloane.

"Oh, there's activity, all right," said Crockett.

"It would probably be better if you waited inside," continued Sloane. "For your safety. Agent Scott should be back in another hour and a half."

Ricky stifled a slew of f-bombs. "Hour and a half? Can't *you* help us?"

"I'm actually heading out just now myself," said Agent Sloane, looking at his watch. Then he raised his gaze to Ricky and seemed to come to a decision. "But if you'd care to ride along, we can talk, and then I'll have Agent Simons drop you both back here."

"Thank you!" said Ricky, following as Agent Sloane directed them to a dark sedan that had just pulled up at the curb. He held the door as Ricky and Crockett slid onto the back seat, then climbed into the front passenger seat alongside the driver, who wore a matching dark suit. As the car pulled away from the curb, Agent Sloane turned to talk with them.

"First, let me say that I understand how difficult this must be for you. We're still hoping for a favorable outcome regarding your sister."

"That's why we came to see Agent Scott today!" said Ricky, energized. "There's a note on this map that explains it all. She didn't kill anybody! They were members of a fu—" She stopped short, stifling the f-bomb. "Members of a cult! Oh, and there were some guys with guns who came after us at Clark University."

"Really?" said Agent Sloane. "Do you have a description?"

Ricky indicated Crockett, who recited the physical characteristics of the two he had gotten the best look at. The sedan, maneuvering through heavy late afternoon traffic, turned onto Lakeshore Drive heading north.

"Good," said Agent Sloane once Crockett had finished. "We want to keep you both safe while this is being resolved. Is that what you came to tell Agent Scott today?"

Ricky shook her head and brushed her hand along the top of the envelope on her lap. "The parchment that the research team found. Before she disappeared, my sister slipped it into the Zackenberg mail. I think this is what those men are after." She handed the envelope to Agent Sloane.

"Perfect," said Agent Sloane. "Hopefully the note from your sister will help clear her of any wrongdoing. And now that we have the parchment, you two and Mr. Bishara will no longer have to worry about your own safety."

The light disappeared from Ricky's face. "What did you say?"

Agent Sloane remained silent.

A great, cold weight coalesced in the pit of her stomach. "We never mentioned anything to you about Bash," continued Ricky. "We said we went to Clark University. But no one knew that we had gone to see Bash except me. And Crockett."

"And Betty," said Crockett dryly. "Betty the mole."

After a long, wordless pause, Agent Sloane sighed. "Well played." His friendly demeanor evaporated. "Now, if you wish to continue playing, please do not make any sudden moves or try anything foolish. I have a gun pointed at Miss Crowe. The bullets are perfectly capable of penetrating the seat."

"You fucking murderers!" growled Ricky, her face darkening.

"Easy, girl," said Crockett quietly. Then to Sloane, he said, "You've got what you want, right? Just let us off at the next corner and you'll never hear from us again."

"Patience," said Sloane.

The sedan now veered off Lakeshore and made a series of tight turns, sending them beneath the streets and sidewalks to a dingy, desolate, subterranean world of concrete pillars and foundation walls, empty gravel lots and chain-link fences.

"I was here once—or hereabouts," said Crockett quietly. "My cousin was visiting. Car got towed to an impound lot somewhere around here."

Sloane raised the hand not holding a gun, motioning with two fingers.

"Now why don't you both take out your phones and, nice and easy, drop them over the seat to me."

Crockett reached into a pocket and did as he was asked. However, Ricky noticed that the seat blocked Sloane's view, and he could not see that she already held her phone in her lap. Knowing that this bought her a second or two, she worked it with one hand while going through modest contortions that, to her captor, made it look like she was digging it out of a pocket.

"What are you going to do to us?" asked Crockett haltingly, trying to distract Sloane so that he did not realize Ricky's deception. "We're of no use to you!"

Sloane hesitated, but then, as if it no longer mattered, he said, "You *know* things. This place is discreet. A burned-out rental vehicle. Two bodies with bullet wounds. Business as usual in Chica—"

As they approached a narrow area flanked by concrete pillars, Ricky tapped her phone screen with a thumb, and the sound of a police siren filled the vehicle, accompanied by a flashing strobe light.

Sloane and the driver's heads jerked around, trying to pinpoint the source, which they believed was outside the sedan. But Ricky had already lunged forward and wrapped her arms around the driver's head, clawing at his eyes.

Fuck you and all your murdering buddies from Zackenberg!

He took one hand off the wheel to tear at her forearms. It was enough. The sedan veered right a couple of feet and slammed into a pillar. The airbags deployed, though the passenger bag caught Sloane—who was half-turned and unbelted—awkwardly so that the side of his head still hit the dash.

Ricky wasted no time, opening her door and clambering out. She saw that Crockett had done the same on his side. They sprinted toward a concrete wall and in moments, rested on the other side.

Crockett sucked in deep breaths. "What was that? The siren, the flashing?"

"Thank God for YouTube." She held up her phone. "Could have chosen either 'Police Siren' or 'Noises Under the Hood'. Guess I chose right."

Crockett nodded, betraying a trace of smile. "Genius."

Ricky frowned. "Not really. I spend most of my fucking life online."

"Come on," said Crockett, turning away. "We've got to keep moving!"

They ran on, eventually finding the delivery entrance to a hotel, taking the elevator up, and, minutes later, walking out into the sunshine of Chicago in the late afternoon.

"The envelope!" cried Ricky.

"We can't go back for it," said Crockett. "Keep moving!"

Ricky felt sick to her stomach. The envelope had contained the only real proof that her sister had not been working with the terrorists responsible for the Zackenberg massacre. And her sister had sacrificed everything to get it to Ricky to protect whatever secrets it contained. Now there was no hope of getting it back.

"You've goddamn ruined everything!" she cried. "What do we do now?"

"We've got to warn Bash!" said Crockett, and they hailed a cab.

CHAPTER 9

The cab ride took fifteen minutes, and as they neared The Delray, they could tell that the news was bad. Yellow police tape cordoned off a wide area around the building and several squads and emergency vehicles blocked the road out front.

"God, no. God, no," Crockett muttered as Ricky paid the driver and they climbed out.

They worked their way through the gathered crowd to the tape, where a perimeter control officer, sensing their urgency, moved forward with his hand raised.

"Stay behind the tape, please."

"What happened?" asked Crockett. "I have a friend who is staying here!"

"Ongoing investigation, sir," said the officer.

Crockett pulled out his phone and called Bash's number.

Hi. You've reached Dr. Samir Bishara. Please leave a message.

He cursed and sent Bash a text, muttering "no" over and over as he did so.

Ricky half-turned toward a middle-aged woman whose voice rose above the general din, angrily addressing a male acquaintance, her hands animated, moving about like small, tan barn swallows.

"Worthless piece of trash strangled his wife and little bitty baby, and then the coward blew out his own brains with a gun!"

"Why?" said the male acquaintance, a chinless, balding man in a blue work shirt. "Why would someone do that? To his own kid, no less?"

"They said there was a big pile of bills like electric and student loans and medical scattered all over their room," continued the woman. "They think that's why he done it! I don't know why he didn't just do himself and leave that poor woman and little child! The world is full of sickness!"

Overhearing the conversation, Crockett fell to his knees, doubling over so that his forehead touched the ground. Ricky had no idea what she should do, and so she simply stood above him, glaring at the cordoned-off building with growing bitterness. *I should run.* It might be a mile to her apartment, an easy distance. She would run fast, a good cleansing effort. And when she was locked away in her apartment, lost in the virtual world, everything would again be all right.

Only, it wouldn't.

Her decision to go to the HARP Foundation this morning had set these wheels in motion. Her apartment would offer no sanctuary. But had she really had a choice? Was she supposed to have simply ignored her sister's last request? *Yes,* a voice in her head replied. *If the price of that request was the death of two innocent people and their infant child.* But, she reasoned, how could she have known?

Crockett stayed on his knees for several minutes, his body occasionally shaking with grief or rage. When he finally raised his head, Ricky was certain that she had never seen such dark hatred.

"They're going to pay!" he growled hoarsely.

Ricky could not meet his eyes. "I—I'm sorry."

"It's not your fault."

Part of her realized this. Another part wasn't as sure. "But the map—"

"It's *not* your fault! Those bastards who came after us at Clark own this!"

"What now?" asked Ricky, helping him to his feet. "The cops are right here. Do we tell them the truth?"

Crockett nodded, but then stopped suddenly. "Yes. No. This cult is everywhere! Shit, how can we trust anyone?"

"They must have infiltrated the FBI and..." Ricky stopped, trying to make sense of it.

"Think! Did Sloane or whatever his real name is come out the door of the FBI building?" asked Crockett. "Or did he just come from that general direction? Maybe we just *assumed* that the guy wearing a name badge had come out of FBI headquarters. Saw what we wanted to see. Maybe the cult figured that we'd go to the Feds and they ran a con."

Ricky shook her head to indicate that she was not sure, looked around anxiously. "Let's get away from here. By now, Sloan must have gotten the word out that we got away."

They moved through the crowd and out into the open at its rear. Then they jogged along the sidewalk and into a sandwich shop, hugging the entrance as they talked.

"We can't go to the police or the FBI." Ricky suddenly and viciously punched the wooden wainscoting near the entrance several times, dislodging a couple of live music posters tacked up and drawing stares from several diners at café-style tables.

Crocket leaned in, whispered. "Easy champ. And we can't go home. They're certainly going to be watching those places. They must have been watching Bash's and followed Chione to the hotel." He squinted his eyes closed, mashed his right cheek against the window near the entrance, wiping away another tear.

This confirmation of what she already knew—but was loathe to admit—drained Ricky, who examined gashed knuckles, wiped a thin trickle of blood on her pants. "Shit, where can we go?" she asked, immediately regretting the use of "we". "I can't just wander the streets for the rest of my life!"

"No we can't," said Crockett somberly. "Especially if we want to make these sons of bitches pay for..."

He left the terrible sentence unfinished, closing his eyes once more as they stood in silence.

Then, a light seemed to come into Crockett's face. "Okay, we obviously need help. We've got to trust someone. I say we go to see Leo. Dr. Leo Brenner is the director of HARP, and he's the most decent and ethical man I know. And he has resources that might be able to help us. He's definitely one of the good guys."

Ricky stared listlessly out toward the sidewalk. "What if you're wrong?"

"Then there's no hope for any of us!"

Immediately after saying this, he paused as if an idea had just come to him. "You still have your phone?"

Ricky nodded, retrieved it from a pocket, handed it to him. Stepping out of the entry foyer into the restaurant, Crockett dropped the mobile into the trash receptacle around the corner.

Ricky's mouth dropped open. "Shit! What the hell!

"Think about it!" said Crockett. "Think of what they've been able to do! Cell phones can be tracked! We don't want to end up like..." His voice trailed off again. Then he forced himself to say it. "Like Bash."

I should just run. But she had nowhere to run. No safe destination. Nowhere the cult, which seemed to have eyes everywhere, would not think to look.

"Wait!" she said, and then dug unceremoniously into the trash bin, finding her phone—luckily—near the top. She snapped out the memory card, dropping the phone back into the trash. "It's got the picture of the map!" She held the chip aloft a moment and then stuffed it into a front pocket.

They exited the shop, keeping their eyes always moving, hopped a bus, made a transfer, and twenty minutes later stood in front of Brenner's fashionable townhouse. A nagging uneasiness kept Ricky on the verge of breaking into a sprint toward the maze of alleys and side streets and the anonymity offered by early evening shadows. She fought it off, despite what seemed to her the ultimate futility of whatever plan Crockett envisioned. One of Crockett's coworkers at HARP had already led the cult to them. Would Brenner be any less likely to sell them out?

They were buzzed in immediately, and Brenner met them at the door, a tall man, his dark hair graying at the temples, but with a firm, square chin and piercing blue eyes that seemed to radiate leadership. He wore khakis, slippers, and a white dress shirt, though it was open at the collar with no tie.

"Mason, this is unexpected," he said, ushering them in to the hallway. Then, as he appraised them more closely, he added, "You look awful."

"It's been an awful day," said Crockett. "Worse than awful. Leo, this is Ricky Crowe."

Brenner shook her hand and then held onto it in a kind gesture. "Miss Crowe, I'm glad to meet you finally. I believe we spoke on the telephone," he said, recalling his contact with her after the first wave of news out of Zackenberg. "We all love your sister, and hope that there is a positive resolution to all of this." Despite his politeness, she felt the same sense of appraisal that others gave her when they looked at her scar or considered how different she looked from Sasha.

"Leo, Bash is dead."

Brenner seemed momentarily stunned, his smile disappearing, and he turned slowly toward Crockett. "Dr. Bishara? Your friend? How?"

"That's what we're here to talk about, Leo."

The news clearly disturbed Brenner. When he recovered, he ushered them into the living room. "Can I get you something?"

"Beer."

He then looked to Ricky.

"Do you have tea?"

"Coming right up."

As he turned to leave, Crockett stopped him. "Can we talk somewhere else? Somewhere without so many windows facing the street?"

"Sure, Mason," said Brenner, his forehead creasing in concern. "We can use my office in the back."

He directed them down a hallway decorated with tasteful, earth-tone wallpapers and old-fashioned crystal light fixtures. Several gorgeous watercolor landscapes adorned the walls. They took seats in comfortable leather chairs in front of a massive, antique, oak desk while Brenner excused himself to get their drinks.

"Better bring at least two beers," Crockett said as Brenner retreated.

The office featured all the stereotypes: one wall filled with books, floor to ceiling, a tile-faced fireplace, a huge braided rug that covered most of the wooden floor, and a few framed photographs of memorable events on the back wall. Wine-colored curtains were drawn over the only window. There was one shelf that was apparently reserved for family photos, including one of a much younger Leo Brenner standing next to a pretty, smiling woman.

"Mary," said Crockett, catching the direction of Ricky's gaze. "His wife. No kids. She passed away six years ago. Cancer. Since then, he's been married to the Foundation."

A minute later, Brenner arrived with a serving tray, which he sat on the desk.

"Your tea," he said, extending his hand toward the cup. "There's also honey, sugar, and milk if you wish."

Ricky nodded curtly and noticed that Crockett was already halfway through the first beer.

"So what's going on here, Mason," said Brenner, settling into his high-backed leather chair. "Bash? Dead? My God, how? And why the secrecy?"

They spent the next half hour filling him in, starting with Ricky's receipt of the envelope from Sasha. They described the envelope's contents, including the map, its possible Celtic connections, and how they had taken it to Bash for interpretation of the hieroglyphics.

"Leo, we think there is a mole at HARP," said Crockett, who explained their suspicions about Betty. Leo listened raptly to this and to the details of how they had eluded the cult thugs at Clark University, how they had accompanied Bash to the Delray, and how Crockett and Ricky had been kidnapped by cult members pretending to be FBI agents.

"Good Lord!" exclaimed Brenner as they described their escape. "I can see why you're reluctant to go to the police! You're lucky to be here!"

"We should have stayed with Bash," said Crockett, somberly.

"No," said Brenner. "Then you'd all be dead. Don't put this on you. These people, whoever they are, *they're* the ones responsible, period."

"Leo, they killed him because he had seen the map. And they made it look like he killed his family! Made it look like he was some poor, desperate, unhinged sap! Sons of bitches!"

Brenner seemed lost in thought for a minute. Then he said, "We need to know more about these people. They obviously have financial resources. And they have connections. But so do I. They must have left a footprint of some sort."

He flipped out his cell and tapped the screen several times.

"Tom? Hi, Tom, this is Leo! Yes, it is. Good, good. Hope you've been well. Look, Tom, I know this is short notice, but can you drop by tonight? Within the hour, if possible. Yes. Yes, very. It's linked to what is being falsely framed as a murder-suicide that occurred in the city tonight. And are you familiar with an organization that worships or idolizes someone called Cessair? C-E-S-S...yes. Yes. Yes, there will be two others here. Good. Thank you, Tom. I look forward to it!"

He signed off, leaned forward onto his desk, lacing his fingers together.

"Tom is an old friend. Has written a dozen books on world cults. If anyone knows anything about these murderers, Tom will know."

Dr. Thomas Campion arrived half an hour later.

CHAPTER 10

"So good of you to drop everything and come, Tom," said Brenner as he ushered Campion into the room. Then he excused himself for a moment, pulling in a padded chair for the new arrival.

"Well, when you mentioned Cessair, how could I say no?" asked Campion playfully, shaking his head. Dr. Thomas Campion —medium height and about sixty with wavy, silver-flecked hair the color of straw—wore baggy khakis and a long-sleeved navy t-shirt under a black leather vest. His kind smile radiated a sincerity that eased the tension in the room significantly.

Brenner introduced Ricky and Crockett. Then they took turns bringing their new arrival up to speed.

"Incredible!" Campion remarked several times as the other three narrated. "Incredible!"

At its conclusion, Campion removed and slowly cleaned his round, wire-rimmed glasses, staring across the room at nothing, considering the immensity of what he had heard. Brenner finally broke the silence.

"What do you know about these people, Tom?"

Campion twisted the spectacles onto his face and looked to each of them in turn. "The Cult of Cessair is very secretive. And very old. Yes, perhaps 5,000 years. The details of their leadership structure are difficult to come by. In fact, it has often been assumed there is no structure. Just random individuals or small groups devoted to Cessair. However, recent events seem to suggest otherwise."

"I still can't figure out how all of this fits together, Doc," said Crockett, addressing Campion. "Egypt, Ireland, Greenland. How are they all connected? And what is the Scroll of Life and Death?"

Campion pressed his fingertips together and seemed to be collecting his thoughts. "Let me start at the beginning. According to legend, Cessair was a granddaughter of Noah, who lived in Egypt or Mesopotamia. When news of the flood reached her, she went to her grandfather, seeking a place on the ark, but was refused."

"We know that," said Ricky curtly. Then, realizing that she might have responded too abruptly, added, "I mean, if you believe in the story of the ark, why would Noah do that? Turn her away, I mean?"

Campion's face became rigid, deadly serious. "There are several versions of the story. But based on today's events, it seems one of them has moved to the front of the line. Apparently he turned her away because of what she brought with her. The Scroll of Life and Death. According to myth, an Egyptian sorcerer had created that dark magic, and Noah would almost certainly have felt that it was God's intent that it be destroyed in the flood along with the other evils of humanity. That's why she was refused."

Crockett interrupted. "So whatever this cult is after, it's not gold or money?"

"Something far more valuable in their eyes," said Campion.

"What was the purpose of this scroll?" asked Brenner.

"It contained the secret of immortality," stated Campion.

Silence gripped the room for several seconds.

"But… that's just legend, right?" asked Crockett. "I mean, that's not possible."

"Whether it is possible or not, the devotees of Cessair *believe* it is true," said Campion, "and this is why they have been searching for 5,000 years. Even if it is merely a folk tale with no basis in fact, these people are tremendously dangerous because *they* consider it the truth! You've heard of Giordano Bruno?"

"Astronomer, right?" asked Brenner.

Campion nodded. "Was tried for heresy in 1593. Said lots of things that upset the church. For instance, that the earth was not the center of the solar system, that there was no center of the universe, and that the stars might have planets revolving around them complete with intelligent life! He also questioned the Trinity and Transubstantiation—you know—the idea that, during communion, the wine and the wafer actually *do become* the blood and body of Christ. Whether these things are possible or not, the Roman Catholic Church believed them passionately, and that made the church an enemy to people like Bruno. He was burned at the stake!"

Brenner cleared his throat. "I get your point. Myth or fact, these believers in the scroll are dangerous."

"Like conspiracy theorists today," chimed in Ricky.

"Exactly!" nodded Brenner. "Like the Heaven's Gate cult whose members passionately believed that a spaceship was trailing Comet Hale-Bopp, so much so that thirty-nine of them committed suicide, thinking their deaths would transport their souls to the spacecraft and they'd be taken to another, higher level of existence."

"Look at some of today's Internet conspiracy groups," added Campion, "whose faithful advocate taking up arms against the government or renouncing established science based on the slimmest evidence and wildest theories. Unfortunately, some are all too willing to 'believe'."

"But I still don't get where Greenland comes in," said Crockett.

Campion tapped an index finger on the desk excitedly. "Cessair went to Ireland to escape the flood and took the scroll with her. Again, this is all according to the old legends. She felt God's punishment of humanity was unjust, and so *her* plan was to create a race of superhumans who would no longer need to fear God, for they would not be touched by death. But her plan began to unravel. Two of her three ships were lost in storms on the trip."

"Divine intervention?" asked Crockett smugly.

Campion smiled. "Who can say? In any case, there remained Cessair and forty-nine other women, along with three men, Fintan Mac, Bith and Ladra. These were to populate Ireland with a race of immortals. Then, Bith and Ladra died. Fintan began to appreciate the evil of Cessair's monstrous plan. And so he escaped."

"Yeah, I heard he turned into a salmon," said Crockett. "I guess whatever works for you."

"Folklore frequently uses symbolism and allegory, either to make a point, or to make the story more interesting for listeners in that age," said Campion with a grin. "I think it's more likely that he took the boat that we've heard about."

"And he was apparently heading for Egypt," said Brenner. "Or at least some place to the south where he could secure more reliable passage to Egypt."

Crockett nodded. "The map showed Memphis. But why was he going there? I thought you said that Cessair had the scroll with her?"

"Remember that Fintan had rebelled against Cessair and her unholy plans," said Campion, "so it's likely that he destroyed the scroll. But remember, the sorcerer who created it was in Egypt."

Brenner nodded. "I see. So he was going to kill the sorcerer."

"Or maybe he believed there was another scroll," suggested Ricky. She was again surprised—as she had been at the Del Ray—at how empowered she felt discussing the old Celtic myths, and how easily she found it to share what she knew. "I mean, it stands to reason that the creator of such a powerful magic would have a duplicate for himself."

Campion nodded. "Yes, it appears the cult believes in a second scroll as well. But until the map was dug out of the ice in Greenland, no one knew that the second scroll's hiding place was in Egypt. Or where in Egypt, specifically. They could only guess. Blindly, for 5,000 years, Cessair's devotees have searched for the scroll that legend told them existed somewhere in the world."

"So Fintan borrowed a boat and went after the sorcerer... or the scroll... or both." Crockett considered this for a few moments. "Too bad he didn't have a better sense of direction."

"I've been thinking about that," said Campion. "There are currents that could sweep someone to the north and west. And if the waters were rising due to a great flood, this could increase their power and the distance they would drive Fintan Mac off course."

"If you believe in that sort of thing," said Crockett.

"Cessair and her followers believed in the danger well enough to travel to Ireland," said Campion. "And the earth periodically suffers catastrophic weather events. So was it a Great Flood like the one described in the Bible? A freak storm? A tsunami? Just bad luck with the currents? Impossible for us to say. But the fact remains, Fintan's boat and the parchment map ended up in the ice at Zackenberg."

"What do you think happened to Cessair?" asked Ricky.

"No one knows," said Campion. "Fifty women on an island

with no men? Her tribe may simply have died out. Or scattered to other places in northern Europe where they were absorbed into existing tribes—or perhaps they joined tribes that they found in Ireland, contrary to their belief that it was uninhabited. Or they may have perished in the Great Flood, if you prefer that explanation. On the other hand, maybe it's all myth. Maybe Cessair never existed. Yet, flood or not, it's beginning to look like there's some degree of truth to the tales, since a map was indeed recovered from the ice. Regardless, the legend behind the scroll persists, and so generation after generation, that legend has been passed down, as are the myths and traditions in all cults or belief systems. The cult of Cessair, however, has become quite powerful, despite the fact that they've been operating far under the radar."

"But they're not really going to find anything," said Ricky, surprised by her own boldness.

"Perhaps not," said Campion.

"Perhaps?" Ricky looked around the office for support. "Immortality? Really? Let's say they go to Egypt and find nothing. Won't that be the end of them? Won't they realize that it's all a sham?"

"I don't know," said Brenner. "Perhaps their organization will finally break down. But it's more likely that someone in their leadership circle will declare the map a fake or suggest that it has been altered, and their search will continue, leaving more bodies in their wake. Fanatics like these aren't slowed down by the truth."

"I remember reading about a pastor who predicted the world was going to end on May 21, 2011," said Crockett. "People sold their possessions, their homes. When it didn't happen, he said he'd miscalculated and changed the date."

Brenner nodded. "I could see that happening here. If reality doesn't match your version of the truth, just tweak reality. These zealots have invested too much over too long a period to *allow* themselves to be wrong. That means they'll continue to be dangerous. And we have no idea if the passage of time will cause them to lose interest in you two. No, these people are a cancer. They must be brought to justice."

"How?" asked Crockett, massaging his forehead. "We can't go to the police or the FBI because the cult may have infiltrated them. Maybe it's the beer. Or Bash. But I can't think of anything that will help."

Brenner stroked his chin, staring at the blotter on his desk. "Do we know exactly where they are going now that they have the map?"

Suddenly, Ricky felt like retreating into the shadows again, embarrassed that she had eagerly handed the map to cult members. Aware that this probably meant there was nothing they could do.

"I suppose we could remember most of what's on it," said Crockett in what almost seemed to Ricky like at attempt to rescue her. "That might give us an idea. There were four groups of hieroglyphics…"

Brenner took out a legal pad upon which to jot notes.

"Wait!" said Ricky suddenly remembering. "I took a picture!" She retrieved the memory card she had removed from her phone. Brenner took it, inserted it into his own device, and a minute later brought the picture onto the large screen.

"All right!" said Crockett, leaning in to see her screen. "It's almost like having the real thing!"

"I'll print out a copy, too," Brenner said, handing the SD card back to Ricky. "This is very helpful."

"Bash gave this spiral a name" she said, pointing to the torn symbol on the map.

Campion strained forward for a better look at her screen. "As

ROD VICK

the rest of these symbols are Egyptian, I'd wager that this is a
mehen."

Crockett nodded. "Yeah, that's what Bash called it." He
suddenly looked at the floor, seemed to struggle to control his
emotions. When he spoke again, he was fighting hard to keep from
giving in to his grief. "What does it mean?"

"It means 'coiled one'. You know, like a snake. In Egyptian
mythology, it's often seen coiled around the sun, sort of as a
protector. And the sun is often seen as representing life."

"This makes sense," said Crockett, jumping in with artificial
enthusiasm as if to redirect his focus away from Bash. "*Life*, get it?
We have a map that directs us to Memphis and to a tomb. And I'll
bet somewhere in that tomb is a mehen like this that marks the
location of the hidden scroll!"

Campion pointed a finger at the photo where the torn edge of
the map that crossed the spiral. "This looks new, but it's hard to tell
from a tiny photograph. Your sister wrote on the map?"

Ricky confirmed this with a slight nod. "But we're not sure
why she wrote about the moon."

"Very curious," said Campion. "Could it be some sort of
hidden message? A code, for instance. She may have done it in
case the map was to fall into the hands of enemies. What I mean is,
perhaps she believed it was a clue that you, her sister, might
understand."

Ricky frowned. "I've never heard of freakin' Mare Desiderii. If
it's a clue, it must have been intended for somebody else."

Crockett threw up his hands as if in defense. "I'm just as much
in the dark, Tom."

Campion again turned to the map but continued to speak to
Crockett. "If Sasha used precious seconds to write this message, it
must be significant. And since it's written over part of the spiral, I

114

can't help wondering if Mare Desiderii and the mehen are connected."

"Do you think Cessair's people will figure out that the spiral is a mehen?" asked Brenner.

"I suspect they already have," said Campion. "Even fanatics have access to experts. But it's not a particularly uncommon symbol among Egyptian hieroglyphs. Almost anyone could discover its meaning with a quick online search."

"Then they're probably jetting off to Egypt right now to find the scroll," said Crockett, his excitement gone.

Brenner suddenly sat up straighter in his chair.

"Maybe that's exactly what we should do."

No one said anything for a moment.

"You mean try and find the scroll?" asked Crockett.

Brenner nodded and a smile spread across his face. "Why not? Look, they're already after you, and they'll probably keep looking for you even if you do nothing. For all we know, they may come after Dr. Campion and myself, too, if they suspect you've confided in us. Sorry, Tom."

"No, no, that's all right," said Campion good-naturedly. "I spend hundreds of hours writing esoteric academic papers that will be read by dozens. It's nice to find myself on the periphery of a little *real* adventure."

"It's more than a little adventure, Doc," said Crockett. "Our lives are at risk."

Brenner shrugged. "Our lives are at risk if we sit here twiddling our thumbs. We can't trust the police. But we have Dr. Bishara's translations and our own educated guesses as to what they mean. Well, what if our guesses are better than theirs? I think we have to assume that Sasha's clue was intended for either Crockett or Ricky, something only one of them could figure out. That could give us an advantage. If we can find the scroll first and get it to the FBI—the legitimate guys, not the imposters—then there will be no motivation for the cult to silence us! Knowing that the scroll is out of play may, in itself, be the end of the cult. Or it may lead them to be reckless enough to expose themselves to authorities."

Ricky sat there stone-faced. *Egypt? No fucking way.*

As if he had heard her utter the sentiment out loud, Crockett let out a short laugh and addressed Brenner. "You're kidding, right? We're not exactly the Marines. Plus, they've got a couple hours head start. And lots of guns."

"I've already acknowledged that it will be dangerous," said Brenner. "But so is sitting around and waiting for them to emerge from a dark alleyway or fail to stop for you in a crosswalk four or five weeks from now. Look, money isn't an issue with me. I've got resources. If we can travel to Egypt, stay under the radar, so to speak, perhaps we can get our hands on the scroll first. Now, let's take a closer look at that map."

They returned their attention to the screen.

"We know we have to go to Memphis," said Brenner. "But where after that? There are hundreds of tombs of one sort or another. We can't visit every one, looking for a... a...?"

"Mehen," volunteered Campion.

"Right. So, is there anything on the parchment that will narrow it down for us?"

"I wish to hell Bash was here to help us," said Crockett, his voice cracking.

"The help he has already given may end up defeating this great evil," said Brenner. "Now try and remember what those hieroglyphics mean."

Crockett cradled his head in his hands for a moment, then sat up. "I think the first column was just the name. Scroll of Life and

Death. The second was—damn, I'm a mess."

"It was the tomb," said Ricky. "And something about it being in the shape of an X."

Campion suddenly nodded as if this made sense.

"There was also something about a river—a river of milk," said Crockett. "And then the last one was a reference to the Nile, I think. Great river."

Brenner scribbled all of it onto his notepad.

"What about these repeating symbols at the perimeter?" asked Campion.

"Mythological characters," replied Crockett. "Gods and goddesses."

"Back up," interrupted Ricky. "The X-shaped tomb column. There was something else. Follow the sun."

"The sun shows the way," nodded Crockett. "Something like that."

Brenner raised an eyebrow. "Something like that?"

Crockett threw up his hands. "That's the best I've got without Bash's notes."

Campion sat back. "Fascinating."

Brenner looked to Campion. "I really can't make much of all this. Tom, how about you?"

"Well, I think we may have turned our needle in a haystack into a needle in a... much smaller haystack," said Campion. "Keep in mind, I can't interpret hieroglyphics like this. I'm familiar with a few symbols, but for the most part, I'll be relying on the certainty of your memories."

Crockett smiled through clenched teeth. "Way to put the pressure on us, Doc."

"According to the parchment," continued Campion, "we're not just looking for any tomb. It's a tomb with a specific design. Like

117

an X. In other words, interior passages in the shape of a cruciform. Like a cross—one long main passage with a shorter cross passage. Most of the Egyptian tombs weren't designed like this, so that narrows it down considerably."

"Wait!" said Crockett, raising a finger. "We also know it's got to be an old tomb. Bash said the types of hieroglyphics meant it was Archaic Egyptian. So we're talking something constructed between 4,000 and 5,000 years ago."

Brenner nodded, adding to his notes. "Great. And you said it's probably located at Memphis?"

"That would make sense," said Campion. "Memphis was known as the city of white walls. White walls could be interpreted to look like a river of milk."

"And great river means Nile, which also makes sense," said Brenner.

"So what do we do now?" asked Crockett.

"Now, we eat," smiled Brenner.

Ricky remained stone-faced. She had felt miserable all night. The day's events had been horribly unsettling. Her head was pounding, and she felt a growing sense of unease approaching panic. She belonged at her apartment in front of a brightly lit screen, the world's real problems locked outside of her digital parallel universe.

She was also starving, and Brenner's mention of food made her stomach rumble.

"I don't have much of an appetite tonight, Leo," said Crockett.

"Of course." Brenner patted him on the shoulder. "Tom?"

Campion nodded. "I could do with something."

Brenner tossed Campion his cell phone and a credit card.

"Pizzeria Da Nella. It's in the contacts. Order a couple of larges. And bread." He then turned to his computer keyboard and began tapping.

Ricky asked for directions to the bathroom and then headed back down the hallway in the direction from which they had come. She emerged a few minutes later shivering, despite the comfortable environment inside the townhouse.

He can't be serious. Fucking Egypt!

She dug a couple of aspirin out of her backpack and searched out the kitchen to find a cup of water. However, as she opened cupboard doors, looking for a drinking glass, she discovered a bottle of whiskey, more than three-quarters full.

Shit.

Ricky found a drinking glass in another cupboard, took the two aspirin with a gulp of water. Then she opened the door to look at the whiskey again. She stared at it longingly.

I don't need it.

But she knew this was a lie. The framework of her life lay in ruins. Her sister, missing. A man she had only just met, murdered along with his family. And didn't she share some of the blame? People trying to kill her. Her apartment a place of safety no more. And now a wild plan to jet off to Egypt to compete with psychopaths over a bit of folklore that probably did not even exist —but which might succeed in getting them killed.

She could imagine the whiskey on her tongue, its healing warmth as she swallowed.

I don't need it!

But suddenly, her previously empty drinking glass was half full. She stood staring at the copper liquid, unable to think of a single reason to not drink it, although on some level, she knew there must be dozens.

It occurred to her that she should leave right now. Out the front door. Back streets to her apartment. Surely she could sneak in without anyone seeing. She could lock herself in, call in sick for a few days until it all blew over.

Then she thought of Bash.

She detected movement to the left and turned quickly. Crockett stood in the entrance to the kitchen, expressionless. After a few moments, he turned without comment and walked away.

Ricky shivered, picked up the glass.

Down the fucking drain.

But then she took a sip. A minute later, the glass was empty.

CHAPTER 11

She returned to Brenner's office, sat, avoiding Crockett's gaze. *It's one goddamn glass. Half a glass. No big deal.*

And she felt a little steadier, a little warmer, a little less likely to run to her apartment and curl herself into a ball in a dark corner.

"You're certain of Bash's translations?" Brenner was asking Crockett.

"Yes, sir. Sort of. As certain as Bash was, anyway. And our memories."

Brenner nodded. "We're staking an awful lot on the accuracy of his translation. And our analysis of it. How certain are we that this tomb is located near Memphis?"

"There's always a chance for misinterpretation," Campion acknowledged. "But the city location on the map, the river of milk... it all seems to fit."

Brenner considered the matter quietly for a moment and then stood. "I'm going to excuse myself to another room to make a few calls. I think we should act quickly if we're all agreed. Mason? And you, Miss Crowe?"

"How quickly?" asked Crockett.

"If you're game, I can have a private jet and a couple of

security personnel ready to go in an hour. I think if we really want to have a chance at beating these villains to the prize, we have to act immediately. We can continue our research on the way."

"What about me?" asked Campion.

"Tom," said Brenner, slapping him on the shoulder, "it could be dangerous."

Campion smiled. "Great! I wouldn't miss it for the world!"

Then all eyes were on Ricky.

Although her headache was gone, her stomach had begun to roll again, and she felt completely off-balance, the way one might when carried along by a mob toward the smoldering stake in the village square. Everything that she had come to know as a constant in her life had collapsed, half of it in the past twenty-four hours.

Noting her hesitation, Brenner said, "If you'd rather not, I can put you up in a safe house of sorts until this is resolved. Until we've found that scroll, I don't think you should stay at your normal living quarters."

Ricky stiffened. She was not going to live out of a hotel room or basement like some prisoner.

But how was Brenner's suggestion any different than barricading herself in her own apartment playing video games? Just two different versions of the same prison. And that wouldn't change until the cult was neutralized.

In Egypt, perhaps she would at least have the satisfaction of helping fuck-up the bastards who were responsible for her sister's disappearance.

"No. I'll go."

Her decision was immediately followed by the arrival of the pizza.

Ricky ate ravenously. Crockett, who had earlier confessed to having no appetite, seemed to have recovered his nicely. However, after polishing off his third thick slice, he brought a problem to the group's attention.

"Passport," said Crockett. "Mine's sitting at home in my sock drawer."

"I have to pick up mine, too," added Ricky.

"Take a cab," said Brenner. "I'll give you the address of the corporate airfield. Be there in an hour. And keep thinking about what Sasha might have meant by her reference to the dark side of the moon. Considering the circumstances, it has to be vitally important. I'm sure it's driving the cult crazy. And speaking of the cult, be very careful retrieving those passports. In fact…"

He left the sentence unfinished, disappeared down the hall and up a flight of stairs. Several minutes later, he reappeared, clothing draped over his arms.

"Put these on. You'll look like a nicely dressed couple returning from a movie or dinner. If there are people looking for you, the disguises might throw them off. It won't be the clothing they've been told you're wearing."

Ricky slipped into the bathroom and examined the dress. Very nice and very expensive. Black, falling to just below her knees. Fairly modest neckline. Brenner had also selected black pumps, probably suspecting—correctly—that Ricky was not adept with spiky high heels. Or perhaps it was simply the style that Mary had preferred. The finishing touch was a blonde wig, shoulder length, wavy and formal. It fitted easily over her own hair once she skewered it with bobby pins that had been affixed to the wig's liner.

When she emerged from the bathroom, she was greeted by a whistle from Crockett. "My, you dress up nicely!"

Crockett wore an expensive looking charcoal suit, a pin-striped dress shirt beneath the jacket, and a cherry-colored tie that matched the stripes. He also wore a fedora.

"You look like fucking Clark Kent."

"I'll take that!" he said jovially.

"It's probably a little out of fashion," said Brenner, "but I needed to find one that would fit. Take a cab. When you get out at your apartments, talk loudly, laugh as if you've had a wonderful evening. Be everything they'd expect you not to be, just in case they're watching. They'll be expecting cautious, plainly dressed individuals, not an obnoxiously happy couple. And when you head for the airport, switch cabs, make sure you're not followed. Good luck!"

They headed to Ricky's apartment first. As they approached the building, Crockett asked, "Are you sure you can do this?"

"Get my passport?"

"No, laugh like you're having a good time. It's kind of important, and so far, I haven't seen any evidence of you being capable of expressing any form of humor or happiness."

She glared at him as if she wanted to rip his face off, then suddenly broke into a raucous laugh as if she were the life of the party.

"All right, all right, good to know," said Crockett. The cab pulled in front of the building and Crockett paid the driver. They got out, talking loudly, laughing convincingly, trying to avoid the temptation to look around. Ricky was sure their performance was so badly overdone that it fooled no one. Once inside the security door, Crockett exhaled noisily.

"Keep your eyes and ears open," he said.

"My eyes and ears have been open ever since that damned package came in the mail," Ricky replied.

"I mean anything that doesn't look right, even in here. They caught us with our britches down earlier today, and I don't want to end up in the back seat of a cultmobile again."

They took the elevator to floor nine, and then climbed the stairs the last two floors. The door to her apartment was locked and appeared to have been untouched. Slipping inside, she locked it behind them."

"I'll just be a minute."

Crockett gave the tiny living room, which opened into an even tinier kitchen area, a quick appraisal. "Nice place," he said, even though it wasn't particularly nice. However, a 60-inch flat screen TV stood in the living room, wired, it appeared, to the latest in gaming technology. In addition, a shelf along the wall was filled with movies. He stepped closer, inspecting the titles. *Casablanca* caught his eye.

"Nice movie collection."

He did not quite catch her muffled response from the bedroom.

"I said nice movie collection."

Ricky emerged, carrying a small backpack. "I said those are Sasha's. I don't watch that shit. Or TV."

"You don't watch any TV?"

"It's all piss."

"You wouldn't say that if you had NFL Network. What's this?" He indicated a new backpack she carried as she arrived at the door.

"Change of clothes. And some personal none-of-your-fucking-business items."

She unlocked the door, switched off the light and they moved into the hallway.

"I was just going to grab my passport," said Crockett, eyeing her bulging pack.

Ricky regarded him with barely restrained impatience. "What about a toothbrush? A change of underwear?"

"Have you ever heard of 'going commando'?" said Crockett,

smiling as they headed toward the stairwell.

She shook her head. *Goddamn hick.*

A few minutes later, their cab arrived at his apartment. Ricky noticed a drugstore on the corner. "I'll just be a sec," she said. "You go up, get your things."

"I'm on the second floor, apartment D," he called after her, and then turned toward the older brownstone.

Rushing into the well-lit store two houses away, Ricky withdrew cash from an ATM, using some of it to purchase more aspirin and two no-contract mobile phones. Then she jogged back to Crockett's building.

What's the point in going up? The fool isn't even packing underwear!

She waited. For a man who was packing light, he seemed to be taking a long time.

Too long.

She cautiously mounted the front steps, entered the common hallway, started up the open staircase, trying to make as little noise as possible. The old, wooden steps, their dark varnish worn away down the middle by decades of traffic, groaned at even the lightest footfall, until she placed her feet at the extreme ends.

It's nothing. His passport isn't where he thought it was, that's all.

But with each step, her heart sounded a more insistent alarm. As she reached the landing, she found two doors, C and D. Guitar music boomed from behind D. She hesitated.

'Keep your eyes and ears open to anything that's out of place,' Crockett had said.

Ricky leaned close to the door. The music continued, but there were no sounds of footsteps pounding across the room or drawers being slammed open and closed. The fact that Crockett had chosen to play music alarmed her even more, since their goal had been to slip in and out quickly and unnoticed.

They've got him, Ricky thought. *They must have broken in and were waiting for him.* He might be dead already or they might be waiting until he helped lure her into their trap.

She had no intention of giving them the chance. Crockett was a dead man. Whether now or ten minutes from now, it made no difference. The Dixie-glazed man-child had been careless, and now he was done. There was no way she could rescue him without assistance or weapons.

But she might still be able to save herself.

Ricky backed away from the door, crept silently down the flight of stairs, and emerged onto the sidewalk. Jogging to the main street, she hailed a cab, and moments later was speeding away to the rendezvous at the private airfield.

CHAPTER 12

Crockett sat at his desk, listening to Lynyrd Skynyrd's "Gimme Three Steps" pouring like audible whiskey through small but powerful Bose speakers on his bookshelf, looping over and over again, his passport in his pocket.

A passport he might never get a chance to use.

Come on, Ricky!

Unless she understood his signal, they were both doomed. But she *had* to understand. He had tapped on that specific song as soon as he had heard the faint scraping of tiny tools in the lock mechanism on his apartment door, hoping it would be interpreted by the intruders as an innocuous behavior, just a guy putting on some background music while he got his things together. There really had been no time or opportunity for him to do anything else to help his cause. Ricky would get impatient, he knew. Come up the stairs, knock on his door. Calling out a warning to her at that point would probably earn him a bullet from the man in the red polo shirt and sport coat sitting across the room with the barrel of his Sig Sauer aimed at Crockett's forehead. A second thug in a white polo pressed his ear against the wall beside the door, his gun also drawn. But if Crockett's music choice tipped her off *before* she rapped on the door, maybe she would summon the police. At least their arrival would give the two of them a chance.

But Ricky had been gone a long time.

And the police were slow in arriving. Chicago was a big city with infinite chaos, yet finite numbers of men and women in blue. Maybe they had not believed her. Or worst case, maybe Ricky had not understood his message.

No. She would come through. She was clever, he could see that. Still, the clock ticked with no sounds from the hallway.

Sirens wailed nearby—not unusual for Chicago. Crockett noticed a stiffening of both body and facial features of his captors. He grew hopeful for a moment before realizing that the sound was growing more distant. The thugs reverted to their alert and business-like demeanors.

Crockett began to notice the two men casting doubtful glances at each other. Would they decide that too much time had passed, put a bullet in Crockett and resume their search for Ricky elsewhere? The music looped on.

In walked a man
With a gun in his hand
And he was looking for you know who!
I was scared and fearing for my life
I was shaking like a leaf on a tree
'Cause he was lean, mean
Big and Bad, Lord
Pointin' that gun on me!?

She'd hear the words, get the message, make a call. But... what if Ricky could find no help? What if no rescue was forthcoming? He had tried to evaluate his situation, searching for some escape option that he might exercise on his own, if it came to that. If he tried to move from his chair, he would be shot before reaching a standing position. He might succeed in ducking down behind the desk, but it offered scant protection, and the thugs would only need to walk over and pump a few shots into his cowering form.

Think! There must be a way!

Sirens sounded again, and this time Crockett smelled smoke. He realized this might be a coincidence, but the emergency vehicles seemed closer now, and in another minute, he could tell that they had rolled to a stop in the street outside of his building. The acrid smell was more obvious now.

What the hell?

Red Polo slid to the window and peered out. The other kept his gun trained on Crockett.

"I think the building's on fire," said Red Polo levelly.

White Polo said nothing. Slamming doors sounded on the first level. The amplified voice of one of the firefighters ordered residents out of the building. The first thug aimed an urgent, questioning glance at the second.

"They're going to come in," blurted Crockett, this unexpected development offering hope, making him bolder. "They'll go door-to-door to make sure everyone's out."

He knew that the thugs saw no favorable outcome in that scenario. Discovered with a hostage, they would be trapped in the building by the several squads of police who had no doubt already arrived along with the trucks. Now they needed an escape route. They pulled Crockett out of the chair, thrust their gun hands into a pocket of their sport coats, and used their other to guide him out of the apartment and down the stairs.

"Away from the building quickly, away from the crowds," said White Polo. "We'll worry about the girl later."

As the trio descended the stairs, sooty smoke billowed from the back hallway, making an unnoticed retreat in that direction impossible. They elbowed past a pair of firefighters and out into the muggy twilight where two fire trucks rested at the curb and at least three police cruisers stretched out to the west. A modest crowd had gathered in the street.

"Nothing stupid, pal," said White Polo as they started down the concrete steps toward the sidewalk. Halfway down, a figure burst from the crowd, a young, blonde woman in an expensive dress, catching up with them at the bottom of the steps, trailed by two firefighters, in full view of the gathering crowd, police officers, and rescue personnel.

"Oh, I was so worried!" Ricky cried loudly, throwing her arms around Crockett's neck. Still hugging, she lowered her voice to the thugs. "Either he goes with me, or you're going to have to shoot us both right here in front of all these spectators. And these are Chicago cops. They'll gun down both your sorry asses in about five seconds, and there goes your shot at goddamn immortality!" Both thugs' eyes widened, realizing that she understood their end game, and then, reluctantly, their grips relaxed. Ricky pulled out of the hug and Crockett shook himself free of his captors' hands.

Ricky spoke again, loudly enough for most of the onlookers to hear. "Thanks, guys! Sweetheart, you're wheezing! Let's get you over to the ambulance where you can get some oxygen."

She led him away, and the polo shirts, seeing that they were the center of attention, could do nothing but stand there and seethe.

Ricky and Crockett veered past the ambulance, broke into a run toward the main street and, seconds later, were in the back seat of a cab heading for the private airfield.

Crockett beamed a broad smile and pumped the air with a fist. "Damn, that was close! But you, little lady, you have balls made of frickin' titanium!"

Ricky's reaction was reserved. "Yeah, I guess."

"I had a feeling you'd come through!" Crockett was smiling

like he'd just won the lottery. "I knew you'd figure out the clue."

"The music?"

"Yes, ma'am," beamed Crockett. "I'd locked my door when I went in and heard them picking at the tumblers while I was throwing things together. Figured they had watched us arrive and didn't want to kick the door in, so that they could surprise you when you came back. I was trapped, but I just had time to turn on the ol' sound system to play 'Gimme Three Steps'!"

Ricky shrugged. "What's that?"

His smile drooped. "That was the clue. The *words* to that song. They were a warning!" Crockett began to badly speak-sing the words. "'In walked a man, with a gun in his hand, and he was looking for you know who.'"

Once again, Ricky shook her head.

"Lynard Skynard? 'Gimme Three Steps'? It's a *great* clue! 'Man with a gun!' 'Looking for you know who!' It's about a guy who's trapped, trying to get away! Skynard!"

"Sorry," said Ricky. "Guess I'm not familiar with his music. I got spooked because you were taking so long. Why would Captain Commando need so much time to pack? And why would you play music if you were trying to sneak in and out unnoticed?"

Crockett slumped back against the seat. "Well, you just ruined it! Not familiar? Lynard Skynard is a great American institution!"

"I'm sure he's very nice." She felt suddenly queasy.

"*Very nice*. And it's *they*!" He stared at her as if she were an eggplant. "You never heard 'Free Bird'? 'What's Your Name'?"

She shook her head.

"How about 'Sweet Home Alabama'?"

"Oh, I think I've heard of that one!" said Ricky.

"There may be hope for you yet, darlin'," said Crockett, folding his arms across his chest and allowing himself a modest smile.

"Wasn't that a shitty movie with Reese Witherspoon?"

"I'm gonna ignore that. I'm not gonna let any of it bother me because, regardless of how or why it happened, you were brilliant. You literally saved my life!"

"Why don't you just shut the hell up." She rubbed her own arms.

Crockett's expression went slack. "I don't get it. You were great."

"You don't know shit."

"What are you talking about? What...?"

"I goddamn bolted on you."

Crockett struggled to understand. "No, you—"

"Shut the hell up!" cried Ricky, suddenly furious. "When I heard your goddamn music, I figured they had you, and I didn't want to get caught, so I ditched you! I was halfway to the airport!"

Crockett blinked, processing it. "But... the fire..."

"I felt shitty, okay?" Ricky bit back tears. "An attack of conscience or something. Call it whatever you want. I had the cab drop me back at the drugstore two doors from your apartment." There, she explained, she had bought a bottle of rubbing alcohol and a disposable lighter from a display at the checkout. "Call 9-1-1," she had told the cashier as she tossed her money onto the counter. "Fire in an apartment two doors down!" With the wig and dress, she had figured she looked respectable enough that the cashier would take her seriously and comply. Then she had raced out onto the sidewalk and back to Crockett's building, following the first floor hall the short distance to the rear exit, bursting into the back alleyway. There, she had dug three bulging trash bags from the dumpster, dragged them into the hallway, doused them with rubbing alcohol, and ignited the heap with the lighter.

"You set the damn building on fire to save my life!"

"It was mostly smoke. Lots of plastic and coffee grounds and soggy paper. I figured it was too wet to burn the building down. At least right away."

"The point is, you came back."

"No."

Crockett raised an eyebrow. "No?"

Ricky looked him in the eye. "The point is, they could have shot you before I resolved my little moral crisis and made the cab turn around. And Jesus, it was more for my sister than you."

"I don't follow."

"She sent me that goddamn map." Ricky struggled to keep her voice low, though the cabbie seemed completely uninterested in their conversation, and in fact had seemed to possess a working vocabulary of about ten English language words, based on their conversation at the start of the ride. "And I don't think she intended for her actions to start a John Wayne Gacy body count among her circle of friends! If I let that happen, what sort of sister does that make me?"

Crockett shook his head. "You've gotta give yourself more credit. What happened to Bash was... it was awful. But you didn't do that. Neither did Sasha. And yeah, that little thing in my apartment could've gone bad, but all that really matters is that, in the end, you made the right choice."

"Just the eternal optimist, aren't you? What happens if I kick you in the balls? You petition the mayor to name a street after me?"

"Just giving credit where credit is due," said Crockett as the cab veered onto the access road leading to the airfield. "And so I should probably add that the hug was a nice touch. And the 'sweetheart'."

She flipped him a middle finger. "Next time I let you die."

Crockett smiled as they pulled up to the hangar. "Bet not."

CHAPTER 13

Ricky had never flown in a plane as small as the Gulfstream G450, but her initial misgivings were forgotten less than an hour into the flight. The fourteen-seat private jet was quite comfortable, had tables for their laptops, and a kitchenette and lavatory near the rear.

Crockett sat with one arm stretched out onto the back of the seat beside him, the other hand holding a can of beer from the refrigeration unit at the back. He still wore the dress pants, shirt, and fedora that Brenner had given him, but the tie and jacket lay on the floor of the plane. Brenner and Campion both stared intently at notepads on the table surfaces in front of them. Ricky sat by herself in one of the forward-most seats while Brenner's two security men in polo shirts chatted quietly near the back. Ricky still wore the black dress, although she had removed her shoes and the blonde wig.

"Leo, you must be making a helluva salary at the Foundation to afford luxuries like this," said Crockett, a broad smile on his face. "And it explains why mine is so low. I want a raise."

Brenner grunted a smile that looked like a grimace, finished tapping at his notepad, and then sat back.

"This isn't Foundation money." He swept a hand around to indicate the interior of the jet. "I've invested well, it's true. But I was born with the proverbial silver spoon in my mouth. You know those estates you see in films? A Greek revival mansion with a Bentley on the circle drive and six more in the heated garage? That was us. And by the time I was a teenager, I felt guilty as hell. Don't know precisely why. I suppose there was more than a bit of rebellion against my parents in it. And there was a girl—this was before Mary. An art major, who introduced me to all sorts of bohemian ideas."

Crockett raised his beer in salute. "Why Leo, you rascal!"

"Got me thinking about social justice. About our responsibility to each other in the world. Even after we went our separate ways, that became a guiding force in how I invested. And eventually, I formed HARP."

Crockett's head swiveled, appraising the interior. "Usually I'm stuck on the delayed flight to hell via Sardine Airlines, between a guy with flop sweat and a mom with a crying baby. But this... Pretty sweet ride, Leo."

"Sweet or not, it's a long flight," said Brenner. "We'll be making two short refueling stops, but we'll need to be well rested. Tom thinks we're right about Memphis."

"In ancient times, Memphis was the Egyptian capital," said Campion. "The people called the city Hikuptahl, which meant white walls. We're even more convinced that this is what was meant by needing to cross a river of milk."

"It sure would be nice if this map had been created by some literal son-of-a-bitch who just said, 'Go to this longitude and latitude and dig to a depth of thirty-five inches and that's where you'll find Waldo,'" said Crockett.

"Someone's had too many beers," said Ricky.

137

Crocket raised his can. "Just getting started, sweetheart."

"The tomb we believe is our target belongs to a princess, Itet," said Campion, ignoring Crockett. "Well, one of the Itets. Down through the many dynasties, we see a lot of the names repeated. Did you know that there were at least ten Cleopatras? We only remember number seven, and that's because of her dalliance with Julius Caesar."

"People always remember your dalliances," said Crockett, though he seemed to be talking to himself. Campion continued.

"Remember, the map tells us that the sun will show the way. Itet's tomb is notable in that it is not only laid out in a cruciform, but also the princess appears to be a devout worshipper of the sun god."

"Ra?" asked Brenner.

"Ra decorates the tombs of many in the Valley of the Kings," explained Campion. "But in Memphis, we find Hathor taking a greater role. Hathor was female and sort of a human-animal hybrid among the deities. She is often pictured with the horns of a cow or bull, reinforcing the river of milk connection once again. And many pictures of her—such as in Itet's tomb—show her with a sun disc between her horns. Itet's death and the construction of the tomb also seem to correspond with our time frame of roughly 5,000 years ago."

Brenner appeared impressed. "It all seems to fit."

"Of course," added Campion, "we are making a few assumptions here. Although the tomb of Itet seems promising, it's always possible that the tomb *we're* looking for was destroyed or buried in antiquity and has not been rediscovered yet."

"Pessimist!" said Crockett.

"It's a place to start," said Brenner. "The cult of Cessair has now been in possession of the map only a few hours. I'm guessing that they're going through the same process as we are. And I'm certain they have far greater numbers of human and financial resources at their disposal, if what we've seen from them so far is any indication. There are other cruciform tombs. Let's just hope we're better guessers. And I'm still convinced that Sasha's mention of Mare Desiderii was intended as a coded message to one of you two." He waved his hand in a general gesture toward Ricky and Crockett. "That gives us an ace they don't have."

Ricky shook her head. If it had indeed been intended as an "ace", it was still hidden deeply in the deck.

"Leo," said Campion, turning to face his friend, growing more serious, "there's something I've been thinking about. Perhaps you'll think it silly of me, but I wanted to get it out on the table."

"By all means," said Brenner. "You know that I value your opinion immensely."

Campion nodded as if to say thank-you before proceeding. "Leo, had you ever entertained the possibility..." He paused, shook his head.

"Go on, Tom."

"You're going to think I'm foolish," said Campion, "but... what if it's true?"

"About the scroll?" asked Brenner.

"What if there was a good reason for it to be so carefully hidden away?" said Campion. "For this cult to use such deadly force to find it. For the legend to burn itself so fiercely into the souls of generation after generation of followers for a span of fifty centuries?"

No one said anything to this, and after a moment, Campion continued."And the scroll is a sword that cuts in two directions. Life and death! Yes, it promises immortality! But we haven't really talked about death. Does it mean the ability to destroy one's enemies? Perhaps it's a formula for a deadly poison. Or a virus of some sort. Or a curse. Something that could lay waste to a single individual, to a city, to a nation!"

Suddenly, he began to chuckle. "I don't mean to sound melodramatic, like some corny adventure movie, but... oh, I don't know what I mean!"

"I think what Dr. Campion is saying," said Crockett, who seemed suddenly more focused, "is that we need to be cautious. And that means not ruling anything out."

"But," said Ricky with a sneer, "magic?"

Crockett took another drink before responding. "A thousand years ago, this jet would have been regarded as magic." Then he smiled glassily. "But a dalliance was still a dalliance!"

"Magic or not, our best chance of avoiding a confrontation with this cult and beating them to the scroll is to be prepared," said Brenner. "I'd suggest that we be well rested. Get some sleep!"

He turned to Crockett.

"Especially you!"

CHAPTER 14

They touched down in Cairo, stowed their baggage at the hotel, met the driver Brenner had arranged for in advance to take them to Memphis. Five minutes in the van convinced Ricky that the driver was insane. He weaved in and out of traffic, ignoring even the most basic rules and courtesies, flashing his lights, honking his horn, ignoring pedestrians who, thankfully, managed to narrowly avoid death.

Ten minutes into their trip, she realized that his driving was not so much different from many of the other vehicles on the road.

"This is why I hired a driver," said Brenner, reading the looks on their faces. "Cairo is a huge city. About seven million people packed into a very tiny area. The only rule of driving seems to be that there are no rules. But automobile ownership is growing dramatically. Many drivers don't understand the driving laws. Some got their licenses fraudulently. They say, up to thirty percent of all truck drivers are likely to be under the influence of drugs! For most people, the best course of action, if you're from out of town, is to find a native to drive you!"

Crockett, who had been listlessly leaning against the window, asked, "What's the best course of action if you're from out of town and you have a hangover and feel like your stomach's about to go inside-out?"

The driver pulled over near a grove of date palms and Crockett spent five minutes among them on his hands and knees.

Ricky watched him without pity, yet without judgment, remembering that she had woken up on the floor of The Edsel's back room two nights earlier.

It seemed half a lifetime ago.

"Better?" asked Leo, after Crockett had finally shuffled back to the van.

"Yeah, I've been better," said Crockett, resuming his seat and putting his head down on his forearms. Ricky noted that he was still wearing his clothes from the plane. Ricky had changed into black pants, a zebra-striped t-shirt, and dirty gray jogging shoes.

After more than half an hour of driving, the city lost some of its frenetic density and traffic thinned, allowing them to hurtle along the Cairo-Aswan Agriculture Road at a strong clip. Ricky found the scenery fascinating and more varied than she had expected. Flanking them at times were wide, planted fields, rows of doom palms along the highway, and occasional stands of sycamores. Then there would be stretches where there was nothing but sand dotted with tough grasses or tangles of tiny flowers. The beauty and strangeness occasionally succeeded in keeping at bay both her anger over the turn that her life had taken and her fear of what might lie ahead.

The driver, who spoke reasonably clear English, although usually not without being prompted, had suggested the trip to Memphis would take about forty-five minutes. An hour and fifteen minutes after leaving the hotel, they finally turned west, away from the Nile, onto a rougher stretch of road. A short time later, their driver brought the van to a stop in a gravel parking area. There were two cars—probably rentals—a tour bus, and a police vehicle. A small cloud of locals hovered near the bus, following the tourists, offering to sell them bottled Coca-Colas from buckets full of ice that they carried, or promising that, for a price, they could deliver special tours of wonders that would not be seen by the official groups. A few of these entrepreneurs broke off and shuffled toward Brenner's company, and though he shook his head and waved them off, they lingered at a short distance as Ricky and the rest moved away from the van.

They faced a modest museum housed in a modern-looking building, fanning themselves in the ninety-five-degree heat. Brenner took out a small paper notepad, consulted it, and occasionally glanced around. More palms hung overhead but failed to modify the oppressive heat.

"Fascinating place!" said Brenner, glancing alternately at his notes and at the landmarks that now surrounded them. "There is a gorgeous garden here, an alabaster sphinx, and a gigantic, broken statue—the Colossus of Ramses. It's too bad we don't have the time. What we're looking for is this way." He raised his arm and pointed.

They began to walk, Brenner in front, Campion and Ricky slightly behind, Crockett another couple of steps back, the two security men, and finally, a couple of the locals.

"Keep your eyes open," Brenner reminded them.

"I was afraid you'd say that," mumbled Crockett who, Ricky noticed, was now wearing sunglasses."

They stopped outside the visitors center, and Brenner entered. Ricky saw that Crockett was drinking from a plastic water bottle, probably from the hotel. She thought that this was a good thing. She took a long swig from her own bottle and cursed the heat and the fact that she had not worn light-colored pants. It simultaneously occurred to her that she probably did not own a pair of light-colored pants.

A minute later, Brenner returned, looking concerned.

"If I was able to understand correctly, the tomb is about two hundred meters from here." He waved his right hand to indicate the direction. "But there may be a problem. Cairo University apparently has a new dig at the Itet site."

"What does that mean?" asked Ricky.

"Does it mean we can go someplace that has air conditioning and beds?" asked Crockett.

"It means," said Brenner, "that we may not be welcome."

"I've been feeling like that a lot ever since that map showed up," said Crockett.

As they moved away from the visitor center, the landscape became more barren. Here and there they passed a tumble of cut stones poking out of the dust.

"This place redefines the word 'desolate'," mumbled Crockett, peering wearily over the top of his sunglasses.

"Yet, at one time, Memphis was the pulsating heart of Egypt," said Campion. "But then came the Romans, who established Alexandria as the seat of government, and people moved out. Memphis literally became a graveyard—and a source of stone to build new cities and monuments."

"A source of stone?" repeated Ricky.

Campion nodded, shrugged. "Why expend the tremendous effort to quarry new blocks and transport them long distances when you can simply disassemble an abandoned building?"

It did not take long for them to see a square, white tent shivering in the torrid breeze. As they approached, they saw that the tent had been erected in front of a slight rise in the landscape, presumably the entrance to the tomb. Several smaller tents stood off to the left, possibly sleeping quarters for those working the dig, or perhaps work areas for cleaning and studying artifacts. A linebacker-sized, dark-skinned man sat in a camp chair in the shade on the tent's right side, seemingly half-asleep. However, as Brenner's party approached, he stood.

Although not many words were exchanged, it became clear that he had no intention of allowing them to enter. Eventually a man who spoke some English emerged from inside and apologized for not being able to allow them into the tomb, but that it was closed to all except those on the Cairo University team. Despite repeated attempts at diplomacy and, eventually, bribery, Brenner came away frustrated.

"Not that I can really blame them," said Brenner. "We could be a group of foolish American tourists who would disturb their digging or research or whatever they're doing. Or we could be looters, for that matter."

"I doubt that looters would come up and introduce themselves," suggested Crockett. "We could come back after dark, but then we actually *would* be looters."

"That guard or another would probably still be watching over the tomb," said Brenner as they trudged back toward the van.

"The good news is that it doesn't appear that the cult of Cessair has been here yet," said Campion.

"How can you tell?" asked Ricky.

"Because," replied Campion, "the people working at that tomb are still alive."

When they climbed into the van, Ricky offered another question.

"Cessair's cult had a head start on us, so how come we got to the tomb first?"

"We don't know whether that is the right tomb," said Campion.

"Or perhaps it is, but the cult is looking elsewhere. Remember, there are multiple cruciform tombs."

"I wish we could be surer of the location," said Crockett.

"The only way to be sure is to get inside that tomb," said Brenner resolutely. "Maybe we'll have to risk coming back after dark. When the rest are asleep, perhaps we can reason with the guard. Or offer him a bigger bribe. Or, if necessary, overpower him."

Ricky looked shocked. "What does that mean?"

"Not kill him," said Brenner. "But some physical force may be necessary. You have to remember what the stakes are. We're trying to stop a very large, very well-financed coven of rattlesnakes."

They piled back into the van, and a few minutes later, turned onto Cairo-Aswan Agricultural Road heading north.

"There's got to be another way," said Ricky, seething over the idea that a single sweaty security guard might hold the power to thwart justice for Sasha.

"I'm open to any suggestions," said Brenner. "I did find out that one of the absent Cairo dig leaders will be returning this evening. I'll come back later and try reasoning with him. Academic to academic. Perhaps I'll be able to connect."

Loud engine sounds interrupted them, and Ricky noticed that a stake truck, at least thirty years old, had pulled up close behind them. The driver of their van stared into the shimmering distance ahead as if he had not noticed.

"I say try more money," said Crockett, who appeared to be somewhat more animated than he had been an hour earlier. Ricky supposed hydration had played a role. "Throw enough green at people, and you can always get them to cooperate."

"That's not true with all archaeologists," said Ricky, thinking of David Gates—who she supposed she should text about taking a few days off of work. "Some have real respect for the dead, for history, for the integrity of their digs."

"Everyone's got their price," said Crockett, the fedora tipped down over his eyes.

"I don't think it has to be posed to them as anything unseemly," said Campion. "I mean, if we can communicate to them that we're a respected research institution ourselves—I'd like to think the reputation of the HARP Foundation carries some gravitas—and that their cooperation would earn the university a very tasty grant, they might be quite agreeable about allowing us a window of access."

The loud blat of the truck engine behind caught the attention of them all. The stake truck swerved into the passing lane and accelerated past the van.

"Jesus, when did NASCAR start holding events in Egypt?" asked Crockett, sliding the hat back on his head so that he could watch the truck rocket past.

Ricky grunted, replied without looking at him. "You should feel right at home."

Once the stake truck had passed, it remained in the oncoming traffic lane until it was six or seven car lengths in front of them. Then it moved over so that it was straddling both lanes while still pulling away.

"You were right, Leo," said Crockett. "These people drive like —Jesus!"

The stake truck now passed a white sedan that had been cruising along a couple hundred feet in front of the van, cutting back into the right lane too soon, causing the driver of the sedan to slam on his brakes and plunge into the ditch to avoid a collision. Their own driver also hit the brakes as a cloud of dust obscured their view.

"Stop! Pull over!" shouted Leo, and their driver obeyed, bringing the van to a full stop about fifty feet behind the white sedan, which was pitched forward down a slight embankment.

The stake truck had, by this time, disappeared into the distance.

"I take it back," said Crockett, exiting the van with the others. "NASCAR is much safer than this!"

"Hello?" called Leo toward the sedan. "Is everyone okay?"

The driver, a dark-haired man in a suit, was already out of the car and around to the passenger side, where he was helping a woman from the vehicle. It took them a minute to reach the level of the road, but when they did, it seemed to Ricky that the woman looked familiar. She appeared about thirty-five with rich, dark hair and nutmeg skin. Trim and athletic in appearance, she wore hiking boots, tan pants, and a light, cotton blouse.

"Damn!" said Ricky. "I know her! I think that's Rio Armstrong!"

Campion squinted. "I think you may be right!"

Crockett seemed to squint as well, though it was difficult to tell behind his dark glasses. "Who's Rio Armstrong?"

Ricky took a few tentative steps forward. "A freakin' goddess!"

Suddenly, the dark-haired woman let out a whoop.

"Whoooeeeeee!" Then she glanced back at her car, smiled, and shouted, "Ain't that a rodeo!"

"She sounds like the goddess of Dodge City," said Crockett, who Ricky noticed had removed his sunglasses. "How do you know her?"

Ricky increased her pace. "Ten years ago, she saved my life!"

CHAPTER 15

Their party sat on the outdoor deck of the Casa Mia Restaurant at Hotel Sofitel Cairo El Gezirah, sipping cool drinks and waiting for their dinner entrees. The deck, suspended just a few feet over the Nile itself and accessible from two gangplank-style walkways, offered a gorgeous view not only of the legendary river, but of the eastern Cairo downtown skyline. The hotel itself rested on the southern tip of Gezirah Island in the middle of the Nile, almost as densely developed as Manhattan and home to the Cairo Tower, northern Africa's tallest building.

Brenner's two security men sat inside at the bar, sipping club sodas, their eyes always moving.

Under the umbrella tables on the terrace, Brenner, Campion, Crockett and Ricky enjoyed the company of the woman they had "rescued".

"All in all, I got off lucky," said Rio, who seemed to have a nearly endless energy reserve. "Not even a bruise! I've seen much worse in my visits here. Drivin' in Egypt is not for the faint of heart!" She raised her glass. "Nor is this wine! Woo!"

Ricky hung on every word. She had not been lying to Crockett about Rio Armstrong saving her life, though she had not exactly

149

put it in context for him, either. Ten years earlier, at sixteen years of age, Ricky had been nearing the end of two years of binge drinking and near-constant inebriation, a dark period that had plunged her deeper and deeper into hopelessness and depression. She had entertained suicidal fantasies daily. *What would it be like to just open that window and jump? What if I swam out as far as I could swim, and then just tried to keep going? How many of these pills would it take for me to go to sleep and not wake up?*

But there had been a part of her that did not want to die, and this part also knew that time was growing short to turn things around. And so, one morning, she emptied her secret stashes into the toilet, then turned on the TV—which she rarely did—in order to try and distract herself. And there on the science channel was Rio Armstrong.

She was beautiful, rich, an expert in her field, and refreshingly irreverent. Technically not an archaeologist herself, she financed and oversaw some of the most productive digs across the globe. Her stated goal was the preservation of the world's most important antiquities. It seemed that some archaeologists despised her because of her brashness, her outspokenness, and her tendency toward self-promotion—although almost all respected her mission.

Ricky had begun to read more about her, and the more she read, the more she liked. Thus began an extended period of sobriety and an interest in archaeology as a career.

Neither the sobriety nor the career had worked out quite as planned.

Or had they? After all, Ricky *was* working for a corporate archaeology firm, she *did* have a fairly solid fundamental knowledge of how a dig worked—at least in the corporate world—and now, here she was, *set to explore* rare and important tombs in Egypt. *Goddamn Egypt!*

It was funny how life sometimes played out. She knew people who had gotten master's degrees in archaeology who were waiting tables and working in car washes, who had never even traveled to a dig in Canada.

And to top it off, she now sat across the table from the most famous woman in the field who, despite being both wealthy and respected, behaved more like a sorority girl.

Rio held up her wine glass. "I think I could finish the bottle myself and still drive better than the feller who ran me off the road today!"

Crockett turned to Ricky. "I like her."

Ricky wrinkled her nose at him. "Not surprised one bit."

"What's her story?" whispered Crockett. "Millionaire, right?"

Ricky nodded, leaned in close. "She inherited a frickin' fortune. And she took over the reins of TROVE from her reclusive mother about a decade ago."

"TROVE?"

"It was formed just after World War I." She paraphrased what she had learned watching the science show and her subsequent online research. "Back then, it was called The Global Art and Antiquities Preservation Society. I think Rio's family has been involved in it for a long time. Today, TROVE is mostly known for their recovery and restoration work. And for Rio Armstrong. I've seen photos of her skydiving, running with the bulls, going up Everest..."

"You all will have to come out to the ranch some time, north of Missoula," said Rio, raising her glass again, and then sweeping it across the table. "This place puts out a pretty nice spread, don't it? Who'd a thunk we'd find first-rate Italian in Egypt, right? But you come visit me, I'll take you out to Zimorino's Red Pies Over Montana! Best damn pizza on the planet!"

Ricky noticed that Crockett was studying the phone that Ricky had purchased for him in Chicago.

"Wow!" he whispered, holding it slightly below table level. Ricky raised an eyebrow in question. "Looks like her family has its fingers in dozens of industries, all quite profitable, I might add." He then read in a mumble, directly from the screen. "'In the twenty-first century, TROVE employs a team of respected archaeologists and restoration experts who handle everything from excavations to the gifting of entire collections to museums or a country's national archives. As a result, the antiquities communities of the world and their respective governments typically open their doors wide to Rio Armstrong.'"

"Dinner is the least I can do for you folks," said Rio, city lights shimmering off the water behind her. "Who knows how long we would have stood there in the heat, waiting for someone to pull us out, if you hadn't come along!"

Earlier, after they had returned to the Hotel Sofitel—which was also where Rio was booked—Brenner and Rio had spent the afternoon in the hotel bar.

"Ahwa ariha," Campion had noted when Crockett had wondered what Brenner and Rio had been drinking. "No alcohol. It's a slightly sweet coffee. Very big here. Devout Muslims don't drink alcoholic beverages, although booze is allowed in the tourist hotels. I think Dr. Brenner is making some sort of business proposition."

"Did you see the look in his eye?" Crockett had asked. "Oh, he's got *business* in mind, that's for sure."

Now, as dinner drew to a close, Brenner attempted to bring the others up to speed.

"Rio and TROVE are working a dig a few miles south of where we were this morning," he explained.

"We were led to believe that it was intact, undisturbed," said Rio, still passionate, yet more businesslike. "However, we found that it had been cleaned out and then sealed up again. Disappointing. Happens a lot, as a matter of fact. But there is one exquisite wall, untouched, beautiful pictographs. We're focusing our attention on that."

"And Rio may have found a way to help us," said Brenner, smiling broadly.

Ricky whispered in Crockett's ear. "Look at his face. It's like he's a proud father whose daughter has just won the spelling bee."

Crockett, who still seemed to be drinking only water, turned his head to whisper a reply. "Look closer. That's not the proud father look. That's the 'I wonder what she's doing after dinner' look."

Ricky looked again. "Oh my God."

"I simply made a few inquiries," said Rio. "Turned on the Armstrong charm. One nice thing about having an old family business. It can open a few doors."

"The long and the short of it," said Brenner, "is that tomorrow evening, Cairo University has agreed to give us an hour in the tomb of Itet."

The last of the tension around the table seemed to evaporate with this announcement, though Campion posed a question.

"What if they—" He thought better of the question and rephrased it. "How do we know the tomb will be safe until tomorrow?"

"Look, I'm no dummy," said Rio, addressing the group in a frank yet friendly manner. "Once I learned who you all were, I was able to connect most of the dots. Leo's the head of HARP. That's a name that's been in the news a lot lately, ever since that Zackenberg fiasco. So has the name Sasha Crowe."

Now she looked at Ricky, who stiffened.

"Miss Crowe, that must have been very difficult for you. It is, in a word, unthinkable. Naturally, I'll help in any way I can."

Ricky felt her ears warm, and she nodded slightly.

Rio returned her attention to the group. "There are rumors about Egyptian hieroglyphs on the Zackenberg artifacts. And now, here you are, the employer of Sasha Crowe and the sister of Sasha Crowe, in Egypt. I have no idea what it is you all are looking for here, thousands of miles from Greenland, but it's pretty obvious it's connected and it's important. And like I said, I'll help in any way I can."

"Tom and I have identified two more tombs that might fit our profile," said Brenner. "We can visit those during the day, prior to our visit to Itet. Rio has agreed to accompany us."

"Well, since it sort of petered out, my crew can handle our dig without me for a day," said Rio. "So y'all are stuck with me, I guess."

Their entrees arrived. An hour later, too full for dessert, they felt reluctant to leave the gorgeous outdoor venue.

"I'm calling it a night," said Campion. "Jet lag, you know."

"Of course," said Brenner. "And I believe Rio and I have a few things to go over."

Ricky got up to leave.

"Where you off to?" asked Crockett.

Ricky curled her lip. "You a cop?"

"Just concerned."

"Going to take a walk." Ricky inclined her head to the north. "Along the river."

"Not alone, you won't," said Brenner. "Crockett, go with her. You never know if they're watching."

Crockett stood, extended his palm theatrically. "Lead on, m'lady." Ricky gave him a dark look, like she might spit on it.

After expressing their gratitude for dinner, they crossed from the terrace to the hotel, wove their way through the crowds, and a minute later stood outside on the walkway.

"You don't have to come," said Ricky. She felt awkward. Crockett had been too eager. And the fact that she felt awkward about it angered her.

"No, Leo is right," replied Crockett. "You never know. And it's probably best if we don't stray too far from the hotel."

They walked north-east, along the side of the island that fronted the widest portion of the river.

"God, this is all so unbelievable!" said Ricky.

"That we're here in Egypt, or that Leo's getting lucky tonight?"

Ricky made a sour face. "I really don't care who anybody hooks up with, but..."

"But what?"

"I mean... what would Rio Armstrong see in him? He's at least twenty years older!"

"Just like cars," said Crockett breezily. "Some prefer the classics."

She suddenly felt inordinately annoyed by Crockett and wasn't sure whether it was this conversation, her frustration over her sister's unsolvable moon crater clue, the fact that everybody seemed to think she needed a chaperone, or something else that fed the flame. "Let's change the subject," she said. "What if we come up empty tomorrow?"

Crockett shrugged. "We keep looking. More research, I guess."

"Yeah, but there are so many ruins just in Memphis. And what if we're wrong about the location? We could spend our lives looking for this thing!"

"What makes you think the cult is having any better luck?" asked Crockett.

"They've got more money," replied Ricky. "Leo said so."

"Well, now we've got Rio Armstrong. And one or both of us —" he gestured back-and-forth between the two of them "—is supposed to know something about Sasha's clue, something that the cult doesn't know. Even though we're clueless as to what it might be at the moment."

Bringing up Sasha's clue again deepened her foul mood, for it seemed to underscore her failure to grasp the message her sister had felt certain she would understand. A message she had risked everything to send. A sacrifice that weighed more heavily on Ricky every time she thought of it.

On the other hand, Ricky had to admit to a subtle flicker of... something. As far as she could recall, she had never heard of Mare Desiderii, yet when Bash and Campion had talked about the mehen and the dark side of the moon, something very faint had seemed to register. Or perhaps she was so eager to fulfill her sister's wish that she had merely imagined it.

They walked along silently for a bit.

"So if no one finds the scroll, what then?" asked Ricky. "Do we have to enter the goddamn witness protection program? Does anyone ever pay for the shit storm at Zackenberg?"

Crockett shrugged. "Don't worry about things that may never happen. Worry is like a rocking chair: It gives you something to do but never gets you anywhere."

"Wisdom from the Deep South?"

"Ohio. Erma Bombeck. Just trying to keep things light."

"Yeah, it's all a big joke, isn't it?" Ricky could feel herself growing angrier, knew that it would be best if she let it slide. But Crockett's seeming cavalier attitude had set her off again. "Fucking rocking chair?" echoed Ricky coldly. "I lost everything. I can't go home. I'm running for my life, trying to spot enemies who could be anywhere! And I lost my sister…"

Crockett nodded. "I get it. I lost a good friend."

"It's not the same!" The tears came, taking her completely by surprise. *Damn it! No! Not now!* She realized it was the first time that she had spoken of her sister in the past tense, acknowledging that she was probably dead. Crockett tried to put an arm around her shoulders but she shook him off. "Don't!"

He looked at her sadly. "All right then. Get it all out. This is probably good."

"Don't analyze me!" she snapped, her cheeks wet. Suddenly, she wanted to make Crockett hurt, too. "You and your glib, good-old-boy, country-fried, Alabama honky-tonk bullshit!"

"Charlotte, North Carolina, acually. Is that different from your angry, Irish, chip-on-your-shoulder, mad-at-the-world bullshit?"

"Fuck North Carolina!" She knew the ferocity of her reply was completely irrational, but her shame in failing Sasha washed away all of the remaining pretense and civility, goading her to lash out. "Your fucking receptionist set those bastards on us! It was your fucking idea to get Bash involved!"

Crockett looked at the ground, shook his head, then returned his gaze to her, his eyes now dark and dangerous. "And don't think I won't carry that with me every day the rest of my life. You're not the only one hurting here! And if you don't like the way I deal with it… well, that's your business. Y'know, I had trouble figuring how you coulda got into a bar fight the other night. I guess, when one finds out all you got inside is anger, it's not so difficult to imagine after all."

Then he turned and strode back toward the hotel, leaving Ricky shaking in the warm, Cairo night.

CHAPTER 16

Ricky said little at breakfast in the hotel restaurant the next morning. Rio supplied most of the good-natured banter while Brenner listened raptly.

Damn, Crockett was right.

The thought of Crockett and their argument last night made her stomach hurt. Her emotions lurched sluggishly from muted anger to guilt to depression to some impossible-to-pin-down fear, and then began the whole cycle again.

Meanwhile, Rio spun stories of fascinating digs and related adventures across the globe. Normally, Ricky would have been enthralled by the narrative, but today her mind was elsewhere, and the star of the show was the strong Turkish coffee.

Crockett did not appear at breakfast.

Dr. Campion, on the other hand, seemed well-rested and cordial. He listened cheerily to Rio's entertaining tales, though he eventually noticed the dark circles beneath Ricky's eyes.

"You don't look like you slept well."

She nodded toward her cup of coffee. "The antidote." Ricky estimated she had slept maybe two hours, getting up early to work out. Pushups and sit-ups on the floor of her room. Then she had heaved the mattress off her bed, set it on end against the wall, and had beaten it mercilessly for half an hour, prompting multiple indignant verbal rebukes—in a language she did not understand—from the room next door.

The argument with Crockett had left her agitated, and this had shredded even the brief hours of sleep she *had* managed. But there was something else. Inevitably, her thoughts had settled on the coming exploration of Itet's tomb. Her fight with Crockett had left her feeling unsteady and foul, as if she stood on an emotional fault line that shifted without warning. But it had also returned her thoughts to Sasha's clue and the seed of a memory about the mehen that she could not quite nurture into germination. Her gut told her that Sasha really *had* intended the clue for her. Somewhere inside, Ricky *knew* something, though she could not quite put her finger on what it was that she knew. It did not seem particularly logical that she should feel this way, for she knew little about the moon or Egyptian history and had never heard the word "mehen" until Bash had used it. Perhaps whatever it was that she could not quite remember was related to her knowledge of archaeology.

Stop thinking about it and then you'll remember, her mother used to say when Ricky had forgotten some important detail as a young girl. Not that her crack-and-grass-dependent mother had been able to remember much of anything herself. However, last night, Ricky had not been able to shut down the chaotic interplay of concerns and horrors.

Her sister.

The mehen.

The fight with Crockett. And why he bothered her so much. The first two seemed to be riddles without a ready answer. The last she was pretty certain she could put her finger on.

She had been thirteen at the time. Ricky, Sasha and their

mother had driven from Chicago to Huntsville, Alabama, where they had stayed three nights with her mother's sister, and Aunt Connie's new husband, Uncle Willis. The two had met through a dating service, and Willis had whisked his bride away from Chicago six months later to answer a lucrative new job opportunity in the state where he had spent his youth—a move that seemed to exacerbate Rose's melancholy and eccentric behaviors, for without her sister nearby, she was once again a soul adrift, as she had been since the death of her own husband. Only this time, she was adrift in Chicago, a new and unfamiliar city.

But seeing Aunt Connie in Alabama had seemed to restore her mother somewhat. Ricky and Sasha had enjoyed the visit as well, particularly Uncle Willis's cookouts on the deck in back of his house. Often, up to a dozen neighbors attended, each bringing a dish to share. Ricky admired their closeness, how each family seemed to trust and look out for the others. She especially liked her new 24-year-old cousin Paula, from Willis's first marriage, and Paula's fiancé, Drew, 25, who had grown up next door. Paula was kind, quiet and gentle, while Drew was a clowning storyteller. He had seemed to take a special pleasure in making Ricky laugh. He was cute, and she found his thick Dixie accent charming. He had sat up late with Ricky and Sasha and Paula the second night of their visit, telling hilarious stories after the adults had gone off to bed. And then Paula had excused herself on account of having to work early the next morning. Eventually even Sasha said goodnight, leaving Ricky laughing in the wake of yet another outlandish anecdote.

And then, in the dark backyard, on Aunt Connie's padded chaise, Drew had raped her. The amusing stories had given way to more personal conversations about their likes and dislikes. One of his hands had suddenly been on her back, quite naturally and innocently, it had seemed, as they chatted quietly under the stars. Then, softly, onto her neck. In her hair. He had leaned in close, his breath warm on her cheek. She had felt herself tremble. She felt afraid, unable to connect this behavior with anything familiar. His charming drawl had tried to sooth her at first, had flattered her as the prettiest little thing he had ever seen, eventually had become cruel and threatening as Ricky protested and became more frightened and anxious. She had run into the dark and silent house afterwards. Aunt Connie had come awake, and in the kitchen, Ricky told her aunt what had happened. Aunt Connie made her a cup of warm milk, took her into the downstairs bathroom, undressed her, scrubbed her thoroughly, threw her clothing into the washing machine and started the load.

Then she had hugged Ricky and explained that boys liked kissing and hugging, and sometimes they got a little worked up.

Ricky told her it was more than kissing and hugging.

Aunt Connie had smiled and told her that it had probably *seemed* like more than what it was because Ricky was only thirteen. That there was no need to let our emotions and imagination cause us to say things that might *really* hurt people. After all, Drew and Paula were getting married in the fall. It was going to be a big wedding. The gorgeous white gown was already hanging in the front closet in a plastic bag. Ricky didn't want to ruin everything for Paula, her cousin, did she?

The last of this had, behind her aunt's smile, the hint of a threat in it, and Ricky had suddenly felt both frightened and angry. After a sleepless night, she had sought out her mother, but it was clear that Aunt Connie had already spoken with her and Ricky's mother believed—or wanted to believe—that her daughter had exaggerated a few minor encroachments, the sort of foolish things that boys do. Ricky really didn't want to tear down someone's reputation over a few ill-advised kisses, did she?

But it wasn't just…

However, her mother would hear nothing of it, hurrying off into the backyard to smoke a joint.

The day crawled forward, threatening and unfamiliar, despite that it was the same house and the same people she had taken comfort and pleasure in the day before. That night, as she lay on the sheet-covered chaise on the front porch—her bed during the visit, with Sasha asleep on the sofa in the living room just a few feet away—Drew let himself in to the dark porch, quietly knelt down next to the chaise.

Had she said anything, he asked? He had figured no, or that if she had, no one had believed her. They would have sought him out and said something otherwise. So it was all good.

Then he had smiled at her, and she had felt the bile in the back of her throat, lying on her side on the chaise, her head resting on a thick pillow. She was a pretty one, he had said. Had done real good for a first time. Was going to be real popular when she got a little older. And he was going to miss her because, let's face it, Paula was just sort of average-looking, and she hardly ever wanted to fool around.

He undid the front of his jeans, bringing himself out, putting a finger to his lips with his free hand.

Just one more little favor before she headed north the next day, Drew had whispered, and she could feel the heat radiating off him.

Ricky had sprung up from the chaise so quickly that Drew was caught off guard and fell backwards onto his rear. He scrambled forward to grab her, but Ricky had retrieved one of the two weapons she had taken to bed with her and hidden beneath the blanket to protect herself from a repeat of the previous night's horrors: Uncle Willis's nine-iron from the golf bag leaning against the porch wall. She swung it viciously, tears streaming down her face, remembering not only how she had been violated the previous night, but how she had been betrayed by those who were supposed to protect her. It connected with a dull crack on the left side of Drew's face, knocking him sideways. He emitted a muffled bark, reached up and felt blood.

"You bitch!" he hissed. "I—you—you knocked out two of my fucking teeth!"

He rushed forward on his knees, catching the shaft of the golf club before she could administer a second crusher, and this was when she had pulled out her second hidden weapon: one of Aunt Connie's sharp kitchen knives.

"Get out!" she had cried, but Drew had delivered a stinger to her wrist with the nine-iron, and a moment later, the knife had been in *his* hand.

The rest was hard to remember, although the memory of the pain she felt when the knife traveled down the side of her face was as fresh as yesterday. She learned later that he had been going for her eye, but in the dark, and with her struggling so, he had missed.

Lucky her.

The next thing she recalled clearly was the nine-iron in her hands again, swinging viciously and being pulled off of Drew, who was slumped on the porch floor in a pool of blood, his pants around his knees, unconscious.

There followed conflicting stories and lies and the sorts of assumptions people make about women in cases like these, even if they are completely innocent. Even if they're pretty thirteen-year-olds. There were some who believed her, but the water had grown pretty muddy. And Drew's considerable injuries—broken jaw, loss of sight in his left eye, skull fracture, two broken ribs—did not cast Ricky in a particularly favorable light. Before a fairly accurate version of events had been settled upon by the lawyers and the courts, she had spent two months in a juvenile detention center.

And that was the beginning of the time of not trusting. Of the search for comfort in a bottle. Of the darkness that was reborn whenever she heard a drawl.

After breakfast, Brenner called their driver. Rio told Brenner she would meet them at the site. They had agreed to leave at 8:00, but Ricky could see that Brenner was champing at the bit, distracted yet anxious to get to it. Ricky's watch read 7:40 as the van pulled to the curb and Brenner opened the door.

"Crockett's still not here," she said, looking around. She tried texting him, but several minutes elapsed without an answer.

"Go get him," instructed Brenner coldly. "Knock on his door!"

She made a pained face, rolled her eyes, but jogged off toward the elevator. Having to confront Crockett was the last thing she wanted to do this morning. Two minutes later, she pounded on his door. It opened almost immediately, and Crockett stood there with a toothbrush clamped between his teeth, his shirt open, exposing a trim, hairless chest. Although he was still wearing the same clothes from the night before, she noted that he had at least scrounged a toothbrush from somewhere.

"Relax," said Crockett with the toothbrush still in his mouth. "We've still got ten minutes."

"I think Leo's trying to impress his new girlfriend," said Ricky, an assessment that normally would have struck a mildly humorous note, but came off as awkward after their argument the previous night. "They're at the van right now, waiting for us!"

Her cell dinged and she quickly dug it out, groaned.

"They're *not* waiting! They said to grab a cab, they'll meet us there!"

Crockett disappeared inside, reappearing a few moments later, sans toothbrush. He pulled the door closed and buttoned his shirt on the way to the elevator. When the doors closed and it was just the two of them, he said, "Look, about last night..."

"Screw last night," said Ricky. "It is what it is."

Crockett sighed. "I'm not sure what it was. But I'm sorry it happened."

The doors opened and they jogged through the lobby and out to the curb, quickly finding a taxi. They sat in silence for a minute, their eyes on opposing side windows, as the taxi driver, hemmed in on all sides, waited for the cab in front to finish loading an inordinately large quantity of heavy luggage. Crockett broke the silence.

"You were right."

Ricky continued to stare out her window.

"We've each got different... demons. I shouldn't be sticking my nose in where it doesn't belong."

He paused for a moment, as if considering his words, and then continued.

"I just... don't want to be your enemy. For whatever reason, we're on this journey together."

Ricky still said nothing.

Crockett returned his gaze to his window, and Ricky, settling back in her seat, briefly considered making some reply, even if it was just "Sure, okay," which she knew would break the uncomfortable stalemate. But she did not.

He continued to look out the window. Then, suddenly, she felt him lurch forward. She turned and saw the muscles in his neck tighten.

"Shit!"

"What is it?" asked Ricky, just as their cab began to pull away.

"That man on the sidewalk back there—that was Porn Star Moustache!" Crockett's eyes were wide.

It took a moment for Ricky to make the connection. "One of the cult guys from Clark in Chicago? Are you sure?"

"I'd bet the farm on it," said Crockett. "They're here! Cessair's thugs! They're in the same damned hotel!"

CHAPTER 17

It took forty-five minutes to complete the trip to Memphis. Spotty cell phone coverage kept them from calling or sending a message to Brenner.

"The cult bastards must have thought we had all left with Brenner," Crockett had said on the way. "So they weren't as careful as they should have been. Remind me to sleep in more often. We should reach Memphis ahead of them. I'm sure Leo will find this very interesting."

Once the cab dropped them, it took another ten minutes to reach the tomb of Seti—one of the Setis—where Dr. Campion stood waiting with one of the HARP security men.

"Well, that was a wash-out," he said, jabbing a thumb toward the tomb entrance. "Leo told us to wait for you here and then bring you to the other tomb that looks promising. It's about a quarter mile in that direction." He pointed off to the left. "He just can't sit still! Like he's supercharged with adrenaline this morning for some reason."

"More likely with testosterone," said Crockett with a wry smile, though this did not seem to register as significant with Campion at all. Then Crockett brought Campion up to speed on what he had seen at the hotel.

"We need to let Leo know right away," said Crockett.

"And Rio," added Campion. "Since she's helping us, she's probably in just as much danger."

"Isn't she with Leo?" asked Ricky.

Campion shook his head. "She had to attend to some problem at her own dig at Saqqara."

"That probably explains why he's so antsy," said Crockett with a smile. "Yin has been separated from yang."

Ricky frowned. "What are we going to do? How are we going to let Rio know?"

Crockett thought for a moment. "Leo's probably got her cell number, but that doesn't do us much good if we can't contact him. And who knows if his cell service is any better?" Then he addressed the security man that Leo had left behind. "Jim, let Brenner know that the cult is at our hotel, and that they may be following us out here. Let him know that Ricky and I are going to warn Miss Armstrong."

Jim nodded and trotted off.

Ricky and Crockett turned to retrace their steps toward the parking lot. "Wait!" called Campion. "I'm coming with you. I think Jim and Hector will do an adequate job of looking after Leo, and I'd love to take a look at one of Rio Armstrong's projects in action!"

They reached the visitors center, where they found their driver, whose name was Amet, lounging on a bench inside.

"Saqqara is only about four miles from here," said Crockett. "We should be back long before Leo is done at the next tomb." Minutes later, the van hurtled them past a landscape that, in many respects, had changed little in 5,000 years. They passed a billboard-sized, greenish sign as they neared the site:

GOOD LIFE, IMMORTALITY AND HAPPINESS ARE
FOUND IN EGYPT

"Now there's a good omen," said Crockett.

"Hopefully the shit-heads didn't read it first," responded Ricky.

They arrived at Saqqara a few minutes later. Their driver, Amet, an NFL lineman-sized Egyptian in Dockers and a sports coat, accompanied them, as there was no visitors center in which he could sit. The most imposing structure was the funerary complex of King Djoser.

"There it is," said Campion, pointing. "The first of Egypt's step pyramids. Over two hundred feet high, and it predates its more famous cousins at Giza."

Djoser's pyramid was easily visible over the thirty-foot walls of his funeral complex.

"The bricks used to make this... they're so small!" noted Ricky.

"Excellent observation," said Campion. "The man who built this was a genius. The Egyptians of that time were so impressed by the craftsmanship that they regarded him as a god!"

"Rio said she was working in the South Tomb," said Crockett.

Amet tapped him on the shoulder, pointed.

They altered course slightly.

"No one knows exactly why the South Tomb was built," noted Campion, who seemed to be enjoying his role as a tour guide. "It's a maze of tunnels and chambers, as are many mastabas."

"What's a mastaba?" asked Crockett.

"Most were intended as funerary monuments and contain burial chambers," explained Campion. "Initially, they are constructed at or slightly below ground level. Then the exterior walls are built up at a slight angle. They're either made of mud brick or from stone. Stone slabs often form the roof, supported by the interior walls.

Sometimes that doesn't work out so well."

"What do you mean?" asked Crockett.

Campion pointed to the huge step pyramid. "The pyramid of Djoser started out as a mastaba. Then, they decided to add more rooms, presumably so that the good king would have more space to stroll around in the afterlife. Each time they got a new idea for renovations, they added a new layer to the cake, so to speak, making it slightly smaller than the preceding layer. This, of course, accounts for the step appearance. Unfortunately, the sub-structure was not strong enough to bear the weight, and it began to crumble. Recently, they've restored and improved upon the footings and supports. They inflated huge balloons in the passageways to keep them from caving in while work proceeded. Quite clever. I'm not sure whether they've finished yet. Of course, not all mastabas have that problem. Most don't have pyramids built on top of them. And many, I suppose, are still lost beneath the sands."

They reached the south tomb and stopped, surprised.

"I think I see Rio's problem," said Crockett.

"I don't see any signs of activity here," said Campion, running his fingers through his hair.

"Yeah, that's the problem," said Crocket. "Are you sure she said 'South Tomb'?"

"Yes," replied Ricky.

"Yeah, I was sure, too."

Ricky turned to Amet. "Is there another South Tomb?"

Amet shook his head. "This is the deal," he said in a deep, quiet voice.

"I'm getting a bad feeling," said Crockett, turning slowly, letting his eyes travel the expanse of the funeral compound.

"What do you mean?" asked Ricky, suddenly feeling anxious herself.

"I don't know what I mean," said Crockett, his voice rising. "It's just that when someone you really respect, one of the world's most prominent archaeologists, tells you that she has a dig somewhere and then there's no dig, it gets you thinking! Why would she tell us that? Why would she mislead us? I know I've got an overly active imagination—even more so, since you brought that parchment to my office—but I don't like *any* of the answers I'm getting!"

"Do you have any signal yet?" asked Campion, holding his cell phone a few inches from his face. "I'm still at nothing."

"Same," said Ricky. "We've got to get back and tell Leo!"

They began retracing their steps toward the car. As they emerged from Djoser's compound, Crockett skidded to a halt.

Ricky glanced around anxiously. "What is it?"

"Yesterday when we rescued Rio, what was she doing on Cairo-Aswan Agriculture Road?" asked Crockett.

Ricky blinked. "What are you talking about?"

"Yes, now that you mention it, that's a good question," said Campion. "If she were heading back to Cairo from here, her supposed dig, she should have been on Mariotta Road. Cairo-Aswan would have been well out of her way."

"She set us up!" said Crockett.

They resumed walking.

"Wait, are you saying that she had someone deliberately run her off the road?" asked Ricky.

"That's exactly what I'm saying," said Crockett. "Notice that he waited behind us for quite a while... until he found a place he could do it where there was little chance of serious damage to her car!"

"But why would she do it?" asked Ricky.

"She's in on it!" said Crockett. "She's part of the cult!"

Ricky could not believe it. "That's crazy! She's already rich!"

"But she's not immortal," said Crockett.

"That's just a fairy tale," Ricky countered.

"Doesn't matter whether someone believes in fairy tales or cold science," said Crockett. "If they shoot you, you're just as dead. In fact, it all makes sense now! Who better than the head of TROVE, who has access to every dig on the planet, to lead the search for the scroll! It's the perfect cover!"

Ricky shook her head. "That's fucking nuts! There's got to be some mistake. It's got to be a misunderstanding. We messed up the directions, that's all. Or misheard her. And then when you saw those guys at the hotel, it made you paranoid!"

"That's another thing," said Crockett. "More than a little coincidence that, with all the hotels in Cairo, they were staying at ours!"

They reached the parking area and were about to get into the van when a bearded man in dress pants and a Hawaiian shirt stepped out of a nearby sedan. Two other casually dressed men followed him, as well as one woman.

Rio Armstrong.

"I knew it!" said Ricky. "There she is now." Then, as they drew close, she spoke brightly to Rio. "We came looking for your dig, but we couldn't find it! We must have got our directions wrong!"

Rio smiled, reached inside her bag and pulled out a derringer. "My dear, I don't think you realize how wrong you got it!"

CHAPTER 18

"These gentlemen are all very well-armed," said Rio, the cowgirl accent gone, replaced by something difficult for Ricky to pin down. "And they won't hesitate to do exactly what I say. So in that spirit, I'd like *you* to do exactly as I say. Turn around and start walking. We're going to visit a little attraction that's a bit off the beaten path."

"And if we refuse, what then?" asked Campion. "Would you really shoot all of us right here with dozens of tourists milling about?"

"Certainly," said Rio, and Ricky noticed that all the playfulness and warmth that had formerly characterized her speech had vanished, an actress dropping a role. "But then we'd have to kill every single one of the tourists as well, wouldn't we? After Zackenberg, you know that's not an idle threat. So, if you please?"

They turned and walked to the south of the Djozer compound, into the shimmering heat of the desert, with Rio and her associates a few steps behind. They walked for several minutes before Crockett yelled out a question.

"Where are we going?"

"To a place I think you'll find fascinating," replied Rio. "It's just over the rise ahead."

A few moments passed before Campion spoke up.

"We're all intelligent, civil individuals. There's no reason this has to end badly for anyone. We can help you."

"You *were* helping me," said Rio. "You were working on the same problem I was. My people had not yet come across the tomb of Itet, so thank you for that! I'm hoping it turns out to be the one. In case it isn't, we had planned to let you lead us to other tombs as well. But, unfortunately, you were only useful if you remained ignorant."

"What you're looking for," continued Campion, a hint of desperation in his voice, "if it's about the market value of such an unusual antiquity, Dr. Brenner is quite well-off. I'm sure something can be arranged. There's no need to do anything drastic."

Rio laughed. "I have all the money I'll ever need. But as they say, there are some things money can't buy."

Jesus, thought Ricky. *She believes the scroll can really make her immortal!*

"You're a woman of science," countered Campion. "You surely can't believe the old legend!"

Rio flashed him a cruel smile. "All science starts out as myth, Doctor."

Ricky had trouble controlling her voice. "You killed my sister!"

Rio gave her a sideways glance. "I can't say for sure what happened to your sister. I do know that sending the map to you made things… inconvenient. However, I suspect she is at the bottom of the sea with the team I sent to Zackenberg. If so, a fitting end."

"Fucking bitch!"

"Such kind words," said Rio, showing a trace of smile. "And

utterly irrelevant."

They crested the rise and started down a mild slope toward an area unremarkable except for a few weathered, cut stones protruding from the sands and a narrow, rectangular pit to the right of them. Stacked next to this were three slabs of limestone and what appeared to be a Bobcat with a wide front shovel and a backhoe at the rear.

"This is the Hollow Tomb," said Rio. "It was uncovered about twenty years ago. No one knows who built it or who was buried here—if anyone. It had already been looted and the plaster had crumbled off the inside walls so that no writing survived. Its story is a mystery. The sand has partially covered it so that one could easily miss it. The only remarkable thing about it is that it contains a wonderful maze of passages and rooms, about thirty. Please."

With a polite hand motion, she directed them toward the pit, which Ricky now noticed was the entrance to the mastaba. Stone steps led down into darkness. There was nothing else to do. If they tried to run, they would be gunned down before taking three steps. There was simply no cover to run to, no place to hide. They ducked their heads and descended.

Rio produced a flashlight and lit the way, directing them about twenty feet down a narrow passage and then left, into a larger space. Ricky, Crockett, Campion and Amet stood illuminated by Rio's beam, the stone ceiling inches above their heads.

"Do you like it?" asked Rio, who, receiving no response, continued. "I had my associates inspect it yesterday. It seemed that I would eventually need a place like this near the site of my supposed dig. The only way in or out is the main opening, and soon, a slab of limestone will cover that—along with all the sand we can shovel in fifteen minutes! Did you know that a single cubic yard of sand weighs more than a ton? All four of you together won't be able to budge that slab. Not to mention that it'll be difficult to even spot this tomb from outside—unless you know exactly where to look! It could be years before anyone digs out the entrance again."

"I suppose it would be pointless," said Campion, "to note the folly of your actions. Good Lord, you're an intelligent woman! Again, I implore you! You can't really believe that when you find that infernal scroll—*if* you find it—that it will grant you immortality!"

Rio smiled, though in the harsh shadows, it looked like the grimace of a gargoyle.

"No, I don't."

This stunned the group for a moment. Then Crockett spoke.

"Then why all the killing? Why the deceptions? If it's not for money or immortality, why go after the scroll?"

Without answering the question, Rio addressed Ricky. "Miss Crowe, I don't know exactly what happened at Zackenberg. But your sister did upset my plans when she mailed the map to you. And I hate it when people cause me problems. For that, I am happy to make you all suffer a slow death. But I will give you one chance at survival. If you or Mr. Crockett will reveal to me what your sister meant in writing Mare Desiderii onto the map, you will have your chance. If the information leads us to the scroll, I will inform the authorities of the location of this tomb and that you are trapped in it. I trust that they will waste no time in digging you out. Once I have the scroll, it won't matter."

"But," said Campion, "even with that knowledge, it may take you days—or longer—to find the scroll. We may suffocate or perish from lack of water."

"You may indeed," acknowledged Rio. "But it is, at least, a chance. And if I don't find out the meaning, you have no chance at all."

"We don't know what it means," said Crockett, who looked to Ricky for confirmation. But Rio noticed something flicker across Ricky's face, something secret yet uncertain.

"That's not true," said Rio, a smile creeping across her own face. "You do know, don't you, Ricky?"

Ricky's lip twitched and she had trouble controlling her voice as she spoke. "No. But even if I did, I wouldn't give you information my sister died to protect!"

Rio's smile disappeared. "I suspected as much. I also suspect that even without your help, we will figure out the secrets of the parchment map eventually."

"Wait," said Crockett. "You may not want to seal us in here just yet. You already admitted that our investigation has helped you. Well, we did a lot of research on our way across the pond! We've got quite a few other possible tombs on our list. And if you kill us, that research dies with us."

"You flatter yourself." Rio smiled casually. "I have resources you cannot begin to imagine! And the fact that you're now about to perish in a nameless tomb suggests you're not exactly our intellectual equals. But just in case you've stumbled onto anything, my people will be taking a look at your tablets and laptops. I have associates who are quite adept at that sort of thing. In fact, I'd like your mobiles as well. They might contain useful information. And it's always possible that you might pick up a signal and let someone know where you are."

Facing Rio's armed thugs, they complied.

The bearded thug turned his attention on Amet. "You. Driver. I'll need the keys to your van so that we can leave it a few miles from here."

Amet shook his head.

177

"Don't be a fool!"

Amet shook his head again. "Not my van. But my responsibility."

Both of Rio's men took a step forward. Crockett spoke up quickly, sliding in front of Amet.

"You'll have to shoot all of us if you want those keys! Then there goes that 'slow death' you want us to suffer!"

Rio stopped her men with a motion, her lips curling into a bitter smile. "Let him keep them. They won't do them any good. Brenner hired the van for at least a week. By the time it's missed, it will no longer matter. And even if someone came looking for it today, once we've covered the mastaba's entrance and moved the Bobcat, no one will have any idea where they might have gone... or where they're buried."

"Look, you said it yourself," Campion chimed in desperately, "you don't need money. But you're a reasonable person. Can't you see how wrong this is?"

"The one who holds the power determines right and wrong, Dr. Campion. And now I must say goodbye. I enjoyed our dinner last night. It was rather fun while it lasted. A pity that you discovered our intentions so quickly."

"You can thank porn-star moustache over there for that," said Crockett bitterly.

Rio shot the man a dark glance, but quickly recovered herself and turned to her captives with a look of smug superiority.

"Two words of advice: First, don't waste your time trying to move the entrance slab. There's a reason we borrowed that Bobcat from a nearby excavation. And second, it's going to get very dark in here in a minute. So watch your step. There's a sixty-foot-deep burial pit near the center of the maze of rooms. Wouldn't want to stumble around in the dark and fall in."

Rio and her associates backed up the steps. Crockett and Campion rushed toward the base as the engine of the Bobcat roared to life. Almost immediately, the great stone plug lurched as the bucket lowered its elevated end into place. It fit snugly, and Ricky uttered a curse as the tomb was plunged into darkness.

CHAPTER 19

The few cracks of light around the edges of the plug stone disappeared as Rio's associates shoveled sand loosely over the entrance to conceal its location.

"Don't panic!" cried Campion.

"Why not?" replied Crockett. "Buried alive under tons of stone and sand. Pitch black. No food or water. Air will eventually run out. Did I miss the silver lining?"

"Leo!" cried Ricky. "Leo and the security team! Leo is still out there!"

"But we've got no phones," said Crockett. "Even if we could contact him, I'm not sure how to tell him to find us. 'Walk a half mile into the desert and start digging!'"

"I don't think it was that far," said Ricky.

"It doesn't matter," said Crockett. "Unless we can find a way out of here ourselves. And I don't think that's likely. Our friend Rio already had her apes check this place for soft spots."

"Perhaps they missed something," said Campion hopefully. "History is full of tales of giant slayers who, intoxicated by the conceit of their own superiority, proceeded to stumble upon pebbles."

Crockett's voice broke as he replied. "So whatever pebble they possibly missed, we're going to find it in the dark?"

Suddenly, the chamber lit up as if someone had flipped on a wall switch. All eyes went to Amet, who stood holding a long, silver flashlight.

"Always carry it," he said quietly. "Never know."

"Amet, you're a man of surprises." Crockett, whose voice steadied somewhat at the new source of illumination, slapped their driver on his broad back. He looked around the room they occupied, sucked in an unsteady breath, and turned to the others. "Okay, trying to stay cool here. Think about it: People bust into tombs all the time. How difficult can it be to bust out of one?"

"I think most tomb robbers use tools," said Ricky.

"Maybe there's something in one of these other rooms that we can use," suggested Crockett. "Something Rio's boys missed."

"Well," said Campion, "I don't know if we want everyone wandering around in here getting lost."

"Okay then, Doc and I will poke around in some of the other rooms. Ricky and Amet, you can start by checking out this room. Look for loose bricks or stones. Maybe you'll feel a draft from somewhere. Or a trip stone that opens a door to an escape passage."

"It doesn't work that way in real life," said Ricky.

"Unfortunately not," agreed Campion. "In the world of cinema, tomb raiders always seem to be the beneficiaries of spring-loaded mechanisms and counter-balanced doors. But in the real world, people thousands of years ago had no technology to make metal springs or hinges. And any rope slings or pulleys would have long ago succumbed to mites and rot."

"Problem," interrupted Ricky. "We've only got one flashlight."

Crockett smiled. "Unless Amet brought another?"

Amet shook his head.

"Then Doc and I will check in this direction. If we don't have any luck, we'll come back and send you and Amet the other way. You'll just have to sit in the dark for a few minutes until we get back."

The big man nodded.

Ricky watched as the light disappeared into the narrow passage, felt for the wall, and lowered herself into a sitting position. After a few seconds, she heard Amet do the same a few yards away. Ten minutes after they disappeared, Crockett's voice sounded from around several bends in the passage. "We found the pit! And no, we didn't fall into it!"

The news did nothing to improve Ricky's spirits. It simply seemed to underscore the hopelessness of their situation.

"The walls are strong, thick," said Amet suddenly.

"I wish we had shovels," said Ricky.

"Maybe some dynamite," added Amet.

Ricky shrugged her shoulders against her sweat-soaked shirt. "It's so fucking hot! I'm drenched!" She shook with the effort it took to keep from breaking down. *Damn it! Don't go to pieces now!*

"Don't cry, pretty lady," said Amet from across the room.

Pretty lady. Eight-inch goddamn scar.

"I'm sorry," said Ricky, impressed with their driver's hearing. "I'm goddamned afraid."

"I am afraid, too," said Amet.

"You don't seem afraid," said Ricky.

"I am pretending," he replied. "I am doing it so my customers will not worry so much."

They were silent again for a minute before Ricky spoke.

"Do you think there's a way out?"

"I don't know," replied Amet. "But an hour ago, I didn't know this tomb existed. Now, here it is. Just because I don't know it now doesn't mean there isn't one."

At that moment, light spilled around the corner and Crockett and Campion shambled back into the chamber, carrying a length of rope and a four-by-four timber about six feet in length.

"Time for a little physics experiment," said Crockett, good-naturedly.

"What did you find?"

"Maybe a way out," said Crockett. "When we came across this stuff, it gave Doc an idea."

"The rope and timber are relatively new, probably used by folks poking around in this place in the last year or two," explained Campion. "This board was set across the top of the burial pit back there, and the rope was tied to it so it dangled down to the bottom. That gives us over sixty feet!"

"Is that all you found?" asked Ricky, her voice edged with disappointment.

"Actually," said Crockett, "we also found a set of car keys."

"I mean, how is a rope going to help?" she asked.

Crockett extended his hands toward Campion as if introducing a guest speaker.

"Er, well, you see, there's no pyramid on top of this mastaba now, is there? That means maybe six inches—possibly a foot—of rock above our heads. And maybe a thin dusting of sand. Not really such a great distance between us and freedom, eh?"

"No," said Ricky, "except that it's heavier than hell!"

"Yes," agreed Campion. "Impossible for us to lift, no matter how vigorously we should push."

"So we're still stuck."

"Maybe not," said Campion. "If I make a stack of six bricks, will it be easier to lift up the pile or to push it over?"

"To push it over, obviously," said Ricky. "Wait. Are you saying that we're going to try and push over one of these walls? Are we strong enough to do that?"

"By ourselves, no, probably not," said Campion. "But this rope might help."

"Shine your light on the ceiling up here, Amet, my friend," said Crockett, giving the torch back to the driver and walking to the wall. "Here, in the center of the room, there's one wall holding up the roof. That's a lot of weight on these stones right here. They're going to be hard to move." Then he walked over to where the passage exited the room. "Here, there are two walls close to each other. That means each is carrying half the load. That's half the weight of the wall in the center of the room. In theory, it should be twice as easy to push these stones out of line. And the rope can help."

He took one end of the rope and walked to where the passage exited the room. "There's a hole in the wall up here. Just a couple of badly set stones that fell out of place after three thousand years. But I can pass the rope through to the neighboring passage and then bring it around and through the opening back into this room, like this."

He passed the end of the thick rope through the eye-level bowling ball-sized hole a few feet from the passage, brought the end around the supporting wall and then walked it to the opposite side of the room. Here he looped it around a stone pillar, also at eye level. He finished by tying the two rope ends together with at least half a dozen knots before standing the timber between the two lengths of rope that ran horizontally across the room like slightly sagging parallel clotheslines.

"The principle is the same as one of those rubber band airplane engines that children used to play with," said Campion. "The more times you wind the propeller, the more tension you place on the band. The rope loop is like our rubber band. The timber is our propeller. Each time we wind it, the rope will exert more pressure on the sides. Hopefully enough to pull the stones out of place!"

"All right, Amet, you and me, we're going to wind the propeller," said Crockett. "Doc, you and Ricky go out into the passage, get behind the wall—right where the rope is—and when we crank, you push!"

Ricky nodded and she and Campion headed for the passage.

"Wait!" called Crockett. "I should point out that there is more than a small amount of danger. Of course, there's always the chance that we won't be able to budge these sons of bitches. The other danger is that we will, and that the roof will come down on top of us. Those aren't cedar shingles up there! If it starts to go, get out of the way!"

Ricky and Campion disappeared behind the wall and called out to indicate that they were ready.

Crockett rubbed his hands together. "Let's hope this works." He held the ropes against the center of the timber as Amet rotated it once, twice. Now that the ropes were twisted into place securely around the center of their timber, Crockett got on the opposite side of the contraption to assist with the winding. The first few twists were easy enough, but then the ropes lost their remaining slack, and lifting the end of the timber felt like lifting a refrigerator.

"All right Doc, Ricky, put your shoulders into it!"

The sounds of grunting and boots scraping against the floor filled the chamber. Sweat poured down their faces. Another twist and their efforts resembled trying to budge a BMW.

"Come on, Amet!" said Crockett hoarsely, straining against the timber, shaking with the effort. "A little more!"

185

Aside from a bit of dust, it didn't seem that they had moved any of the stones at all. Ricky could tell that if the wall did not start to go in the next few seconds, they would be physically unable to continue. She tried to ignore the pain, focused solely on her hatred of Rio Armstrong and the evil that had swept her beautiful sister into the sea.

"Come on, you son of a bitch!" cried Crockett.

Suddenly, Campion stopped pushing, bent to the floor, where he picked up one of the melon-sized stones that had fallen out of the wall years ago, raised it over his head, and slammed it into the wall just above the vibrating rope.

Nothing.

"A little more! Just a little!" grunted Crockett, and in response, Amet dug in his cross trainers and let out a low sound that was half moan, half growl.

Panting, Campion went to the floor, lifted the stone over his head again, backed up two steps, roared as if he were charging into battle, and brought the stone forward on a run against the wall.

And suddenly, there was a crack in the ancient mortar.

"I think... you got it started!" wheezed Ricky, her muscles burning.

Another crack. A stone fell. Then a second.

"More!" cried Crockett.

Then a large slab, followed by prolonged thunder, and the support column began to topple toward the middle of the larger chamber.

Crockett called out, "It's going! Get out of the way!"

Ricky dived as far down the passage as she could. The ground shook. Behind her sounded the throaty screech of rock scraping against rock like the death cries of prehistoric creatures. Debris exploded down the passageway, and she was pummeled by a few potato-sized stones. Then it was over, except for choking dust everywhere.

"Hello?" she called out, then was seized by coughing.

She pulled the neckline of her shirt over her nose, recovered, listened. No answer.

She rose tentatively, called out again. "Crockett? Dr. Campion?"

A wave of coughing rattled her, and with it, real fear. Had the others been killed in the cave-in, leaving her still trapped, alone, the air so thick with dust that she would suffer wretchedly until she choked to death? A weak glow from around the corner provided scant illumination.

Then she heard a voice. "It's my leg! It's pinned under some of the fallen wall!"

Dr. Campion.

This was followed by coughing from the chamber beyond the wall. "We're—we're okay. Damn, that was an awful plan!"

She pawed her way quickly to Campion, covered in dust and rubble. It took her a minute to move enough stone to free his leg, but he gritted his teeth and stifled a cry in attempting to stand. Ricky helped him to one foot and supported him as they picked their way around fallen rock and reentered the larger chamber where Amet stood holding his thin flashlight, illuminating the remains of an entire wall strewn across half the room. The gray powder that covered both the big man and Crockett gave them the appearance of living statues.

Crockett doubled over, hacking, spat on the ground.

Panic welled in Ricky, something darker and far worse than before, fed by the extinguishing of hope. Her voice cracked as she spoke. "Now what?"

"Now we climb out of here!" Crockett pointed up and to the

left. "Thankfully, our awful plan worked!"

She now noticed that not all of the chamber's illumination came from Amet's flashlight. A beautiful shaft of sunlight spilled onto a broken slab of limestone sitting at an awkward angle.

"I-I don't think I can do it," said Campion, grimacing.

Amet carried him, squeezing through the narrow opening in the roof of the mastaba. The others followed.

Crockett turned his face toward the sun and raised his hands into the air. "We are alive!" Then he turned to the driver. "Amet, you are amazing! Best driver ever! My friend, if there's ever anything I can do for you, just name it!"

"I need a new flashlight," said Amet, showing them the spider web of cracks in the lens. Then he smiled and began the trek to the parking area, carrying Campion.

CHAPTER 20

They had Amet take them to the Anglo American Hospital a mile west of the Hotel Sofitel.

"We can't go back there," said Crockett, indicating the direction of their hotel. "Once they see we're alive, now that we're on to them, they'll try to finish the job. I hope Leo has managed to stay out of their sights."

As they waited for the staff to patch up Campion, Crockett borrowed a mobile and called Brenner.

"For the love of God!" Brenner began. "I can't tell you how good it is to hear from you. I thought something awful might have happened!"

"Oh, it did, Leo, it did," said Crockett. "We can't come back to the hotel. We're going to get a room in some cheap place near here and wash the desert off. I'll call when we're settled and you can meet us. In the meantime, lay low." He explained that Rio had tried to kill them.

"I could almost hear his heart breaking over the phone," said Crockett after he had ended the call. "Poor bastard. As far as I know, that's the first time he's let himself be vulnerable since Mary. And Mary was his world."

After that, they waited. Crockett dozed in the seat next to Ricky. Amet sat with eyes straight ahead.

"You can rest, too, if you want," Ricky told the driver.

Amet shook his head. "On duty." Then he smiled and Ricky returned it.

A minute later she excused herself to use the restroom. While there, she took the opportunity to wash the dust off her exposed skin.

I can't wait to take a bath or shower.

She toweled off her face. They had come so close to dying today. And for what? Rio had said that she did not expect the scroll to make her immortal. Then what was going on? Why was the cult of Cessair so fanatical about possessing the artifact if not for money or immortality? There was some part of the puzzle they were not seeing—or which, perhaps, had not been revealed to them yet.

Her eye fell on the wall-mounted plastic container for medical waste next to the sink. On it was emblazoned the international bio-hazard symbol:

Something stirred in her memory.

Stop thinking about it and then you'll remember.

The mehen. She had stopped thinking about it. For a long time. And then she had come into this restroom.

The bio-hazard symbol was three crescents, each forming a circle and then drawn together like a three-leaf clover.

Like a three-leaf clover.

Her breathing quickened.

Mare Desiderii. A place on the dark side of the moon. Why would Sasha have chosen to write the name of that place on the map? Ricky knew nothing about the geography of the moon except that it had so-called seas. Not actual seas, of course, but rather shadowy, cratered areas that ancient people had assumed were seas. The tradition had been continued in modern times after it had become possible to photograph and map the moon's dark side.

She knew something, and now it was right there, close to the surface. She burst from the restroom, saw an open door on her left —an office or unattended nursing station. Thankfully, the last user had not logged out, and so Ricky sat, quickly changed the language setting on the browser to English, and typed *Mare Desiderii* into the search engine.

Mare Desiderii (Latin for Sea of Dreams) was an area of the Moon named after Luna 3 returned the first pictures of the far side.

The epiphany came to her so suddenly and so clearly that it made her gasp. Ricky returned to the restroom, splashed cold water on her face again, this time to calm herself. Racing back to the waiting area, now occupied by half a dozen other people, she grabbed a very confused Crockett by the arm, pulled him along the

191

hallway and through the entrance doors.

"This must be important," said Crockett. "My arm nearly came out of its socket."

"Shut up!" cried Ricky, then lowered her voice. "Listen! I know where the scroll is!"

Crockett's eyes widened. "You do?" then they narrowed again. "How? What do you mean?"

"Sasha told me! Told us! In her note!"

"Why didn't you say something earlier?"

"I just figured it out! She made it into a clue only I would understand in case the map fell into the wrong hands!" Ricky was so excited that she felt light-headed. She tried to slow her breathing, take deeper breaths. "Remember that Bash said someone had torn off a piece of the parchment?"

Crockett nodded.

"Sasha did it! She couldn't read the glyphs, but she knew it was a map and that the cult wanted something it could lead them to! So she fucked it up so no one would see the whole symbol!"

"The mehen?" asked Crockett.

Ricky shook her head. "It's not a mehen!"

"But both Bash and Doc—"

"Listen! Sasha wrote Mare Desiderii on the spiral."

Crockett grunted an affirmation. "One of the seas on the dark side. Sea of Dreams."

"If someone would have translated the name earlier, I would have known!" hissed Ricky. "*Sea of Dreams* is a place Sasha and I went!"

Crockett raised an eyebrow. "On earth, I assume."

"Of course, you asshole! It's the name of a tattoo parlor we went to on our eighteenth birthday to get matching tats!"

Crockett struggled to make the connection. "Tattoos? Of a

mehen?"

"I told you, it's not a mehen!" cried Ricky. "Sasha tore the map so that you can't tell what the whole figure really looks like! Confuse the bad guys, but give *us* the clue! If I had a phone…"

Then, she realized that she didn't need one. Ricky suddenly spun away from him, leaned forward, and pulled up her shirt so that he could see her bare back. There, between her shoulder blades was a three-lobed symbol:

"It's a triskelion," she repeated giddily. *"It's not a mehen, it's a fucking triskelion! We got the tats when we turned eighteen!"*

Crockett whistled, impressed. "Okay, you definitely have my attention. But isn't this a pretty unlikely coincidence. You having a triskelion tattoo, and a triskelion being on the parchment?"

Ricky shook her head. "The triskelion is one of the most common symbols in Celtic mythology. The three spirals can have many meanings. I chose it to represent mind, spirit and body. The symbol has been around for much longer than the scroll."

"Okay," said Crockett, rubbing his chin. "Let's say you're right and the missing symbol is a triskelion. You said it's a Celtic symbol. Why would a Celtic symbol be carved onto a wall or door of a cruciform tomb in Egypt?"

Ricky took a deep breath. "It wouldn't."

"O-kayyyyy." Crockett shook his head. "Now I really don't get it. I thought the mehen—I mean triskelion—was supposed to mark the location of the scroll. Now you're telling me there's no tomb with a triskelion marking!"

"No tomb in *Egypt*!"

Crockett let the thought hang there for a moment. "Then where?"

"One of the most famous cruciform tombs on the planet! But we're on the wrong continent!" She had grown up with the monument in her backyard. She had read all of the myths, knew its history.

Crockett's eyes lit up as it became obvious. "Ireland!"

CHAPTER 21

Three hours later, they sat at a table in the bar at the surprisingly named Swiss Inn, which they had found a short distance from the hospital. They had also found a store where they had been able to purchase clean clothing and a few personal items. Then they had taken turns showering off the grime, in the bathroom of the room they had rented.

While dramatically cheaper than the Hotel Sofitel, the Swiss Inn was clean, up-to-date, and boasted all of the amenities of the better three-star hotels in the States—and then some. Amet had produced a spare cell phone from the locked glove box of the van, and Crockett had used this to inform Brenner of their whereabouts.

Brenner joined them a half hour after they checked in, taking the chair at the end of their table. The rest sat on sofas, one on each side of the table, forming a kind of booth, with Ricky and Crockett on one side, Amet and Campion—his splinted and bandaged leg extending to the side—on the other.

"Tom, your leg!" exclaimed Brenner.

They took turns filling Brenner in on the rest of the details of what had happened, keeping their voices low, though the restaurant and bar did not have many customers in the mid-afternoon. Ricky saw the sadness in his face as Rio's role in the affair was fully explained.

When they had finished, he shook his head. "Damn! I can't believe what a fool I've been! I put all of you in jeopardy!"

"Not at all!" Campion scolded him brusquely. "When she staged her accident on the Cairo-Aswan, she did it to infiltrate our group. If you had not been a part of the group, she would have simply struck a friendship with someone else."

While it was clear that Brenner appreciated the comments, it was equally clear to Ricky that it would take a while for his bruised emotions to recover.

Then Ricky dropped her bombshell. She first had Brenner bring up the photo of the map on his mobile.

"We thought it was a mehen," said Ricky, pointing to the torn edge that Brenner had enlarged to fill the screen. "But there are actually three spirals!"

"What makes you so sure?" asked Brenner.

She explained the clue left by Sasha. "It was a reference to my tattoo! It's a common Celtic symbol! Sasha tore off the edge of the map so only I would know!"

"Is that all?" asked Brenner, unimpressed.

"The map mentions that you need to cross a river of milk." She now unfolded a sheet of paper showing a photo of an unusual earthen mound. "The hotel clerk printed this out for me at the desk after I brought it up online at the business center."

Brenner adjusted its position in front of him. "What's this?"

"Newgrange," replied Ricky. "As soon as I figured out the meaning of Sasha's message, I thought of this place. It's one of the most famous tombs in Ireland. It's older than the Great Pyramids. Built around 3200 BC."

Brenner rubbed his chin. "Okay, that's the right time frame. Is there more?"

Ricky nodded. "The tomb we've been looking for has a cruciform-shaped burial chamber. Here's the burial chamber at Newgrange." She indicated a sketch of the tomb's passageway that she had penciled onto the back of a paper place mat.

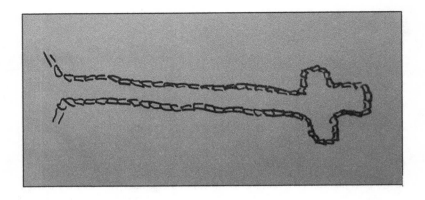

Brenner nodded slowly. "All right, I'm definitely intrigued."

"There's more," said Ricky, who had used every spare moment of the afternoon to arm herself with information on the site. "If you look at the photograph, Newgrange has a white stone wall built up against its earthen sides. But it doesn't extend all the way around. And the wall wasn't put there by the original builders of the mound. The wall was built as part of a controversial restoration project in modern times. But they built it less than halfway around, partly because many archaeologists believed there never was a stone wall surrounding the original. They believe that the stones, which are quartz, by the way, had originally formed a *walkway* that *encircled* the mound 5,000 years ago."

"A white quartz walkway all the way around it!" exclaimed Brenner, his eyes widening. "A 'river of milk'!"

Ricky could not contain a miniscule smile over his reaction. "On the winter solstice, the sun shines through the tomb opening and illuminates the burial chamber on the far end of a ninety-foot passage," she continued. "That fits, too! The map says the sun will show the way! I wouldn't be surprised if it also points to our symbol! Triskelions were often used to decorate Celtic tombs and ritual sites. And that would mark the location of the hidden scroll!"

"You realize that we're half a year away from the winter

solstice," noted Brenner.

"There has to be someone there who knows where the sunlight falls inside the tomb," suggested Crockett.

Brenner shook his head. "This changes everything. Ireland! We all rushed here to Egypt like first-class idiots!"

"So did the cult," said Crockett philosophically. "But it's easy to see why. Whoever was carrying the map—"

"Fintan," noted Ricky.

"Right, Fintan started out in Ireland. It was only natural for us to think the scroll would be in Memphis, which is the only other location on the map."

"And whoever made the map, from their perspective, the English Channel or the Irish Sea or both probably seemed like a 'great river'," said Ricky. "We all guessed the Nile."

"We were rushing," added Campion, "working against the clock. I'm afraid we didn't proceed very carefully or scientifically."

"We won't have the luxury of making that mistake again," said Brenner, coolly. "But I still don't understand. If the scroll was in Ireland instead of Egypt, where was Fintan going? And why did he hide the scroll rather than destroy it?"

"Maybe he wasn't coming to Egypt at all," suggested Campion. "Maybe it was just a reference point that he figured the reader would recognize. Remember, Memphis was the center of the known world to him, a point everyone could use to orient themselves."

Crockett nodded, a smile creeping across his face. "That makes a whole lot of sense."

"All right," said Brenner, "but that still doesn't explain why he didn't destroy the scroll. If he didn't want Cessair to use it, wouldn't the best course have been to get rid of it?"

They sat silently for a few moments. Then, unexpectedly, Amet spoke up.

"Maybe he wanted to keep it in a safe place so he could use it."

Crockett nodded. "To become immortal himself?"

"Or as a weapon," suggested Campion. "Remember, it's the Scroll of Life *and* Death."

Brenner cut the discussion short. "We can't know the answer to all of these questions right now." Then he turned to Ricky. "I think you are absolutely correct. We have to go to Ireland, and quickly, before Rio figures it out, too. But there are a few problems."

"Only a few?" asked Crockett. "You're talking to folks who were buried alive a couple of hours ago. How bad can they be?"

"Bad enough," said Brenner. "After you called, I was pulled aside by the hotel manager who informed me that the police were on their way."

Campion, who had been using Brenner's phone to learn more about Newgrange, snapped to attention. "The police?"

"Yes, Tom," said Brenner. "Apparently Rio told authorities that we have been disturbing historical sites without a permit and looting tombs. I'm told there have been some artifacts worth a small fortune planted on our jet."

"Why would she bother to do that?" asked Crockett. "As far as she knows, we're dead."

"I think she must have put that part of her plan into action before she cornered you at Saqqara," said Brenner. "Or maybe it was simply a kind of insurance. But it creates a huge problem for us now. If we are recognized, or if we break the law in any way, we'll be arrested. They may try to track our movements if we use credit cards. And oviously we can't use the jet. In fact, it's going to be very difficult for us to leave the country. With the police looking for us, we'll be stopped at any airport or border crossing."

Ricky's features went slack. "Then we're finished."

"What about getting fake passports, Leo?" asked Crockett.

Brenner nodded. "That's what I was thinking. They'll be pricey. Money isn't an issue. I carry plenty of cash. But getting papers like that so that we can leave the country is going to take time."

Amet cleared his throat and spoke softly.

"I have an uncle. He can get you those papers by tomorrow."

Then he smiled.

CHAPTER 22

Surprisingly, the easiest part of their journey was securing the bogus documentation from Amet's "uncle". He arrived at the hotel with a laptop pack and a large, square-sided suitcase. They went directly to their room where he revealed an impressively compact and sophisticated counterfeiting operation.

He started by taking each of their photographs—twice, having them change clothes and comb their hair differently for the second so that the passport photo and their drivers' license photos would not look like they were taken in the same place on the same day. He fed the digital images into a compact desktop printer, which spit out an ID for each of them. A second, slightly larger apparatus printed their photos onto a passport page and expertly bound it into the finished product. Then he handed each of them a different credit card with their new name on it.

"I'm Andrew Gorski," said Crockett, examining his documents. He held up the card. "Is this legit?"

Amet's uncle nodded. He also dished high-end, no-contract, pay-as-you-go mobiles.

Brenner paid him—handsomely—and he left. The whole thing had taken less than an hour.

"He doesn't stay around long when it's business," said Amet.

"The man is slick," said Crockett.

After that, Amet had driven them to the Turgoman Garage in Cairo, where they had booked bus passage to Tel Aviv. Then they said goodbye to the big man.

"Amet, my friend," said Crockett, giving him a hug, "you don't know how much I'm going to miss you! If not for you, we'd have cashed in our chips long ago!"

Ricky gave him a hug, and he surprised her by lifting her off the ground.

Brenner gave him an enormous tip.

Ricky and Brenner sat next to each other on the bus, and Crockett and Campion took the seat behind, though Campion had a difficult time keeping his wrapped and mostly immobile leg out of everyone's way.

"It should be easier crossing the border as part of a tour than if we had rented a car and tried to do it ourselves," said Brenner, speaking softly. "We'll stand out less. The authorities in Tel Aviv won't be looking for us, so we should be able to book a flight."

"You'd think there'd be an easier way to travel to or from Egypt," said Ricky. "I mean, other than by plane. Why don't they have ferries that cut straight across to Greece or Italy? That would make so much sense!"

"Such routes used to exist," said Brenner. "Not long ago, you could take a ferry from Alexandria to Venice. But that's all changed. Hard-line Muslims have more influence in Egypt than they had twenty years ago. Civil wars are being fought right next door in Libya on one side and Israel on the other. There are fears of terrorism. Ship owners fear attacks on their vessels. And some ports are leery of allowing the vessels to dock. Until the political dynamic in the Middle East improves, we'll have to continue to take the long way around. If we can't fly, that is. Besides, you wouldn't have wanted to take a ferry from Alexandria to Venice."

"Why not?" asked Ricky.

"When they used to run that route," replied Brenner, "it took four days!"

The bus shuddered to life and they settled in for the long ride.

Brenner fell asleep almost immediately. They rolled on through Madinaty, Suez, and then across the Sinai Desert toward Nekhel. Ricky again found herself unable to sleep, anxious about the border crossing into Israel at Taba. However, the stop and the inspection of their documents went off smoothly. As a result, five minutes after crossing the border, she nodded off as well, waking more than three hours later when the bus made a rest stop outside of Be'er Sheva. Crockett and Brenner helped Campion down the bus steps, taking care not to bump his heavily wrapped right leg.

"You doin' okay, Doc?" asked Crockett.

"Goodness, yes," said Campion, hobbling along a half step behind them on his crutches. "Time of my life. It'll take more than a little pain to dampen my spirits!"

As they stretched their legs and bought Cokes, Campion posed a question.

"How long do you think it's going to be before Rio figures out we're not dead and starts looking for us?"

"That's hard to say," said Brenner.

"I mean," continued Campion, "we need a head start. We're traveling by bus, which is tortoise speed. Once Rio figures out where to go, she's going to be able to hop on a plane."

"How is she going to figure it out?" asked Ricky. "There's no way she can know what Sasha's message means."

"She may not know where we're going, but she'll still come after us," said Campion.

"But unless she knows Amet's uncle, I don't think she'll be leaving Egypt any time soon," said Crockett.

They all looked at him.

"What do you mean?" asked Brenner.

"You want to tell them?" he asked, looking toward Ricky.

"She fucking tried to kill us," Ricky said evasively. "Bitch."

"What did you do, Ricky?" asked Brenner.

"I gave an anonymous tip to the police. I told them that Rio was working with the 'other Americans' to steal Egyptian artifacts."

"What would make the authorities believe that?" asked Brenner. "It was just an anonymous tip. There's no proof of any collusion."

Ricky hesitated. "I may have suggested that they look at hotel security tapes."

"Which would show?"

Her eyes darted around the group, and then she plunged ahead. "You going into Rio's room to spend the night."

Brenner's mouth opened slightly as if he might say something. But he did not.

"Yeah," said Crockett, a smile on his face. "That should do the trick."

"Of course, it shouldn't take them too long to figure out the truth," said Campion. "Still, it might buy us a day. Maybe two. Or three."

"I guess we sort of threw you under the bus," said Ricky hesitantly.

"No, no," said Brenner, recovering himself. "It was brilliant. Just... unexpected."

Campion spoke up. "Leo, have you given any thought to our next move when we get to Tel Aviv?"

Brenner held up his cell phone. "Finally got a decent signal about half an hour ago. Booked us a flight to Ireland. There's a connecting flight in Frankfurt. We'll have just over a two hour wait. I booked the first flight available. I don't want to sit around and take a chance that we'll be detained."

"Then we're almost home free," said Crockett.

"Not until we're successful," warned Brenner. "Once Rio and Cessair's cult learn you're still alive, we'll be in more danger than ever. We need to be even more wary."

Crockett nodded soberly. "You know, when you put it that way, I really miss Amet."

CHAPTER 23

They arrived in Frankfurt at 08:30 a.m. local time and prepared to settle in for a two hour wait for their connecting flight. Ricky had to admit that she felt much better, now that they were far from Egyptian authorities. Yet, for all she knew, what lay ahead might be more dangerous than what they had already survived.

They had slept during the four and a half-hour flight. Now they were hungry, as they waited in line at customs in the bright, modern terminal.

"We can just grab something in the concourse," suggested Brenner, tapping at the screen of his phone, delighted to have a decent signal. "They've even got a McDonalds."

Ricky agreed that McDonalds sounded pretty good right now. However, they first had to get through customs. Brenner was first in their group, and Ricky could see from the flicker of concern in the eyes of the agent who inspected his passport that something was wrong. Speaking in a thick, German accent, the agent told Brenner to step off to the side. Moments later, Ricky, Crockett and Campion stood beside him.

"Follow me, please," said a second armed agent wearing a white service cap, dark pants, white shirt, and protective vest. A third brought up the rear.

"I think there must be some mistake," said Brenner.

"Just routine, I assure you," said the agent in the lead. "Hopefully it will not take long."

They were taken to a secure room where the first agent left. The second remained, sitting quietly in a chair but saying nothing. His presence discouraged most conversation among the group, although Brenner did try to assuage their fears.

"Like the man said, it may simply be a part of the routine. Perhaps we were pulled out of the queue randomly."

"I don't know," said Crockett heavily. "I've got a bad feeling and, since about two days ago, a real skepticism about anything that appears random."

Fifteen minutes later, the door opened and the first agent stepped back into the room. With a head motion, he signaled for the other agent to leave. Then he shut the door.

"Please excuse this inconvenience," said the man, whose name tag read KOEHNE. "But we have detected a problem with your documentation."

"This is ridiculous," said Brenner convincingly.

"We're just tourists, sir," added Crockett. "I'm sure this is a mistake."

"We've traveled all over the globe without an issue," said Brenner, jumping back in with added indignation.

"And we're getting kind of hungry!" stated Crockett. Brenner looked like he had been about to say something, but instead, turned to raise an eyebrow at his colleague.

"I'm sorry," said Crockett. "I'm starving and my stomach's been growling ever since you mentioned that McDonalds!"

"Perhaps there is a mistake," said Agent Koehne politely. "But your documents were red-flagged by a security program."

"What sort of red flag did we raise?" asked Brenner.

"I'm sure it will all be explained," said Officer Koehne calmly. "I apologize, but anything to do with computers, I must admit, is beyond my understanding."

"I see," answered Brenner brusquely. "But with all due respect, we have a connecting flight to board in about forty-five minutes, a very important flight, and I would hate to miss it as the result of some computer glitch."

"We will do the best we can," said Officer Koehne. "But you understand how it is with security these days. We must be thorough. However, you had mentioned you were hungry?"

"Starving!" said Crockett.

"May I get you something to eat while we wait for verification? Or to drink, perhaps? Coffee? Tea?"

Ricky requested tea. Campion, only water. Crockett asked for hash browns and two of anything with bacon from the McDonalds. "And a large coffee."

Brenner requested merely an orange juice and a couple of aspirin.

Koehne exited, leaving them alone for a few minutes. Ricky tried the door and found, without surprise, that it was locked. When their food and drinks arrived, Crockett tore into his ravenously.

"I will check with my superiors to see if there is any new information," said Koehne, who then disappeared again.

"So, Leo," said Crockett, speaking with a mouth half full of bacon and biscuit, "what are the chances that they decide they've made a mistake and kick us to the curb?"

Brenner scanned the room for cameras before replying, though he still kept his voice low. "Not good, I'd guess." Crockett waited for more, but instead, Brenner dug out two aspirin, washing down both with half of his juice.

Campion chuckled grimly. "And we thought that our toughest challenge would be escaping from an Egyptian mastaba."

"There's nothing more difficult to escape from than a bureaucracy," said Crockett. "So what's our plan B?"

Brenner shook his head. "There is no plan B."

"There's always a plan B," said Crockett. "Isn't there someone you can call? You know a lot of influential people back in the States, Leo."

"Yes," admitted Brenner, "but that would mean admitting that we were using forged documents to travel between countries, which is a serious crime. And I doubt we could justify it in the eyes of the German police by telling them we're heading to Ireland to rob a national monument."

"Yeah," said Crockett. "Now that I think of it, Indiana Jones had problems with the Germans, too."

Brenner rubbed his eyes. "Tom, you're an idea man. Have you got anything up your sleeve?"

When Campion failed to answer, they looked over and saw that he had fallen asleep in his chair.

Brenner smiled. "Well, we're all exhausted, aren't we?"

"I could use a nap," said Crockett thickly, running his fingers through his hair. "Then again, McDonalds food always makes me feel like that."

Ricky had to admit that she could hardly keep her eyes open. She looked toward Brenner and saw that his head was now resting sideways on the table, eyes closed, mouth slightly open.

What's happening?

The last image she recalled before nodding off was Crockett, his cheek mashed into the bacon biscuit sitting on a wrapper on the table in front of him.

CHAPTER 24

A sound like prolonged thunder awakened her. She felt heavy, confused. The smell of freshly turned earth and concrete dust hung in the air.

"Ah, there she comes!" said a heavily accented voice, and after a moment, Ricky realized that the man was talking about her.

As the fuzziness faded, she found herself sitting on bare ground, her back against a concrete wall. Ricky tried to raise a hand to her forehead. Something held it back.

The edges of her reality sharpened.

My hands are tied behind my back!

She also realized that her ankles had been bound together with duct tape.

A stab of panic. She tried to twist and separate her hands, emitting a pathetic grunt.

"Welcome back, Miss Crowe!" said the voice, which she now recognized as the security man from the airport, Koehne. "Please, do not waste your energy struggling."

Ricky looked around. The area seemed to be a wide tunnel whose gray light filtered in from beyond the walls and support columns in the near distance. On her right a few feet away sat

Campion, his hands and ankles also bound, though he seemed to be in considerably more pain, the result of the pressure applied to his wounded leg by the duct tape. On her left was Crockett, and beyond him, Brenner. Koehne stood in front of them, perhaps fifteen feet away, still in his airport security uniform. Four other men, two in suits, two in construction coveralls flanked him.

Crockett spoke to her, his voice low, hoarse. "I wasn't sure you were going to wake up."

Ricky took a deep breath, blinked, trying to make some sense of it.

"Welcome to Frankfurt Central Station, traversed by almost half a million travelers every day," said Koehne. "But none of them can hear you. The noise of the trains and the thick walls make this an ideal meeting place for our purposes. We're actually under the northern part of the station. Just behind you—or rather, behind the wall you're sitting against—is the S-bahn, our underground train."

Ricky looked around. The wall against which she sat rose about twenty feet to a concrete ceiling. How far it extended horizontally she could not say, for a series of concrete supports interrupted the view. Some renovation or repair work seemed to be going on about fifty feet to the right, for there was an orange hydraulic digger next to what appeared to be an open trench, and a cement truck with green markings idling quietly, its great drum rotating lazily.

"Get this tape off me!" growled Brenner, struggling against his bonds.

"I will deal with you in due time, Dr. Brenner!" said Koehne, his features darkening. "But first, we must conduct our business."

Ricky felt a stab of panic, hearing Koehne use Brenner's and her real names. He knew. And that almost certainly meant he answered to Rio.

"I will answer the questions I am sure are on your minds," continued Koehne. "And then you will answer *my* questions. After that, we will go our separate ways."

"Just like that?" asked Crockett.

Koehne smiled and nodded slightly. "Just like that. First, one of our people was responsible for having you detained at the airport. Records will show that you were questioned and released, a common occurrence. What actually occurred is that once the drugs took effect, *our* people transported you in wheelchairs to a waiting van, which brought you here.

"So you're Rio's lackeys," said Crockett derisively. "What do you want from us?"

"We want to make sure we know everything you know," said Koehne. "There was some...*trickery* back in Cairo, I believe, which has delayed Fraulein Armstrong's departure. But you four left quickly. We understand that you were heading to Ireland, that you left Tel Aviv earlier today and then arrived here in Frankfurt. We know that you were scheduled to land in Dublin later today, and then you would be traveling to Newgrange."

"What the hell is Newgrange?" asked Crockett. "Our connecting flight is to Barcelona. We thought we'd try the nude beaches."

"Mr. Crockett," said Koehne patiently, "Your tickets are for Dublin. You have already reserved a rental vehicle that will allow you to travel from there to the Newgrange passage tomb."

"So what are you, some kind of mind reader?" asked Crockett. They had told no one of their plans, except Amet, and Crockett was certain their former driver would never sell them out. They had made all purchases and reservations using faked documentation, which might have been flagged, but would not reveal their real names. "There's no way you and the queen bitch could know our plans!"

Ricky knew Crockett was right. Rio might have guessed that they were alive. She might have even figured out that they were headed to Ireland, although the odds against calculating Newgrange as their precise destination would have been astronomical. But there was no way she could know how they would get there or which flights they would take through which cities.

"Unless…"

They turned to Campion who had begun to speak, beads of perspiration standing out on his forehead.

"Unless one of *us* told her. But that doesn't make any sense."

"No, it doesn't," said Crockett, his brow furrowed as an idea formed. "Or… or does it? Maybe someone made a deal with Rio."

"Who? Ricky certainly isn't going to go in with the people responsible for her sister's disappearance," said Campion. "And Leo doesn't need the money."

"Amet?" asked Crockett. "Tell me it wasn't Amet!"

"Amet didn't know all of our plans," noted Campion, struggling against his pain to keep his voice even.

"What if that person wasn't interested in money?" asked Ricky.

Campion frowned. "I don't understand."

"What if the deal was for immortality?"

"Seriously?" asked Crockett.

"Dr. Campion said it. People can be dangerous when they're after something, whether it's real, or whether they simply think it's real."

Campion nodded as if hardly believing his own words. "But who? Surely none of us believes in fairy tales! And we all nearly died in the mastaba!"

Ricky felt her throat go suddenly dry as the one possibility occurred to her. "Not *all* of us."

They were silent for a moment as it hit home.

Crockett sat back, hitting his head against the concrete. "Oh no! Oh, God, no!"

Koehne laughed loudly. "Dr. Brenner, it looks like you are out of the closet, so to speak."

"Fine, damn it!" said Brenner. "Now untie me!"

"First, the business," said Koehne.

Brenner's face was red, his eyes dark with fury. "How dare you! Don't you know who I am?"

"I confess that *I* don't know who you are, Leo," said Campion. "I dared to think we were friends."

Brenner said nothing, but continued to stare at Koehne with unconcealed hatred. Crockett had pulled his knees up toward his chest and had buried his face behind them.

"I have only a few questions, and then we will go," said Koehne. "As I said before, thanks to Dr. Brenner's communications with Fraulein Armstrong, we know you were going to Newgrange, to the tomb with the X-shaped chamber. And he had mentioned to Fraulein Armstrong that you were no longer looking for—what is it?—a *mehen*? That some other symbol marked the scroll's location."

Ricky realized that Brenner, who knew they were searching for a triskelion, had intentionally withheld this information from Rio. She wondered whether he had decided to keep this ace up his sleeve because he did not fully trust her.

"It wasn't supposed to be this way! They weren't supposed to be harmed!" said Brenner furiously. "You'll get nothing more from me until I'm untied!"

Koehne turned away from Brenner. "Very well. What about the

rest of you? Will you tell me what it is, hmm?"

"It seems to me if we don't tell you what it looks like, you're done," said Crockett. "Good luck finding the scroll without it!"

Koehne gave Crockett a dark smile before moving on to Ricky. He regarded her stoically for a moment, then smiled maliciously, knelt beside her, and stroked her scar lightly with an index finger. "What about you, lovely lady?"

A wave of revulsion washed over Ricky, fed by the knowledge that he was mocking her—and caressing her scar to let her *know* that he was mocking her, that "lovely" was the last thing he considered her. But the other force feeding her hatred was even stronger: the knowledge that this stale-breathed, sociopathic lackey was a part of the pit of vipers that had killed Sasha, and now he knelt over her, sinister and powerful, toying with her with no more regard than if she were an insect he was about to crush. Or a thirteen-year-old girl in Alabama to whom he felt entitled.

In that moment, she had never hated so greatly, had never been so completely overcome by blind emotion, its searing red flames fueled by Alabama, by the cretin who had given her the scar, by her sister's murderers, and by the mocking sycophant daring to touch her. Perhaps it was even amplified by this new betrayal by Leo, a man she had liked. With the suddenness of a striking serpent, she lunged, her teeth snapping down on Koehne's index finger.

At first, what was happening did not seem to register. Then, Koehne emitted a high-pitched scream, struggled to remove his finger, found it impossible. Ricky gripped tighter, the taste of his blood in her mouth, her teeth reaching bone. Koehne grabbed at her hair, yanked hard, released, delivered a punch to the side of her head. This loosened her grip just enough that he was able to pull his finger free.

Although the finger was still attached, blood streamed down his hand. A crimson smear stained Ricky's lower lip and her right ear stung from the blow. Koehne howled again and one of his suited accomplices, who had rushed forward, proffered a handkerchief, helping to secure it around the mutilation.

"*Verdammte fotze!*" wailed Koehne. Then he gestured toward the accomplice. "*Messer! Messer!*"

The man produced a switchblade, and Koehne instantly flipped it open.

"No!" cried Crockett. "Oh, God, no!"

"Stop!" boomed Brenner.

But there was no stopping Koehne, who once again knelt next to Ricky, this time brandishing a blade rather than a digit. He glared at her fiercely, even perhaps with a bit of fear. Then he transferred the knife to his right hand, squeezing it against the blood-soaked handkerchief, and delivered a vicious backhand across Ricky's face with his left.

Her head snapped back, and as she faced him again, he placed the tip of the knife to her lips. "Would you like to try to bite this, you bitch? I should cut out your tongue!" Then his voice lowered and he touched the tip of the blade to Ricky's scar. "Who gave this to you? A playful boyfriend? A jealous lover? Someone you betrayed?"

Ricky was too terrified to say anything. Yet her eyes continued to radiate hatred.

"Whoever it was, he was very sloppy," said Koehne, panting as if he had just run a mile, his eyes gleaming and feverish. "You see? His incision begins up here on the forehead, but it veers to the side, missing the eye, then swings back inside toward the chin. He most certainly must have wanted the eye, his hatred so great, but perhaps your struggles left him... unsatisfied. His work ruined."

217

He grimaced, staring bitterly at his own bloody finger. "It will take only a minute to correct it!"

He barked a command, and the suited man who had given him the handkerchief stepped forward, knelt, and put a beefy hand on each side of Ricky's head to hold it steady. Tears streamed down her face, but she refused to cry out.

"No!" repeated Crockett. "For the love of God!"

As Koehne knelt close, Ricky strained against her captor and her bonds. Koehne slapped her again and then motioned a second man to hold her still. Then he knelt, peeled up her left eyelid. This time, her struggles were completely futile, and she was beyond any sort of dissent other than a low, barely human-sounding moan.

It was done in a motion so swift, it seemed to surprise even Koehne, who grunted an insane bit of laughter and then stared at the glistening, grub-like object on the ground. One of the men holding Ricky turned away, made retching sounds. Tears streamed down Crockett's face. "You goddamn animal!"

For Ricky's part, there had been less pain than she had expected. A sensation like sizzling light, as if someone has poked a Fourth of July sparkler into her face, followed by a migraine-like stab on the left side of her head. And darkness. She could feel wetness down her left cheek and didn't know if it was blood or something else. The fact that she was not screaming suggested to her that she might be in shock.

"Koehne! No!" Brenner's voice boomed.

Crockett: "You sick son of a bitch!"

They heard scuffling in the dirt and turned, realizing that Crockett had pushed himself into a standing position against the wall. "No more!" he cried. "Get away from her!" As if by the force of his words he could get desperate fanatics to bend to his will.

As Crockett took a hop in their direction, Koehne stood, uttered another command in German. The second man released Ricky's head, stepped around her and grabbed Crockett roughly by the shoulders.

"Thank you, Mr. Crockett, for pointing out that there may be other ways to hurt Miss Crowe even more deeply," said Koehne. At a sign, the suited man dragged Crockett the short distance to the nearest excavation and threw him into the first of what now became apparent was a progression of holes about thirty feet apart. One of the men in work clothes got into the cab of the cement truck, while the other went to the rear, climbed up on the rig, and used a thick, green hose to add a bit of water to the tank.

"We have been here for a while, and the mixture starts to thicken," explained Koehne, his voice unsteady, an amalgam of the effects of pain and fanatic resolution. "We must get the right consistency for quality work."

Ricky barely heard him, her head hanging forward.

"What are you going to do?" asked Campion, his voice trembling.

"The excavation over there is six feet deep and just as wide," explained Koehne. "It will be a footing for a new support column. There are several others beyond it intended for the same purpose. In a few moments—when our mixture is ready—we will bury Mr. Crockett in concrete."

"No!" cried Ricky, her head coming up.

"Koehne!" roared Brenner. "Untie me! I can tell you all you need to know!"

They were interrupted by clanking sounds as the other worker maneuvered the delivery chute into position over the hole. Then the thick, gray soup flowed down the channel and dropped sloppily into the pit. Crockett cried out in horror.

"Stop! Stop!" screamed Ricky.

"Willing to talk now?" asked Koehne, his eyes fiery, maniacal, cradling his throbbing index finger in his good hand. When Ricky did not answer, he continued. "It's like mud, harder to move about in the deeper it gets. Mr. Crockett should be all right for a while, as long as he stays on his feet. Of course, that won't be easy with duct tape around his ankles."

She saw the top half of Crockett's head, but then it disappeared and he cried out. Her heart skipped. She heard him making frantic noises that coincided with his breathing, and then the top of his head appeared again.

"For a while he should be able to pick himself up, regain his balance. But soon, the concrete will be a bit too deep. When he falls, it will be a little too heavy, will restrict his movements a little too much, because he will be completely submerged. It might only require that the hole be half-full for this to occur. It will feel like he is beneath two hundred pounds of wet blankets. The effort of trying to move, to raise himself will quickly exhaust him. And then he will have to breathe. But there will be no air. Only darkness and thick, choking gray mud in his mouth, his nostrils."

"Please, stop!" cried Ricky, the effort sending a new wave of migraine-like pain through the left side of her head. "It's a triskelion! Just please, stop! Help him!"

At a signal, the flow of concrete was stopped. Crockett leaned against the side of the excavation, mostly covered in gray, endeavoring to keep his balance.

Koehne frowned at her, a shiver of pain coursing through him for a moment. "A..."

"Triskelion," said Ricky, hanging her head again, exhausted, defeated. But she was not going to show him her naked back. "Look it up. It's a common Celtic symbol."

The second suited goon pulled out his phone, tapped at the

screen, waited, tapped again. Then he rotated it toward Koehne, smiling. Koehne nodded.

"Get him out!" shouted Ricky.

"First, is there anything else we need to know?" Koehne asked.

Tears streamed down Ricky's cheeks. She wanted to tell him to burn in hell, that she would enjoy seeing him roasted alive on a spit above a raging furnace or buried up to his neck and covered in honey in a hill of fire ants. But it would only invite more torture, more abuse, more cruelty for cruelty's sake. He held all the cards, all the power, could act viciously and with impunity.

For a moment, she thought to tell them about the sun, how on the winter solstice it shone through the tunnel entrance, showing the proper location of the correct triskelion. But Rio would figure that out. And if she did not or if it took them longer, well, fuck them.

"Nothing."

Koehne regarded her for a moment, seemed satisfied.

Campion spoke up. "You have everything you need! Now get Mr. Crockett out of there!"

"Getting him out was not part of our deal," said Koehne.

Ricky gasped. "But you said…"

"I said that once you had answered my questions, we would leave you. I intend to do that. But first, we need to tidy up."

The second suit stepped forward and wrenched Ricky to her feet. The two truck operators did the same with Brenner and Campion. Ricky was dragged, screaming, to the nearly half-full excavation that Crockett already occupied and tossed roughly into the slop. She struggled to keep her head up, to push off and come to a standing position.

If I fall again, I don't know if I can get back to my feet!

"I'm sorry," said Crockett, edging along the side toward her, trying to stay upright, his voice cracking. "I'm just... sorry."

Above, they heard Brenner's frantic, angry voice as they dragged him and Campion to the next hole.

"Are you insane? Do you realize what she'll do to you? We had an agreement that none of my people would be harmed!"

Koehne shook his head. "Dr. Brenner, *she* is the one who gave the order to have me do *this*!"

"That's impossible!"

"All is fair in love and war, no? Apparently her trust in you was not..." He searched for the word. "...absolute. And after you were kind enough to provide your group's destination, Fraulein Armstrong felt that allowing you to reach Ireland would only have complicated things. All we had to do was convince you to reveal the final puzzle piece." Then, with a hand signal, concrete again began to pour down the sluice and into the pit that Crockett and now Ricky occupied. She cried out, screaming protestations. Crockett's eyes seemed to be in another place, but his face was contorted in pure hatred.

"Bastards! Sons of bitches! Burn in hell!"

"Ah, yes, it is an awful way to die," said Koehne above the grinding rumble of the truck, his eyes flashing a transparent cruelty. "But in five minutes, it will be over."

"Fuck you!"

"Goodbye Mr. Crockett. Miss Crowe."

CHAPTER 25

Rio supposed she had missed the obvious because she was not a real archaeologist. She was not a lot of things she pretended to be, but one could get away with that sort of behavior if one was rich enough. And Rio Armstrong was rich enough. Wealth beyond what even the popular media, in its insatiable appetite for the sensational, had estimated.

But she had found, as do many inordinately wealthy people, that money by itself is insufficient. Wealth yields little satisfaction when the world is crumbling outside the palace doors. It yields little satisfaction when fools dictate the pace of daily life. Or when the world outside is a vulgar, dangerous, inhospitable jungle. When the world itself becomes a prison.

Yet, wealth can also provide the key to escaping that prison. It allows one certain freedoms, opens the doors to powers that most do not possess.

Power to change the world.

Rio considered the future as she sat in her hotel room. A police officer, his uniform of khaki drill cotton almost indistinguishable from that of the Egyptian army, was stationed in the lobby, just a reminder that she was not to leave Egypt—or, for that matter, the hotel—just yet. Lingering questions about stolen artifacts. Certainly it would all be resolved in her favor, the police had told her. But even Rio Armstrong had to wait until all of the evidence had been examined. Well, a day or two delay was no longer a concern. Her people in Germany were seeing to that. Tomorrow, perhaps. Or, at worst, the next day. Then she would be off in her private jet to Ireland, where the scroll waited.

And then the world would change.

The power to create my own army. An army of immortals. And to destroy my enemies.

That was what the Scroll of Life and Death promised. The chance to remake the world without the mistakes. To get rid of the weak and the unproductive. To silence the thousand voices of dissent that kept the planet in a constant state of war. To eliminate fear, for when one is immortal, there is nothing to fear—not even God.

Her search had been a long one. Then there had been the surprise discovery at Zackenberg. The first Crowe sister had complicated things, it was true, but then the little fool in Chicago had allowed Rio to pick up the scent once again. Rio had followed the pitiful group of crusaders to Egypt. There, it had been simple to gain their trust. And they had proved useful. After all, the map's directions were rather vague, and the area had certainly changed in five thousand years. She had counted on their help in finding the scroll's hiding place among the many tombs.

Unfortunately, it had not taken long for them to discover her deception. And they had been absurdly lucky to escape from the mastaba.

They might have disappeared after that, leaving Rio to search tomb after empty tomb in and around the Valley of the Kings. Except that Rio had an ace up her sleeve.

Dr. Leo Brenner.

Rio had had many men, more than she could remember or count. However, that first afternoon, she had felt the attraction. She realized it was not love. The notion that one could instantaneously connect in a meaningful and lasting way was laughable, a plot device for B-movies or shallow romance novels. The attraction between her and Leo had been based on engaging personalities, physical compatibility, good old-fashioned desire, and opportunity.

They had made love within an hour of returning to the hotel. Then they had spent the afternoon in the bar. Rio could tell that Brenner was smitten. As for herself, she did enjoy his company, and his prowess in the bedroom was superb. However, Brenner was a means to an end. There was no castle on the hill waiting for them at the end of the fairy tale. For her, there was the mantle of leadership, the leader of an army that would be unstoppable and eternal. For Brenner there was, in all likelihood, death.

After dinner, they had engaged in a marathon session of love-making. At this point, she felt that if she had asked him to leap from the hotel's roof to demonstrate his love, he might have done it.

But there was more.

The greatest love of Leo Brenner's life would always be his wife, Mary, who had died six years earlier. As many people with terminal diseases do, Mary had searched feverishly for some sort of miracle cure, spending long hours on the Internet, ordering plant extracts, creams, vitamin supplements, and researching alternative medicines. It was here in her search for a way to cheat death that she had come upon references to a shadow group generally referred to as Alchemy. There seemed to be no official organization, leader, web site, or home base. There were, in fact, only vague hints or indications that it existed at all. Yet, the group was rumored to be vast and dedicated to seeking eternal life—not after death, but in this world.

As Mary's own disease had progressed, she had desperately read everything she could find, participated in online discussion groups, written letters to people whose names and addresses she had tracked down on the chance that they might be connected. She had even met with a group of alleged members of Alchemy, although this had turned out to be three local writers who often posted essays sympathetic to the group.

Eventually, one of the letters had found its mark and was passed along the chain of command until it reached Rio. The letter interested her, not because of Mary's pathetic plea for help, or how Mary had described to Rio the depth and breadth of her desperate search, but because Mary's husband, Leo, was the head of an influential research group. Alchemy was always looking to increase its reach, and Rio had calculated that it might be a good thing to have someone inside the HARP Institute. Ironic, actually, in light of what had occurred.

But before Rio had been able to act, Mary had died and other matters had drawn Rio's attention. Then, when Rio had found herself in Egypt with Brenner and his cohorts, she knew that she could use her slight connection to Mary Brenner to her advantage.

In the early morning hours, Rio had confessed her role as the leader of Alchemy to a smitten Leo, which had at first appalled Brenner. But she had explained the necessity for extreme measures. The scroll, after all, could do great good for the world in the right hands.

"Leo, Mary contacted us before she died," she had told him. "She wanted to live! What if I told you that the scroll could make her live again?"

He had been stunned by her question. "You really believe that the scroll can help you cheat death?"

She had told him that she did. Yes, she had been very convincing.

Very.

Leo had gone completely to pieces, blubbering like a baby, confused and emotionally fractured, finally falling asleep at 4 a.m. The next morning, he was ready to do anything that needed to be done.

For the good of the world.

For Mary.

Of course, it had been a lie, Rio reflected. The scroll did *not* have the ability to awaken the dead, as she had suggested to Leo. And her assurances that Leo's associates would be left unharmed had been hollow. And the lie had worked. Leo had served his purpose. Rio had received Koehne's message just minutes ago. He had extracted the necessary information. Now he was tidying up.

She sighed.

She had liked Leo Brenner. Had he been emotionally stronger, perhaps there would have been a place for him in her new world. Then again, she philosophized, if one is destined to live a thousand centuries, perhaps personal attachments were ill-advised. In any case, there would be other intelligent, desirable men to amuse and satisfy her as the centuries rolled on.

Rio sat back, sighed. In a day or two, she would be in Dublin. A few hours after that, Newgrange.

And then she would have her prize.

CHAPTER 26

An acid fear coursed through Ricky, her mind overwhelmed, unable to process the inevitability of her own imminent and horrifying death. The fear of drowning in the gray ooze, of trying to take a breath, but instead, drawing in the chalky sludge, then sinking into blackness, buried forever in the concrete footings—it was too much. It reduced her to a wild animal, thinking only of survival, yet realizing that there was no chance.

The concrete had risen several inches since she had been tossed into the excavation, and she knew that if she lost her balance, even once, it would be impossible for her to get up.

"Please! Don't do this!" Her piercing cries were almost unintelligible.

Koehne did not stop the concrete. He only smiled down at them, as though they were mongrel puppies that he intended to drown, his eyes shining.

A few feet away, Crockett stood motionless, trying to balance himself against the wall, terrified into a paralysis of disassociation.

"Stop! Please!" This voice belonged to Brenner, calling out from the next excavation, which would presumably be filled after the cement reached the top of the one containing Ricky and

Crockett. "This is all a mistake! I'll do whatever you want! I have money!"

Ricky was now past the stage where she could form words, even in her mind. Searing, ragged-edged terror was all that registered as she faced the inevitability of her own last moments.

Then she heard a shout and both the suited thug and Koehne's heads snapped around to the left. Ricky heard voices in German, confused voices. Koehne replied in German, insistent, threatening. Although Ricky did not speak the language, she recognized one word: apfel.

Apple.

Koehne spoke again, a bit louder, made a hand gesture, and then, stepping next to the truck, returned his attention to the pit.

Dr. Leo Brenner had made many mistakes in his life, and certainly some serious ones in the past forty-eight hours. However, he had always come through by taking action rather than sitting back and waiting for whatever was to come. He had realized immediately that neither Koehne nor the suited thug had a good view of the pit he was in, for they were thirty feet away and standing above ground. They could certainly not see Dr. Campion, who was sprawled on the bottom of the second excavation, his face contorted in pain. Once they finished filling the first excavation and started on the second, Campion would not last long.

Brenner lowered himself to the floor of the pit beside Campion, which rendered him out of sight to Koehne and the suit. First, he had to get his hands in front of him. They were all helpless with their hands behind. Sitting on the ground, he brought his knees to his chest and gradually worked his hands under his heels and around his feet.

Once his hands were in front, he was able to use his fingers to tear the duct take around his ankles. In a moment, he could stand easily, yet, he crouched, watching, not wanting to let his captors know of his progress.

Then he had heard the new voices. He knew German. From the brief conversation, he concluded the voices belonged to three or four homeless individuals who visited the construction site every day. It seemed the heavy equipment operators typically gave them apples and occasionally a half sandwich on their lunch breaks. Koehne had informed them that the workers had the day off, had advised them to leave quickly if they knew what was good for them. Even if they had seen something, no one would believe the ramblings of stinking, ill-dressed derelicts.

Brenner had heard all of this while on the move. As soon as he had seen the thug and Koehne's heads snap to the left to address the approaching beggars, he realized that this was his one chance. The sound of his movements masked by the growling of the cement truck engine, he scrambled up the side of the pit and, moving swiftly, was hidden along the right side of the great vehicle in an instant. He found a rough steel edge on the truck and raked his taped wrists across it, gashing them badly. However, it did the trick, tearing the duct tape enough so that he could finally remove it.

Without wasting a moment, he grabbed a shovel from a cradle on the side of the truck and then opened the passenger-side door of the cab. The driver's eyes went wide, completely taken off guard. Before the man could react, Brenner mostly decapitated him with the shovel. Then he pulled the man's body out the passenger door, climbed in and slid over into the driver's seat.

What do I do now?

The unfamiliar voices had offered a sliver of hope—perhaps

they were police officers or railroad security—but that hope had now passed. The cement had nearly reached Ricky's chest, and her muscles ached from the effort she was exerting to steady herself.

It would be over soon.

Then, without warning and accompanied by a loud, blatting engine growl, the huge truck lurched violently backwards toward the pit. The thug in the suit was completely taken off guard as it slammed into his back, knocking him face-down onto the ground. The heavy back tires then rolled over him, crushing his right leg and pelvis like papier-mâché. His animal screams nearly drowned out the grinding of the motor.

Koehne caught the motion of the truck out of the corner of his eye and spun around instinctively. Unlike the suited thug, he was not caught completely unawares, got a hand up to shield himself and took a step and a half backward—there was no other direction to go in that fraction of a second. While the side of the truck's sluice mechanism slammed into him, his backward motion kept it from being a bone-crushing blow. However, the hinged edges of the articulated channel snagged his jacket. Then one of the truck's back wheels dropped over the edge, and Ricky screamed, almost losing her balance, thinking that the entire rig might come crashing down on top of them. But it stopped there, sagging into the pit, Koehne nearly horizontal and tangled, hanging from the back, his shoes kicking up spatters of concrete, a string of unintelligible German issuing from his mouth, as well as the universal mantra of displeasure:

"Fuck! Fuck! Fuck!"

Crockett seemed to come alive at this, first with startle, then with resolution. Realizing that this was an opportunity that might offer a narrow window for some sort of action, he seemed to come to a decision. His eyes suddenly widened and he swore to himself repeatedly. "Shit, shit, shit, shit, shit!" Suddenly, taking a deep breath, he disappeared beneath the surface.

"No!" screamed Ricky. If Crockett had lost his balance, there was nothing she could do. She was barely able to stay on her own feet. She watched the place where he had gone under.

Nothing.

A scream escaped from her, a hoarse, primal howl that indicted the entire universe for its cruelty.

A minute elapsed.

Then the surface of the ooze bulged, almost as if it were elastic. It seemed to happen in slow motion. Crockett's head appeared, and as enough sludge fell away to render it possible, he drew in a noisy, rasping breath, coughing, spitting, choking. He stood, the concrete up to his chest, but with his hands now in front of him. Ricky realized he had gone into a tuck beneath the surface to step through.

"Oh God!" he muttered, between coughs. "Oh thank God!"

Then he turned to Ricky. Before she could say anything he spun her around.

"Lean into the wall!" he said. She did so, her head turned to keep the ruined side of her face away from the dirt, and he boosted himself up, dropping his feet into the notch formed where her hands were duct taped together. From here he was able to two-hand grasp the rim of the big wheel of the truck and pull himself out of the pit. He found the bloody shovel and slashed his wrist and ankle bindings with the edge. Then he returned to the pit and pulled out Ricky. As they undid her bindings, shots strafed the truck. They ducked, though the shots did not appear to be intended for them.

Crockett spotted the assault rifle that had been dropped by the suited thug, who lay moaning in the dirt, most of his internal organs hopelessly crushed. He grabbed it, edged around to the front of the vehicle.

A couple more shots hit the truck, and Ricky cringed, her head throbbing more insistently than ever. She looked around for something with which to protect herself. Koehne continued to curse as he dangled over the gray mire, and she saw now that the mechanism had snagged him so tightly on the left side that he could not use his left hand to extricate himself. She also noticed that his right arm hung almost motionless and at an odd angle, probably broken when the truck slammed into him. Even if he managed to raise it, his mutilated index finger would render it difficult for him to free himself.

But she also saw, on the far side of the pit, a handgun—presumably Koehne's—lying just inches from the edge. She could not circumnavigate the pit without exposing herself to gunfire. Instead, she got down on her stomach and crawled beneath the truck. The flow of concrete had stopped, as had the truck's engine. Ricky observed that the concrete was within a couple inches of filling the excavation. She did not care to think about what might have been, and so she crawled on. Halfway to the other side, the vehicle lurched and its underside dropped suddenly to within a couple inches of her head. She realized, then, that the cement truck was not stable, as if it had been left in neutral and so was subject to gravity. With one wheel already hanging over the pit, Ricky feared that, if it rolled backward another foot or so, the other wheel would slip into the excavation as well, and the massive vehicle's chassis would crush her.

She kept her head down, scrabbling forward. As she reached the other side, she stopped. Moving cautiously toward the truck's cab was the second workman. He held an automatic rifle and was so focused on the driver of the truck that he had not noticed Ricky. Koehne still hung a few feet to her left, caught in a way that made the thrashing motions of his left hand, repeatedly attempting an ineffective motion, almost comical. Two feet in front of her right eye rested the pistol.

She groped for it but her hand fell short, then clumsily knocked it an inch or two further away, her compromised vision playing tricks with her perception. As if synchronized to her own motion, the truck groaned and shifted another few inches, the chassis now bare inches above her. The thug took another step toward the truck, and as he did, Ricky heard Crockett's voice.

"Drop the gun!"

Instead of dropping it, the thug peppered the front of the truck with gunfire. Crockett retreated behind the front grill.

Now's my chance!

Ricky scrabbled forward, her right arm and her head protruding from beneath the monstrous rig. Her movement caught the attention of the thug, who turned, his eyes wide with surprise, and brought his weapon around to deal with her. Seeing an opportunity, Crockett stepped from behind the bullet-riddled fender and squeezed off a couple of rounds. The thug's eyes rolled back in his head and he collapsed face-down onto the ground.

Before Ricky could celebrate, she heard another, unfamiliar voice from the front of the truck.

"Drop the gun!" said the man, whose German accent was even heavier than Koehne's.

Ricky looked toward the front, saw the dress shoes and pant cuffs of the second suited man, saw Crockett's shoes, and then his gun hitting the ground.

The truck groaned again and shifted backward another inch. Fewer than six inches now and the second wheel would drop into the pit, and she would be crushed into the hard soil like an insect.

"Now," said the thug, moving toward Crockett, "let's go find your girlfriend!"

The truck began to roll again, slowly, and this time, Ricky sensed that it would not stop. She had seconds to get out before tons of steel and concrete smashed her into pulp. The truck creaked, picked up speed, and Ricky lunged for the pistol one last time. Her scrabbling fingers closed on the grip, she brought it back beneath the truck and aimed for the thug's ankles—a clear shot.

She pulled the trigger, three, four, five times, then clawed at the dirt, pulling herself out into the open without waiting to see whether her shots had hit their mark. A scream from the rear of the truck brought her head around, and she just caught a glimpse of Koehne, still hopelessly entangled, his face terrified as the bulk of the truck's wheels collapsed the earthen walls, lowering the back of the truck and plunging him beneath the surface of the concrete in the pit. The truck's backward motion stopped as its rear axle buried itself in the dirt and gravel, but Koehne's motion did not. His left hand—the only part of him above the surface of the concrete—reached out for life, grasping for something, anything— and then it slowed, wavered and almost elegantly, sank into the gray ooze.

Ricky inched her way to the front of the truck, where she found Crockett, breathing hard, holding a rifle barrel, its stock resting on the dirt. In front of him, suited thug number two lay motionless on his stomach.

"Thanks," he said, panting, patting the rifle. "You took him down, and then I whacked him in the head with the butt end of this to keep him down."

She nodded, then laughed, but it almost immediately changed to tears as she dropped to her knees. How was it possible they were still alive? Uncontrollable tremors of grief and shock rolled through her and an animal wail escaped, doubling her over so that her forehead rested on the ground. Crockett, knelt, embraced her. She allowed it, feeling nothing and everything, and they both sobbed raggedly. After several minutes, Crockett found his voice, spoke hoarsely. "We have to get you to a doctor."

"It doesn't hurt." In truth, the left side of her head ached so badly that she could hardly think. But she could feel that the bleeding or whatever had accounted for the wetness had stopped and had dried on her cheek. "I don't need... we don't have time. Just bandages."

"Listen, you need—"

She pulled away abruptly, stood. "We need to move. He" — she motioned toward the back of the truck— "called Rio. She thinks we're dead. But when she finds out her guys fucked up, she'll send people after us again!"

"All the Gestapo are either dead or wishing they were," said Crockett, suddenly refocused on business, getting to his feet, wiping a grimy hand across his face. Then he led the way around to the driver's side door. "Now let's find out who's driving this piece of shit."

He climbed up on the side step, pulled open the door and saw Brenner behind the wheel.

"You son of a—" But then he stopped himself. Brenner's hands were limp in his lap, streaked with blood, and red soaked into his clothing from several ragged holes on Brenner's shirt that seemed to correspond to the height of the bullet holes in the driver's side door.

"Jesus, Leo! Jesus!"

Ricky stepped up to look. "Shit!"

"I'm sorry," said Brenner, sounding tired. He lifted his eyes to Ricky's face. "My God, so very sorry."

"Damn it, Leo," said Crockett, "what were you think—"

"Shut up," said Brenner wearily. "Just shut up and listen. There are some bills in a money clip that the thugs took from me. Multiple currencies. Take it."

"Keep your money," said Crockett. "Let's get you out of there and to a hospital."

"I'm done," said Brenner. "You two and Campion will have to finish the job. And you'll need money to arrange transportation, whatever it takes. You've got to stop them! The scroll is real!"

"What do you mean?" asked Ricky.

"I mean," said Brenner, "that it really does contain the secret to immortality! That's why it's more important than ever to stop them!"

"You're delirious, Leo," said Crockett, leaning over Brenner to pull a first aid kit from the glove box. He frantically grabbed a wad of cotton gauze and tore it into sections, balling them up, pulling up Brenner's shirt, and pressing them against the three oozing wounds. "Lower your arm! Push against the gauze! Try and put a little pressure on it!"

"I'm not delirious! It's how Rio convinced me to help her! She told me she could bring Mary back. I think now that was only a lie to delude me. But the immortality part isn't! I know it isn't!"

"How can you be so sure of that?" asked Ricky.

"Rio is immortal!" said Brenner, and then he coughed weakly before explaining. "She's the first person to use the enchantment of the scroll! And so far, the only one!"

"I don't care what that chick did, Leo," said Crockett. "We need to get you some help."

"Don't you understand?" said Leo, summoning his strength. "Rio is Cessair!"

CHAPTER 27

Their love-making had been wild, yet there had been an artistry to it that had transported them both to a new level of pleasure. They'd lain in each other's arms in the dark for a long while, until finally, Rio had spoken.

"I am glad that we met, Leo Brenner."

"You're an amazing woman," he had replied. "I don't think I've ever met anyone quite like you."

Rio had smiled. "Thank you." They enjoyed the quiet for a while before she spoke again. "But let's be honest. There's someone else, isn't there?"

"What do you mean?"

"Leo, I can tell. Your heart isn't yours to give. It is already possessed by another."

Brenner sighed and took a moment before responding. "I didn't think it was that obvious. I'm sorry, but... I was married. Mary passed away six years ago."

"I'm sorry."

"I'm afraid I haven't really let myself open up much since then. I've devoted my time to my work. Too much, some might say."

"Have you been afraid of being hurt?" asked Rio gently.

Brenner sighed. "Perhaps that's part of it. I suppose I figured if I shut off the part of myself that desired a relationship, there was no chance that those raw nerves would be nicked. But I think loyalty has also been a part of it."

"Loyalty?"

"I know it sounds foolish, but, even though she's gone, there's a part of me that feels like I'm betraying her whenever I'm attracted to someone else."

"How do you feel about tonight?" asked Rio.

"Not the way I expected," said Brenner. "You made me feel so... comfortable."

Rio smiled. "You make me sound like a favorite old pair of bedroom slippers."

"No, not at all!" Brenner apologized. "It's just... your personality is so... full of life! Vibrant!"

Rio laughed lightly. "And vibrant is comfortable?"

Brenner cleared his throat. "Mary was much more reserved, outwardly. Your openness made me feel right about spending time with you. *That* sort of comfortable. Maybe it's that the women *before* were too much like Mary and you're just the opposite."

"I'll assume there's a compliment in there."

"Yes, I meant it in a good way," said Brenner. "A very good way. I've enjoyed my time with you."

"And I with you, Leo."

"Which leaves me wondering," said Brenner slowly, pausing then for a long moment, "what is this, really?"

"This?"

He pointed back and forth at the two of them. "What do we have here?"

Rio smiled coyly. "What would you like it to be?"

Now Brenner grunted a laugh. "To tell you the truth, I'm not sure. Right now, I'm living in a very pleasant moment."

Rio sat up, pulling the covers up onto her. "Perhaps I can give it a name, Leo. Fun. You had fun, and there's nothing wrong with that. And I think that if we wanted, we could have a lot of fun together for a very long time. But I do not think we could ever have something like you had with Mary."

"I didn't mean to imply—" said Brenner, but Rio cut him off.

"Please, I'm not offended. I understand what this is. And I had fun, too—very much so. But what you had with Mary was special. A life bond that cannot be equaled in a new relationship. I sense that if you had the opportunity to revive that love, you would take it."

Brenner nodded. "But as you said, a bond like that can't be equaled."

"Not equaled," said Rio. "Renewed. If you could bring back Mary, would you?"

The question took Brenner by surprise and his tone hardened. "That's an odd thing to ask."

"I'm sorry if it made you uncomfortable," said Rio, "but humor me. I won't be offended, regardless of your answer. Would you?"

"In a heartbeat," said Brenner. "But I hope you won't be offended if we change the subject. The idea is silly, but for me, painfully so."

"Let's talk about Egypt, then," said Rio. "Such a mysterious place, don't you think?"

Brenner nodded, trying to recapture the mood that had preceded Rio's uncomfortable line of questioning.

"Tombs with secret chambers," she continued, "cryptic symbols on the walls, strange legends. But sometimes, sometimes there is truth behind the legend."

"Are we talking about a specific legend?" asked Brenner.

"We are talking about an entire civilization obsessed with death," said Rio. "A people who build elaborate, sometimes massive tombs that are like palaces in which they can reside during the eternal afterlife, palaces filled with foods, games, furniture, even money. People convinced that life goes on, even after the breath has left one's lips."

"I suppose this is what has made the study of ancient Egypt so fascinating," said Brenner.

"There were healers, high priests, sorcerers," continued Rio, "devoted to the science of death. Not only the treatment of the dying and embalming, but death itself. The dead lived on in the mastabas and monuments—they really believed that. But how could they bridge that seemingly narrow gap? If the dead could walk among the dead, why could they not be made to walk among the living?"

"Which brings us to the scroll, apparently," said Brenner.

"One of the sorcerers is successful," continued Rio. "A young woman begs to be given the potion and to have the incantations read over her, but he refuses. He thinks she is too ruthless, that she would use immortality to empower herself rather than for the common good. Then they hear the stories of a flood. Fearing for her life, the young woman flees to her step-grandfather, who lives in the Land of the Hatti. He is building a huge vessel in which he, his family, and whatever animal species he can load aboard hope to ride out the flood. The young woman begs to be given a place aboard the vessel. She is, after all, family. However, her grandfather refuses. You see, he has heard stories of the Scroll of Life and Death. He perceives it as evil and believes God wishes for it to be destroyed in the flood. He wrongfully believes that his granddaughter has the scroll with her, and this is the basis for his denial."

Rio spoke calmly, almost hypnotically, and Brenner wondered where she had unearthed some of the details, for they seemed to vary from the version of the myth with which he was familiar.

"The young woman is enraged by her grandfather's decision, which means she has been condemned to die at God's hand in the predicted deluge. She finds the injustice of it monstrous, and so she turns from God. Returning to Egypt, the young woman begs the sorcerer for immortality, but he again refuses. When she discovers that the sorcerer has sent Ladra to Ireland with the scroll, she gathers a crew and two ships and sails after him."

"I thought the legend said that Ladra was part of Cessair's crew," said Brenner.

"The legend was wrong, as legends frequently are," said Rio. Benner registered a chilling intensity about her as she narrated the tale with a diminishing western lilt to her voice. "One of the ships is wrecked in a storm, but the young woman's vessel, which also carries her father, Bith, and Fintan Mac, a warrior from the north who has made the trip before, arrives at the island. Ireland suits her purposes perfectly. The sorcerer believed that Ireland would not be flooded, since it was uninhabited and therefore sinless. But he was wrong. There are clans living here, farming, hunting, building. It matters not. Here, she will create an army of immortals and eventually preside over a new and better world order, one in which the fear of God is absent. She hunts down and slays the betrayer, Ladra, and recovers the scroll. But when Bith and Fintan realize her intentions, they turn against her. She kills her father. It is unfortunate, but she cannot allow him to stand in the way of her plans. Fintan, however, is cleverer; a beautiful man, but misguided. He steals the scroll, fearing Cessair's loyal clan and how powerful she is growing. What he does with the scroll is a mystery. There are rumors that he has sent trusted messengers back to Egypt with the scroll to hide it there, safely away from Cessair. Others say his men have wandered to the far northern unexplored lands to find a place of concealment. Still others have heard stories of a ship that has borne the scroll to misty, undiscovered islands across the great ocean. Fintan himself flees the island and is heard from no more. But it is said he possessed a map to the scroll's location. And so the search begins for Fintan and this most valuable map, a search that continues for millennia. Some fear the map has been destroyed or is hopelessly lost. But the devout continue the quest. Only recently has the truth begun to surface. Rising flood waters created monstrously strong currents that swept Fintan north to his doom. Yet, the map survived, frozen for five thousand years."

"You should write adventure novels," said Brenner, smiling.

Rio regarded him with deadly seriousness. "You think it's a fairy tale. What if I were to tell you that I know it's true?"

"I'd say you had far too much wine at dinner."

"What if I could prove it to you?"

Brenner smiled a tight-lipped smile. "I'm sorry. I guess I'm not really in the mood for this sort of thing."

Rio regarded him for a moment and then spoke slowly. "What if I told you that the scroll could not only preserve life, but restore it?"

"Rio—"

"Think about it!" she said, her eyes blazing with the notion. "Think about who you could bring back if you could bring back anyone! Think of lost love, blooming again!"

Brenner's jaw tightened and he sat up, swung his legs off the bed. "Perhaps I should go."

"No," said Rio resolutely. "Perhaps I should."

Then she had slipped out of bed. Brenner had regarded her perfect figure, illuminated only by the moonlight pouring in from the seventh-floor balcony. She opened the sliding glass door, stepped onto the balcony, naked in the moonlight and, without hesitation, climbed up onto the ledge and jumped.

His heart in his throat, Brenner leaped up and reached the balcony in half a dozen long strides. He dreaded looking over the rail, and when he did, the awful sight of Rio, lying face-down on the deserted, moonlit courtyard, wrenched a hoarse "No!" He choked back his grief, pulling on his clothes in seconds, and then raced down the stairs, hoping that perhaps something that he had not noticed had broken her fall, that her injuries would not be fatal after all. Yet, he knew in his heart that this was impossible. Although his glance over the balcony had been brief, it had revealed no awnings, no shrubs or tree branches, nothing but a seventy-foot drop onto marble.

No one could have survived such a fall.

Reaching the ground floor, he raced out into the deserted back courtyard. There, with dim patio security lights illuminating the awful sight, he stepped forward, knelt beside her.

Rio opened her eyes. Then she propped herself up on her elbows, threw back her head and laughed.

"Good God!" cried Brenner, falling onto his backside, unable to process what he was seeing.

"Do you believe now?" asked Rio.

"My God, you're alive!" he said, his voice trembling.

"Think of it, Leo!" she said, her eyes glistening with moonlight. "The power to thwart death! What do you think now?"

Brenner picked himself up, took off his dress shirt. "I—I don't know what to think. I—it's impossible. But..." He helped her to her feet, slipped the shirt over her shoulders.

"Think about your love," said Rio. "Think about your Mary! Holding her in your arms again!"

Tears formed at the corners of Brenner's eyes. "It's not right. It's not natural."

"At one time, all science was regarded as unnatural, as witchcraft," said Rio. "There are still those who fear vaccines today, even some who believe the earth is flat. But we know better. Why should we fear *this* amalgam of ceremony and nature? This makes all other healing obsolete!"

Brenner sank to his knees on the cool marble and began to weep. "Mary… Mary…"

Rio went to him, embraced him, holding his head to her stomach. "You are a good man, Leo. You deserve your happiness. The world deserves this gift. You can help all of it happen."

Brenner nodded, stood.

"What next?"

"Next," said Rio, "we must stop those who would kill your love."

"But," said Brenner, "if you're immortal, that means you've used the scroll."

Rio nodded.

"But the scroll has been lost for five thousand years," Brenner continued. "That means you're…"

Rio inclined her head. "You're welcome to call me by my real name, if you wish."

When Brenner said it, it was almost a whisper.

"Cessair!"

CHAPTER 28

"Jesus!" said Crockett as Brenner related the highlights of his story.

"It must have been a trick," said Ricky.

"It was no trick. And it explains why the cult has been able to remain focused for 5,000 years. Even though its membership died out and had to be replaced with every generation, its leader remained, completely and fanatically dedicated to the task!"

"Wait, Leo," said Crockett. "Are you saying Rio has always been the leader of the cult?"

"Yes!" said Brenner, grimacing. Telling the story had seemed to generate some adrenaline, but now he was fading again. "The group calls itself *Alchemy*. Rio Armstrong is simply a name she adopted in the last forty years. As I said, she's really Cessair!"

Crockett shook his head. "Leo, I'm afraid this is way too much for me to process."

"Well then don't process it! Simply act! Our world depends on it! I'd stake everything on the fact that her leap was not a trick. And if I'm right, you can't afford to let her beat you!"

"But I can't leave you here!" cried Crockett, his face contorted in anguish.

"Yes, you can," Brenner implored him, closing his eyes. Then he opened them again, pointed vaguely. "They took the stuff in our pockets and left it in a pile over there. Get your passports. Give me my cell and I'll... I'll call an ambulance."

Crockett slammed the door on the truck. He paced rapidly back and forth for a few moments before pounding the front fender of the vehicle four times. Then he turned to Ricky. "Let's get Campion."

They found him in the hole where Brenner had left him.

"Leave me," said Campion through gritted teeth as they pulled him out. "I know they broke some ribs when they threw me in there. That and my leg, I'll only slow you down. This is the end of the line for me!"

"Here's your cell," said Crockett to Campion. "I don't think Leo's got very long. After we're gone, call an ambulance."

Ricky squeezed the older man's hand, and then she and Crockett took turns stripping off their clothing behind the truck and using its hose to rinse off the concrete and dirt. Since their own clothes were soaked and could not be cleaned and dried sufficiently in the short time they had, they changed into some of the clothes worn by the dead henchmen. Ricky had some difficulty balancing and moving about; more than half her field of vision was reduced to darkness. Once dressed, she pulled a hoodie off one of the men in coveralls, hoping this would hide her wounded, throbbing face.

"You really need to see a doctor," said Crockett, his face dark with concern.

"You really need to mind your own business." She knew he was probably right, but she also knew that a trip to hospital would at the very least delay them when speed was essential. At most, suspicious medical personnel might alert the police and end their pursuit.

Crockett seemed to bite back a rebuttal. "Let's hope nobody realizes the little holes were made by bullets," he said, slipping a finger through one. Before they left, they returned to Brenner. He was pale, in significant pain, and the gauze was soaked.

"Campion's calling an ambulance," said Crockett. Brenner sat slumped back against the seat, eyes closed, not answering, though they could see that he was breathing.

"Thank you for saving us," said Ricky, the words difficult to voice, her stomach hurting.

Brenner's eyes fluttered open. "Saving you?"

"It was brilliant," admitted Crockett. "Backing the truck toward the hole. Caught the assholes completely off guard."

"I had no clue what to do," said Brenner weakly. "I think I panicked. I didn't know—" His voice trailed off.

"You didn't know what, Leo?" asked Crockett.

"I didn't know the truck was in reverse!"

After borrowing a large gauze patch from the medical kit to tape over her empty socket, Ricky followed Crockett up to the main floor of the train station. She kept her head down. In the restroom, she did a more thorough job of cleaning herself up and inspected her eye socket. She felt light-headed at first, and she had not stopped trembling since she had fired the gun. *So cold. Definitely in shock.* She washed and dried the area around the eye as best she could, then used more bandages and tape recovered from the cement truck's first-aid kit to create a new patch to cover the socket. The left side of her head throbbed, and she wished there had been a couple of Tylenol in the kit.

"We can't go back to the airport," said Crockett, now somewhat less gritty himself and squinting at the schedule by the time she returned. "We already know Cessair's people are there.

But we can pay cash, hop on a train, take it to Brussels and try to get a flight from there."

They used a fraction of Brenner's anaconda-choking wad of cash to purchase tickets, then bought a change of clothes from one of the shops in the train station—and a bottle of extra-strength pain killers, two of which Ricky swallowed in the check-out line. Crockett purchased a white, button-down shirt with vertical blue pinstripes and added dark glasses, a navy-blue windbreaker and a stocking cap, which helped to camouflage his features somewhat. Ricky wore dark glasses and a black Deutschland Soccer hoodie that allowed her to cover most of her hair.

"I feel like a character from a Hitchcock movie," she said, as they settled into seats on the train. The shivering was intermittent now, though the pain level had not diminished. She was surprised that she didn't feel more distraught about the loss of her left eye—another argument in favor of her being in shock. Or perhaps it was the adrenaline boost that came from escaping almost certain death and now being on the move again.

"If Leo wasn't hallucinating, this is going to get a lot scarier than any Hitchcock movie," said Crockett. "I mean, it's impossible, isn't it? But I doubt Leo would feed us bullshit with his—"

Ricky understood. *With his last words.*

Crockett turned away. Ricky knew that Brenner's betrayal had stung him badly.

"He wasn't thinking clearly when he did the things he did," she said. "But I can't imagine him making up that balcony scene. If Rio is really Cessair, how can we ever win?"

"Older doesn't always mean wiser. We have to be smarter... and faster," said Crockett. "We have to operate under the assumption that your tip to the police slowed down Rio...

Cessair... whatever her name is... enough that we'll get to Newgrange first. She may be immortal, but she's not omnipotent. If we can get the scroll, we can stop her from forming an army. One immortal bitch, maybe the world can handle that. Five hundred? A thousand? Yeah, that could be a problem."

"I just thought of something," said Ricky. "Cessair has people all over the globe, right?"

"Yeah," said Crockett. "One of the benefits of extreme wealth. I guess when you're five thousand years old, you have a lot of time to accumulate cash, power, and contacts. By simply increasing her financial worth a small amount each year, she could easily be a billionaire many times over in fifty centuries."

"But if her influence is so vast, she must have operatives in Ireland, right?" asked Ricky. "Then why doesn't she just have one of them get the scroll? They could be there within an hour or two."

"I suppose it boils down to trust," said Crockett. "Think about it from Cessair's perspective. She tells one of her goons in Dublin to go to Newgrange and grab the scroll. What happens if Goon Number One decides to keep the scroll for himself, become immortal and form his own army?"

"I thought there was supposed to be honor among thieves," said Ricky.

"That was only for a short period in the 1950s when they were making bad crime movies," said Crockett. "Remember, Cessair was burned pretty badly 5,000 years ago when she trusted Fintan and Ladra. She won't be wanting to make that mistake again."

"At least you hope she won't."

Crockett nodded. "At least I hope she won't."

The train rattled into motion and they were soon speeding along on their way. Within five minutes, Ricky had dropped off to sleep. When she woke an hour later, she noticed that the left side of her head felt thick and achy, but that the intense pain was gone—for now. Crockett had fallen asleep, too. She quietly slipped out of her seat and found the lavatory, keeping both hands up in a kind of defensive position, struggling to keep her balance, hoping not to blunder into something that her left eye would normally have detected. In the mirror, she examined herself more closely, trying to determine whether she had successfully rinsed all of the concrete out of her hair. She took another look at her eye socket as well, cleaning up the pinkish fluid that had leaked from the corners. *It's like it belongs to someone else. It can't be me.* She recalled the bastard Bricker's "Bride of Frankenstein" comments that, today, seemed centuries ago. It occurred to her that if Leo's story about Rio being Cessair was true, this seemed to argue in favor of the existence of some sort of Supreme Being, and as Ricky examined her reflection, she wondered what she had done to piss Him or Her off. After deciding that she had cleaned up the best she could, she pulled up her hood and exited the lavatory. Crockett slept on. Ricky tried unsuccessfully to resume her own nap, but apparently her body had now passed through the needs-sleep stage to the point where her fatigue could no longer overpower her worry and the horror that she had suffered.

We've got to find the scroll first.

Any thoughts about the scroll eventually brought her back to Leo. As awful as his betrayal had been, she actually felt pity for the poor man. This made her angry with herself. They could have died. They *would* have died. And it would have been horrible. She wondered whether bleeding to death in a truck cab, knowing that you had sold out those who believed in you, was truly justice.

So many had been killed. Could there ever be any real justice?

Leo, Bash, the researchers at Zackenberg, Sasha.

And those were only the deaths they knew of. Who knew how

many thousands Cessair had silenced over the millennia in her pursuit of what turned out to be dead ends? Now the tears came. Perhaps she was more distressed about her lost eye than she had first admitted to herself. Perhaps it was the enormity of the evil they were up against. Or the weight of their task. A one-eyed gamer and a pencil-pushing environmentalist against a superhuman being.

Leo may have deserved his fate, but he had been right about one thing. Cessair needed to be stopped.

CHAPTER 29

Despite their fears to the contrary, both the trip through airport security and their flight from Brussels were uneventful. Ricky popped a couple more painkillers an hour before the recommended dosage time.

Crockett noticed and sang his one-note refrain again. "We should really get you to a doctor."

"You should *really* mind your own fucking business, though I'd say that's pretty unlikely considering you've already turned a ten-minute meeting in Chicago into a freakin' globe-hopping tour of cruelty and nightmares."

"Maybe a doctor could do something."

"Like what? Put the eye back in? It doesn't work that way. And besides, it's back in that goddamn tunnel in Germany."

They arrived in Dublin, passed through security, and then Crockett bought a newspaper. "You need a credit card to rent a car," he explained. "But I don't want to put us on the grid unless it's absolutely unavoidable. So might as well buy one!"

"A car?"

Crockett smiled. "Don't expect a Ferrari."

"But why would it matter if we rented a car?" asked Ricky.

"By now Cessair already expects us to be in Ireland."

"True," replied Crockett, "but if they can hack rental car company records, we don't want them to know what we're driving. Plus, some rental car companies use tracking technology on their vehicles. Again, we want to stay out of their crosshairs."

In the paper, he found a notice for a 1999 Daewoo Matiz SE plus with 264,000 miles. A taxi dropped them at the seller's house. The man, an enormous fellow in overalls, with an accent so thick he could hardly be understood, was happy to part with the vehicle, which had a crack running the length of the front windshield, and whose rear bumper covering was gone. And just like that, they owned a car.

"It's yellow," observed Ricky.

"It's a means to an end," said Crockett. "When you get home, you can buy any color car you want."

"I don't want to buy a car," said Ricky. "But I definitely don't want to buy a yellow one."

It so happened that the man, whose name was Patrick, was happy to sell them a few other items from his tool shed that they thought might come in handy to perform minor excavations at the tomb. His stout and bubbly wife, Elizabeth, impossible to say no to, pulled Ricky aside.

"What happened here?" said the woman in a motherly way, gesturing toward Ricky's eye.

"It's nothing."

"It's not nothing. It happened recently, didn't it?" Then she gestured toward Crockett and spoke in a low, accusing voice. "Was it him?"

"God, no," replied Ricky. "I got mugged." Which, she rationalized, was sort of true.

Elizabeth brought Ricky into their tiny cottage and exerted

motherly authority that overrode Ricky's protests, removing the gauze patch and dabbing into the socket with hydrogen peroxide-soaked q-tips. It hurt like hell, but in the end, her efforts produced a pile of brownish-tipped swabs and scabby material, and once the initial pain subsided, Ricky detected less irritation. After re-bandaging the socket, Elizabeth cut her a thick slice of crumb cake.

When Ricky popped two more pain pills and emerged from the house, she found Crockett strapping a hunting knife in a sheath to his calf, a purchase from Patrick's collection.

"Insurance."

"I take it Patrick didn't have an AR-15 in his shed," said Ricky.

"Pity."

"Yeah. I keep forgetting this isn't the States."

After saying goodbye to Patrick and Elizabeth, it took them forty-five minutes to drive to Brú na Bóinne Visitors Centre, just across the River Boyne from the impressive Newgrange passage tomb, rising above the Boyne Valley. Modern and full of displays, films, and even a scale model of the Newgrange passages, the Visitors Centre was also the starting point for the only public access to the tomb. They purchased their tickets, exited the building, crossed a pedestrian bridge that spanned the River Boyne, and found themselves waiting with others at a turnaround where they boarded a tour bus that would take them the remaining distance.

"This is good," said Crockett. "If Cessair had been here already, this place would be closed down today."

The bus, they noticed, was not full, but contained a group of thirteen, not counting Ricky, Crockett, and the driver. There was a well fed, fifties-ish couple from the States in matching plaid shorts; a prim looking, red-haired woman and her two teen-aged daughters; a slim, dark-skinned, fortyish fellow with a neatly trimmed beard; two senior citizen couples traveling together; and a young French couple—the woman appearing to be in the late stages of pregnancy—and their two-year-old, curly-haired daughter.

Ricky felt a few glances linger a bit too long, no doubt assessing and drawing conclusions about her patched eye, which continued to throb. But it was the younger teenager who seemed to steal glances the most frequently. The kid seemed in pain—not physical, but the kind of palpable discomfort that comes with being dragged along on the vacation from hell. Her appearance suggested artistry or defiance or both: bright blue spiked hair, jeans riddled with fashionable holes, a t-shirt with a slogan calculated to embarrass the mother, and pen drawings and a couple of cut marks on her arms. The mom, by contrast, wore a conservative yet fashionable skirt and blouse, as did her older daughter. She bravely smiled and pointed out interesting sights through the window, in answer to which the blue-haired girl adopted an increasingly bored and disgruntled demeanor, and occasionally quarreled with her sister. Father working? Dead? Disinterested? Divorced? Mom perhaps trying to find an experience for the girls to share? The younger daughter was having none of it.

"I don't like this," whispered Crockett as the bus got underway.

"What do you mean?" asked Ricky. "Do you think someone in this group is part of Alchemy?"

"Not really," replied Crockett. "It's just that if something happens, these folks could get hurt."

Although they could see the burial mound atop the hill less than a mile to the west, the bus headed north along a narrow, paved country road, past farms, fields, and an occasional sheep pasture. While Crockett had purchased the tickets, Ricky had examined some of the displays in the Visitors Centre. The Newgrange mound was set above the Boyne River, part of a lush agricultural region dotted with cottages, farms, and several other burial sites, known as the Boyne Valley. Now, as they rattled along the narrow road, knifing through the verdant countryside, Ricky noticed that even the smaller cottages were kept storybook neat, and many bus passengers responded by clicking away with their cell phones or digital cameras.

After a few minutes, the bus rumbled across a cattle guard, and shortly thereafter took a left, heading now more directly toward the mound. Trees crowded the roadway, but away from it, much of the land had been cleared for cows, goats, sheep, or crops. Despite the overcast conditions, the eyes were overwhelmed by an explosion of vivid greens, punctuated occasionally by a cluster of beehives set far off the road, or by yellow fields of rapeseed.

"All the people who live in this valley, they have to be able to access these roads," said Crockett, leaning toward her. "That means we could have driven to the tomb ourselves."

"But they said at the Visitors Centre that only tour groups get to go inside," noted Ricky.

"Yeah," acknowledged Crockett, "but I don't see Cessair and her lackeys following the rules."

The road came to a junction, and the tour bus veered left. Now the tomb rose above them almost immediately on the right, breathtaking. Less than a minute later, the road took a sharp right. They slowed, pulling onto a roadside drop-off area marked by traffic cones. There was no public parking lot.

Ricky surveyed the sprawling countryside as best she could. "It's in the middle of goddamn nowhere."

"Reminds me of the Field of Dreams in Dyersville, Iowa," said Crockett.

"What's the Field of Dreams?"

257

"You haven't seen the movie?" asked Crockett, truly shocked. "They build this big ol' ball field right in the middle of a cornfield. Nothing around but farmland on all sides."

"Why'd they do that?"

"So some baseball players could return from the afterlife to play on it."

"Sounds like a great movie."

"There's more to it than that," said Crockett. "It's a classic. I can see you're going to need a little course in film appreciation when this is all over."

Ricky shook her head, then regretted the movement. "Yeah, if we survive this, the first thing I'm going to want to do is watch a movie about zombie baseball."

They disembarked and were greeted by a woman who seemed to be in her late sixties—Mavis—who was to be their guide on the tomb tour. She welcomed everyone cordially, yet with an air of officiousness, made a few general remarks about what lay ahead, and then marched them along a paved walkway through an opening in the thick, vast hedge that completely boxed in the area surrounding the tomb, an area roughly the size of a Major League Baseball stadium parking lot. They moved slowly, conscious of the ages and delicate conditions of some in the group. As they did, Mavis nattered on.

"This is the Newgrange passage tomb, visited by more than 200,000 people each year! It was constructed more than 5,000 years ago, making it about 600 years older than the Great Pyramids. And Stonehenge? Very nice, but forget it! Newgrange is 1,000 years older!"

They continued their gradual ascent. Crockett walking on Ricky's blind side. So far, nothing seemed to indicate the arrival of Cessair.

"The mound is about seventy-six meters across," continued Mavis. "The wall built up along the outside is made of quartz, though it extends less than halfway around."

The river of milk.

Ricky reminded herself that the appearance had been more truly like a river when the milky quartz had formed a kind of walkway around the outside of the tomb 5,000 years ago.

"From our perspective, the mound appears to be circular in shape," said Mavis, a treasure trove of minutia. "However, from the air, one can see that its shape is more like a fattish kidney bean."

As Mavis continued her narration, they approached the entrance, and Ricky gasped. There, as if on guard a few meters in front of the entryway, rested a horizontal boulder that Mavis referred to as a "kerbstone".

"It is thought to weigh about five tons," she added.

A long pause for more photographs.

The stone caught Ricky's attention because of what appeared to be triskelions carved into its surface, as if to confirm that they were in the right place.

Her pulse quickened.

But she also knew this was not their destination. The triskelion they sought had to be inside the tomb.

The triskelion kerbstone was one of several that blocked their path to the entrance, but stiles had been built over this stone wall. It took a few minutes for the tour group to surmount it and follow Mavis inside.

The long passage—about nineteen meters, according to Mavis —was generally straight, though it seemed to rise slightly the further they advanced. They finally reached the intersection point which formed the inner chamber, revealing much shorter chambers off to either side and straight ahead. These created the cruciform shape of the tomb. The inner chamber had a high ceiling at the intersection—a corbelled ceiling, according to Mavis, with overlapping horizontal stone slabs creating an upward-spiraling cone. At the end of each of the three short side chambers—roped off to allow visitors to look, but not touch—rested a stone that might have served as a bench, altar or basin. Ricky noted that the basin in the north chamber, directly ahead, was broken into several pieces. As if reading her mind, Mavis remarked about this.

"The basins you see were likely used for rituals for the dead. The bones would be placed in the basin, along with offerings such as stone beads, flint arrowheads and carved bone figures. No one knows for certain, but the north basin was probably broken some time shortly after the tomb was re-discovered, probably by careless amateur explorers or looters."

Figures had been carved into the walls, including a number of spirals and triskelions. But which was the one they sought?

It was somewhere in this tomb that, on December 21st, the sun would shine through the opening and cast its rays on the farthest reaches of the passage. According to Bash, the map indicated that the sun would show the way. That seemed to suggest those rays would mark the spot where they would find the Scroll of Life and Death.

"I can't believe we're here," whispered Ricky. "My palms are sweating." She was still popping questionable dosages of painkillers to deal with the migraine-like pain in her eye socket.

"I can't believe Cessair isn't here," said Crockett. "That's got *my* palms sweating."

Mavis now explained the possible uses of the far chamber and the phenomenon of the sun lighting it during the winter solstice.

"Because the winter solstice happens only once a year, it's a very special event," said the guide. "Only a small group of distinguished visitors are allowed in this room for the occasion. Some of the spots are available through a special lottery."

"Where, exactly, does the light shine?" asked Crockett. "I mean, what does it illuminate?"

Mavis indicated a spot beneath the corbelled ceiling. "Hereabouts, I believe."

As Mavis backed away, both Ricky and Crockett knelt to examine the floor, wiping back a layer of loose dust.

There was no mehen. No triskelion. In fact, there were no carvings or symbols at all on the floor.

"Ma'am," said Crockett to the guide, "are you sure this is as far as the light extends?"

"Oh yes," said the guide. "It's very impressive. Lights up the inner chamber. Very other-worldly!"

Ricky felt her heart pounding in her chest.

"I was wrong!" she whispered.

"No, no," said Crockett, bending to her. "Maybe we're just not looking at it right. We'll figure it out."

Ricky shook her head. "That's why Cessair's not here! She knows we're on a wild goose chase. She figured out the real location, back in Egypt! The scroll is 3,000 miles away!"

CHAPTER 30

The pregnant woman said something to her husband in French, a question. He shook his head, keeping his gaze on Ricky and Crockett.

"You're sure this is where the light falls every December 21st?" asked Crockett, his gaze on the floor beneath the corbelled ceiling.

Mavis, whose normally cheery expression now hovered somewhere between annoyed and alarmed, answered, "Yes." Then after a pause, "Well, no. Not *every* December 21st."

Crockett looked up. "No?"

The guide, summoning up her official stature and command of tomb lore, explained. "In modern times, on the morning of the winter solstice, the light illuminates this center area. But this tomb is 5,000 years old. In ancient times, it was different."

"How is that possible?" asked Ricky. "How we revolve around the sun doesn't change."

"Actually, it does," said Mavis confidently. "In the past 5,000 years, the earth's rotation on its axis has changed very slightly." Raising fingers to her chin, she stared at the floor in concentration. Then she sighed. "I used to know this all by rote. But..." she reached a hand into her vest and removed a lavender-colored index card, "I have a little cheat sheet in case I forget!"

A whisper of polite laughter rose and quickly dissipated.

Mavis blinked, squinted, cleared her throat, and explained. "Earth's tilt—it's called *obliquity* or more accurately, *obliquity of the elliptic*—varies over long periods of time. It's influenced by the motion of other celestial bodies—planets, stars, even the sun's course .in the galaxy. These influences are called perturbations. Currently, earth's obliquity is decreasing at a rate of 47 minutes per century."

Mavis saw confused looks on some faces. Her eyes returned to the card, took a moment to refocus. "A minute is one-sixtieth of a degree in measuring angles."

The expressions on the faces of the two teen-aged girls seemed to go from bored to hopelessly bored as they realized that they were not only stuck in a tour group, but were receiving unexpected, spontaneous geometry instruction.

"So yes," said Mavis, clearing her throat again as a prelude to summing up. "When the tomb was constructed, the light probably shined a bit farther back, into that recess."

Crockett and Ricky moved up to the rope that prevented visitors from entering the shallow northern chamber. Within rested a rock slab, and atop it, the several pieces of a broken basin.

"The tomb was discovered in the late 17th century," said Mavis. "Unfortunately, early visitors were not always as respectful of the site and its contents as we are now. In the late 18th century, a group of peasants looking for treasure dug up much of the floor, but found only bone fragments and small carvings."

They peered into the recess and dimly made out a carving on a slab to their right j.

Ricky elbowed Crockett. "Definitely a triskelion!"

"Bingo!" he whispered.

"Triskelions occur commonly in Celtic tombs and architecture," said Mavis. "Do you find them interesting?"

Crockett turned, went over to Mavis and kissed her on the cheek, leaving her momentarily stunned.

"Ma'am, you may have just saved the world!"

Ricky followed Crockett as he moved back toward the tunnel entrance, leaving the group behind.

"Where are you going?"

"We found what we wanted," said Crockett. "But we can't go digging around in front of all those people. In fact, if the scroll is behind that slab of rock, I have no idea how we would go about moving it. It must weigh a ton! Maybe several! We've got to think this through."

As they emerged into the natural light, Ricky froze.

"Shit. So much for time to think."

Cessair and four large, stern-looking men were striding toward the tomb along the paved walk. Cessair's eyes went wide when she recognized her two adversaries. She shouted commands to her thugs, who pulled guns from beneath their jackets. Shots cracked and Crockett and Ricky retreated into the tomb.

Crockett reached down, pulled the knife from the sheath on his shin. "Not going down without a fight!"

Ricky reached into the pocket of her pants, brought out a pistol, stepped to the cave entrance and clenched her teeth while firing off three modestly inaccurate shots.

Crockett's mouth fell open. "Holy—! Where did that come from?"

"Elizabeth," said Ricky. When it did not immediately register, she added, "Daewoo Elizabeth. When I told her I'd been mugged, she showed me her nice little collection of unregistered handguns."

"This is better," said Crockett, eyeing the pistol. "Now they know they can't just walk in here and take everyone out. They've got to play it cautious. They don't know how many guns or what kind we have. And it's easier to defend a bunker than it is the wide-open area they're coming from."

"Those kerbstones make a nice barricade, too. So what's our next move?"

"Not a clue.

They heard their names being called from outside. It was Cessair.

"Come out now and you'll live!"

"Rolling on the cave floor laughing!" shouted Crockett. "You betrayed Leo!"

Ricky whispered to Crockett, "Why doesn't she just march in here? She's immortal! Our bullets aren't going to affect her!"

"She's immortal, not all powerful," said Crockett. "Our bullets wouldn't hurt her, but we could grab her and tie her up. We just couldn't kill her. And her men *are* mortal, so they can't just rush us."

"You have my word," said Cessair. "After I've found the scroll, I have no need for the two of you."

"We already have the scroll!" shouted Crockett.

Ricky looked at him as if he were crazy. Her head was beginning to pound more vigorously.

"One false move and I put a match to it!" added Crockett.

"It would be nice," Ricky whispered, "if we actually *had* the scroll we're using to negotiate a way out of here." She thought for a moment. "Here, take the gun. You know how to use one, right?"

"Give me a break. I'm from North Carolina."

"Give me your knife. I'm going to start an archaeological dig."

"What am I supposed to do?"

"Keep her talking. You should be good at that. And if that

doesn't work, start shooting stuff." Ricky turned, then whirled back to face him, grabbed his hand. "Extra ammo," she said, slapping a second clip into his palm. Then she returned to the far chamber where the guide and the other tourists were huddled.

"Good heavens, what's happening?" exclaimed Mavis.

Ricky looked around at the frightened faces, resisted the urge to tell them that they would all probably be dead in a few minutes. "Bad people. Nothing my friend can't handle. He was a special ops marksman. But I need to take a closer look at the back wall."

She pushed aside the rope barrier, knelt, and, using the tip of the knife, began to scrape around outside the edges of the triskelion. Her head was pounding again but she had no time to take pain killers.

"For the love of God!" cried Mavis, watching horrified, as Ricky worked. "You can't do that! This is a national historical site!"

"I'm an archaeologist," replied Ricky, as if that would make it all better.

"Are those real guns?" asked the American man in plaid shorts.

Ricky replied while she dug at the wall. "Fuck, yeah."

"It's not part of some tourist act?" he asked, his eyes widening. "Jesus, Louise, we should have stayed in Detroit!"

Cobalt Blue Hair shot her mother a this-is-all-your-fault look.

The pregnant woman muttered something in French.

"My wife, she wonders if there is a bathroom?"

Ricky swore, let the knife tip drop. "It's solid rock!"

Mavis looked at her as if Ricky were mad. "Well, of course! These great stones support the ceiling!"

"What are you looking for?" asked Plaid Shorts.

"The people shooting, they want something that's hidden in this tomb," said Ricky. "We have to find it before they do."

"What, is this some sort of spy thing?" asked Plaid Shorts.

"I have to remind you," said Mavis, "people have been searching through this tomb for centuries. If there were something to find, they'd have found it!"

Ricky ignored her and backed away from the wall, looking at everything. They were so close. What were they missing? Other triskelions were visible, but the slabs they had been carved into looked no more moveable than the one in the recess. And they would not have been illuminated by the farthest reaches of the light 5,000 years ago. Her eyes traveled to the floor, to the places where the slabs met the roof of the passage, and finally, to the high ceiling directly above her. The corbelled vault was a marvel of Stone Age construction, solid, unyielding, allowing not a trickle of moisture in fifty centuries. It rose above them twenty feet, stone slabs laid in a circle, then overlapped with another circle, slightly smaller, continuing this pattern of spiraling, concentric circles to the top.

"There has to be some secret hiding place," she said aloud. "A hidden door or something."

"Like in that Nicholas Cage movie!" said Plaid Shorts. "Maybe some spring-loaded trapdoor!"

Ricky ignored him and returned to the triskelion slab in the north chamber, assessed its immense size. "This lump of stone can't be hiding an entrance, can it? How would anyone move it to find out if something was behind?"

"Maybe not behind it, but underneath it," suggested Cobalt Blue Hair. "Like a gravestone? Maybe right under the triple-spiral thingy."

Ricky knelt, and with the knife, began to dig.

"But the floor has been dug up by treasure hunters," protested Mavis, as if she were watching moths converge upon the wardrobe holding her grandmother's beloved bridal gown.

"Maybe they didn't dig *here*," said Ricky, desperately hoping this was true. The bearded man knelt to help. "Name's Peterson," he said as he dug with his car keys. After a moment's hesitation, Plaid Pants joined them, shoveling away dirt bare-handed. "And I'm Stan, since we're getting all friendly and cozy," he said.

The knife, large and sharp, helped them make good progress, and in short order, a suitcase-sized depression had been cleared at the base of the great slab. Ricky had hoped to discover a niche or even a leather bag that had survived the millennia, but there was nothing.

Perhaps the treasure hunters that Mavis had mentioned *had* found something after all. Perhaps the scroll had been uncovered, but the finders had not realized what they possessed and had destroyed it. Or it was sitting in an attic or a lighted display case in the trophy room of some clueless aristocrat.

"Look at this," said Peterson suddenly, rubbing his thumb across the surface of a curved stone tucked beneath the immense slab. Where his thumb cleared away some of the dirt, Ricky saw a tiny triskelion no larger than a silver dollar carved into the stone.

Without another word, they quickened their pace, trying to find the edges. As they gradually uncovered more of it, they observed that the stone buried at the base of the larger slab had clearly been chiseled into something other than its natural shape. Ricky wondered whether its purpose had to do with the strange ceremonies that had been performed in this place, or whether it was somehow related to her search. In a few moments, they had cleared enough along the sides and gained a solid enough grip to be able to slide it from beneath the vertical slab and pull it out into the central chamber beneath the corbelled roof.

The carving was the size of a Thanksgiving turkey but roughly

L-shaped with chiseled, rounded edges. Peterson reached into the cavity created by its removal, shook his head. "Nothing."

Ricky finished her examination of the stone. Other than the single, small triskelion, it bore no markings.

"Well that was a waste of time!" grunted Stan. "Some treasure!"

Then they heard the sound of stone scraping against stone, and someone shouted, "Look out!" Ricky dove toward the south end of the chamber, away from the noise and a blooming dust cloud that accompanied it, at first thinking that the entire passage tomb was caving in. However, as the dust settled, she saw that the great wall slab above the hole they had dug had tilted forward, falling onto the already-broken stone basin and shattering it into even more pieces.

Mavis stepped gingerly forward, examined the basin, shell-shocked. "Well, I guess we now know how *that* happened."

Ricky took a cautious step toward the slab resting at an angle against the stone platform that had held the basin. Behind the slab, there appeared to be a recess, perhaps a hiding place for the scroll. Peterson beat her to the wall and emitted a gasp when he peered behind the refrigerator-sized block of stone.

"My God!"

"What is it?" Ricky quickly moved up behind him. He stepped aside to allow her to see. Peterson's gaze, she noticed, was on the back of the slab, rather than the dark recess. And Ricky was just as shocked to see that the great block of stone had been chiseled out on its hidden side, removing most of the mass of the stone, giving it the appearance of an Egyptian sarcophagus from the rear. The result was a stone shell that, while still heavy, would have been possible for several men to lift into place to conceal the hidden passage. In addition, the inside surface was filled with intricate, beautifully rendered and colored carvings that appeared to represent the construction of the Newgrange passage tomb. And in the middle of it all, another triskelion.

"That L-shaped stone must have been buried there to wedge it in place," said Peterson. "But this is extraordinary!"

Ricky nodded, trying to reconcile what she was seeing with what she knew of Irish history and archaeology. "It doesn't make any sense! The Celtic tribes who built this tomb 5,000 years ago worked with Stone Age tools. Bone chisels and flint. They *couldn't* have hollowed out this stone with those!"

Mavis took a tentative step closer, nodded, her expression stunned. "Yes. There's nothing else like this in the whole Boyne River Valley."

Peterson stepped forward again and peered into the recess, illuminating it with his cell. "That writing... it reminds me of Egyptian hieroglyphics."

Ricky stared at the slab for a few moments, and then the realization came to her.

"Yeah, Egyptians."

Mavis blinked at her. "What?"

"The people with the guns are looking for a scroll hidden by Egyptians who sailed to Ireland 5,000 years ago," explained Ricky. "They would have brought metal tools and Egyptian stone-working technique to do this." She passed a hand over the hollowed-out slab, used her mobile to take a couple of quick photographs of the hieroglyphics. Then, remembering the imminent danger, she faced into the black recess, testing the stability of the tilting block of stone as she squinted. She had expected to find a small niche where the scroll would have been secreted away. Light from her mobile phone found no scroll or other human-made objects, but did reveal a passageway disappearing into the ink.

Crockett arrived on the scene at this moment. "Bad news."

"Fuck. Listening."

"I think Cessair is going to have her goons storm the place," said Crockett. "I think she's afraid that the police are going to show up and complicate things."

"Did she say anything?"

"She said we had three minutes to turn over the scroll."

"When did she say that?"

"A minute and a half ago!"

Ricky considered the dark opening behind the stone. What other option did they have? "Let's go this way."

"Wait!" cried Stan. "I thought you said your pal here was special ops?"

"Would you have felt better if I told you he was a goddamn moron who drives a yellow Daewoo?" shouted Ricky.

Stan eyed the opening anxiously. "And now you want us to go in there? I suppose you're going to tell me it leads to Narnia! We could end up trapped in there!"

"We're fucking trapped in *here*!" cried Ricky. "There's always been a theory that there might be more tunnels in this mound. Maybe it'll take us... somewhere where there aren't fucking bullets!"

"Somewhere without bullets seems better than here," said Peterson. Mavis nodded, although it was clear that the revelations about the tomb as well as the shooting had introduced an unwelcome chaos into her guide world and had left her in a state of shock.

Crockett gestured wildly toward the hole. "Go!"

Ricky climbed through and Crockett assisted Mavis over the angled stone.

"My wife, she is afraid of caves," said the French husband.

"Then this was a pretty dumbass choice of tourist attractions," said Ricky. Her head felt like it might explode.

"I'm afraid she's going to hate what will be coming down that passageway even worse," said Crockett, helping them through the aperture.

Ricky removed a six-inch flashlight from her pocket, flicked it on.

"Another shrewd purchase from the Elizabeth collection?" asked Crockett.

"No," said Ricky. "Found this earlier in the glove compartment of the Daewoo."

"Told you that car was a great deal. Forty-four miles to the gallon and a flashlight in the glove box."

"Fucking yellow."

Mavis suddenly perked up and also produced a flashlight.

"For emergencies," she said. "I guess this is one." She laughed inappropriately, like a woman who believed she was about to die.

The new passage was similar in height and width to the one that they had left, but was strewn with rocks, and there were no carvings on the walls.

"Did you get the scroll?" asked Crockett, inching close to her.

"No," hissed Ricky. "The only thing behind that symbol so far is this tunnel."

"This is bad," said Crockett. "We don't have anything to bargain with, and this is not feeling like the way out!"

The passage stretched straight ahead, following the line of the original. They moved along cautiously, yet as quickly as they could.

"Why isn't this on Fintan Mac's map?" asked Crockett.

"Don't ask me," said Ricky, squinting ahead. "I didn't build it!"

She knew that any minute now, Cessair's thugs would charge into the passageway and see that they were not there. Then the goons would see the opening behind the displaced slab and come through that. It would not be long after that and they would catch up to the pokey group of tourists.

"This is definitely bad!" said Crockett, sounding like a broken record, although he was simply articulating how she felt.

Ricky stopped and shined the light on the way ahead. In the beam, they saw the tunnel split into three separate passageways.

"This is definitely worse," said Crockett. "Which way do we go? If there's a right answer, we've got one chance!"

Ricky considered the matter. "There aren't any markings." She thought about the map. It had contained no clues to guide them.

Or had it?

"What?" asked Crockett, seeing a light in her eyes.

"What if the triskelion were more than just a symbol marking the hiding place? What if it was a map? Three underground spiral tunnels!"

"Interesting theory, Sherlock, but that still doesn't tell us which one to take."

Peterson peered over her shoulder. "I was listening to what you were saying, and if you don't mind? The spiral on the triskelion you were looking at, it goes in a counter-clockwise direction. Maybe that's significant. That could mean an angle to the left."

"Are you sure about this?" Crockett asked him.

"Of course not," said Peterson. "But what else have we got? And hell, I'm on a roll. You know what they say: You don't bet against a streak."

"I don't follow."

"Lucky streak. Paid for this trip with poker winnings."

"What else have we got?" said Crockett in surrender.

They went left, moving swiftly now as the passage curved counter-clockwise. The distant echoes of voices informed them that Cessair and her men had discovered the opening at the end of the cruciform tomb.

"It'll be all right, Louise," said Stan, "but you can't stop to rest now!"

"My wife, I think she may start screaming very soon," said the Frenchman.

"No talking," said Crockett. "When they come to the three passages, if they don't know which way we've gone, maybe it will slow them down."

They proceeded in silence, turning off the guide's flashlight and continuing to the left. Suddenly, Ricky skidded to a stop.

"Shit!" Her smaller flashlight illuminated a dead end, and in the floor, a circular hole about two meters across.

"Burial pit?" asked Crockett, recoiling in terror. "That looks just like the one in that mastaba. God, no!"

The thought that this might be their grave—dark, cold, narrow, and sixty feet deep—shot a wave of panic through Ricky, but as she stepped closer, the opening seemed more than it had first appeared. "I don't think it's the same." She examined it quickly with the flashlight. "It's only about seven or eight feet to the bottom. And then it seems to… spread out."

Crockett recovered, grabbed her flashlight and immediately climbed over the side, dropping to the floor of the pit. He disappeared for a moment and Ricky motioned for Mavis' light, waving it into the hole, illuminating as much area as she could, barely daring to breathe. Then Crockett reappeared.

"Get everybody down here, quickly! Jesus, you've got to see this place!"

Peterson smiled. "Like I said. Lucky streak."

CHAPTER 31

In less than a minute, all of the tourists had been lowered to the floor. With their lives in danger, the four senior citizens had shown themselves to be surprisingly agile. The French woman took the longest.

"We must be careful with my little girl," said the husband, helping Crockett and Peterson ease her through the opening. Crockett realized he was not talking about his wife or the two-year-old they had lowered into the abyss moments earlier.

"You know that the baby's going to be a girl?"

The husband nodded. "My wife, Nicole, had the tests."

What had appeared at first to be a hole in the floor of the tunnel proved to be a circular opening in the ceiling of a vast room that stretched out beneath the Newgrange passage tomb. Massive slabs above their heads rested on hundreds of chiseled stone support columns. In some respects, it reminded Ricky of an ancient, very creepy underground parking structure.

Or a mastaba, she thought, and then shivered at the notion of again being cornered in a tomb by Cessair—this one much larger and with thousands of additional tons of earth and stone above their heads.

The pregnant French woman raced off, disappearing behind one of the columns.

"*Toilette.* Bathroom," said the Frenchman with a sheepish smile. The two-year-old giggled.

"Oh my," said Mavis, taking in the vast area. "Who would have thought!" They could almost hear Mavis's brain sizzling in the grease of chaos and unexpected discovery.

"This is all your fault!" complained the older teen-aged daughter, her voice echoing. "Mom only brought us to this creepy place because of you and your death fixation! Nobody normal wants to go around visiting tombs!" Then she looked around guiltily at the other tourists, seeming to have second thoughts about her choice of words.

The younger girl kept her back turned to her sister. "Just leave me alone, Kel!"

Their mother said nothing, her face a pale mask of hopelessness.

Nicole returned, and they all moved away from the hole, knowing that Cessair and her men would soon find it too.

"I suppose this shouldn't surprise us too much," said Ricky to Crockett, digging out two more painkillers and chewing them dry. "Egyptian Mastabas often had multiple layers and mazes of passageways and rooms. And if Egyptians helped build this…" She allowed her voice to trail off.

"You'll forgive me if I'm still very much surprised," said Crockett.

As they moved along, following what appeared to be a more or less central corridor through the columns, they noticed stone platforms built up from the floor a foot or two, upon which rested bones or mummified remains. Ricky noticed Cobalt Blue's eyes widen in what might have been fascination or horror.

"Keep your eyes straight ahead, Ester," said the prim woman to her daughter, though both of them stole glances at the remains.

Ester! No wonder she's rebelling.

"Fascinating," exclaimed Peterson.

"My wife, she hope the tour is over soon."

They reached the far side of the great tomb, where they found a cairn of bowling ball-sized stones, piled about two meters high. However, this was not the only unusual sight that greeted them. While passing through this tomb beneath a tomb, Ricky observed that vertical slabs of stone, similar to those in the cruciform passage tomb above, defined the perimeter wall—except behind the cairn. As their lights penetrated the darkness beyond the stone pile, they discovered that the walls here had been covered with a smooth skin of plaster. Upon this backdrop, which measured about forty feet in width, had been painted figures and symbols that, like the glyphs on the back side of the hollowed-out support stone, seemed Egyptian in origin.

"If I wasn't scared to death, I'd be downright fascinated," said Crockett, staring.

Just in front of the cairn rested a squarish block of granite, perhaps three feet tall, into which was carved yet another triskelion.

"Perhaps this is it," said Crockett, scrambling up the cairn and tossing away stones. Then he glanced back at the group. "It'll go quicker if everyone helps!"

"What sort of *it* are we talking about?" asked Stan. "Is this what the crazy people chasing us are after?"

"If it is," said Crockett, tossing a couple of rocks to the side, "it might give us a little bargaining power."

Peterson, the Frenchman, Ester, and one of the seniors moved forward to help.

"Wait!" cried Mavis, her words echoing off the stone walls as if she were a deity. "This is a national monument!" she reminded them. "We can't simply upend or destroy things that have been lying undisturbed for thousands of years! These treasures must be examined carefully by trained professionals!"

"Ma'am," said Crockett reasonably, "in a few minutes, some very nasty, heavily armed people will come through that hole in the ceiling. There might be something in this pile of stones that they want, and if that's so, we might be able to strike some sort of bargain with them. If we don't get it first, we will never leave this place alive. And after we're gone, they won't hesitate to disturb these stones."

Mavis sighed, and when she spoke, her voice was resigned. "You won't mind, I hope, if I don't watch."

"I'd prefer that you didn't, ma'am," said Crockett.

Mavis executed a rather ceremonious turn, faced away from the pile, and began humming "The Soldier's Song", the Irish National Anthem.

Crocket reached into his pocket, tossed the handgun to Stan. "Go back to where you can just see that opening in the ceiling. If you see anyone come through it, shoot! We'll hear it and come to help!"

He hurried off into the gloom, and most of the others joined in the effort, putting aside stones as rapidly as they could.

"Wait!"

This time, the voice belonged to Ricky.

"If this violates your sense of archaeology ethics, maybe you should turn around and join Mavis," said Crockett, panting as he tossed aside more stones.

"It does," said Ricky. "Though I'm willing to put my life ahead of archaeological ethics. But…"

"But what?" asked Crockett, pausing in his efforts. The others paused as well.

"That wall in back of the stones... it's incredible. But is it just a ceremonial decoration? Or is it something else?"

"You mean like in the B-movies?" asked Crockett. "A warning? If you disturb the resting place of the scroll, you'll be the victim of a 5,000-year-old curse?"

"I don't believe in curses."

"I do," said Crockett. "Hell, I feel like I've been cursed ever since I first heard of this thing!"

Ricky glared at him. "I meant we should be careful. What if the scroll isn't under these rocks? What if we tear this hill apart and find out we've destroyed the next clue?"

Crockett held up an index finger. "We don't have much time. And we probably won't be able to figure out what those paintings mean. But... you're right. We should at least take a look."

They climbed down from the cairn and trained their lights on the wall. While some of it was indeed a mystery, other figures seemed to tell a story they recognized.

"Three ships," said Crockett, pointing. "Like in the myth of Cessair."

The tableau seemed to agree with what Leo had told them, that Cessair's initial calculations had been wrong, that Ireland had not been deserted. The three ships were shown meeting people with spears and curved clubs who showed the Egyptians the partially completed passage tomb. The next panel seemed to depict a split, with some of the Egyptians joining the tribes and working together, but others clustering around a figure with a crocodile head.

"Good ol' Ammit," muttered Crockett.

Ricky stiffened, remembering Bash's description. "Devourer of souls."

"Gotta be Cessair." Crockett glared at the symbol darkly.

The scene showed the tribes working with Egyptian defectors, an uprising it seemed, stealing and hiding the scroll. Toward the end, Ricky counted human figures—clearly Egyptians—lying horizontally.

"Forty-eight," she said. "All of her followers died in battle. Everyone except Cessair and Fintan Mac."

"Interesting," said Crockett. "There aren't any Celtic tribal warriors lying dead beside them. Was the battle that lopsided?"

"Maybe that's just the way the winners painted it."

Crockett shook his head. "I don't know. But I also don't see anything that tells us to stop throwing rocks."

They returned to the cairn, and in surprisingly short order, several layers had been removed, exposing the top of a three-foot-square stone sarcophagus.

"Frenchy, Peterson, give me a hand here!"

"I am named Paul," said the Frenchman.

Together, the three men and Ricky horsed the lid off the sarcophagus. The effort brought pain like an arrow piercing her skull. Crockett peered inside.

"What do you see?"

He reached in with both hands, pulling out an ornate, clay jar with a tightly fitting cap. For a minute, he struggled with the lid and then, mindful of the passing time, grabbed a stone and used it as a hammer to smash a hole in the jar. Reaching inside, he pulled out a black bag made of animal hide, incredibly, still pliable after fifty centuries. He unraveled the tough, dry laces and searched inside.

"My God!"

"What is it?" asked Ricky.

He withdrew a parchment whose ends were wrapped around

two ornate, gold-colored handles.

"This has to be it!" said Crockett. "I can't read any of it, but this has to be it!"

It was hard to stop looking at the scroll, but Ricky urged, "Put it away and let's find a way out of here!"

Crockett carefully replaced it in the satchel and clambered down to the rest of the group.

"What do you think the chances are of us finding a way out of here?" asked Peterson.

"Slim to none," said Crockett. "So I'm pretty optimistic, because that's been our chances all along, and yet we're still here. Like you said, don't bet against a streak."

An explosion startled them, reverberating throughout the huge chamber. Even the air seemed to tremble.

"What the hell?" cried Crockett.

Screams, shouting, anxious chatter. A second explosion followed half a minute later.

"Stay here," said Crockett to the group. He was going to follow this up with some advice on what to do next if he did not come back, but he had absolutely no idea what they should do, so he said nothing.

He made his way toward the source of the explosions, which almost certainly was the entrance hole. As he got closer, he saw the rolling cloud of dust and rushed forward, no longer bothering to conceal himself behind the stone pillars, meeting a coughing Stan after only a few steps.

"I didn't see anyone come down! But then, boom! I don't know what happened!"

Crockett took the gun and sent him back toward the others. Then he edged forward, gun drawn, looking for signs of light or movement in the dust. Eventually he drew close enough to see the grim truth.

Cessair had apparently set off explosive charges above the hole, dropping the ceiling down on top of it, plugging the entrance with tons of stone and rubble. They were trapped.

Why would she do it?

Trapping them here would keep Crockett and Ricky from making off with the scroll, but only for a short while. At the Visitors Centre, they would notice that a tour group had not returned. They would send people to investigate, eventually summon the police. Soon, they would find the bus parked near the tomb, driver probably dead. Inside the tomb, they would find the newly discovered passage, assume that the tour group had gone through it, and eventually come across the area where the explosion had been set off. Then they would dig. It might take a few days, but Crockett, Ricky, and the others would be rescued. All they had to do was wait.

And that's what bothered Crockett. Cessair would know all of this as well. So it defied logic that she had trapped them in the tomb. In effect, it would be as if she had conceded the prize.

And Cessair was not about to concede something she had pursued for five thousand years.

There was something he was not seeing, or perhaps something only Cessair could know.

Whatever it was, it meant that they were all still in terrible danger.

CHAPTER 32

"The good news," said Crockett when he rejoined the group, "is that we're not in immediate danger. The bad news is that we definitely can't go out the same way we came in."

He explained what had happened.

"Mavis, why don't you turn off your flashlight to conserve battery power," said Crockett.

"Before we do anything," said Stan, coughing and covered in dust, "now that we're not being chased, I got a few questions. Who the hell are you and..." he gestured vaguely at Ricky, uncertain, and finally settled on "the chick?"

Crockett assessed the group and proceeded with something resembling the truth. "We work for the HARP Foundation. It's in the U.S., Chicago. When we get out of here and have cell phone reception, you can look it up. We're researchers. We've been trying to find that scroll" —he pointed to the pouch that Ricky now held — "to protect it from poachers. Its historical value is immense, and as you can see, the poachers are quite ruthless."

"I could never understand why someone would pay a million bucks for something that's been buried for a couple thousand years," said Stan. "Archaeologists must be lunatics, every damn one of 'em!'"

"I don't have any evidence to suggest otherwise," replied Crockett, casting a sideways glance at Ricky. "Lunatics or not, we want to get everyone out of here safely. So we'll have to look for other passageways or structural weaknesses."

"Structural weaknesses?" said Stan, grunting a miserable pebble of laughter. "With all this stone, this place is Fort Knox!"

"I'm afraid he's correct," said Mavis weakly. Peterson nodded his agreement.

"We could make some torches," suggested Crockett. "We'll save some battery life."

"I don't think that's such a good idea," said Peterson. "Torches will burn the oxygen faster and produce carbon monoxide, which in an enclosed area like this could be deadly."

Crockett nodded. "Well, hopefully the phones will last long enough for them to find us and dig us out." He checked his mobile. "No bars." He was not surprised, considering the tons of rock and soil heaped above them.

"We're supposed to meet the Gables for dinner at the Boar and Hare," said Stan. "Is that going to be a problem?"

Nicole chattered away angrily to her husband. Although she did not understand a word, the tone sounded to Ricky like she was arguing for a divorce.

Red and her daughters stood silently, the mother behind, one hand on each of her children's shoulders. Ricky noticed that the girls made no effort to pull away. The four seniors shuffled back and forth between the group and the cairn, carrying a single, bowling-ball-sized rock each trip. This puzzled Ricky, until she realized they were creating rock piles upon which to sit.

"Mavis," said Crockett, "you know this place better than any of us. Can you think of anything that might be helpful?"

Mavis' eyes went out of focus as she thought, but then she slowly shook her head. "I'm afraid I'm not much help." She retrieved her lavender card, studied it listlessly for a moment, slipped it back into the pocket. "This spooky old cellar is all new to me. I don't know what to think." Crockett was about to turn toward Ricky when Mavis spoke again. "Oh, I did try my radio."

"Radio?"

Mavis patted a black two-way radio clipped to her belt. "In case of emergency during a tour. That's what it's for. I'd say this qualifies! Well, fat lot of good it is under all of this stone! No better than your mobiles."

Crockett nodded and joined Ricky, who had wandered near the wall.

"I really hate being trapped in tombs," she said.

Crocket smiled, though it was too dark for her to see. "Then I guess you chose the wrong career." He looked at the rock above them. "Can't bring the roof down this time. A ceiling of stone with a million tons of rock and dirt heaped on top of it. Don't want that coming down on your noggin."

"If we had cell service, at least I could call the Gables and let them know we'll be late," said Stan.

Oh, you'll be late all right, thought Crockett.

They resolved to split into two groups and work their way around the perimeter, searching for anything that appeared to be a weakness. Crockett pointed to Peterson. "You head to the wall and work your way to the right. Take him" —he jerked a thumb at Stan — "with you so he doesn't keep belly-aching about dinner with the Gables. Ricky and I'll work our way to the left!"

Crockett was glad for the chance to leave the group. Nicole was crying, and the teenagers had resumed fighting. The senior citizens had brought out a deck of cards and, sitting on rocks in a circle, seemed to be playing Euchre.

They moved slowly, looking for any oddity that might suggest a point of egress. Ricky knew that tombs sometimes had access shafts or second entrances which, after construction, were filled with stone or sand to discourage plunderers. If this tomb contained such a thing, perhaps it could be excavated.

As they worked, they began to reach the unfortunate conclusion that the place had been masterfully built. The flat stones of the perimeter wall were stacked tightly, and the ends of the roof slabs rested upon these.

"This place is a damned fortress!" said Crockett.

"It always amazes me that people without heavy machinery could build places like this, the Mayan temples, the Great Pyramids," said Ricky, a touch of awe in her voice.

"I've always figured they had help from aliens," said Crockett. "Sure wish they'd visit us again right about now and help us build an exit."

They inspected the wall in silence for a few minutes.

"They'll come looking for us, won't they?" Ricky finally asked. "Not the aliens. The Visitors Centre people, I mean."

"That seems likely. But I'm really missing Amet right now."

Ricky made a doubtful noise. "I don't think a hundred Amets could bring down this ceiling."

"Let's try and put a positive spin on it for the others," said Crockett without taking his eyes off the gently curving surface of the wall. "In any case, we still have the ceiling to inspect. Maybe the rabbit hole we came down wasn't the only rooftop entrance to Wonderland."

"Yeah, well, keeping things positive is not exactly my forte," said Ricky. "And it's going to get worse. The flashlights and cellphones only have a few hours of battery power. So... very soon, we're going to be sitting in total darkness. Once that happens, what can we do?"

"I don't know that there's much we can do anyway," said Crockett soberly. "That leaves us with one option."

"Which is?"

"Destroy the scroll. That will keep Cessair from carrying out her plan."

"I've been thinking about that," said Ricky. "Earlier, Brenner asked why Fintan Mac didn't destroy the scroll 5,000 years ago. That would have at least kept Cessair from expanding her power."

Crockett nodded, his eyes traveling up and down the current section of wall. "Right. So if he kept the scroll around, he obviously had a reason. And the local tribes were on his side. They must have been finishing up this mega-mastaba at the time and helped him to hide the scroll here."

"Until it was needed again."

Crockett looked at her. "What are you getting at?"

"It's the Scroll of Life *and* Death, right?" asked Ricky rhetorically.

"Right. So maybe it can create some sort of plague or virus."

"What if it can be used to kill Cessair?"

Crockett stopped walking. "Whoa! That would explain a lot. Yeah. She's been looking for it obsessively for fifty centuries not just because she can use it to create an army, but because it's the only thing that can kill her. Mind blown!"

"It would also explain why Fintan hid it rather than destroying it," noted Ricky. "And made a map so that he—or someone—could come back and finish off Cessair. But why do you suppose he left?"

"Sounds like Cessair was on to him," said Crockett. "Things got too hot in Ireland, so he decided to take a little hiatus."

"Do you think he intended to go to Egypt? Kill the sorcerer and then come back for Cessair?"

"I thought maybe so at first. But that seems like a pretty crazy trip for one guy on a raft. Now I'm more inclined to think he was just tryin' to get out of Dodge for a while. Maybe come to the mainland or a neighboring island to recruit some help so he could get to her and use the scroll."

"But he ended up in Greenland." Ricky pondered the ill-luck that had brought the map into her—and Sasha's—lives.

"He ended up in Greenland," Crockett repeated. "Talk about a guy with no sense of direction."

"So we might have the power to stop Cessair right here!" She tapped the pouch. "If only we could read Egyptian."

"Or get out of here. Guess we'd better treat that scroll like a winning lottery ticket."

"But help *will* come for us," said Ricky, "a rescue group, right? How could they not? Cessair won't stick around once the police respond. And they'll dig us out."

"If that's true, why did Cessair trap us here?" asked Crockett. "When they dig us out, the authorities get the scroll, and game over for Cessair. That doesn't sound like a scenario she would favor."

"Maybe her people have infiltrated the Garda," suggested Ricky, referring to the Irish police force.

"Maybe. But not all of them would be Cessair's people. Sounds too chancy. Something else is going on here."

A few moments later, they saw the flicker of Peterson's phone along the wall ahead.

"Nothing," said Peterson, making a thumb's down gesture as they met. Stan simply shook his head in a desultory fashion and headed back toward the group. They stood watching him for a beat or two, and then Peterson turned to Crockett and Ricky.

"Who are these people? I mean really? The ones who trapped us here. Something tells me they're not your typical tomb raiders."

"Goddamn murderers!" muttered Ricky.

"No," sighed Crockett, "they are definitely not typical. Part of a cult that calls itself Alchemy."

"Never heard of 'em. And they're pretty hot for that scroll," observed Peterson. "What's so special about it?"

"They think it has magical powers."

Peterson raised an eyebrow. "So these folks are crazy?"

"Most of the evidence points that way."

After a moment, Peterson smiled ironically. "Not the sort of magic that can get us out of here, I suppose. And you two are really trying to recover it for some foundation?"

"Mostly to keep more people from being killed."

Peterson seemed startled by this. "More? You mean they've killed people already?"

"My sister!" said Ricky bitterly.

"I'm so sorry."

"Ricky's sister was one of the climate scientists killed at Zackenberg in Greenland."

The other man's eyes widened again. "Holy mother of pearl! I saw that on the news! Good Lord! *That's* who trapped us in here?"

Crockett and Ricky both nodded somberly. They stood silently for a bit before Crockett spoke.

"You're American, right? What's your story? Why are you so far from home?"

Peterson seemed to reluctantly pull himself away from his grim musings. "I'm on vacation." He chuckled at this. "I'm the tech specialist at one of the hospitals in Columbus. My partner, Jim, he was a security guard there. We had planned a trip to Ireland to celebrate our tenth anniversary together, but that crazy-ass virus a year-and-a-half ago… well, that got Jim."

Ricky and Crockett muttered condolences.

"We thought it would be a hell of an adventure. And after Jim died, I decided to come anyway. I've got a tiny bit of his ashes in the rental car. Was gonna sprinkle them off the Cliffs of Moher, which Jim had really wanted to see." He paused, smiled. "Hell of an adventure, indeed."

They trudged toward the rest, using their light to examine the ceiling along the way. Still nothing.

"We'll start looking over the rest of the ceiling in a minute," said Crockett. "Before we do, Mavis, you don't recall any old maps of this place that might show possible secret tunnels or anything of the sort?"

Mavis shook her head slowly. "No, nothing like that at all. I'm so sorry I can't be more help. There's a second tunnel at Knowth."

"What's Knowth?" asked Crockett.

"It's another burial mound not far from here. It has an east passage and a west passage. They almost meet in the middle. I've always wondered why they weren't connected. But as I said, that's Knowth. People have often wondered whether there were other passages in this tomb, too. I guess we don't have to wonder anymore."

The red-haired woman spoke, her lower lip quivering, her voice shrill. "We're all going to die, aren't we?"

"Oh, Janet, you mustn't give up hope," Mavis said.

Crockett smiled a thin, tight smile and flicked his eyes toward the woman's daughters so as to remind her of their presence. "We still have options, things to check out. Plus, the folks at the Visitors Centre have probably already reported this. They'll dig us out."

"We're going to be in the dark, soon, aren't we? In the dark, frightened, trapped underground beneath a mountain of earth, struggling to breathe!"

"Does anyone have any Valium?" asked Crockett.

Stan's wife began to cry, and this set off Nicole again.

He inclined his head in a whisper toward Ricky. "Why is there no Valium?"

Red took up her phone, punched at its screen viciously, crying out shrilly, "Nothing! Nothing! No one's coming!" Then she hurled it at the plaster wall, against which it shattered and created a tiny indentation.

Then the anxiety seemed to erupt from everywhere, and it took ten minutes to restore a kind of nervous truce.

"Is she right?" Ricky asked, pulling Crockett aside between the cairn and the plastered wall. "Are we all going to go mad in the dark waiting for a rescue that's not coming?"

Crockett let out a long breath. "I've been trying to figure it out. I mean, why Cessair would trap us here. You're not going to like what I have to say."

"That'll keep your record perfect."

"What if Cessair had her thugs put the slab back in place in the passage tomb? The one with the hollowed-out back?"

"I don't understand."

Crockett spoke quietly, earnestly. "The tour bus doesn't come back. They eventually send someone to find out why. They find the bus... driver is dead. Police are called. They search around the tomb, nothing. They search inside the tomb, nothing—because the slab is back in place! Maybe they get a ransom demand, or maybe 'terrorists' claim to have kidnapped and murdered the group. No one searches under the tomb, because no one knows there's anything under the tomb to search."

"Shit!"

"And all Cessair has to do is wait. A few weeks. A few months.

Five years. We'll be long dead and won't put up a fight. Move the hollow slab, blast a new entrance hole a few feet from the original. Walk away with the scroll."

"Shit!" She suddenly felt the enormity of the tons of earth and stone above her, the futility of any struggle. She recalled the crippling sense of futility she had felt as the concrete had poured into the excavation in Frankfurt and understood the crazed fear that had taken hold of the girls' mother.

Ricky looked again at the gouge created by Janet's cell phone. It wasn't the only blemish in the plaster-covered wall, Ricky noticed. Over the years, fragments had fallen off in a dozen places, though no blemish was larger than a baseball. Occasional cracks skated diagonally across the plaster surface as well, another completely understandable consequence of the passage of fifty centuries.

Yet, something caught her attention. Something near the middle of the forty-foot-wide mural. Something to which most people would assign no importance. A horizontal crack in the plaster, perhaps two feet in length. And below it a few inches, another, parallel to it, but only about nine inches.

Crockett heard her breath catch and looked toward her, alert.

"What?"

Before Ricky could answer, Nicole cried out. Paul's voice followed. "*Mon dieu!*"

"What is it, my dear?" asked Mavis, hurrying over to Nicole.

The husband looked up, his eyes wide. "My wife, her water!"

Crockett took a step forward. "Oh, please no! Not now! Not here!"

"She says baby is coming!"

CHAPTER 33

"It can be hours after the water breaks before the baby is born," said Stan. "My wife was in labor with our first for twenty-seven hours!"

"Will we be rescued by then?" asked Paul.

No one had an answer.

Ricky did not think Nicole would be in labor for twenty-seven hours. Her contractions were close—already three minutes apart—and increasing in intensity, to judge by her gasps.

She looked over to the yoiung French girl. Would she watch her little sister be delivered into a tomb that would become a grave for both of them?

"Hey!" called Crockett, shaking her from her thoughts. "A few minutes ago, you saw something. I heard you gasp. Please tell me it wasn't a ghost."

Ricky recovered, grabbed his hand, drew him over to the wall. "I'm hoping it *was* a ghost. Look at the cracks on this wall."

Crockett shrugged. "So?"

"The jagged ones and the diagonals, those are perfectly natural results of the aging plaster, settling of the earth and so forth," she explained, drawing upon her knowledge of archeology. "They seem to travel across the plaster surface randomly. But look at these two." She moved in front of the horizontal lines. "A perfectly horizontal line and then another parallel to it just a few inches apart…"

Crockett saw where she was headed. "Perfectly parallel lines don't occur naturally. You think there's something different behind this section of the plaster wall. Tiers of brick, maybe, instead of big rock slabs."

Ricky nodded.

"But why?"

Rick glanced back at the group, then took a deep breath. "You've heard of Nefertiti?"

"Vaguely. Go on."

"Egyptian Queen. The location of her tomb was a mystery for decades," explained Ricky. "Then archaeologists spotted some odd cracks in the plaster walls in King Akhenaten's tomb. This suggested that a secret door had been built in the wall behind the plaster and then covered up. They sometimes refer to these as 'ghost doors'."

Crockett pointed. "And you think there's one here?"

"It's worth checking. I don't see anything else that looks door-like anywhere."

"But," continued Crockett, "why would the Egyptians build it? As another way out?"

"Maybe. Or to hide something really valuable."

"More valuable than the Scroll of Life and Death?" Crockett breathed a mirthless chuckle. "Fat chance. I'm putting my money on a stairway to freedom. Let's find a couple of rocks and give this wall a little beat-down."

Using stones from the cairn and Crockett's knife, they began to chip plaster from the section of the wall that Ricky had indicated.

Peterson soon arrived to help.

"Contractions are getting closer," he reported. "Any of you know how to deliver a baby?"

"Why don't you try?" asked Crockett. "You're on a lucky streak, remember?"

Peterson grimaced but stooped to pick up a rock and help. As Ricky had suspected, behind this section of the plaster was a brick wall, erected in place of one of the refrigerator-sized slabs. With the plaster façade extending in both directions for twenty feet, tomb raiders would have had no clue that this narrow section was any different from the hundreds of other stone slabs. Within this brick wall was a smaller area about a meter square that seemed to have been erected to seal shut an opening.

"And there's your ghost door!" pronounced Crockett.

"Is it a way out?" asked Peterson.

Crockett narrowed his gaze. "We don't know what's behind it. But I aim to find out. I'd hate to die curious."

Am echoing shriek sounded. Paul's voice could be heard offering worried assurances in French.

Crockett shook his head. "I don't see this ending well."

"Maybe if we get through this wall..." Peterson's voice trailed off and he began battering the bricks.

"Just lost a cell phone," shouted Stan from the circle around Nicole where the rest were gathered. Ricky could not see how announcing this was in any way helpful. And she did not want to think about what might happen if the ghost door failed to provide an exit. Any complications in the birth, and Nicole could die a horrible death. They had no medical gear. Something that could be routinely handled in an emergency room could prove fatal here.

Ricky and Crockett joined Peterson in working on the bricks mortared into the low opening. At first, they seemed fused together like a solid piece of granite. Then their blows generated a few cracks, pushed one in a couple millimeters, then a couple more. After the first few bricks, the rest broke loose easily. They stared dumbly at the dark opening, collecting their strength, drenched in sweat. Another cry from Nicole brought them round. This one sounded more anguished, fearful.

Stan uttered a vulgarity.

"What is it?" shouted Crockett.

"I think we got a problem," said Stan anxiously.

Nicole let out another particularly woeful wail and, without thinking, Ricky moved away from the wall and slid over to the huddled group, kneeling beside the panting woman.

She's in a lot of pain. No way I'm ever getting pregnant.

Someone knelt next to Ricky, and to her surprise, she saw it was Cobalt Blue.

"Ester, don't interfere!" said the mother. Ester ignored her.

"What the fuck do you want?" asked Ricky.

Ester looked at her impassively. "You say 'fuck' a lot." Then the young girl put a hand under Nicole's blouse and felt her abdomen, probing and tapping. "I think the head is up. It's a breech."

"What makes you a fu—" Ricky stopped herself. "What makes you an expert on childbirth?"

"Nothing," replied Ester. "I mean... I just had a friend whose ma got remarried and had a baby at home last year. With a midwife."

"And you were invited? Creepy."

"It happened during a sleepover."

Ricky considered this, realizing how little she knew about anything related to childbirth. "How do you know the baby's a breech?"

Ester pulled up Nicole's blouse, exposing her abdomen. "If you tap on the top here, and the whole thing moves, that's the baby's whole body. Its head is down in the right position."

"But the whole thing didn't move when you tapped it," said Ricky. "Just that one small area."

"That's the baby's head," said Ester. "It's supposed to be down, not up."

A string of back and forth conversation in French erupted between the husband and wife.

Shit! Ricky knew little, though she was aware that the usual procedure in a breech was a C-section. But those were done in sterile hospital procedure rooms surrounded by state-of-the-art equipment and people with medical degrees. Here it was cold and filthy, they had no medical training, they had no antibiotics or anesthetic, nothing to stitch up the mother afterwards, and only Crockett's unsterilized knife for a scalpel.

Shit!

Mavis loomed over the group with her flashlight, reminding Ricky that however terrible the birth, it would all become more terrible still when the lights went out. They would all end up in pitch darkness with a screaming woman who might die along with her unborn baby. A look around the circle at all of the worried, horrified faces confirmed that everyone else was imagining this same, grim future.

Goddamn Cessair!

She rushed back to the ghost door and shined her own smaller flashlight into the space. Then she bent and slid inside. *This has to be a way out!* Crockett and Peterson followed. They discovered a room about ten feet square, its smooth walls filled with symbols and illustrations of human figures.

"What is this?" asked Peterson.

Crockett shook his head. All of them scanned the walls for some sign of a second door. There had to be one. Otherwise, the French woman would die, and then they would all follow as starvation or lack of oxygen took its toll.

But there was no second door. The room was a dead end.

CHAPTER 34

Although there was no second door, the room was not empty. Their eyes were drawn to an object resting on the floor in the center of the room—a small, stone sarcophagus, a twin to the one they had uncovered beneath the cairn.

"Something more valuable than the Scroll of Life and Death?" Crockett asked Ricky, indicating the sarcophagus.

Ricky grimaced. "If it is, I don't think I want to see it. It doesn't matter anyway if we can't get out of here."

"Maybe it's a map of an escape route," suggested Peterson. Ricky doubted it, but could not imagine what the ancient Celts and Egyptians might want to hide to an even greater extent than the scroll.

Crockett and Peterson knelt at opposite sides of the stone box and hoisted the heavy lid. As they set it down, Ricky reached into the box, then lifted out another pouch bearing another scroll.

It appeared identical to the first. When Ricky removed the first from its pouch, this was confirmed.

"Why are there two scrolls?" asked Crockett.

They chewed on this question silently for a few moments before Peterson spoke. "I think it's obvious."

"Enlighten us," said Crockett.

"The first one is a dummy. A fake. If anyone came looking, they'd go away with the counterfeit scroll and leave behind the genuine article."

"That makes sense," nodded Ricky.

"We'd better take them both," said Crockett. He picked up a stone chip from the floor and placed it inside the pouch. When Ricky gave him a look, he explained. "It's so we can tell which we found first. So we don't get them mixed up."

They emerged from the room and rejoined the others, the looks on their faces telegraphing their failure. The French girl cried out again as Ricky settled beside Ester.

"Sometimes," said Ester, "you can make a baby flip."

Ricky looked at her eagerly. "Flip? A breech? How?"

"Sometimes it doesn't work after labor starts," said Ester. "That's what the midwife said."

"But sometimes it does?"

Ester nodded.

"How?"

"You need something cold," said Ester.

Ricky looked around. It was now difficult to see anybody outside of their little group of helpers. "Can someone find something cold?"

"Like a rock?" asked Crockett.

"I don't know! Anything!"

After a moment, one of the senior citizen women came forward, carrying a small, insulated bag. "I'm Frannie. Bill and I are from Wisconsin. Bill keeps his insulin and other medicines with him when we travel," she explained, reaching inside and handing Ricky an ice pack. Ricky passed it to Ester, who positioned it at the top of the French girl's abdomen.

"Try and relax," said Ricky, who reasoned that, if something were going to change position, it would be easier for it to do so without clenched muscles around it.

They waited. The French woman let out another cry.

Ricky stood, slid next to Crockett. *Nothing's happening. It's not working.*

Peterson leaned between them. "It might be okay." Both Crockett and Ricky turned toward him. "Really. Babies are born breech. It's just..."

"Just what?" asked Ricky.

"Well, the chance that it won't make it is higher."

"How much higher?"

"About four times," said Peterson.

Behind them, another cell phone pinged and went out.

"Don't use all of your cell phones for light!" instructed Crockett. "Maybe one or two. We need to conserve."

For what? thought Ricky. There was no way out. They had no way of contacting the outside. The hidden room had been a dead end.

Another cry from the French woman. Simultaneously, Crockett grabbed Ricky's hand in a vice grip.

"What?"

"Come with me," said Crockett, who led her back to the wall and through the ghost door, using the light of his own cell phone to guide them.

"I thought we were supposed to conserve," said Ricky as she rose to a standing position in the small room.

"I just had an idea," said Crockett excitedly. "The cell phone might work in here!"

At first, Ricky did not understand. Then it hit her: "This room...it's not under the passage tomb!"

"That's right!" said Crockett. "Instead of thirty or forty feet of packed earth and stone sitting over our heads out there—" He pointed back toward the huge room beyond the ghost door—"we've got a stone slab and a foot or two above us here! Maybe it's enough to get a signal and call for help!"

He moved around the room, staying close to the outer walls and holding the phone up toward the ceiling, first moving methodically, but eventually, frenetically.

"Shit!" he cried, and looked as if he too wanted to hurl the phone against the floor.

Another wail from the outer room, this one the loudest yet.

"Shit," he repeated, with less enthusiasm. "When all of the lights go out, things could get really ugly."

"They're already really ugly."

"I'm talking *Lord of the Flies* ugly," said Crockett.

A movement caught Ricky's attention and Stan's head popped through the ghost door. "You've got to see this!"

They scrambled out and returned to the dimly lit circle. The French woman had stopped screaming, though she was bathed in sweat. Across her chest lay a baby, wrapped in a light cotton jacket supplied by one of the seniors.

"What the—!" breathed Crockett.

"It worked!" beamed Ester. "The ice."

"There was a big move," said Peterson, who knelt next to the woman and Ester. "Like a shudder! You could almost see the baby flipping!"

"Ester caught the baby when it came out!" added the sister. Ester nodded, but then her smile faltered and she began to sob. Her sister knelt beside her, wrapped her in an embrace.

Ricky sat on the floor, drained, staring into the scene, sensing Crockett's presence nearby. *Thank God for diabetes.*

The two-year-old French girl sidled up close to her mother. *"Mama, c'le bébé?"*

Exhausted, the mother smiled at the older child. *"Oui, Angela. C'est Ester."*

Peterson rose and Crockett slapped a hand onto his shoulder. "You helped?"

Peterson nodded.

Crockett smiled. "Don't bet against a streak."

Now Peterson smiled gratefully and nudged Ricky and Crockett away from the group. "You went back into the hidden room," he said, speaking lowly to them as the others huddled around the birth scene, doing their best to keep the mother and child warm. "Did you find something?"

Crockett shook his head and explained what they had tried to do.

Peterson considered this for a moment. "You used your mobile?"

Crockett nodded.

Peterson seemed lost in thought again and then crept to where Mavis stood, returning with her radio. He led them back to the ghost door and, a moment later, stood facing the outermost wall in the small room.

"Won't that be the same as using a cell phone?" asked Crockett.

Peterson shook his head. "I won't bore you with the details, but some walkie-talkies—I think they call them personal mobile radios here on this side of the pond—are powerful enough to carry even through stone or buildings, as long as the distance isn't too great. He held the radio up toward the ceiling and pushed the button. "Mayday! Mayday!" A static click followed, but nothing else. He tried again. "Hello! Help! We're trapped underneath the tomb!

Mayday!" Again, silence answered his effort. He shifted position. "Don't worry. We have a couple other channels we can try, too." Then he raised his voice. "Mayday! Mayday! Tourists are trapped at the passage tomb!"

This time, a longer crackle of static greeted him, and then, after a few more seconds, a fuzzy-electric voice.

"Who the bloody hell is this?"

Crockett smiled. "The streak continues."

CHAPTER 35

They dug with the heavy equipment at the north side of the mound—the side not covered by the quartz wall. Several of the massive kerbstones encircling the mound were removed once they had determined the approximate position of the hidden room, and then an excavation was commenced, digging carefully and efficiently until the ceiling slabs were exposed. It was not difficult to dig the hole, as there were few of the complications that accompany trapped miners or cave explorers, and so work progressed quickly—once approval for the excavation had been granted.

More than the usual amount of hemming and hawing had accompanied the decision, since the site to be desecrated was one of Ireland's most-visited tourist attractions, as well as a site of tremendous historical importance. In the end, the significance of the discovery of a tomb *beneath* the tomb, combined with the fact that they could excavate in a manner that would leave the original mound intact, along with the additional fact that a woman had just given birth to a child—and the knowledge that if this did not end well for the mother and infant, it would be a public relations fiasco —spurred the bureaucrats into action more briskly than might have been expected.

Those in authority had quickly decided not to try and clear the rocks dislodged during the explosion. Getting heavy equipment through the narrow tunnel, they reasoned, would be nearly impossible, and setting off charges to clear the fallen rock or to blast a new opening beside the original might accidentally bring the ceiling down on them. They would have to create a new point of egress.

Three hours after little Ester arrived, a tennis-ball-sized hole was drilled through one of the ceiling slabs above the room behind the ghost door, which allowed not only a bit of fresher air, but water, protein bars, and some fully charged flashlights, as well as necessary medical supplies, thin insulated body wraps, and chemical heat-generating pads.

Then everything slowed down again as they drilled additional holes, which would be utilized to lift the roof slab.

While they waited, Crockett pulled Ricky aside.

"Have you thought about what happens when they open this tomb?" he asked.

"You mean beyond a shower? I've still got dried placenta on my goddamn shirt."

"There's going to be lots of questions," said Crockett. "The police are going to talk to all of these people, and it's going to come out that the so-called terrorists were chasing you and me, and that's going to focus a lot of attention on us. As much as I've come to love Amet and his lowlife, criminal relatives, I doubt that our documents are going to hold up under the scrutiny of these folks."

"And the cairn," said Ricky. "They'll know we opened it and took something. And from the sarcophagus in the ghost-door room."

Crockett nodded. "That means we'll be detained and they'll

take the scrolls from us. That could be a good thing, of course. I'm assuming one of the scrolls is the real deal. That could take it out of play for Cessair. Game over. No more ruler-of-the-world fantasy. Unless she has people in the police force. Then everyone's screwed. And I mean everyone!"

"I wish you hadn't said anything about her having people in the rescue group," said Ricky. "I mean, I'm glad you did. But now I'm scared as hell! It's dark. There will be plenty of confusion when they open the roof. One of Cessair's goons could come in dressed like an emergency worker, slip a knife in one of us, grab the bags, and disappear in the confusion."

"You're paranoid," said Crockett. "That's good, though. It'll probably keep us alive a little longer. We should each take a bag to increase our chances. Here." He pressed one into Ricky's hand.

"Which one do I have?"

"Don't know," he replied. "Probably best that way."

"Even if the Garda isn't infiltrated, Cessair still gets away clean if we give up the scrolls," noted Ricky.

"Yeah," agreed Crockett. "She'll disappear, assume a new identity. A year, five years, twenty years, she'll be back to get the real scroll, no matter who has it. When you have unlimited time, there's always a way."

"No matter *who* has it," repeated Ricky. "I was just thinking about that. Which government would you trust with the secret of immortality? Or a plague that could kill all your enemies?"

"Not a one of them, come to think of it," said Crockett.

They let this conclusion sink home for a few moments.

"God, I just want to go home," moaned Ricky, resting her forehead on her palm.

"Then you shouldn't have asked who we could trust," said Crockett. "But now it's done. You went all sensible."

She closed her eyes, shook her head. "No."

"We've got to finish what Fintan started," said Crockett. "So I guess I can cross that little post-rescue nap off my list."

"Wait, wait! What do you mean, finish?" She tried to wrap her head around it. "You mean kill Cessair? Do we look like superheroes? The most dangerous thing you've ever done is buy a Daewoo! I almost threw up when the French woman delivered her placenta a few minutes ago! We need to find someone with the skills and nuts to do this right!"

"We found the scroll," noted Crockett.

"So we're good puzzle solvers. That's not quite the same as assassinating a vindictive, immortal Celtic deity!"

"Okay, we'll get someone else to do it," said Crockett. "Give me names."

"What?"

"Names. Who should we hand this thing off to? Who do you trust?"

Ricky glared. "I don't know."

"That's right," said Crockett. "There's no one else, is there? Unless we do this, Cessair lives forever."

"There's always another way!"

Crockett nodded. "Let me know when you think of it. In the meantime, we need a plan to save our derrieres until we can argue some more. When they open this tomb, we keep our eyes open and we find a way to ditch."

Two hours later, Mavis's radio contact, a man named Welch, informed them that the removal of the ceiling slab was expected within the hour. Then they would be transported to hospital, either by ambulance or bus, depending on their needs. There, they would be examined, treated if necessary, and would offer depositions to the Garda.

Almost an hour later to the minute, Welch told them all to move to the far side of the tomb.

"When we pull this piece of stone out, we don't know if everything else will hold, or whether it'll be like dominoes," said Welch.

"Comforting," Crockett replied.

They did as instructed, then heard the muffled roar of a big engine, followed by the sound of scraping stone. Simultaneously, a cloud of dust erupted and light from great portable work lamps poured out of the ghost door.

"Don't move!" A voice echoed through the underground, and Crockett realized it was one of the workmen, crawling through the small doorway, warning them to hold their positions until the opening had been stabilized. This took a few minutes, and then men entered the tomb to lead them out.

"Eyes moving," whispered Crockett. "Anything that doesn't look right."

Ricky nodded as a man in uniform approached. She tightened her fingers on the bag nestled beside the pocketed pistol that Crockett had returned to her.

"Are you hurt?" he asked, first Ricky and then Crockett.

They shook their heads.

He pointed to his own left eye, and Ricky realized he was inquiring about the patch. "No, this was... before."

The man nodded and led them back through the ghost door into the small room where several aluminum ladders now stood. As Ricky climbed, she saw that it was night, but the area was brightly illuminated by portables and the spotlights of news cameras. A significant crowd cheered the apparent happy ending. Security personnel and police formed a sort of gauntlet, guiding them toward a bus, parked next to an ambulance on the paved drive that encircled the mound.

Most in the gauntlet wore smiles. A few clapped their hands in celebration as they passed. Once they were on the bus, it would be more difficult to extricate themselves from the grip of the authorities. Ricky looked ahead. Through the open bus door, she saw the driver in profile. Clean-cut and about thirty, he stared straight ahead out the front window of the bus.

She gripped Crockett's arm. "It's the bus driver!"

"What? How?"

"Look at him," hissed Ricky. "We're the biggest news event that the Boyne Valley has seen since they built this mound. Everyone else is curious, happy, relieved. This prick is staring out the window, avoiding eye contact."

"Okay, makes sense," Crockett nodded. "Brilliant, really. They let us find the scroll. Let the people of Ireland pay to excavate it. Then get the two of us away from the crowds, and bingo! So what are we going to—"

Ricky had already approached a man in the line who wore the uniform of a monument employee rather than that of the Garda. "The jacks? Bathroom?" she said, adopting a pained expression. "I really have to! Bad!"

"There are restrooms at hospital," he said kindly.

"We won't be there for an hour! If I don't go now, I'll pee all over the floor of the bus!"

The man looked momentarily conflicted, then motioned for her to follow him to a portable toilet hut that had been brought in on the back of a flatbed trailer for rescue workers. Dublin Dunnies was painted on the side in cheerful blue letters.

"Thanks," said Ricky. "I'll be back in a minute."

She headed up the steps. Her new friend hesitated a moment, unsure whether he should escort her back, or whether that would simply be awkward. Apparently concluding that there was no logical reason she would not return to the gauntlet and go to a place where she could get cleaned up and then give the police testimony to catch the creeps that had trapped her in the tomb, he turned and walked back the way they had come.

Immediately, Ricky skittered back down the steps, almost bumping into Crockett, who had apparently executed a similar ruse. They cut behind the Dublin Dunnies trailer and then headed along the right side of the mound on the grass, keeping wide of the paved access road.

"Thank God for the baby," said Ricky. "Everyone seemed focused on the French couple."

"Just walk, just walk," said Crockett. "In the dark, no one can see how filthy we look. We're just interested neighbors, that's all. Show's over. We're headed home."

They angled toward the opening in the hedge along the road, noticed that the gate next to it had also been opened for the heavy equipment and emergency vehicles. They passed through without incident, breezing past a few small groups standing in conversation, their bodies turned toward the mound. Veering to the left, they kept to the right edge of the road for about a hundred meters until the main road turned sharply to the left and a dirt access road ran off to the right. They took the dirt road, but almost immediately climbed over a metal rail gate to reach the adjacent meadow, in which they had noticed sheep grazing earlier in the day.

"This way," said Crockett, pointing across the meadow toward the river. "It's about half a mile to the Daewoo...which I'm hoping is still there."

They ran, but not all out, not wanting to trip over stones or sleeping sheep in the dark. However, they encountered neither, and the going was slightly downhill and easy. Surmounting another fence, they found themselves on a dirt path that looked like it had been made by a tractor or all-terrain vehicle. The path ran parallel to the River Boyne, branching in two directions as they came upon a farm.

"Farms usually mean dogs," said Crockett.

They took the right branch, away from the buildings, covering the last hundred feet to the river. Their hearts pounded, partly from the exertion, partly from the knowledge that they had certainly been missed and that a search for them was probably underway. At this point, it was reasonable to assume that no one suspected them of any subterfuge. However, the sooner they were in the Daewoo, the better.

The last stretch near the river was riddled with ATV tracks. Just feet from the bank, they stopped to consider their next move. As they did, Ricky pointed to flashing lights ahead.

"That looks like the place the bus picked us up near the bridge," she said.

"The lights might not be for us," said Crockett. "They might be trying to keep people from coming across the bridge from the Visitors Centre."

"So how do we get across?"

Crockett took a step closer to the Boyne. "Do you know how to swim?"

"Are you crazy?"

"It's been the subject of some discussion. But that doesn't answer the question."

"Yes, but—"

"Give me your pouch."

Ricky surrendered it.

"I'm going to try and keep these above the water," said

Crockett, holding both in one hand. "Just follow me. Doesn't seem to be moving too fast. Can't be more than about fifty feet to the other side."

He waded in, keeping the arm carrying the pouches extended above him. After a few steps, he started paddling. "Whoa. Okay, there's a bit of a current."

Ricky followed, using a combination of strokes she had not tried in a dozen years. A minute later, they sat on the far bank, realizing almost instantly that it was not the far bank, but rather a narrow island only a few meters across. However, the remaining fork in the river was quite narrow, and moments later, they splashed ashore, dripping.

Crockett pointed. "Through the woods and we should be close to the Visitors Centre. Parking lot's just the other side."

The going was tougher here, the vegetation thicker, keeping them completely concealed from the Garda. Reasoning that two soaking wet individuals might attract the attention of any stragglers, they bypassed the Centre in favor of an unpaved, overflow parking area to the south and finally arrived at the lot where Crockett had parked the Daewoo. Only a few cars remained, most probably belonging to members of the tour group Ricky and Crockett had fled.

The Daewoo started like a champ.

"I wonder how much it would cost to bring this baby back to Chicago with me," said Crockett with a self-satisfied smile.

"Ireland will probably pay you to take it with you."

"Hey, you made a joke," said Crockett, pulling out onto Staleen Road. "I may have to write that down. I think it's your first!"

"Shit!"

"Yeah, it was shit, but it was still a joke."

"No," said Ricky, alarmed, "the gun. I think I must have lost it in the river."

"Well, that's not funny," said Crockett. "But if you don't mind, we won't go back and look for it tonight."

"So what *are* we going to do?"

"We've been over that," said Crockett. "We've got to go after the eternal bitch."

"And kill her? You're freaking out of your mind."

Crockett nodded, spoke in a whisper. "Right."

"Just put me on a plane back to Chicago."

"Right. Then you'll hole up in your Fortress of Efficiency. You might even get a few hours of me-time before Cessair's goons break down the door."

"Then I'll go somewhere else."

"Yeah. Somewhere Cessair doesn't have people."

"Damn you!" Ricky rode quietly for a few minutes. "If you're so fucking smart, have you come up with some sort of plan?"

"That's where it gets a little fuzzy," said Crockett. "But I suppose the first thing we've got to do then is find someone who can read that scroll."

CHAPTER 36

Crockett checked the rearview mirror relentlessly during their trip back to Dublin. Once in the city, he randomly cut down side streets, doubled back, sat waiting in side lots, until he finally concluded that they had probably not been followed.

"I'm a little surprised," confessed Crockett.

"I'm freezing," said Ricky, hugging herself to try and conserve body heat.

"Yeah, we'll have to pick up a change of clothes real quick. But like I said, I'm surprised. I thought Cessair might have stationed one of her thugs in the parking lot, just in case we came back to the car."

"Cops must have spooked her," said Ricky.

"Yeah, that must be it," said Crockett, but Ricky noticed he began to fidget as he drove. "Nope. That's not it. That was easy. Way too easy."

"Relax. If somebody had followed us, with all the detours you took, we'd know. Or we would have lost them. Now find a store that's still open."

Crockett pulled to the side of the street, got out of the car.

"What?" asked Ricky, following his lead.

"I was just thinking," said Crockett. "What if Cessair had one of her human bricks put an electronic bug on our car? That would explain why we haven't seen any sign of pursuit."

Ricky looked at the Daewoo, which simply sat there in all its innocent yellowness. "How would she even know which car is ours?"

"She's Cessair," said Crockett, his eyes traveling back and forth along the length of the vehicle. "She's got people and connections. Eliminate the rentals. Check registrations. Or maybe she just figured it was the biggest pile of junk in the lot."

"So how will we know?"

Crockett knelt and bent beneath the right front fender. "Poke around underneath. Check for anything that moves or doesn't seem to belong there."

She used the light from her phone, expecting the task to be like looking for a needle in a haystack. However, she found the needle almost immediately, retrieving a round, black object a bit smaller than a hockey puck.

"This is it," said Crockett, taking it from her. "Come on."

They found a parked car and attached the device beneath the rear bumper.

"All right, now we've got to disappear," said Crockett.

"Now we've got to get out of these wet clothes!" Ricky's teeth chattered.

Crockett took another circuitous route to a different part of the city where, unable to find any clothing stores that had not closed for the night, they looked for a coin-operated laundry. On their sixth try, they found one that was still open. Having no time to wash the clothing before closing, they took turns standing in the shop's bathroom, handing out clothes to be dried, washing up in the sink as effectively as possible.

"We'll have to find a place to keep our heads down for a few days," said Crockett as they returned to the Daewoo. "Doesn't help that this car is about as inconspicuous as if it had been set on fire."

"*You* were the one who picked out the yellow car."

"And it's still running. Now maybe *you* can contribute something useful."

"More useful than saving our asses by spotting the creep bus driver?"

"All right, I'll give you that," said Crockett. "What I was thinking is that this is your turf! Your backyard! Your hood!"

"Shit."

"You must know some place we can go,"

"I haven't lived here for seventeen years," retorted Ricky.

"No friends?"

Ricky frowned. "My friends were nine at the time. I have no idea where any of them would be living now."

"Aunts? Uncles? Grandparents?"

"No good. Cessair will almost certainly be checking out anyone related to me. But..." An idea flashed into her mind, and she began to offer him directions.

"Just where is it we're going?" asked Crockett.

"My grandmother's."

Crockett shook his head. "Whoa! Didn't you just—"

"Cessair won't be watching this one," said Ricky. "She's kind of a secret."

Crockett raised an eyebrow. "A secret grandmother? That's a new one."

"Grandma Neve was Grandma Amelia's lover," she said.

"Didn't see that one coming."

"Neither did my mother. I was only a year old when my grandfather died, and I guess Amelia and Neve started doing things

317

together."

"Things."

"Asshole. Socially, at first. Spending time together. I suppose it grew out of that. Nobody ever talked about it, really. I just had two grandmothers on my mom's side. They never even moved in together. But sometimes Sasha and I would go to Grandma Neve's to spend the day or if mom got called in to work. As far as we were concerned, she was family."

"But there's no record?"

Ricky shook her head. "Don't see how there could be. Haven't seen or heard from her in the seventeen years since we moved." This admission brought a pang of guilt.

"Think she'll help you out?"

"She's my grandmother."

Crockett smiled. "Sort of. And you're not nine anymore. She may not even recognize you. Plus, you've got baggage: me."

"She'll help us," said Ricky resolutely.

They left the lively sections of Dublin, well-worn by the hooves of tourists, and wound their way to a dingier area of storefronts. Ricky squinted uncertainly at the darkened buildings.

"Turn around," she said after several minutes. "We must have passed it."

"Maybe it's on a different street," suggested Crockett.

"This is the street," Ricky said resolutely. "I just missed it. It's been seventeen years."

Crockett turned the car around. "What sort of business are we looking for?"

"It's called Anu's Closet. Jewelry. Handbags. Silk scarves that Grandma Neve dyed herself."

Crockett nodded. "Why Anu?"

"Celtic goddess of the moon, fertility, and prosperity,"

explained Ricky. "I think Neve just thought it sounded cool. Should be on the left side."

Crockett drove slowly and they both looked. Ricky suddenly pointed to a storefront. "I'd swear it's this building. See how every other brick sticks out about four inches near the top of the building? When I was a kid, I always wondered why the builders did that. And there was a grocer next door with big blue and yellow awnings. See?"

"But that's not Anu's Closet," said Crockett, pointing. The sign in the storefront window read GREGOR'S LIQUOR & WHISKEY.

Ricky's spirits sank. "Oh no. Maybe she retired or..." Her voice trailed off.

"It's late," Crockett said. "Even if her store was still here, it wouldn't be open at this hour."

"No," agreed Ricky, but then she brightened a bit. "But Grandma Neve lived in the apartment above the store. Maybe she still lives there."

They parked, exited, stood in front of Gregor's. The entrance to the shop was through a door at the approximate center of the building. Ricky led Crockett to a second door at the far left edge of the building. "Through here are stairs leading up to the apartment."

Crockett rattled the knob. "Locked."

"Neve had a hiding place for the key," said Ricky. "If it's still there, that means Grandma Neve still lives upstairs."

"Or that the new tenants liked your Grandmother's security system."

Ricky stepped up onto the stoop and swung open a glass panel on a hanging electric carriage lamp next to the door. Reaching inside, she found the key resting on the bottom, out of sight unless one was seven feet tall. She inserted it in the lock, heard the satisfying click, replaced the key, and then led Crockett up the darkened stairway.

At the top, Ricky knocked and then waited. After about thirty seconds, she knocked again.

"Maybe she's asleep," offered Crockett, but then they heard movement behind the door, followed by a voice.

"Who is it? How did you get in?"

Ricky spoke tentatively. "It's Ricky, Grandma Neve."

After a pause. "Who? How did you get in? What do you want?"

"It's Ricky," she repeated. "Rose Crowe's daughter. One of the twins."

This time the pause was longer, but then they heard a metallic click, and the door opened as far as it could before being stopped by a security chain. The wary face of a white-haired woman in her seventies peered through the opening at them.

"What do you want? How did you get in?"

"I'm Ricky. I was nine the last time I saw you. That was before my mother, my sister Saoirse, and I left for Chicago."

The old woman seemed to be trying to process this information. "But... the door was locked."

Something was wrong. Neve seemed more confused than Ricky had expected. Perhaps it was the late hour, the passage of so many years. Or the fact that Ricky's hair was now black and the left side of her face looked more zombie than human. "I knew you kept the key in the lantern. Saoirse and I visited here a lot when we were younger."

Neve seemed unconvinced.

"You had a cat named Plato."

"He's dead," said Neve. "But I have another."

"That's good. Grandma Neve, can we come in?"

The old woman thought about it for a long time. "Saoirse and…"

"Ricky," said Ricky, patting her own chest. "I'm Ricky."

"Limerick," said Neve. "Little Limerick and Saoirse." The door closed, and they heard the sound of Neve fumbling with the chain. Then it reopened, Neve peeking around its edge as it swung wide.

Ricky and Crockett stepped across the threshold. As Neve moved out from behind the door, Ricky embraced her. Neve slowly raised her arms to deliver a weak pat upon Ricky's back. This was not the woman Ricky remembered. Neve had always been strong and loud and full of humor. Something was wrong.

"Grandma Neve, are you all right?"

Neve pulled away and shut the door behind them, latching it. "I'm tired. A lot. And you're little Limerick. But this isn't Saoirse."

"I'm Mason Crockett, ma'am," said Crockett, extending his hand, though Neve made no move to take it.

"You're taller," said Neve, turning back to Ricky. "And your hair. But you're still little Limerick. What happened to your face?"

Ricky's right hand went to the bandage over her eye. "Just… just a little bad luck. Neve, your shop. You closed it?"

"You've been gone for such a long time," said Neve, as if she had not heard the question.

"Rose took us to Chicago. We were there for years. But now I'm back and I need a place to stay tonight."

Somehow, this registered with Neve. "I have a spare room. It's late. Are you hungry? You always loved toasted brown bread with raisins."

Ricky brightened, for this was true, and the mention of it seemed to bring out a bit of the Neve she remembered. And as a matter of fact, she realized that she was starving.

"I would love some brown bread, Grandma." As Neve turned

toward her small kitchen, Crockett silently indicated to Ricky that he was starving as well. "And some for Mason, too, please." They followed Neve down the short hallway and into the kitchen, noticing a general cluttered dinginess. Opened boxes sat here and there as if movers had brought them into rooms, unpacked half of their contents, and then simply left. A bookshelf and rocking chair seemed out of place in the kitchen alongside the small dining table, and there was scarcely room to move around. Clean dishes and unopened cans and boxes of food sat out on table and countertops rather than being tucked away into a cabinet. As Neve puttered, Ricky returned to her earlier question.

"Grandma Neve, why did you close Anu's Closet?"

A dark, tortoise-shell cat gazed down at her from atop the refrigerator.

This time, Neve registered the question. "I had to close it when I went to hospital," she said. "It was a bad time. Maybe someday, again."

Crockett mouthed a guess to Ricky. *Stroke?*

"But I still make scarves," added Neve.

Ricky noticed, through the doorway, several scarves hanging from a length of clothesline. "They're beautiful." And they were. "Grandma Neve, are you always alone here?"

"Alone?"

"Is there anyone who helps you?"

"Tim drops off groceries."

"Tim?"

Neve chuckled. "You know Tim."

It seemed that she did remember the name, a nephew, she thought, although she could not recall ever having met him.

Neve brought the toasted bread on tiny plates. It was as good as Ricky remembered. Crockett, devouring four slices, showered

Neve with praise.

"You came back," said Neve as they ate.

"I'm sorry I didn't write you, Grandma," said Ricky. "I had—I had some bad times."

"Is Saoirse coming?"

Ricky tried to hide the tightness in her voice. "Saoirse didn't come with us, Grandma. Just me."

"And the young man," said Neve.

"Mason," Crockett said, realizing that she had probably forgotten his name. He held up a last small bite of brown bread. "This is delicious."

"It's late, isn't it? And the door was locked. And it's been so many years." Neve's eyes met Ricky's. "Are you in trouble?"

"We have important business," said Ricky.

Neve stepped closer, leaned in. "Are you pregnant?"

Crockett nearly choked on his bread.

"It's just business," said Ricky, unamused.

Neve showed them to the small spare room, which contained a standard-sized bed, a dresser, a night table with a bedside lamp that was not, despite its garish, multi-color shade, so completely ugly, as much as its odd proportions failed to please the eye. Encircling the bed was an array of boxes that looked to be partially unpacked, a drying rack covered with half a dozen colorful scarves, stacks of dusty books and an exercise bicycle. The clutter required that they climb over objects to reach the bed.

"Will you be here in the morning?" asked Neve.

"Of course," said Ricky, turning to her grandmother, who stood behind them.

"Good," said Neve. "I was hoping this wouldn't turn out to only be a dream."

Ricky embraced Neve. "Grandma, this is no dream. This is the best I've felt in the past seventeen years."

Neve patted Ricky's forearms as she released her. "Maybe tomorrow."

"What about tomorrow?"

"Maybe tomorrow I'll feel well enough to open the shop again," said Neve, and Ricky noticed a tear slide from the corner of her grandmother's left eye.

As Neve turned and tottered off, presumably back to her own bed, Crockett jingled the Daewoo's keys in the air and informed Ricky that he was going to find a more discreet parking spot before settling in for the night.

"Good idea," said Ricky. "Then when you get back, you can settle yourself onto the floor."

"Look around. There is no floor. That mattress appears big enough for two. We're both adults and I'm sure you can be expected to behave accordingly."

"Me?"

"I'm already drawing an imaginary boundary line down the middle of the mattress in my mind. If you can't trust yourself to do the same, maybe *you* should sleep elsewhere."

Ricky flipped him off. "Fine."

Dividing line or not, when Crockett returned, they both fell asleep almost instantly.

CHAPTER 37

The following day, Crockett rose, meandered down the hall, washed his face in the sink, returned, and noticed that the bed was empty. Ricky returned ten minutes later, carrying a bag.

"I needed to pound on something," she told him.

"Like pound with a hammer?"

"Like with my fists," said Ricky.

Crockett nodded dubiously. "Did you find something?"

"I found a heavy rug over a clothesline out back. But... I only took a few swings. I feel beat. Tried to go for a run—felt like crap and walked most of it. There's a second-hand shop about half a mile away. Here."

She tossed him a pair of jeans and a faded rugby jersey. Then she turned with the rest of the items in her bag and headed off to the bathroom.

When she returned, she still looked ragged. Crockett felt her forehead. "I think you've got a fever. Maybe an infection from..." He waved a finger vaguely, unable to bring himself to say "the eye."

"And I've got a headache."

"I think we need to find a doctor. Get some antibiotics into you."

"Fuck it. I'll just crawl back into bed."

Crockett watched her crawl beneath the covers, then took the walk down the hall, cleaned up, dressed in the new acquisitions, whose sizes Ricky had estimated well enough. He was also glad to see that Ricky had left a new toothbrush for him. When he returned to the room, Ricky was curled under the blankets, changing position every time it looked like she might have gotten comfortable.

Crockett retraced his steps to the bathroom and opened the medicine cabinet. Neve had quite the candy store. Toward the front were aspirin and a blood thinner that suggested he had been right about Neve having a stroke. He found a couple over-the-counter cold remedies, as well as a prescription antihistamine and a couple of medications with baffling names, whose purpose he could not determine. There were also six different plastic containers of antibiotics of various types, which looked as if Neve had begun taking them and then forgot to finish the entire 7-to-10-day course, as there were a few pills remaining in each. None was newer than six months old, and two were dated a decade earlier, expired and certainly lacking potency. In two separate bottles, he eventually found six of one type, both less than eighteen months old. "Take one each morning with food for ten days." He hoped it would be enough to help Ricky get on top of the infection.

Returning to the bedroom with the antibiotic, an aspirin, and a cup of water, he forced Ricky to sit up and take the medicine. She swallowed, cursed him weakly and then pulled herself back beneath the covers.

"All right then," he said quietly. "We probably won't kill Cessair today." He doubted she heard.

Settling onto one of the unpacked boxes, he tried to pull his thoughts together. They had the scroll. He was sure Cessair would have people watching all the airports. Probably the ferries and cruise ships, too. As a result, they weren't going anywhere any time soon and would probably have to find someone in Ireland who could interpret the scroll. Maybe at one of the universities.

They needed Internet access, but they would have to be careful how they used it. They certainly did not want to reveal information that could lead Cessair to them. However, there might be others out there looking for the ultimate salvation—or the ultimate weapon. Perhaps individuals even worse than Cessair, if that were possible.

Of course, this assumed that the scroll was the real deal. He considered the possibility that Cessair had somehow tricked Leo. But Leo had been a pretty level-headed guy. Before Cessair messed him up, anyway.

If there was any chance that the scroll's powers were real, they had to figure out how to harness them. And that meant finding a translator—which would not be easy. By this point, Crockett was just paranoid enough to believe that Alchemy had tapped the phones of every professor of Egyptology in Europe. To get started, he would need to pick up a laptop, set up a ghost account. He wondered if Neve had Wifi.

He found her in the kitchen, puttering together a simple breakfast for them. She paused to direct him to a desktop computer tucked into the corner of a small room containing a reddish leather armchair, a three-foot-tall snake plant that occupied the opposite corner like an iridescent Danny DeVito, an inconveniently placed clothesline draped with more scarves, and a single, octagonal window too high to offer a view of anything except sky. While not cutting edge, he decided it would meet their needs. "Tim brought this," explained Neve. "I sometimes like to see the cute pictures and videos of Corgis."

"Tim knew what he was doing," said Crockett after examining the system. "Neve, you've got a faster Internet connection than I do back home."

Neve patted her palms together soundlessly. "Did you say Saoirse would be arriving later today?"

"Not today," said Crockett gently. "But is it okay if Ricky and I stick around for a while?"

Neve adopted a worried expression. "You're in trouble, aren't you?"

"Maybe a little."

"You can stay right here," said Neve. "You'll be safe here." And for a moment, Crockett believed it. Then Neve added, "And so will Saoirse. When did you say she will be here?"

He spent several hours conducting research, checking the directories of libraries and universities for faculty who might have a shot at translating the scroll. He found few leads and, frustrated, eventually went out on foot to find a cheap, pay-as-you-go cell phone. When he returned, Ricky was awake and admitted to feeling a little better. He reported his scant progress and tossed her one of the new phones.

"Can never be too careful," said Crockett. "They could have slipped a tracer or bug or something in our phones when they had them in Germany."

"Why would they bother to do that?" asked Ricky. "They never expected us to leave. As far as they were concerned, we were dead."

"Humor my paranoia," said Crockett. "Who knows? Maybe they figured out the phones came from Amet's uncle and there's some way calls from them can be tracked. And when I'm looking for translators, I'd rather call than leave an email trail. We don't want some clever hacker of Cessair's to trace my conversations back to your grandmother. And by the way, when we phone each other, we need a code word."

Ricky looked at him, still groggy, and now puzzled. "A code word?"

"I was thinking about that this morning," said Crockett. "It bothered me that you went out by yourself. What if you'd been spotted? Or worse, picked up by Cessair's thugs?"

"You really think they're looking for joggers in thrift shops?"

"The point is," continued Crockett, "we might have to go out by ourselves occasionally. So, what if one of us gets caught and the other doesn't know it? If I texted you, how would I know it was *you* texting me back, or one of *them* trying to lure me into a trap?"

"Couldn't you just call me?"

"They might have a gun to your head."

She smirked. "Now who's paranoid?"

"Under the present circumstances, paranoia may keep us alive."

Ricky considered the practicality of the matter. "What sort of code word did you have in mind?"

Crockett thought for a moment. "How about 'Daewoo'?"

"You really have a thing for that car. I think you need professional help. Besides, I can't even spell that."

"All right, how about 'chicken fried steak'?"

"How's that work?" asked Ricky.

"I text 'How are you?' You text back 'Chicken fried steak,' and I know it's you."

"That doesn't make any sense."

"It doesn't have to make sense," said Crockett. "It just has to be something that no one else would think to use."

"All right, 'chicken fried steak' it is," she said, shaking her head ruefully. "It sounds awful."

Crocket licked his lips. "Darlin', you've got a lot to learn about food."

Her temperature was still slightly elevated and she had little appetite. Nonetheless, they walked to a gloomy pub for dinner, found something greasy to eat, and then slouched back to Neve's. Ricky crawled back into bed while Crockett resumed his search of Irish schools, their faculty and the courses in Egyptian history or language.

The process was slow and the pickings slim.

"I suppose I shouldn't be surprised that Ireland doesn't appear to be the hub of the Egyptology universe," said Crockett.

He continued to plug away, noting one potential lead: The library at Trinity College in Dublin contained an impressive collection of papyri that included portions of the Egyptian Book of the Dead. Reasoning that they must have someone on staff who could do translations, he switched off the computer and called it a night.

Ricky spent most of the following day in bed while Crockett was out at Trinity. Though she slept fitfully, in the moments of leaden, shivering wakefulness in between, she obsessed over the misgivings of their mission. When they had been on the move, everything had seemed to make sense. Now, tucked away out of the line of fire, with sufficient time to think about their next step rather than the barest of time to run, confronting such vast and powerful evil seemed ludicrous. Two people against Alchemy, a well-financed cult whose poison might have seeped into even the most remote and unexpected recesses of the world. Realistically, what were their chances?

On the morning of their third day, Ricky got out of bed and was relieved, and even modestly surprised, when her legs didn't buckle beneath her. She observed, almost immediately, her own pungent

Black Hole of Calcutta aroma, and the acumen to be offended by this observation along with the modest physical act of standing convinced her that she was getting better. Rustling clean underthings and a black WE BANJO 3 tank top, she headed for the bathroom.

Emerging scrubbed and renewed, she slipped on dark-brown pants and found Neve in the kitchen. "It's noon!" said the old woman, sounding more like the Neve Ricky remembered. Perhaps it helped to have people around. "Here, I've made you something. You must be feeling better."

"A bit," she said, reaching for what appeared to be a pastie, realizing how hungry she was. "Thank you."

"Your friend is in at that computer again," said Neve. "I don't use it very much. How's your eye? Can you take the patch off soon?"

It seemed to take more out of her today to think about the eye than it had a few days ago. The fact that she now cared about its absence seemed another indicator that she was getting better. "Not today."

Neve rose, exited the kitchen, and returned half a minute later with a stunning green scarf with blue, gold, and white highlights. "Well, maybe this will make you feel better." Although Ricky meekly protested, Neve deftly wrapped it like a pirate bandana, but in such a way that it plunged diagonally across her left eye, concealing the bandage. "There. Don't you look pretty?"

She tried to make the smile seem sincere. "Thank you. And you're right. I feel much better."

Neve smiled broadly. And suddenly, Ricky's smile was no longer forced. She *did* feel better. And she loved this woman, and after everything the world had dumped on Ricky, particularly in the past week, the fact that this love remained and was reciprocated was everything.

Neve leaned in, gave her a hug and a kiss on the bandana-covered forehead. "So, is Saoirse still sleeping?"

Ricky choked back a tear, wrapped her own arms around Neve. "Still sleeping," she said softly.

Finishing the pastie, she found Crockett hunched over the computer.

He swiveled to face her. "Look who's awake!"

"Yeah. Already did that routine with Neve."

A gesture toward the scarf. "New look."

She gave him the finger.

"Looks like someone's feeling 100%!"

"Fifty-one. Maybe. Sorry I've been so useless."

"It's all good. We're both still cheatin' death." He glanced back at the monitor. "Well, it's not *all* good. I went over to that Trinity College. They've got an impressive collection, but it's in Greek, not Egyptian. As far as I could tell, after poking around most of the afternoon—as thoroughly as I dared without drawing any attention to myself—there's no one at Trinity who could translate Archaic Egyptian."

"Well, that sucks." She went to rub her eyes, changed to just the right eye as her fingers encountered the fabric. "How long have we been here?"

"Three days."

"Cessair must think we've fallen off the map."

Crockett logged off Neve's computer and stood, stretching. "That's good. I'll bet not knowing what we're up to pisses her off."

"I'm definitely for anything that pisses her off."

Crockett smiled. "Then maybe we should just stay here. Your Grandma Neve's brown bread with raisins is a hell of a temptation."

This even got a wistful smile from Ricky. "I'm glad I got a chance to see her again before..." She let her gaze fall. "Before whatever happens next."

"Well, I wouldn't bet against us," said Crockett. "We've had a pretty good run of luck so far. There's an old gambler's saying..."

"I know. 'Don't bet against a streak.' You stole that from Peterson."

"And it's still working for him!"

Ricky frowned. "Here's even better advice: Don't gamble."

"We're already in the game. And everything we have is in the pot. Only one sensible thing to do."

"Run away as fast as we can?"

"Walk. To the nearest pub. I've been staring at that screen so long my eyes are buggy. I think I need a beer."

"A beer." She chastised herself for momentarily expecting a serious response.

"Several. I was going to try that little pub this afternoon. The sheep one."

"The Red Goat."

"That's it. Think you'll be up for a walk?"

"Really? You're asking *me* if I want a drink? Asshole."

"You can drink ginger ale," said Crockett wearily.

"Pass." She turned and headed for the bedroom.

"Really? You're going to make me drink alone in a strange city?"

"I'll bet you've drunk alone in lots of strange places."

Crockett sat staring after her for a few moments after she disappeared. "Well," he said to himself, "yeah."

It was after supper before he took the stroll several blocks to the Red Goat, a completely unremarkable pub with the exception of a menacing looking stuffed goat, painted red, mounted high behind the bar. Several patrons sat at intervals along the bar with a few others at tables, a slow night, for which Crockett was thankful.

He ordered a draft.

Two minutes later, he ordered another.

The bartender, a rough-faced older man wearing a wool vest and a homburg, squinted at Crockett as he pushed the second drink in front of him.

"No need to race, now," he said.

Crockett smiled, took a more relaxed sip. "Been a nut-punch kind of day." After a moment, he added, "Come to think of it, it's been a nut-punch kind of week."

"American?"

Crockett nodded, took another sip.

"Things can be hard when you're away from home," said the bartender, "but you'll find we Dubliners will lend a hand if need be. And if we can't lend a hand, we'll pour you a pint!"

Crockett smiled again. "Thanks. But unless you can read Egyptian, I don't know if there's much you can do." He stiffened for a moment as he realized his folly, wondering whether it had been wise to even mention this casually. Who knew where Cessair had ears? He endeavored to pass it off lightly and refreshed his smile. "Except keep the beer coming."

Unfortunately, the bartender seemed intrigued by this notion. "Egyptian, eh? Why you need that? Get a letter from your mummy?" He laughed at his own weak joke.

Crockett smiled nervously. "Just some old papers. Not a big deal."

But the bartender would not give it up. He called to one of the men at the table. "Hey, Roger! Don't you know some Egyptian woman? Claire has that jewelry from her."

"Roger only knows doxies!" said a middle-aged man at the

table, a statement that generated considerable laughter.

Jesus, they're shouting it across the bar now! "Really, I was just kidding arou—"

"I don't, now!" said Roger, a flush-faced man with a neatly trimmed white beard. "Neither the doxie nor the other."

"We're just coddin' ye," said the bartender.

"It's my wife," said Roger.

"Your wife knows doxies?" said Roger's friend, feigning shock. More laughter.

Crockett leaned toward the barkeep. "What's a doxie?"

"A hoor," replied the bartender with a wink. "Woman of loose morals."

Roger, clearly flustered, attempted to gain control of the moment. "My wife's yoga instructor gave her that thing…" He struggled for the word a moment. "The ankh. It's some sort of life symbol. She—my wife, Claire—she says the woman is some sort of mystic. Knows everything about ancient Greece and Egypt and Africa. Went to university in Cay-row."

Despite his apprehension at the public nature of the conversation, the mention of "Cay-row"—more likely a butchered pronunciation of "Cairo"—intrigued Crockett. If the yoga instructor had studied Egypt and had connections to a university in Cairo, perhaps she could discreetly put them in touch with someone skilled in ancient languages. This round-about method of contacting a translator might just keep them below Cessair's radar.

Roger gave him an approximate address, which turned out to be about six blocks away. Then Crockett bought a round for the lot before gliding out into the chill of the evening.

CHAPTER 38

Crockett and Ricky arrived at Síochána Yoga Studio just after 11 a.m. to find a dozen earnest and lean individuals of wildly diverse ages focused on the session in progress. Each performed the requisite stretches, poses, and meditations on his or her personal, pastel-colored mat. The building itself was an old storefront whose cream brick outside was laced with painted-on vines. The one large room had a polished wooden floor.

They waited patiently in chairs that had been set up near the front windows, and forty-five minutes later, when the session ended, they stepped forward to talk to the tall, thin, agreeable man who had been leading the group.

Yes, he was the owner of the studio.

No, there was no woman instructor.

Yes, he was sure. He would definitely know, being the owner.

Yes, he did know a woman named Claire. She usually attended a Wednesday session.

No, he had not given her an ankh.

No, he was not a mystic of some kind.

No, he had never been to Cairo.

Nor did he know anyone in Cairo.

Yes, he was absolutely certain that no woman taught classes at the studio. It was only him. Then he excused himself to prepare for the next session.

"So, I suppose trusting drunken Irishmen in a pub to offer reliable information seems, in hindsight, a bit foolish," said Crockett as they emerged onto the street.

"Telling an entire pub crowd that we're looking for an Egyptian language translator seems, in hindsight, a bit foolish, too," said Ricky, focused straight ahead as they walked back in the direction they had come.

"I don't think any of them will tell a soul," said Crockett.

Ricky grunted, kept moving.

"Hell, I don't know if any of them will even remember it. But you're right. I was careless. That's the type of thing that could get us killed. It won't happen again."

When she failed to reply, he decided to try and change the subject, see if he could lure her back into an agreeable conversation. "Y'know, those scarves your grandmother makes are amazing," he said, recalling the green beauty that Ricky had worn briefly before picking up a common black eye patch at the chemist's. "Maybe that nephew of hers could help her set up an online store and she could sell—"

Crockett realized, suddenly, that Ricky had stopped walking several moments earlier and stood in front of an eccentric little storefront, staring at the building. Not only was it the only single-story building on the block, its simple brick front had been painted purple. A cornucopia of plants in mismatched pots sat on the uneven, dirty sidewalk in front, and hanging vines and herbs were visible through the large, rectangular window to the left of the entrance. A variety of crystals also dangled against the inside of the window from threads and slim chains. Above the door, an iron arm protruded, from which hung a neat, hand-painted sign:

MADAME LUJA
Spiritual Guidance
Readings

Greek letters and Egyptian hieroglyphs formed a border around the large front window.

Ricky pointed to the hieroglyphs. "Coincidence?"

Crockett, who had backtracked and now stood beside her, said, "Probably. Maybe. What are you thinking?"

"I'm thinking it's really strange that Claire's husband—"

"Roger."

"Roger, thinks Claire's yoga instructor is a woman from Cairo. What are you thinking?"

Crockett squinted through the large front window. "That Claire is telling Roger she's going to yoga classes, but instead, she's got something going on with a street vendor who sells cheap jewelry?"

Ricky shot him the Not In The Mood glance, and so he smiled and started again. "Or… that Claire stops by Madame Luja's shop every now and then after yoga class, and that's where she gets the ankh. Roger, a half-listener like most husbands, mashes the details." He paused, taking in the startlingly purple front of the building. "Now, in the sober light of day, it really doesn't sound like a very promising plan, does it? I mean, even if this Madame Luja did attend Cairo University, what are the chances that she is going to know anyone in Egyptian studies? I mean, I graduated from UI Chicago and can't even remember the name of my English professor."

He was about to ask if they were going in, but Ricky was already up the single concrete step and pushing open the door of the shop. Crockett noticed a sign in the window of the door that read PLEASE ENTER. As they did, a bell above the jamb chimed playfully.

Inside, they were greeted by the scents of teas and incense. A small, round, wooden table, around which rested five mismatched chairs, sat in the center of the room. A fat, partially consumed but currently unlit candle reposed at the table's approximate center. A heavy, black curtain was bunched along one side of the front window, presumably for darkening the room during the day if ceremony required. Odd charms and symbols hung by threads or slim chains from the ceiling—except in the area of the table, where the tongue-and-groove boards above were bare, even of paint. A natty blue sofa rested against the right-hand wall, above which were shelves, bulging with tattered books. stretching to the ceiling. Brass figurines, clay pots, walking sticks, oil lamps and many items that were difficult for Ricky and Crockett to describe rested against the left-hand wall, some on makeshift shelves. The back wall was completely consumed by a mural of a deep blue sky across which stars were scattered, except in the lower right corner where the sun—which looked to be a glowing, golden cat's eye—was rising. Or setting. The only other item on this wall was a Hello Kitty calendar. A doorway on the left, over which strands of beads hung, led, perhaps, to Madame Luja's office or living quarters.

"To tell the truth," said Crockett, his eyes still traveling the room, "after I saw that the outside was painted purple and belonged to a palm reader, it's pretty much what I expected."

"Shut up!" Ricky whispered aggressively. "Don't put her on the defensive! She may know someone."

"Yeah...someone who can score us some LSD," grunted

Crockett. "I can see what's going to happen here. We'll pay fifty bucks to some old crone to learn that we'll meet a tall, mysterious stranger descended from Egyptian royalty who will solve all our problems."

"Shut up," Ricky repeated, glaring, gesturing for Crockett to lower his voice. "It doesn't hurt to ask a few questions."

Crockett rubbed his eyes with his fingertips. "I'm not thinking straight. It's the—the stress of all this. Some drunk in a bar mentions Cairo and I get as excited as if I just bought a 'Rolex' for ten bucks from a guy in an alley. We're wasting our time."

The beads rattled and a woman glided into the room. "I am Madame Luja. You are welcome here." Madame Luja stood almost six feet tall, was quite thin with high cheekbones and uniformly unblemished mahogany skin. She wore wrinkled, khaki pants, a light-blue denim shirt, and a gray, knitted shawl wrapped across her shoulders. What surprised both Ricky and Crockett was Madame Luja's youth. She appeared to be no more than perhaps twenty-five.

Ricky twisted her gaze from Madame Luja to Crockett and back again, finally saying. "Hi. We, uh, don't want a reading."

"No," said Madame Luja, gesturing toward the table. "Sit."

"We don't want to take up too much of your time," said Ricky, "but we were wondering if you could help us find someone who can translate something."

"What is it?" asked Madame Luja.

Ricky motioned to Crockett, who set a small, recently purchased yellow sports bag on the table. Ricky unzipped this and brought out the two dry, leathery satchels. Setting one aside, she opened the other and produced a scroll.

"It's very old," said Ricky, stating the obvious, setting it gently on the table. "We've spent the last couple of days trying to find someone who might be able to read this. We heard you might have gone to school in Cairo—"

"Yes. Alexandria University."

"Right. If you wouldn't mind taking a look at this, we were hoping you might be able to help us."

Madame Luja slowly, carefully unrolled the scroll. She looked at it for a long time. Then, without a word, she rose from the table and disappeared through the beaded doorway.

Crockett whispered, "Why do I get the feeling that she just went back there to call Cessair?"

"Don't be ridiculous," said Ricky, who almost immediately felt far less certain of herself. "She would have taken the scroll with, her, wouldn't she?"

A very long minute passed.

When Madame Luja emerged, she was holding a tall cup filled with steaming tea and carried a yellow legal pad in her other hand. She sat at the table and scratched a few words onto the pad. Another silent minute passed as she wrote. Then a third.

"Did you think of someone?" asked Ricky after watching Madame Luja jot away a fourth minute.

Madame Luja looked up. "I'm sorry?"

"Aren't you writing down names and contact information?" asked Ricky.

Madame Luja regarded Ricky curiously. "Names?"

"You said you attended Alexandria," said Ricky. "I wondered whether you were familiar with anyone who might know how to translate the old Egyptian."

"Yes," said Madame Luja. "It may take awhile, but I think I can translate it. If you want to wait, there's tea in the back."

CHAPTER 39

Madame Luja finished the translation ("To the best of my ability.") three hours later, consulting half a dozen obscure and ancient-looking books from her "library" in the process and pausing occasionally to be social. "I'm sorry to take so long," she apologized. "It's just that I don't have much opportunity to work with language from this period. It's been years."

Crockett and Ricky had taken turns dozing on the sofa. Finally, Luja stood, disappeared into the back room, re-emerged with a freshened cup of tea. By Ricky's estimation, she had consumed gallons during the translation. She sat down, invited the other two to the table, tapped the pouch containing the scroll she had recently finished examining and said, "This is bad shit."

Madame Luja knew her bad shit. She had told them, during breaks to replenish her tea, a few things about herself, including the fact that her real name was Luja Issa, that she was twenty-four, and that her journey across the waters of formal academics had ended at age nineteen when she found herself mired in the bottom sludge of meth addiction.

Really bad shit.

A friend had helped her through withdrawal and recovery,

using an unorthodox recipe of meditation, calming teas, and New Age mysticism that had literally saved Luja's life. Being a voracious reader, top-one-percent brilliant and curious, Luja had begun to consume everything she could find on mysticism and alternative religion, hoping to pull back the curtain to determine what miracles, if any, had contributed to her salvation, and whether these truths were shared by other belief systems. She studied symbols, dead languages, history: a virtual sponge with nearly unlimited capacity. If Dr. Robert Oppenheimer had decided to devote his life to mysticism instead of creating the atomic bomb, he would have been Luja. Initially, she had believed that, behind all magic, if one pulled back enough layers and examined the inevitable cause and effect relationships, that one would find science. In recent years, she had become less certain of this.

"There is so much energy in Egypt," she told them. "It radiates to us through the millennia from the ancients. In order to fully study it, I had to, of course, study the language."

Crockett shook his head. Here was one of the most brilliant minds he had ever encountered, and instead of a house with an Olympic-sized pool and an 80-inch flat-panel TV, she lived in a tiny shop in a grimy neighborhood on a scruffy backstreet of Dublin. Then he laughed at himself. What, after all, was so bad about a life that allowed one to pursue one's passion, surrounded by one's favorite books and with a ready cup of warm tea? Wealth, he supposed, was relative. For Luja, this might be Nirvana, and a pool-and-limousine life, with all its accompanying obligations and moral compromises, would be hell.

"Before we begin to talk about what the scrolls say," said Luja, "I have a question. What will you do with them?"

In the preceding hours, they had been the recipients of such candor from Luja, regarding her own hells and triumphs, that they

343

did not hesitate. They told her the story, starting with Zackenberg.

"If not for Cessair, we would destroy the scrolls right now," said Crockett.

"But she needs to answer for what she did to my sister," said Ricky.

Luja met Ricky's gaze. "And for what she did to you."

"And what Cessair still plans to do is far worse," added Crockett. "If we're right about the scroll, then it's is the only way to stop her."

"And then you will destroy it?" asked Luja.

Ricky was not sure what to say. She wondered whether Luja, who had made the study of myth and magic a kind of religion of her own, would consider the destruction of the mystical artifact a kind of sin in itself and would resist the idea.

However, she could see no point in lying.

"Yes."

Luja nodded. "Good." Then she turned her attention to the notepad. "On these next pages, I have a general translation in English. The language used in the recitation of the ritual is irrelevant."

Ricky and Crockett nodded.

She carefully removed the second scroll from its pouch, then did the same with the first, setting it just to the side. "These are the symbols for life and death," said Luja, pointing at the second scroll and then at her sketches on the legal pad. She continued this process of pointing out an item on the scroll and then explaining it on the legal pad. "Beneath those is a warning. In essence, it says that if you choose to walk in the footsteps of the gods, don't stumble."

Ricky frowned. "Don't stumble?"

"Perhaps it means that you may be crushed by the feet of those many behind you also hungering for such power," suggested Luja. "Or, more likely, ground into the dust by the heel of a disapproving deity. Following this warning are the two rituals, the first for everlasting life, the second, death. Each ritual is divided into five parts corresponding to the five ancient elements."

"Wait," said Crockett, "I'm only familiar with four. Earth, air, fire, and water."

"The fifth does not appear in the records of all cultures," said Luja. "It went by many names. Aristotle called it aether. In Hinduism, it is akash. It is, essentially, a term used to describe that which is beyond the material world."

Crockett nodded. "Like magic."

"Magic seems an insufficient term," replied Luja. "Spirit. The energy of the soul. Insight. Healing powers. Forces that we can neither see nor understand. By utilizing the first four tangible elements, the ritual stimulates a *fifth* element reaction."

"Okay. How does it work?" asked Crockett.

"First is the pricking of the clay. On a clay tablet, a person's mark is made. It could be a name, a thumb print, a blood spot. Then the priest or leader makes a mark next to it or a scratch over it."

"Why clay?" asked Crockett.

"I misspoke," said Luja. "It would not have to be clay. The scroll says it must be made *'of the earth'*. We spring from the earth, we return to the earth. Life, death. Thousands of years ago, clay tablets were commonly used for purposes of keeping records. But the marks could be made on stone, wood, paper, even traced in the dirt."

Ricky was about to question Luja's inclusion of paper, but realized, it was really simply pressed wood pulp, *of the earth*.

"The second part is the mixing of the elixir. This is the liquid or *water* element of the ritual. I've listed the recipe. It's an interesting little chemistry experiment."

"Do people pass around a cup, like communion?" asked Crockett?

Luja studied her notes for a moment. "Each person must consume some of the elixir."

"So you could drink a bit?" pressed Crockett.

"I suppose any sort of consumption would work," said Luja thoughtfully. "Injection, inhalation as a mist, absorption through open wounds or mucous membranes. Perhaps even absorbed through the skin."

"My God."

"This is followed by the incantation," said Luja. "Spoken words in this case are synonymous with the *wind*. The leader faces the east—the rising sun signifies life—and recites a simple line: *Let our lives follow the light*."

"That's it?" asked Crockett.

"Yes," said Luja. "The sun, represented by facing east, is the fourth element—fire."

"How can something so…voodoo-crazy be so simple?" asked Ricky.

Luja smiled. "How simple is breathing, yet, what a miracle." Then she continued. "You can see that the next section is clearly separated from the first," noted Luja. "The ritual is almost exactly the same. Again, there is the preparation of the clay or stone—this time presumably a tablet bearing the name or names of one's enemies. Then the elixir, made from a much different recipe. The same incantation finishes the spell," said Luja. "Except this time, the leader faces west—the setting sun. Symbolic of death."

"Wait," said Crockett. "After the second ritual, the people whose marks or names are on the tablet just die?"

"Yes," said Luja.

"Jesus!" exclaimed Crockett. "If this thing is legit, it's the most dangerous weapon in the world! Imagine some psycho-nutjob tyrant getting hold of this, finding a way to mix it into the drinking water of an entire city!"

"Or aerosolizing it," suggested Luja. "Or seeding it into rain clouds. The world at the time of the scroll's creation was a much different place. While great numbers of people could be killed, the ancient Egyptians did not have the sort of modern technology and delivery systems that could expose millions of people."

"And only the people on your list would die, leaving behind the faithful who are devoted to you and the cause," said Crockett. "Except how do you get all your enemies to face west at the same time?"

"For the people in the ritual, the direction they face is irrelevant," said Luja. "Only the leader must face the east or west in order for the fifth element to be activated."

"But what about Cessair?" asked Ricky. "She's immortal. Will the death ritual have any effect on her?"

"Yes," said Luja. "If her mark is on the tablet, the death ritual will kill her as well. But not immediately. The ritual will restore her mortality, and she will perish with the next sunrise."

"That works," said Crockett. "That's better!"

"But," warned Luja, "if one who is immortal *already* takes part in the *life* ritual a *second* time, she will no longer be vulnerable to the death ritual. There will be no way in heaven or earth to stop her. Ever."

They considered this silently for a moment, stunned.

"That's got to be Cessair's plan," said Crockett. "This is the only thing that can threaten her!" He pointed to the scroll. "No wonder she wants it so bad! She's going to go through the life ritual *again* so that she'll never have to worry about death!"

Ricky rubbed her face with both hands. "What the hell are we going to do?"

Crockett shrugged. "Capture Cessair. Mix some poison. Get Cessair to drink it. Recite a few phrases in Egyptian. Doesn't sound too hard."

Ricky spoke through her hands. "Impossible is the word."

"If the deceit is bold enough, even a god may be tricked," said Luja. "Or goddess."

"Do you have something in mind?" asked Crockett.

"The other scroll," she said, pulling it in front of her, "is almost identical."

"That doesn't make sense," said Crockett. "Why hide a second identical copy behind a ghost door?"

"I said that they were *almost* identical," continued Luja. "The only difference is that the formulas for life and death have been changed."

"Changed how?" asked Crockett.

"Switched."

They considered this silently for several moments before Ricky spoke. "So if thieves had broken into the passage tomb and discovered the first scroll, they would have had no clue that it wasn't legit. They would have performed what they thought was the life ritual, hoping to achieve immortality..."

"And died," said Crockett, finishing the thought. "Son of a bitch!"

"What?"

"If we'd have just gone to the beach in San Sebastian after we left Egypt, Cessair would have broken into the passage tomb first, found the bogus scroll, performed the ritual..."

"And she would have turned mortal," said Ricky, now finishing

Crockett's thought. "And then died at sunrise."

He nodded. "And any minions she tried to make into part of an immortal army would have died. And we'd all have great tans. Son of a bitch!"

"That can still happen," said Luja. "You must get the trap scroll into this Cessair's hands."

"Easier said than done," said Crockett. "We have to find a way to do it without making it seem too easy or like we want her to have it."

"The only way she won't be suspicious is if she takes it from one of us by force," said Ricky. "How's that going to work without getting one or both of us killed?"

"We'll think of something," said Crockett. Then he regarded Luja for a moment. "All this knowledge about mythology and mysticism... the languages you know... the symbols... you're an amazing woman, Luja. You asked us what we would do with this information."

He paused. Lula regarded him stoically, unblinking.

"In a little while," he continued, "the scroll will be gone from your shop. But you're sharp, you are. You won't be able to forget what's on the scroll. Not ever. You'll remember every word."

Luja stared at him, then nodded.

"So," continued Crockett. "What will *you* do with the information?"

Luja looked him in the eye.

"I will take it to my grave."

CHAPTER 40

She checked the time on her mobile. 02:45. Ricky had slept
raggedly the past four hours, never for longer than thirty minutes.

The doubts had started after their return from Luja's. True,
there had always been doubts, plenty of them. But before she and
Crockett had found the scroll, the quest for it had always seemed to
promise a victory. Just get the scroll before Cessair. Simple as pie.

Learning what was written on the scroll had changed
everything as far as Ricky was concerned. The scroll had not
meant victory at all. Its acquisition had not defeated Cessair. It had,
in fact, simply revealed to them how far they had still to go. And
how impossible it would be.

In order to kill Cessair, they had to first make her mortal.

In order to do that, they had to get the bogus scroll into
Cessair's hands and hope she would not realize that the potion for
immortality had been changed to a death cocktail. This seemed
possible, for if Cessair could recall the exact recipe after 5,000
years, she would have no need of the scroll. Perhaps she had never
seen the formula. It was possible that someone else had mixed it
and then performed the ritual on her.

But they couldn't just leave the bogus scroll on a street corner hoping Alchemy fanatics might wander along and spot it. Or put a notice on eBay. Cessair would know that Ricky and Crockett would attempt to conceal themselves, and that they would never give up the scroll voluntarily. Getting Cessair to believe she had discovered it "accidentally" would be risky. They could book a rental car or a ticket on an airline, hoping that going on the grid would draw out Cessair, but she would surely recognize such an obvious move as a trap. Cessair needed to feel that she had earned a hard victory, to feel drunk with her newly acquired power—so greedy and eager to take the next step that she would not question the scroll's authenticity.

And a *convincing* victory surely meant confronting not only Cessair, but also her equally fanatic minions, all heavily armed, all fully ready to empty a magazine of hollow points at anyone deemed to be a threat.

In short, any attempt to derail Cessair was suicide.

They had nothing that could compete with her firepower. No guns, explosives, protective armor. They could probably find weapons of some kind, but even then, they were only two people against Cessair's army and her infinite resources.

The only weapon they possessed was the scroll, and Cessair currently seemed insulated against its powers. Trying to bring her down was simply throwing their lives away.

On the other hand...

What if the scroll was bogus? Ricky had no doubt it was 5,000 years old and had been created by some Egyptian holy man, but that didn't make it magic.

And if the scroll was not legit, then Rio Armstrong was not Cessair. She had managed to trick Leo.

But why?

This line of thinking certainly suggested that Rio believed in the scroll, even if the reality was otherwise. Perhaps Rio had thought that the role playing was the only way to elicit Leo's cooperation, knowing that he would do anything for a chance to bring back Mary. Knowing that it was the only way he would ever betray his principles.

And if Rio was not immortal, but believed the scroll could make her so, then she *could* be stopped. However, that would not change the fact that they would have to face an army of her cult of psychopaths in order to do so.

Or would they? If the scrolls were really just a lot of mumbo-jumbo that could no more grant immortality than they could grant Rio a pumpkin coach to take her to the ball, they could simply hand them over to Alchemy and that would be the end of it. Rio's movement would fizzle. Or perhaps she'd claim the scrolls were just another clue toward a destination that was always just over the next hill. Still dangerous, but not a goddess. A mortal fanatic in a world with no shortage of them.

And if she and Crockett could no longer help or hinder Rio's efforts, perhaps Ricky could go home. Other more capable forces would eventually end Rio's quest, once and for all.

Ricky thought of her dark apartment, thousands of miles away —the security it had always offered. Her online friends, faceless yet dependable. And there had been comfort in her routine: the gym, work, *Clandestia*. The online game was set in a mythical, semi-primitive world of tropical islands, deserts, remote mountain regions, forests, and jungles, filled with the remnants and ruins of an advanced civilization that had existed millennia before—an apt choice of gaming recreation for someone interested in archaeology. Players worked with others online to solve challenging puzzles and logic problems to open passageways, move into previously sealed or forbidden areas and accumulate artifacts necessary for solving future riddles. It had, at times, been maddeningly challenging, even with three or four others in her online group adding their cleverness to the tasks. Yet, in the end, there had always been a solution. And there were no deaths. Only problems to be solved.

But this was different.

There was no solution—assuming the scrolls possessed the power they promised. And unless they stuck a sword through Rio's heart and she responded with laughter, how could they know for sure? Since that wasn't likely to happen, they had only Leo's dying words to go by, and Rio's claim that she was Cessair. For the sake of the world, they had to assume the reality of the scroll's magic. And in that scenario, every path led to death—except one. The path of retreat.

They had egged her on with talk about saving the world, about the need for justice for innocents like Bash—and for her sister. Sasha had, after all, risked everything to send the map. Ricky had even convinced herself of the need to avenge her sister, had actually talked herself into believing it was something Sasha would expect.

But certainly *this* was not what Sasha had wanted—to send Ricky to certain death.

And why should she risk everything for Leo, the betrayer? Or for Campion, whom she had only just met? Or Crockett, for that matter, a wise-cracking boy in a man's body whom her sister had been wise enough to keep at arm's length? Or for anyone in the world? She owed the world nothing. It had responded to her overtures with only more betrayal. The rapist Drew in Alabama, betraying both Ricky and Paula. Her aunt's subsequent denial and deceit. Her mother, looking the other way, dissolving into her own mess of alcoholic and drug-induced stupor. Even the Fates or God or whoever pulled the golden strings behind the backdrop of the heavens had turned from her, taking her father, then Sasha, and leaving Ricky a twice-mutilated, awkward outsider.

So what exactly was supposed to motivate her to take the next step, the one that would put her on that path almost certainly leading to her death? Pure altruism?

The hell with that.

Ricky carefully slid off the bed. Crockett moved slightly, sluggishly, then settled into an easy, rhythmic breathing. She found his wallet, removed a portion of Brenner's money. She would need some funds to disappear. Brenner owed her this, at least. The price of an eye. Grandma Neve snored lightly beneath a patchwork quilt and heaps of laundered but unfolded clothes that covered her bed, her cat curled into the crook behind the old woman's knees. Ricky padded into her room, knelt, gently touched her lips to the wrinkled forehead.

Finally, she grabbed the yellow pack.

She could not leave the scrolls here, particularly if they really did possess the power to make one immortal. If Crockett persisted in trying to stop Cessair alone, he would fail and Cessair would take over the world. Better that Cessair alone be immortal than allow her to create an immortal army and have access to the death ritual.

Ricky would destroy the scrolls. Then no one would ever see her again. She would run, disappear, go someplace where people didn't care about your past and didn't ask questions. There were people who were paid to take chances, risk their lives, protect and serve. Let them take on the immortal witch.

Sorry, Saoirse.

But she wasn't really.

And then she was gone.

CHAPTER 41

Crockett slept in the following morning. Ricky was not there when he woke, which did not surprise him. Yesterday, because she was feeling better, she had gone out to punch the rug. That was where she was now, no doubt. Maybe she would try a jog today. He had never seen anyone so fit. Was that the right word, he wondered? Had rolled up against her in the small bed, accidentally of course, on more than one occasion. She was all sinew and angles, like rolling up against a saddle.

While her morning outings did not surprise him, they did not particularly please him, either. He knew it was a thousand-to-one shot that anyone connected to Cessair would see her, but they'd already survived some pretty long odds, showing that in the end, odds were simply numbers that, in the face of bullets and bombs, mattered little.

He took the walk down the hall, took a bath, pulled on jeans as well as a red-striped, button-down shirt with rolled up sleeves that Neve had said was her Tim's, but which Crockett was free to wear. When he returned to the room, Ricky was still not there.

He wondered if she was in the kitchen attempting to have a conversation with Neve, to try and coax another brief window of the verve and fire that had radiated from her grandmother seventeen years earlier. "Have you seen Ricky?" he asked Neve, who was leaning over the sink with her back to him.

"She was always such a beautiful girl," Neve said wistfully. "Do you think her face will heal?"

"Did you see her go out this morning?" asked Crockett, trying a different tactic. This seemed to register with Neve.

"No. I haven't seen her. I thought maybe she was still sleeping."

Crockett pulled out his phone, reluctant to call. After all, Ricky was an adult and could go where she wished—and when. Yet, they were also a team—sort of—and needed to be alert to very real danger. If something had happened to her, he wanted to know and deal with it.

He tapped her number.

No response.

He texted.

JUST WONDERING WHERE YOU ARE

He waited.

Nothing. His phone said 11:42.

It's all right, he told himself. *When she shows up, there will be a simple explanation.* Yet, he had to admit that he was worried. Very worried.

She'll be back for lunch.

But she was not. Crockett's soda bread and bowl of coddle that Neve had prepared went nearly untouched. He texted and called again. Still nothing.

His mood darkened. Something was definitely wrong. What if Cessair's thugs had found her? He did not want to think about it. How could he even consider pressing on without her? Despite her tough looks, he knew that she was frightened, vulnerable. It made him sick to think that, after losing so much, she might now be suffering at the hands of a monster.

He wondered if he should venture out, guess which streets she might have taken on her morning jog or whatever it was she did. Ask people if they had seen her. It would be easy enough. The girl with the patch on her eye. Maybe someone had seen which way she had gone, had seen her get into a car, had seen her talking to someone.

He still had the knife. There did not appear to be any formidable weapons in Neve's house, so it would have to do. Crockett rose, turned toward the hallway and heard footsteps on the stairs.

Ricky!

But it was Gregor, the seventy-something owner of the liquor store beneath Neve's apartment. Crockett had made a few purchases over the last couple of days and the two had talked a bit. Gregor appeared worried.

"I just stopped in at the Goat for some chips," said Gregor. "Toby was watching the store."

Crockett wondered why Gregor thought he might find this interesting or important. Gregor continued.

"Your wife's the one with the scar, ain't she?"

"She's not my—" Crockett stopped himself. "What? Why do you ask?"

"She's in a bad way," said Gregor. "You best go to her."

"Where?" cried Crockett, nearly screaming it.

"The Red Goat!"

Crockett maneuvered around Gregor and shot off down the stairs, wondering what he would find when he reached his destination. *She's in a bad way.* Did that mean she had been shot? Beaten? Was she even alive? *She's got to be alive,* he repeated over and over to himself as he sprinted.

He skidded to a stop at the entrance, pushed open the heavy door just in time to see Ricky's fist slam into the face of a stocky, middle-aged man wearing a jeff cap, probably breaking his nose, judging by the sound. He went down like a bag of sand tumbling off the rear of a speeding pickup truck, pushed himself away, stood, dabbed at the blood oozing from his nostrils.

"Ricky!"

She turned toward him, her eye glassy, her face raging, like a cornered animal.

He took a step forward, intending to join the fight against what he presumed were Cessair's thugs. Then he looked around the pub. In addition to the man with the broken nose, there were three other individuals, all somewhat older and less than streamlined fighting machines. He now recognized the man with the broken nose as Roger's sharp-tongued friend.

"What is this?" he asked.

"You *know* her?" asked the man with the probably broken nose, rubbing away most of the blood with his jacket sleeve. "Get her out of here!"

"I don't understand," said Crockett. "What happened here?"

"Fuck you!" shouted Ricky, more or less focusing on him, her bearing unsteady. "That's what happened here!"

The bartender with whom Crockett had spoken two days earlier now took a cautious step forward and pointed across the room. "She threw a tumbler through my bloody window!"

Crockett turned, saw the jagged hole.

"And she insulted my customers. Attacked Roger!"

"Is he all right?"

"He's in the loo," said the bartender, inclining his head. "Cleanin' up. She broke *my* nose, too, I think!"

Crockett took two more steps. "Ricky, let's go."

"You know, I could be home right now!" she said. No trace of humor. Only sadness and desperation. "Nice and safe and sober. But now, everything's fucked."

He stepped closer. "Come on, let's go."

Lightning fast, her fist shot out and caught him on the left side of the face. He staggered back, for a moment wondering whether the jaw was shattered.

"Jesus!" exclaimed the bartender.

Crockett worked the jaw, waited a few moments for the sting to subside. "We need to get out of here. If you don't leave, they'll call the cops."

"Tell them to bring guns. Those Garda pussies don't even carry guns."

He stepped forward again. "Don't hit me. I'm your friend."

She stood poised for battle. "You're not my friend. You just wanted to screw my sister!"

"Ricky…"

"Sasha was your friend. And Bash. And Leo. And they're all dead. And I'm fucked."

"We'll talk about it," he said, inching closer. "Let's go someplace else. Give me your hand."

Her right shot out again, just grazing him. She stumbled slightly but recovered herself.

"I don't want to go someplace else. This place has whiskey."

He decided to charge her while she was speaking, diving toward her midsection to grab her around the waist. Although her reaction was delayed, she brought a knee up into his chest and then threw another right, which glanced off his shoulder. Without thinking, his own right fist shot out, catching her square in the face and sending her to the floor in a heap, unconscious.

"Jesus!" said the bartender, even louder.

"Shit!" He bent down to check, saw that she was breathing. Then he paid the bartender for the window and threw in a generous extra amount to help him and the other casualties forget about their bruised faces. Returning to Ricky, he picked her up and made his way to the door, which one of the other patrons was gladly holding open for him.

"Hold on!" called the bartender as Crockett prepared to exit. He walked over to where Ricky had been sitting and picked up a yellow bag from the floor. "I think this is hers."

Crockett barely stifled a gasp. They had almost left behind the scroll. *Why the hell did she bring it here?*

The bartender looped the strap around Crockett's neck and then Crockett passed through the doorway, hearing the bartender chatting good-naturedly with the remaining patrons as he did.

"Pretty generous haul! I should get m'nose broken every afternoon!"

It was 18:00 before Ricky woke in her bed back at Neve's. She wondered almost immediately if she had been in some terrible accident, or whether she was simply experiencing the worst hangover in history.

"My face hurts," she said sluggishly.

"Your nose is broken," said Crockett, who sat next to the bed in a simple chair whose paint was worn down to bare wood.

She noticed a wet cloth lying next to her face on the bed, a few nubs of ice still unmelted. "How did I break it?"

"I punched you in the face."

She made a move to sit up, but decided the effort was, at the moment, not worth it. "I don't remember a damned thing. Did I deserve it?"

"I don't know. It was a reflex. And it seemed like the only way to stop you at the time."

Now Ricky did sit up, which she was surprised to find was easier than she had expected. "Stop me?"

"You beat up a couple customers, broke the bartender's nose, and threw a mug through the front window of The Red Goat. Oh, and you nearly broke my jaw with a little roundhouse right."

She closed her eye. She did not want to tell him the real reason she had gone there.

"On the plus side, I think the ice helped a lot. Swelling is down. Nose looks almost normal."

"Great."

"I wouldn't be surprised if you have a concussion, though," said Crockett. "Better take it easy for a while."

"I feel fine."

The silence grew long and awkward before Crockett finally continued.

"Look, this is a crazy situation, and we're getting toward the end game. I understand how tough this must be for you."

"Don't say that," said Ricky tersely.

"I'm just saying that you don't have to face this alone."

Ricky tried to hold her feelings in check, but her voice wavered as she responded. "I've been alone ever since they dug that map out of the ice. And now I'm even more alone than ever. You heard Luja. How impossible this is. No hope."

"That's not what she said," said Crockett, trying to turn the conversation. "Besides, maybe there's a little hope."

"What do you mean?"

"First of all, I'm going to get a tracking device for that bag."

"What good will that do?"

"When Cessair gets her hands on it, it's going to contain the bogus scroll. We're going to want to know where she takes it."

"To make sure she performs the death ritual."

"Right. And…" His voice trailed off.

"And what?"

"Well, the ritual will make her mortal. But someone is still going to have to kill her."

"She'll die when the sun comes up."

Crockett nodded. "True. But I'll bet she figures out she's been duped before then. Someone has to either kill her or keep her from performing the other ritual on herself until sunrise. Otherwise we'll be right back where we started."

This news did not improve Ricky's mood. "What if she ditches the bag?"

"It's a nice bag!" said Crockett irritably. "Do you think she's got something better to carry scrolls around in?"

"Where are you going to get something like that?" asked Ricky.

"You'd be surprised what's available," said Crockett. "Google 'tracking devices' and see what comes up. People use 'em for their keys, their cars, to keep track of their kids or a shifty spouse."

"Tell me you didn't put us on the grid by ordering something online."

"Give me a little more credit than that," said Crockett. "But there's a place I'm going to visit in about half an hour. And pay cash, of course."

"Great." Ricky's head felt like it weighed fifty pounds. "Then we just have to find a way to let Cessair get it without getting ourselves killed."

He pulled car keys from his pocket. "It must be killing her, the fact that we've dropped completely off her radar."

"Aren't you afraid Cessair's people might spot the Daewoo if you go driving around?" asked Ricky, who realized how much her entire body ached. "That thing's a goddamn beacon."

"Yeah, I am," said Crockett. "Which is why I'm taking your grandmother's Volvo. Twenty-two years old but, according to Neve, still purrs like a kitten. Not that she uses it very much. Or at all."

Her evening appointment had left. No more were scheduled, but she usually kept the light on until late. The night seemed to draw questions out of people. Luja put on another kettle of water, allowing her thoughts to return to the Scroll of Life and Death.

It was the most extraordinary mystical artifact she had ever handled.

And the most frightening.

She also thought of Ricky and Crockett.

Some people's paths were easier to read. Less conflicted. But these two...their futures appeared in greater flux than most. Particularly the woman's.

She sensed darkness. Some great chill.

Luja had focused most of her energies on the scroll that day. If she could spend more time only with Crockett and Ricky, she might be able to better sense whether their destinies tended toward light or dark.

The bell over her door jingled merrily. She turned down the gas, walked through the beaded opening.

Before she saw who it was, the energy hit her like a dark wave.

No! It can't be true!

CHAPTER 42

Ricky lay on the bed. Crockett had now been gone for a couple of hours, and she felt anxious, unable to focus. She had gone for a walk, just to try and clear the cobwebs. But now her head throbbed worse than when she had first awakened after the bar fight. So much had changed in the past few weeks. And many of the changes could not be undone.

As they frequently did, her thoughts drifted to Sasha.

As messed-up as it had been before her sister's disappearance, now, Ricky's life and her place in the world seemed more muddled than ever.

There had been times, however, when they had been hunting for the scroll in Egypt, or even at the Newgrange tomb, when she had felt something akin to hope and even purpose. There had always been a plan, a clear objective. She had felt alive in a way that she had not felt in thirteen years, had felt herself learning to live again. Now that they had the scroll in their possession, the pathway was obscured and terrifying. The mice had succeeded in stealing the cat's prized toy. But dispatching the cat itself was a far more daunting task.

And her own actions today had made things worse.

Despite her troubled mind, she eventually fell asleep, the first deep and meaningful sleep she had had in days. When she woke, it was dark. She clawed through the clutter and found her way to the kitchen.

"Oh, hello dear," said Neve, sitting at the small table, a travel magazine open in front of her to pictures of tropical beaches. "No, Mr. Crockett isn't here. He went out."

"Yeah, I know, Grandma."

They were silent for a few moments, during which Ricky opened the refrigerator and poured a glass of orange juice. Then Neve spoke.

"I'm glad you're here, Limerick."

"I am too, Grandma."

Neve looked down at the magazine, but her eyes moved as if searching for something not on the pages. "I missed you. And Saoirse."

Ricky walked over to where Neve sat and kissed her on the forehead.

"It's late," said Neve. "You haven't eaten. Would you like something?"

Ricky told her that would be nice. When this was all over, she would find some way to repay Neve. And she promised herself that she would visit regularly. Perhaps it was time that she moved back to Ireland. There was no longer anything for her in Chicago.

While Neve fixed supper, Ricky found some fruity antacids in the bathroom medicine cabinet. Then she took a quick bath, washing off dried blood and whiskey. She wandered back to the kitchen where Neve had made her a sandwich, and for a moment as she ate, Ricky felt as if she had drifted twenty years back in time. She almost expected her Grandmother Amelia to glide through the doorway.

Neve watched over the rim of her own teacup as Ricky again checked her phone. "He'll be fine, dear," Neve said, sipping tea at the other side of the small table. "If you're really concerned, why don't you call him?"

On the one hand, calling him made perfect sense. It would give her an immediate measure of relief when she knew that, at least for the moment, Crockett was all right. He had given her the impression that his destination was less than half an hour away. Yet, he had now been gone almost four hours. How long did it take to buy a tracking device?

I'll wait a bit.

At 23:05, Neve said goodnight, the flame of her maternal instincts doused by the first trickle of an impending river of dreams.

Ricky returned to her own room, curled onto the bed, pretended to sleep. The night crept along like death's housecat.

At midnight, she could take it no longer.

I'll just text. When he texts back, then maybe I'll be able to sleep.

She started to text WHERE THE HELL ARE YOU? Then she stopped. Deleted it. Started again.

IT'S LATE. ARE YOU OK?

She waited. A minute passed. Two. Then three. Finally, the reply ping, and she breathed an enormous sigh of relief.

FINE.

She froze. That was not the code word they had agreed upon. Had he forgotten? She typed another message, her mouth suddenly dry.

ARE YOU SURE?

Again, she waited, and then:

YES. RELAX. B BACK SOON

She knew then that she was not texting to Crockett. Crockett would not have made the mistake twice. A sudden hoarse gasp escaped, and she considered how she should respond. She had no idea whether she was texting one of Cessair's thugs or with Cessair herself. Finally she typed:

NXT TIME, DON'T B PRICK. CALL IF LATE! GOING 2 SLEEP!

Whether that would convince them that she did not suspect, she did not know. She sat on the end of the bed, cradled her head in her hands. *What do I do?*

She could not call the Garda. Leo was dead. Campion was hundreds of miles away and of no use. Crockett had been captured. Neve was asleep. There was no one to help her. She shook her head violently, trying to stifle the screams that threatened to burst forth. Lurching to her feet, she paced the room like a death row prisoner.

Neve!

She had to get her grandmother out of there to a safer place. If Cessair had Crockett, she would try to get him to reveal where Ricky was. *He won't say anything.* But even as she thought this, she knew Cessair would find ways to hurt Crockett. Unspeakable ways. And she would keep hurting him until he told her anything she wanted to hear.

Ricky moved into the darkened hallway, heading stealthily for Neve's room. She paused as she passed the locked door leading to the stairs. Something far away sent a barely discernible metallic echo up the staircase—the key turning in the lock of the door at the bottom of the stairs.

Crockett! But she knew better. Crockett would have texted the code.

Cessair's men were already here.

CHAPTER 43

She believed they would want the element of surprise, and so they would proceed cautiously up the stairs. They knew that she had possessed a gun at the passage tomb. Even so, she guessed she had no more than half a minute. Ricky rushed into Neve's dark room, shook her grandmother until her eyes fluttered open. Then she whispered desperately.

"Come with me, Grandma. Now. It's an emergency."

Neve seemed completely alert. "Is it a fire?"

"Yes," said Ricky, nodding. If that would do the trick, fine. She would hustle Neve down the back stairway that opened into a back room of the liquor store. Ricky had played there when it had formerly been Neve's office. She would hide Neve in the closet there and lead the men away. Trying to keep ahead of them with Neve in tow would be futile.

As Neve sat up, Ricky heard muffled movement just outside the locked stairway door. She pulled Neve off the bed, out into the hallway and past the door, stopping in the kitchen.

"I'm frightened," said Neve.

Ricky attempted to shush her, pulling her toward the door to the back stairs, opening it with her free hand.

Please don't let them be coming up that stairway too.

But the stairwell appeared clear. Ricky now pushed Neve into the opening. "Down to your old office," she whispered. "Hide. The closet!"

Neve appeared confused. "But the fire?"

Ricky had no time to respond. She heard the liquid metallic click of the lock—they had either discovered the hidden key or picked it—and realized the door to the other stairway would be open in a moment. Her eye darted desperately around the kitchen, searching for a weapon of some sort. Unfortunately, there were no knives or iron skillets lying about, and Ricky had insufficient time to search. On a whim, she pulled the small, wooden kitchen table the few feet into the hallway and in front of the door, just as it began to open. The table, which only just fit into the hallway, allowed the door to open only an inch or two before becoming wedged against the opposite wall. Ricky heard a curse from behind the door as the first man apparently realized what had happened, and then three dull shots from guns with silencers tore alarming gashes into the door.

Now someone was throwing his shoulder into it, and she could already see the upper door panels beginning to give. The hiss of more shots sounded as the barrel of a gun was angled through the slim opening and dull metal clanging rang from bullet strikes in the kitchen. Ricky dove away from the sounds into her bedroom, stumbling over the junk that filled the room. "Shit!" she muttered, scrambling to her feet, hearing the splintering of the door's wooden panels. In only seconds, Cessair's thugs would destroy enough of the door so that they could push the table aside. A few more steps, and they would have her cornered in the bedroom. If she and Crockett were both caught, that ended any hope of stopping Cessair.

The only other way out of the room was a window. She might be able to drop to the alley below without injuring herself, but it was likely that someone had been left behind to cover that possibility.

She twisted her neck, looked up.

The roof loomed only a few feet away, and a dull, gray length of vertical conduit just inches from the window looked like it might offer her a handhold. Pulling back inside, Ricky slammed the bedroom door, pushed boxes in front of it, and then pushed the bed against these. It was a poor bulwark against vastly superior manpower and firepower, but she guessed it would buy her some time. Seconds might be enough. Then she returned to the window and climbed out.

Standing on the sill and holding the conduit for balance, Ricky found that her fingers were only inches from the lip of the parapet. Jumping back into the room, she found a small but sturdy box as bodies thumped against her bedroom door. Setting the box on the sill, she stepped onto this, allowing her to reach the parapet, and then pulled herself up, using the space between bricks for toeholds.

Though exhausted, she wasted no time. The neighboring buildings were close enough that moving between roofs required little effort. As she ran, she hoped that Grandma Neve had found her way to the closet. She hated the thought of leaving her on her own, but if Ricky had stayed with her, she knew that both would have been caught. She hoped that Cessair's thugs would be so consumed with chasing her that Neve would go unnoticed in her old office in the liquor store downstairs.

As Ricky scrambled over the parapet of the fourth building, her thoughts traveled to Crockett. Was he dead? The idea made something twist painfully in her gut. However, she wagered that Cessair would not kill him until both of her most dangerous adversaries were apprehended. As long as Ricky was on the loose, Crockett could be used as a resource or bargaining chip.

But how would she ever find him?

She stopped, looked to the street that ran past the front of the shops. At this hour, it was deserted, except for a black SUV in front of the next storefront. It had to belong to Cessair's thugs, who had parked it several buildings away to effect a more discreet arrival.

Crockett had talked about a tracking device. *If only I had one now,* she thought, looking wistfully at the SUV. *They could lead me to where they've taken Crockett.*

Then she looked at her phone.

It was much larger than the tracking device that Crockett had wanted to plant in the bag, but that wouldn't matter if she could get it into the SUV. Her fingers racing across the screen, she turned off the ringtone, opened her phone's device manager and tapped "Location". Scanning the rooftop, she noticed the curved iron anchors of a ladder, which took her to a fire escape and the alley. Cautiously peering down the sidewalk, she saw no movement and darted to the SUV.

Be unlocked.

To her relief, the back passenger door opened, and without hesitation, she slipped the phone into the pocket on the back of the front passenger seat. She closed the door, sprinted back into the alleyway, out the other end, and kept on running.

She had no idea where she was going.

Something in her brain had rebelled for a few moments at the act of leaving the phone behind. It was, after all, her only connection to Crockett.

But reason ultimately prevailed. As she ran on, putting more space and more turns between her and Cessair's thugs, she knew that, dead or alive, Crockett wasn't going to call.

CHAPTER 44

She waited an hour and made her way back. She had to. Ricky had left her Grandma Neve in the back stairway. Hopefully, Neve had made her way to her old office. If so, there was every reason to believe that she was safe. The thugs had been looking for Ricky. Even if they were aware of Neve's presence, they already had a bargaining chip in Crockett, and so they had no need to harm the elderly woman.

The streets around the liquor store were still deserted under a cool canopy of stars. The black SUV was gone. Ricky spent another hour making a wide circle, staying in the shadows and alleyways, making sure that Cessair's thugs had not merely moved the vehicle and then come back to wait in hiding for her. When she was convinced that they were gone, she slipped inside the front stairway, which had been left unlocked.

She padded silently up the stairs, just in case. At the top, splinters and larger slabs that had once made up the door were strewn across the hallway, and the wooden table rested upside down, two legs broken off. Half a dozen bullet holes peppered her bedroom door, which hung at an odd angle from wrecked hinges.

A quick check of the other bedroom revealed neither Cessair's thugs in waiting nor Neve. The kitchen had survived with no damage, other than a trio of bullet holes in the stove. "Neve?" Ricky called cautiously, in case her grandmother had come back upstairs. She repeated this several times, until she was convinced that the apartment was deserted.

She's still in her old office.

At the foot of the back stairs, Ricky opened the door and stepped into the liquor store. The place was dark except for a dim security light that glowed near the checkout counter at the front. Rows of dark bottles rose before her, but her destination was the door at her left. Seventeen years earlier, it had been Neve's lavender scented office, where she had sat at a broad wooden desk writing checks while Ricky and Saoirse wriggled on the floor, cheating each other at card games.

It was now Gregor's office, though Gregor had gone home hours ago.

She knocked lightly. "Neve?"

No response. Her stomach muscles tightened. *They wouldn't have taken her.*

"Neve?" she repeated a bit louder, pushing the door open.

No lavender aroma wafted from Gregor's office. The desktop was a mess of paperwork surrounding a computer monitor, not the efficient and uncluttered workspace that Ricky remembered. Stacked boxes, some open with the tops of wine or whiskey bottles visible, obscured two of the four walls. A shaggy, green island of carpet that smelled of dog covered the middle of the vinyl floor.

"Neve?"

Still nothing. The twisting in Ricky's stomach intensified.

She moved across the room to the closet just to the right of the desk. This was where she had advised Neve to hide.

Please, please, please...

"Neve, are you in there?"

Ricky opened the door. Neve was there.

She sat with eyes wide open, not fearful but surprised. A wine-colored stain had ruined the breast of her nightgown.

Ricky wailed loudly, scrambled into the closet, embraced her grandmother and pulled her out onto the dog carpet. There she held onto Neve, rocking and sobbing.

For a long time.

Until, gradually, her grief grew into hatred.

She second-guessed herself. *I could have stayed behind, fought off the men.* But she knew this was a lie. There were more of them, and they would have eventually overpowered her. Tied her up or cuffed her. And they would have killed Neve for sport in that scenario, just as they had in this one.

Ricky carried Neve upstairs, placed her into her own bed, closed her eyes. *Guess I disturbed a crime scene. Well fuck me.*

Then she cried again, but only for a minute.

Think!

She went back downstairs, into the liquor store, found a bottle of Glendalough, took a swig that she suspected was worth about one hundred dollars.

Just one.

Returning upstairs, she knew what she had to do. If her phone hidden in the car had not been discovered, she had a chance of finding Crockett.

Then she'd make that bitch and every one of her murdering followers pay.

In the kitchen, Ricky discovered that more than three bullets had found a target. In addition to the three in the stove, two more had traveled through a wall and pulverized Neve's computer monitor.

She needed the Internet to find where they had taken her phone.

Ricky returned to Neve's bedroom, which was somehow more emotionally daunting the second time. Doing her best to ignore the bed, she searched Neve's nightstand and bureau for a cell phone. Either she had none, or it was well hidden. A search of the other rooms proved no more helpful.

Gregor's computer!

She raced down to his office. Weak light seeped in the front windows. A wall clock in the store indicated it was after 05:00. Ricky had no idea what time Gregor came in to stock shelves or do bookkeeping, but she had no intention of being there when he arrived. Hitting the power button, she waited.

ENTER PASSWORD

Ricky pounded the desktop in frustration. *Give me a fucking break!* She began to pull open drawers in the wooden desk, hoping that Gregor had a phone with which she could access the Internet. While she found no phone, she came across a thin, book-sized box containing a tablet. Based on the bag in which it was wrapped, Ricky guessed that Gregor had received it as a premium when he acquired his most recent mobile phone, and had never used the tablet, stuffing it into a desk drawer. Ricky clawed it out of its package, saw that it had no charge. However, it did come with a charger, which Ricky attached immediately.

She rushed back upstairs, giving Neve's apartment one last look. She collected her and Crockett's few items from the bedroom and then returned to Neve's room, pausing to place a gentle kiss on her forehead. In the kitchen, she scrounged a pencil and scrap of paper from a drawer. On the paper she wrote, *The cult of Cessair did this. Alchemy. Same as Zackenberg. They were looking for me. Please treat my grandmother with kindness. Limerick Crowe*

She placed the paper on the kitchen counter, then raced down the stairs once more. She was pleased that the fast-charging tablet was already at fifty percent. Powering up, Ricky found an Internet connection and logged into her own account.

Bingo!

The map showed her phone was somewhere north of Dublin along the coast. Now that she had a destination, it was time for her to go. She powered off, grabbed the tablet and charger, pulled out the keys to the Daewoo. Just before stepping out the back, she stopped, turned, found the bottle of Glendalough where she had left it.

Just one more.

She took another hundred dollar swig, set the bottle on the floor again. She paused. Then Ricky picked up the bottle and headed out the back door into the new day.

CHAPTER 45

Ricky drove north, first through the mostly quiet streets of pre-dawn Dublin, and then along rural roads that were not main arteries. It was the first time she had driven since losing her left eye, and she found herself, at times, disoriented and hesitant.

Caution, she knew, was essential, and so she wanted to make sure that as she neared the location, she proceeded slowly and without being observed. She did not have an exact address, only a general map location. Ricky hoped she would be able to narrow her choices as she got closer. And two questions burned almost as painfully as the lingering sadness over Neve.

What would Ricky do when she got there, wherever *there* was?

Was Crockett still alive?

He has to be!

She could not bear to think about the alternative.

Dublin's urban sprawl gradually fell away to the sort of green countryside she had passed through on her way to Newgrange, first north on highway 3, but then exiting onto side roads that took her through pastures and past farms closer to the Irish Sea.

Occasionally she pulled over, logged on, and checked the location of her phone on the maps. Thirty minutes outside of the city, Ricky realized that she had actually passed the location—and the tablet had run out of juice. She turned and drove back more slowly. The sun had risen, but clouds obscured it, and a patchy fog made it easy enough to miss things. Half a mile back, she spotted an unpaved road extending to her left.

This has to be it.

However, Ricky was reluctant to take it. The road might eventually connect with another. On the other hand, it might terminate at a cottage or barn, and then Cessair's thugs would likely see her. She drove past. Another mile down the main road, she arrived at a tiny farm. Older outbuildings whose roofs had been updated to metal sheathing peppered a yard surrounded by a mix of fencing types: stone, wood and wire. A light shone in the house, and so Ricky pulled her car next to it. Summoning her resolve, she walked to the side door, rapped on it several times. Peering through the window, she noted the light on over the kitchen sink, but she detected no movement inside. She rapped again. Still nothing.

Wondering if the owner of the house had ventured outside, she looked toward the barn and noticed a side door ajar, through which a sliver of yellow light shone.

She swallowed hard. *Nothing ventured...*

Going to the barn, she pulled on the metal handle and stepped inside, the sweet aroma of manure mixed with the sour of urine and mildew filling her lungs. As she squinted toward the glow at the structure's center, a dog began to bark and a collie raced to within a few feet of her.

"Gertie! That's enough!" said a voice from the vicinity of the light.

The dog quieted but stood its ground.

"Gertie! What is it, girl?"

"Hello?" called Ricky.

She moved forward. Gertie retreated reluctantly, and after a few steps, trotted to the man near the light, sitting between her master and the new arrival.

The man now realized that Gertie had been barking at an intruder. "Blazes!" He glared wide-eyed at Ricky, and she realized that he was reacting to her scar and eye patch.

He was short, wide, but not fat, wore overalls and a rumpled, gray work shirt. His formerly dark hair was more than halfway to gray, and he bore a rather remarkably unattractive hooked nose. Now that Ricky stood before him, she was not quite sure what to say.

"Flat tire, is it? Or are you lost? A fool Yankee tourist who can't read a map, are ye?"

"Please," said Ricky, the word feeling foreign and uncomfortable on her tongue, "I only have a quick question for you. Then I'll leave."

"You're Irish," said the man, hearing her faint accent.

Ricky nodded.

"All right, I've got a bit of patience for ye then. But make it quick. These girls aren't going to milk themselves!" He waved a hand toward the herd.

Ricky exhaled, nodded. "There's an unpaved road about two kilometers north of here. Heads east. Where does it go?"

The man thought for a moment. "It doesn't go anywhere. If you mean just the next road up the way."

"That's the one."

"Sure, that's a dead end, little lady. Nothing down there except An Tsuil."

"Excuse me?"

"The old ruin. An abbey, maybe eight or nine hundred years ago. Deserted now."

Ricky considered this. "Does someone live there?"

"Some rich dandy took to trying to restore it about a decade ago. Guess he made a fortune in medical implants, which ended up poisoning people. Lost his shirt. After that, blew his brains out! Never got very far with the restoration, and then part of the abbey fell into the sea. Place sits empty now. Yank, he was, which I suppose I didn't need to tell you."

"Thanks," said Ricky. "How far down the dirt road is the abbey?"

The man squinted with one eye. "I suppose a kilometer or two or three. You aren't thinkin' of going there, are you? And at this hour?"

"I was just curious, that's all."

"Curious, eh?" The man narrowed his gaze on her. "Just curiously driving past at six in the morning, miles from a main highway. Now that, my dear, is indeed a curious circumstance."

"You're certainly no fool Yank, Mr..."

"Brian."

"Brian. You're a pretty smart man. Smart enough, I wonder, to have Internet?"

"Lassie, when you're a bachelor farmer out in this pasture land, you'd better have a satellite dish the size of a goddamn haystack! I suppose you want me to make these girls wait so you can use it?"

"I can make it worth your while," said Ricky.

Brian laughed. "Girlie, you're far too young for me!"

Ricky blushed, floundered for words for a moment. "I meant that I have money."

"I'm not going to drop everything for fifty Euros."

"Add a zero," said Ricky.

"Blazes!" gasped Brian. Then his gaze narrowed on her again. "The early hour, the questions, the money... I'm going to just assume that whatever you're up to isn't exactly within the law. And quite frankly, I don't care. An Tsuil is a wreck anyway. All I want to know is this: Is there any way *I* can get in trouble?"

Ricky smiled. "Not if you stay here with the cows."

Brian let the idea hang in the air for a moment, and then called to his dog. "Come on, Gertie girl!" He stepped forward, kicking hay as he went, turning toward Ricky as he passed. "Darlin', follow me. The girls think it's time for a break!"

CHAPTER 46

Brian fixed breakfast while Ricky plugged in her tablet and completed her research. There were no other roads that would take her toward the general map location. Her phone—and hopefully Crockett—had to be at An Tsuil or very near to it. And she knew that against Cessair and her thugs, knowledge of the playing field would be an asset.

Thinking of Crockett and what might have happened to him made her feel heavy inside. This was layered atop the existing heaviness of Neve's death. Which was layered atop so many other tragedies and failures. However, she knew that wasting time indulging her emotions would not help.

According to her research, An Tsuil was the name given to an abbey that had been built around 1100 A.D. where monks who served the surrounding area received religious instruction and training, and secluded themselves from the world. At one time, there had been vast gardens around the structure, which supplied food for the monks, who distributed the excess to the poor. The abbey had been dubbed An Tsuil, meaning "the eye of God," because of its single tower built on high granite cliffs that overlooked the Irish Sea, watchful and powerful. The impression of permanence was bolstered by the fact that several battles were fought in the area over the years, yet never once was the abbey breached. There was a legend, in fact, that no one in the vicinity of the abbey could ever be struck by lightning, such was its ability to repel assault. Not even the powers of nature could compel the Eye of God to blink.

As with many abbeys, there was an adjacent cemetery, though monks who achieved a certain level of piety were honored with interment beneath the stones of the floor of the chapel, reasoning that if An Tsuil could repel invading armies and lightning, then it could also repel Satan's attempts to swoop down and, after their deaths, carry their souls to hell.

As if the edifice were not formidable enough, it had been built almost at the edge of cliffs that dropped off into the Irish Sea. A single bell tower had faced the sea, but this had been destroyed in an earthquake only a few years ago, during which a section of rock had cleaved from the face of the cliff, carrying part of the tower down with it. A number of smaller outbuildings, also stone, had stood near the main abbey structure, but these were in disrepair, now mere rock piles.

"Are you sure you're wanting to go there, darlin'?" asked Brian, bringing a plate to her. "I'm thinking it might be better if you drove back the way you came. An Tsuil stands empty for a reason, you know. They say the souls of the monks buried there haunt it."

"I have to go," replied Ricky, without looking away from the screen. "Besides, it's not empty today."

"And it isn't something that would be better handled by the Garda?"

She shook her head. "It's something I have to do."

Brian said nothing for a few moments and seemed to be

considering the matter. "Maybe I should go with you."

Ricky shook her head. "No. Just… no."

He searched for words that would make his case without offending or embarrassing her. "I was just thinking… well… having an extra set of eyes might—"

She cut him off. "I—I can't, I just… can't. I've… let too many people get hurt already."

After another silence, he asked, "Whose side are you on?"

Ricky turned to look at him. "What do you mean?"

"Whose side are you on?" Brian repeated. "God? Or Satan?"

Tears brimmed. The lack of sleep. Grief over Sasha and now Neve. The sudden realization that of the seven billion people on the planet, she alone carried their slim chance. And she hated the fact that this burden had been given to her.

"I don't know."

The old farmer nodded. Then he plodded out of the room. Ricky studied the satellite view of the area around the abbey until he returned a minute later.

"Take this," he said, handing her a shotgun and a box of shells. "It won't do any good against the ghosts of those monks, but I have a feeling there might be a few devils there who will bleed."

She expected to not enjoy Brian's scrambled eggs, as anxious as she was about her mission. However, she had to admit, they were delicious. And after the tears, she felt calmer, resolute against whatever was to come.

"A man who cooks like that, I can hardly believe he's still a bachelor," said Ricky, rinsing her plate in Brian's sink.

"I've had my share of lady friends over the years," said Brian. "They always loved my cooking. But they found me difficult to put up with for more than a day or two at a time."

"I'm not sure I believe all of that, either," she said, and smiled.

She picked up the gun, intending to leave, but then another thought occurred to her. "Be right back." She jogged out to the car, returning with the Glendalough, which she deposited on the kitchen counter beside Brian.

"Blazes! Nectar of the Saints!!"

· "It's the least I can do for all your help. And that amazing breakfast."

Brian nodded, narrowed his gaze upon her, smiled. "I think you're on God's side."

She nodded, then was struck by a thought. "Do you have a mobile I could use? Just for a moment."

Brian raised an eyebrow. "Are you serious? You must be the only lass under fifty on the isle who doesn't have one!" He fished in a pocket and pulled his out.

Leo was dead. Neve was dead. Crockett was, at best, a prisoner. No one else in the world understood what was happening —except for Dr. Campion. He was still alive, as far as Ricky knew, and if something happened to her, it would be up to Campion to take the story to people who might still be able to stop Cessair. He had an easy number to remember, which she recalled from when Amet's uncle had distributed their new phones. She hoped he still had it. She texted:

Cessair has Crockett and scroll at An Tsuil

Scroll can destroy her

Going to get Crockett and kick bitch's ass

I hope

Ricky

She sent the message, then erased the record of it from the phone, returning it to Brian. When she drove away, Brian had a much fatter wallet.

The shotgun rested in the backseat and a box of shells bounced gently on the seat beside her. Brian had offered a final question before returning to his girls: "For whatever you're about to face, do you have a good plan?"

Ricky had nodded. "A good one."

Then she drove off. She had no plan whatsoever.

By this time, the sun was well up and the fog had melted away. She drove back toward the unpaved road, but as she drew near, she realized how the Daewoo would stick out like a beacon to Cessair's crew. Half a mile from the turnout, she drove into a meadow and parked behind a rubble wall. From there, she resolved to go cross country on foot.

She considered that the locals might find it somewhat alarming to see a young woman striding through their property carrying a shotgun. On the other hand, it was mostly wide pastures. She would be more likely to run into a herd of sheep than another human.

According to the tablet, the location of her phone had not changed. But that told her little about Crockett. Was he safe and a prisoner? Had he already been killed? Was he even at An Tsuil? She had assumed that Cessair's thugs would travel to wherever Crockett had been taken, but she had no way of knowing whether this was so.

Among Ricky's many troubled thoughts as she sat, reluctant to exit the Daewoo, was the fate of the scrolls. Had Crockett managed to hide them before being captured by Cessair's thugs, or did Cessair have them? If she had both, would she know which to use to create her immortal army and make herself truly invincible?

Had she used it already?

Perhaps it was too late. Crockett dead, Cessair beyond the reach of even God, and no way to stop the madness and horror as she toppled the world's governments and established herself as omnipotent dictator.

It was also possible that she was walking into a trap. Ricky had not hidden her phone in a particularly clever place. They might have found it and guessed her intention. So many scenarios seemed to suggest a bad ending to the business. *I'm a fool. I should drive away. Change my identity. Live away from people.*

From somewhere within her came a reply. *You've been running for thirteen goddamn years.* Whatever lay ahead, she knew it was time to turn and face the devils.

Ricky opened the box of extra shells that Brian had given her and stuffed as many as she could into her pockets. Then she grabbed the shotgun off the backseat and set off across the pasture. She was able to occasionally move along lines of shrubs or groves of trees, but much of the area was open. However, she lost sight of the road fairly quickly and there did not appear to be anyone around to chart her progress in the direction she was heading.

She began to work her way father north, for she still had not encountered the unpaved road. For a while, she feared she had become lost or had missed it, although reason told her that since the abbey stood right at the cliffs, missing the road was impossible.

The crenellated brow of An Tsuil finally crept into view at nearly 9:00 a.m. She moved as close as she dared and found a grove of shrubs from which she could remain hidden, yet which afforded a decent view of the west side of the old abbey.

The building itself was constructed of gray stone that matched the dreary sky. An imposing, intact, wooden door faced the front, and in the stone wall were vertical openings for narrow windows that began halfway up. Rubble tumbled out to the sides from behind the abbey, overgrown with moss and grass.

At the front were a dozen cars, mostly nice sedans looking out of place resting in weeds that, in some instances, reached the gas fill. The number of vehicles surprised her, and as she watched, two more pulled up, weaving onto the grass. Their occupants—a single nicely dressed man from one vehicle, a man and two women from the other—exited and walked through the main entrance of An Tsuil. Ricky did not notice a twenty-two-year-old Volvo in the mix, which did not surprise her. They had likely picked up Crockett elsewhere, abandoning Neve's vehicle before bringing him here.

Or had they killed Crockett, dumping his body and the Volvo in some remote quarry or forgotten shed? She tried to push out the thought, tried to reassure herself with the idea that they would not kill Crockett until they were sure they had Ricky as well.

She shook her head. *Right into their trap, genius.*

On the other hand, maybe things would work in their favor. Crockett had taken the bag with the scrolls. Now Cessair had it. It was what they had hoped for.

Yeah, right. Only about a hundred things have to go just right in order for this to work out. Piece of cake.

There were a lot more people than she had anticipated. Initially, she had imagined she would encounter only Crockett, Cessair, and her henchmen. The dozens that were now arriving here would make it more difficult to sneak in and out. And as she watched, another car arrived, bringing another nicely dressed couple.

What's going on here?

If Cessair's primary purpose was to find an out-of-the-way place to hang out until Ricky showed up, and then spring a trap, what was the purpose of the newcomers dressed to the nines?

Looks like she's throwing a party. She wondered whether the guests had been invited to watch Cessair complete her victory by destroying the last of her enemies.

But then a more chilling idea occurred to her.

She's going to do the ceremony tonight!

That had to be it. It would explain all of the cars and the Oscars-worthy outfits. Cessair was summoning her faithful and would be creating her immortal army in An Tsuil tonight. Five thousand years ago, her plan to create an invincible force of fifty followers had been thwarted. Was that how many would receive the "gift" today? If so, based on the number of vehicles, they had certainly not all arrived. And if Cessair had not completed the ceremony yet, that meant there was still a chance.

She gripped the shotgun more tightly.

Her heart beat faster at the sliver of hope she had imagined. And this led to another epiphany.

Goddamn Crockett had gotten himself caught on purpose.

It was a crazy theory, but seemed less so, the more she thought about it. That was why he had gone out alone. It had allowed Cessair to get the bogus scroll without endangering Ricky. The noble bastard. That had to be the case. How else would Cessair have found him? The odds against a chance encounter at an electronics store in Dublin were pretty steep. And if Crockett had put himself in harm's way, that meant that he had made sure that only the bogus scroll was in his possession when he was caught.

Ricky had to get inside. Unlike the day at the Red Goat, this time she *would* break his jaw. The wise course would be to wait until dark. However, by then, it might be too late. Still, she figured she probably had some time before Cessair would begin, since cars were still arriving. Looking over the abbey more carefully, she noticed movement in each of the front windows and realized these were lookouts. She also observed men standing on the grass at the two front corners of the abbey and two more standing in the shadows at the entrance. Straining to look back down the road, she spotted yet another two men near a rock wall about two hundred meters away who were stopping the cars at a checkpoint.

ROD VICK

Well, if I were cleaned up, had a new suit of clothes, and a nice rental car, I could probably walk right in. And no eight-inch scar. No, no, and no. So what's plan B?

The woods stretched to the right gradually, approaching the cliffs. Ricky decided to use this cover to get a look at the back of the abbey, since entrance from the front seemed doubtful. It took her almost an hour to reach the edge of the copse undetected, and here there was a bit of a ravine filled with exposed roots, bleached tree trunks and boulders that eventually dropped off into oblivion at the edge of the cliff. Although she was now farther from the abbey, she could see that a guard was posted on the ground along the abbey wall, about fifty feet from the cliff. She knew she would find a similar situation on the far side of the structure. Two guards strolled back and forth along the wide, sea-facing walkway at the top of the abbey, changing direction as they neared the caved-in section. However she saw no others. As a result of the fortress's position near the cliffs, it was clear that they expected more serious threats from land than from sea.

The cliffs themselves offered a jagged, irregular ridge, which eventually plunged a hundred feet to a turbulent, rocky inlet. If anyone tried to get a boat close to the shore, it would be ripped to splinters on the rocks. Even if a party did survive the sea, scaling the sheer cliffs would be a monumental if not impossible task.

On the other hand, the irregular character of the rock formations at the ridge offered an opportunity. While climbing *up* the cliffs was out of the question, it seemed to her that it might be possible to climb *sideways* just beneath the top of the cliffs, just below the ridge. None of the four guards watching the back of the castle would have the right angle to see her.

Yet, it was one hundred feet down, an absolutely terrifying scene.

Then don't look down, she told herself.

This brought to her attention the problem of the shotgun. She did not want to leave it behind, but it had no carrying strap, and she knew she would need to use both her hands in climbing. She tried to use the car keys to start a cut in the leg of her pants so she could tear some strips of material, but the fabric was too tough. Her ankle socks were too small to be useful.

Jesus! She thought to herself, removing her bra and underpants to fasten around the gun in two places and create a harness. *Fucking commando!*

Then she crept from the trees into the ravine. She tightened the knots securing the gun and climbed laterally so that she was a few feet below the top of the cliff, doing her best not to look at the roiling waters below.

CHAPTER 47

Cessair smiled at her acquisition. The Scroll of Life and Death. First life, then death, as was the way of the world. Tonight, after the last of her fifty chosen ones had arrived, she would gather them in the great hall of An Tsuil and oversee the ritual. Then, Alchemy could come out of the shadows.

Soon, she would create a small army. As it suited her, she could eventually grow her immortal force to the hundreds or thousands. Against men who could be killed by bullets and explosives and poison gas, her immortals would prevail every time. Cessair would direct them. And she would be the only truly immortal one, and the rest would know that their gift could be revoked by her as easily as it had been bestowed. Their allegiance, therefore, would be absolute and unquestioning. Tonight, she would repeat the ritual that guaranteed life everlasting. Then, not even the powers of the scroll could touch her. Nor God.

Not ever.

She climbed the old stone stairway to the west balcony that overlooked the great hall. The U-shaped balcony stretched the entire length of the room, continued across the south end, and resumed on the east side, identical to the west balcony except that a portion of the back wall had collapsed, affording her a view of the sea and the eastern horizon. Here on the west balcony, tied to a heavy, oak chair, sat Mason Crockett, facing the stone railing with its many missing balusters. He would have the best seat in the house for the evening's performance. First, he would watch as her fifty were transformed. Later, she would allow him to experience the horror of the scroll for himself.

In some respects, it was regrettable. After all, without him and the girl, it might have taken Cessair much longer to be reunited with her prize. Add to that the fact that he was young, bright, good-looking. He might offer her a few years of delicious diversion.

But, sadly, his loyalties could not be coerced.

And Ricky Crowe? How poetic it would have been to have her here for tonight's ceremony. To see the look on her face as her male friend died a terrible death in front of her. And then to suffer the same fate herself. Unfortunately, the girl appeared to be in hiding. She had narrowly escaped from her men at the apartment above the liquor store in Dublin. It did not matter. After tonight, she could no longer hurt them. But Cessair would make her pay eventually. Whether it took six months, a year, ten years. Eventually, Ricky would no longer be able to hide. After tonight, it would become increasingly difficult for any enemy to hide. And Ricky Crowe would pay exquisitely for her defiance and the troubles caused by her meddling sister.

"Why Mason, it's nice to see you're awake," said Cessair with mock sincerity as she approached, stepping into his field of vision.

"Go fuck yourself, Cessair," he said bitterly.

Cessair smiled. "One of the advantages of immortality, Mason. Kings, peasants, generals, slaves… you get to fuck them all!"

"Hope you get an immortal strain of the clap!"

Cessair laughed. "I am going to miss you. I hope you know

that. I'll bet you would have been even more fun in bed than Leo. And believe me, he was quite good. Sure you don't want to give it a go?"

Crockett stared at her darkly.

"Probably for the best. Don't want to betray your little scar-faced Irish strumpet. It's pretty clear she has it for you. You hadn't noticed? Well, let me tell you something. Because I like you, your death will be quick. But your little cyclops? Her death will be slow. Very, very slow!"

"Maybe we can make a deal," said Crockett, a hint of fear in his eyes. "Once you've performed the ritual, you won't need to worry about her! If it's revenge you want, I'm listening! I'll do whatever you want!"

Cessair frowned. "Capitulation, Crockett? How boring! I'd always imagined taking you to bed kicking and screaming!"

"I can do that, too, if you want."

"It's no fun if it's disingenuous," she replied. "Well, not as much fun. However, perhaps if you tell me where you think your girlfriend might be hiding out, my men will go and get her and I'll do you the favor of killing you both at the same time. There would be something romantic in that."

Crockett said nothing.

"Suit yourself," said Cessair with a smirk. She turned to leave, but was stopped by Crockett's voice.

"Why do all of this?" he asked. "You're successful. Why destroy the world order? Why not simply be content with your own immortality?"

"World order?" said Cessair, turning again to face him, the smirk now gone. "You'll forgive me if I disagree. In five thousand years, I've seen very little of what I would call 'order.' What I have seen in abundance is a world filled with the chaos of war, hunger and cruelty! For centuries I listened to the sages say, 'This is God's plan. It will eventually lead to a more enlightened world.' But generation after generation proved them wrong. Despite the advances that humans have made in science, art and technology, the chaos has continued. Worsened, even."

"Maybe the chaos is man's plan, not God's," said Crockett.

"Yet God does nothing to stop it!" retorted Cessair, her eyes flashing. "Does this sound like a *loving* God?"

"One could argue that a loving parent gives his children the opportunity to learn and make mistakes," said Crockett. "We call it free will."

"I call it rationalizations!" spat Cessair. "And all the while, the world sinks deeper into the cesspool. But I realized I had the power to do something about that! I alone stood outside the power of God. But I could not do it without the strong arms and backs of others, even as an immortal. I had to find the scroll. As the years passed, I, of course, worked, accumulated a bit of wealth. Naturally, I had to move around. After a decade or two, my lack of physical change would begin to create suspicion. In modern times, investing was able to accelerate the growth of my fortune. And I was able to surround myself with people who could keep secrets. None of them ever knew who I really was, but there were individuals who built and supervised my organization, who supplied the new technology, who checked out leads in the hunt. Every so often I would rotate those closest to me to hide the secret of my youth. Sometimes I would be introduced to the new group as the daughter of the previous owner or CEO. It was quite an elaborate ruse... a ruse that will now be coming to an end."

"How will making everyone immortal change the world?" asked Crockett.

"That is not my plan," said Cessair. "If everyone were

immortal, everyone could act with impunity. It would be more terrible than it is now, since there would be no consequence or meaning. Instead, my chosen ones will become the leaders. Unable to be killed, it will be easy for us to recruit legions of loyal followers who wish to be on the right side of history. And to earn the reward of eternal life if they are especially helpful!"

"Not many, I'll bet," said Crockett.

Cessair smiled. "Very few indeed. But simply the promise will be enough to keep the gears turning. And gradually at first, then in a wave, the world will be changed. Corrupt governments and regimes will be toppled. The defiant will be exorcised. The unwilling or uncooperative will vanish."

"You don't see it, do you?" asked Crockett.

Cessair narrowed her gaze on him. "See what?"

"You've become what you hate," said Crockett. "A god who offers eternal life, only without the free will. In Cessair's universe, you don't choose and learn. You simply obey."

"Obedience is necessary for the success of any civilization," said Cessair. "Free will is like candy: sweetly seductive and ultimately ruinous. Order is ambrosia, the food of the gods!"

"Your speech writer is good, I'll give you that," said Crockett, "but in the end, you sound like you're selling the same stuff that German fellow with the spider on his arm was selling about a century ago. And you've got the same Messiah Complex. You're going to save the world from itself. Shit, you even have yourself half-convinced that what you're doing is for the greater good. Well you know what I think? That you're no different than the power junkies that come along in every generation. And your frantic search for the scroll wasn't really about a better world. It was because for five thousand years, you've been terrified that someone else would stumble upon it and discover that it's the one thing that can make you mortal!"

Cessair smiled bitterly. "Trying to provoke me with bile? In a few hours, you may be begging to join me."

"Don't bet on it."

"Tonight we begin the process of taking this broken world back from God!" said Cessair. "Once we are immortal, God can no longer touch us! We will scour the globe of decadence, sloth, unrest. Then we will recreate the Eden that it was originally intended to be, only this time, with knowledge!"

"Knowledge approved by you," Crockett corrected her.

Cessair smiled wickedly. "Cheer up, Crockett. You will be witness to the greatest event in human history. And I hope you'll appreciate the appropriateness of the location."

"I'm sorry, you lost me."

"An Tsuil. The Eye of God. Buried beneath the stones of the floor below us are friars, monks, holy men. How appropriate that we dance upon their graves as we take back the world! A finger in the eye of God!"

Crockett looked down at the worn floor in the chapel below, the stone tiles in the center arranged in a pattern that appeared to be an open eye five meters across. He said nothing for a moment, but then: "Well, don't be too surprised."

"Surprised?" said Cessair. "About what?"

"If God has more of a say in the outcome than you anticipate."

CHAPTER 48

As Ricky began inching her way down the rocky ledge just below the ridge of the cliff, she wondered whether she had made a huge mistake. The ledge was sometimes as wide as two feet; at other points, narrower than six inches, the footing always irregular. And she had not anticipated how much her now limited vision would affect her confidence. To her back, she could hear the sea crashing against the fallen rock nearly a hundred feet below, but she dared not look down.

Having the shotgun strapped to her back made it possible to work with both hands—an absolute necessity—but the weapon's few extra pounds upset her equilibrium just enough that she had to constantly reassess her position, making certain that she would not be pulled a centimeter too far in the wrong direction.

Then there was the wind, which she had not noticed in the pasture, but which tugged at her with a seeming malicious pleasure here on the face of the cliff.

As if the narrowness and the need to proceed cautiously did not slow the process sufficiently, she encountered dead ends, requiring frequent backtracking to find new ledges or even single rocks that would move her slightly higher or lower on the face of the cliff. As she crept along, her fingers growing sore as a result of the abrasions and incessant gripping, she imagined a dozen other ways she could have tried to enter the ruin, running each mental scenario. Yet, she realized this was simply an inevitable mental exercise, a coping mechanism for helping her deal with this extreme situation. In the end, the other ways were mere fiction. They either did not exist or would have offered a greater chance of failure. Her route along the cliff was the chink in the ruin's armor. And while it was no sure thing, it was her best shot.

She came to another dead end and looked up. Thankfully, it was impossible to see the guards over the lip of the cliff, and so she also knew that she was still invisible to them. She had visually marked a spot before she started, the point she would need to reach before climbing to the top. However, her destination point was still half a football field away. Turning her head carefully, she scanned the cliff above. She could not spot anything that looked like it might be wide enough to offer her passage.

She looked down. The crashing sea far below gave her a moment of vertigo, which she fought off by staring into the rock in front of her. Then she looked again, trying to keep her focus on the cliff rather than the water. Thankfully, she saw a mossy rock point jutting out about two feet. It was clear that, once she reached this, she could work her way to her right for at least another twenty meters, gradually moving up the face.

However, descending to the ledge would be treacherous. She guessed it to be about six feet below her current position. There were no hand- or footholds below, and even worse, the face of the cliff actually curved inward, making it impossible to slide down the smooth surface.

She would have to jump.

I can't.

How far back, she wondered, would she have to go in order to find an alternative route? She studied the face of the cliff, but it was uncompromising.

She pressed her cheek against the cool stone, her eyelid closed.

I can't.

Another five minutes crept by. She tried to slow her breathing. She thought of her sister. Of Crockett. Of Leo.

And she thought her mother. Whenever Ricky was afraid, her mother had said, "It'll be okay." And then her mother had betrayed her, and things had never been okay again, and now she was on a high ledge and, even if she made it to the top, things were only likely to get worse.

And I led them to Neve. That could never be undone. Tears rolled down her cheek, and she pushed the side of her face hard against the wall to squelch them.

Then she jumped.

Rather than jumping out from the cliff, Ricky dropped almost straight down, scraping against rough stone, unable to stop herself from twisting, landing awkwardly on her side, knocking the wind out. Her hands scrabbled for purchase, and she was fortunate to grab a clump of tough weeds as she hit, which stopped her momentum and kept her from plunging over the lip.

Hold on, she told herself, for she could feel her right hip hanging off the ledge, and that if she transferred weight to it by accident, she would send herself tumbling over. Bit by bit, she inched the center of her mass back onto the ledge and then took several more minutes struggling to her feet without losing her balance.

She rested, sucking in air, trembling. Then she moved on. While the climbing was no easier, at least there was a clear series of escarpments leading her gradually higher. She fought the

400

temptation to relax—ever. One mistake, even something minor, could set in motion a muscle reaction that would move her center of gravity to that tipping point only a few inches from the cliff face.

She came to the end of the current ledge, still about thirty meters short of her goal. Below, the cliff slid away at an increasingly alarming angle, devoid of any hand- or footholds. Above, however, were several creases in the rock into which she could fit her fingers. She would have to climb vertically about two meters to reach them. The handholds on the intervening space seemed far less promising or reliable. Ricky had seen veteran rock climbers use the tips of their fingers to gain ground on such surfaces. It could be done. And, she reasoned, it was only two meters. Or so.

On the other hand, one slip and she would begin sliding down the smooth face, picking up speed until she plunged out into space where the wall curved inward.

Can't think about it. Just do it. And after a moment, she added ruefully, *It'll be okay.*

Ricky reached up, found a slim crease in the stone, worked the fingers of her left hand into it and then did the same with her right. She pulled herself up off the ledge a few inches experimentally, and then returned her feet to the solid footing. Then she took a few deep breaths, worked her fingers into the shallow ridge again, and lifted. Immediately, she looked for the next handhold, found a knob of granite, slid her right hand onto it. With her left hand, she found a tiny crease, and this brought her up another few inches.

The going was made more difficult because her feet kept slipping. The rubber on the edges of her jogging shoes was too pliant, too forgiving, and this kept her feet from grabbing the surface and allowing her to push up. It occurred to her that veteran climbers often had special shoes that allowed them to use their toes to push off, sparing the arms from having to do so much work.

As she reached for the next handhold, the unthinkable happened. Her right foot slipped, and she began the downward slide. She dragged her fingers, hoping for something to stop her momentum. Fortunately, her feet landed on the ledge from which she had started. The drop, while terrifying, had been only a little over a foot.

It's these shoes.

Awkwardly, slowly, Ricky slipped off her jogging shoes, tied the laces together, and looped them around the barrel of the shotgun.

Then she climbed again.

Barefoot, her toes were able to find places in the rock to push and grab, and slowly she covered the distance to where she could stand again. From here, the going became significantly easier, for years ago, a section of the cliff had fallen away, taking the old tower and a portion of the west wall with it, leaving the ground covered with block and rubble, as well as a boulder-filled crevice. The climbing here was routine, and in a few minutes, she found herself at the top of the cliff. Part of the old monastery came right up to the edge, and the rubble field completely covered any area between the structure and the cliff. The guards on the north and south sides were out of sight. The guard on the high balcony could not see her. She lay on her back, panting, giving her fingers and forearms, aching from hours of continuous effort, a chance to recover.

Now all she had to do was sneak into the monastery, avoid Cessair's thugs, find Crockett, recover the scroll, dispatch Cessair, and get out safely.

The easy part was over.

CHAPTER 49

The young woman's appearance at his farm before sunrise had continued to bother Brian McIntyre as the day wore on. He finished with the milking and the morning chores, wrapped a sandwich for himself, filled a screw top container with water, and drove the pickup out to the north pasture. He parked and waited. Here, he had a clear view of the dirt and gravel road that led back to An Tsuil, yet those driving along the road would scarcely think twice, seeing a battered pickup parked in a field.

The dirt road was rarely used, although today, traffic down it had been quite regular.

He thought again of the girl. She was going to An Tsuil too, but secretly, not like these other arrivals. And she clearly expected trouble, the kind that required a gun.

What was going on at the end of that road?

He had conducted a search online before coming out to the pasture. He could find no mention of special cultural events or tours or estate auctions on any calendar. For a moment, he had considered that the old ruin was being sold, and that the cars represented buyers coming for a look. However, why had none of them exited? They had been turning in at the abbey for hours, and

403

not a single one had left.

Something was not right. Either the girl was set on causing mischief, or the mischief was already there, and the girl wanted to do something about it. His gut told him it was the latter. She could have broken in and stolen his guns while he had been milking. She was bold, yes, but he had sensed a frightened child beneath her bravado. And she had been hurt, he could tell, in ways that did not show. But, it was clear, also in ways that did. The scar. Her eye covering. And who knew what other injuries? He sensed that it was somehow connected to An Tsuil, but how?

And if she was sneaking in now while all the rest of the guests were coming right up the road, then it was pretty clear that it was her against at least thirty. Probably a lot more. He didn't like those odds.

In the late afternoon, the flow of cars stopped for almost an hour. Brian had been ready to move, but then four more arrived together. After that, it was quiet again.

It seemed like all of the party guests had found their ways to the cake.

Patting the loaded 30.06 that rested against the seat beside him, Brian drove through the pasture, down into the ditch, across the lane, and onto the dirt road leading toward An Tsuil. After a mile, he saw a line of trees ahead and pulled to the side of the road. He knew from his study of satellite pictures on the online maps site that once he passed that tree line, anyone at the abbey would be able to see him. He grabbed the rifle, carefully closed the door of the truck, and proceeded on foot, hoping that no one else would come from the direction of the main road.

The day had been overcast, but as the sun neared the western horizon, the clouds broke, revealing luxurious reds and purples. It also illuminated the scene ahead, so that Brian could see that there were no watchers on his side of the tree line. The four vehicles that had arrived just before him had parked on his side of the trees, the only ones to do so. He approached them warily, but upon inspection, concluded they were empty. Fortunately, he did not take the road through the tree line, for as he peered out of the brush, he noticed two men stationed on the abbey side, either greeting or perhaps vetting cars that came through the opening. Beyond the trees, the overgrown yard in front of the abbey was littered with expensive sedans and even a couple of limousines.

Brian crouched, scurried quickly, reached the first of the cars, paused to catch his breath, realized how fast his heart was pounding.

Remember, you're no action hero!

He had no intention of taking on the dozens who now occupied the abbey. In fact, he had no proof they posed any threat. He had only the vague indications offered by the girl with the scar. Perhaps she was disturbed. A psychopath. He doubted this. She had seemed afraid. Unsure of herself. Like she was being pulled into a dilemma of extraordinary scope. Something nasty.

And the oddness of so many cars at the old abbey. Something sinister *was* going on. He could feel it. Now, he needed to get a look for himself, to make sure. Then he would call the Garda, if need be.

Who were all of these people? Organized crime? Drug dealers? Devil worshippers? Or maybe just a bunch of fool Yanks who thought it would be smashing to spend a night in an old ruin. He needed to know.

Men stood at the entrance and at each of the front corners of the structure. Were they carrying weapons? The low sun cast shadows in such a way that it was difficult to tell. No sounds issued from inside. If Brian had heard booming speakers blasting

Stairway to Heaven or something by Springsteen or hip hop, he would have turned around and walked to his truck. The silence offered no clues.

He had to get closer. If he saw that the guards carried guns, that would be enough for him to notify the Garda. Squatting, he moved to the next vehicle. The mish-mash of cars parked haphazardly between the tree line and the abbey made it easy to remain concealed from those at An Tsuil.

As he knelt beside a dark sedan, wiping the sweat from his brow, the seconds ticked by, and he felt increasingly inclined to make the call. But he did not want the police to come charging in on a reunion of old army buddies or a former rugby team. He had to keep going. He needed to know that these people were dangerous. He needed a sign of some sort.

The whisper came from behind him.

"Don't move."

CHAPTER 50

Ricky lay draped over several flattish stones, a human dishrag, panting, giving rest to her sore muscles, gathering herself for the next task. It was not her intention to rest for long, knowing that her chances of being discovered had increased as soon as she reached the top of the cliff. But the endeavor had taken a toll. She shook out her arms, let them fall across her face, choked out a muffled sob. Then she untangled the shoes from around her neck, pulled them on. Taking a deep breath, she pushed up, crouched, and scrambled over worn blocks and rough stone to the base of what had once been the tower.

Five hundred years ago, the tower had formed part of the east wall of the monastery, its peak stretching above the structure to a sort of empty belfry with a circular opening on its east and west faces. Each day, the sun would shine through this opening, earning it the nickname The Eye of God.

Now, however, The Eye lay at the bottom of the cliff in a thousand pieces, most of them submerged in the churning water. A section of the old, stone staircase survived against what had been the inside wall of the tower, and Ricky used this to avoid the ground floor of the abbey and reach the east balcony undetected.

Unfortunately, she had no idea where Crockett was being held —if he were still alive. And she had no idea where to find the scroll.

Then, she turned around.

Fifty feet away, facing her from the west balcony, sat Crockett, his eyes wide with surprise as he recognized her. She could see that he was tied, but otherwise, he seemed unharmed. The wave of relief surprised her.

Ricky slid sideways into the darkness of support pillars and assessed the situation. The balcony stretched around three quarters of the room, meaning that she could work her way over to Crockett by remaining in the shadows. Every ten feet, vertical wooden supports rose to support diagonal beams that met high above the floor of the great hall. These thick posts and the shadows in the space behind promised some cover as she moved along, close to the walls. No one other than Crockett appeared to occupy the balcony, although down on the floor of the hall, dozens of individuals chatted in small groups, sat on benches near the wall, tapping away on notepads or phones.

She counted about thirty-five. Cessair had come into possession of the scroll last night and had no doubt alerted her fifty chosen ones. But even with immortality calling, it would take time for some of them to arrange travel.

Keeping low, Ricky slipped along the wall toward the south portion of the balcony. She continued in the shadows, taking her time, taking great care to make sure she made no sound, although it seemed the ambient buzz from below would offer some cover. She soon found herself edging up behind Crockett. Taking a final look in both directions, she darted out from a post, crouching behind his chair.

"How?" he whispered.

Ricky's reply was barely audible but precise. "Shut up!"

She began to fumble with the ropes binding his hands. His whisper stopped her.

"Don't."

"Why not?" she hissed in reply.

"Because if they notice I'm gone and start looking for me, they'll find both of us. How did you get in?"

Ricky moved slightly to the side so that they could make eye contact. "Would you believe I climbed up the cliff?"

"If you could get past all of Cessair's guards, I'd believe you're capable of almost anything." Then his eyes widened in surprise and a thin smile played on his face. "What's that around the shotgun?"

Ricky felt her cheeks warm. "I had to have my hands free to climb."

"You made a sling out of your bra and panties."

She sighed in exasperation. "My pants wouldn't tear."

"How about that," said Crockett. "Commando! I knew you'd come around!"

"Shut up. You handed yourself over to them, didn't you?"

"No! Someone must have ID-ed me. I was on my way back to Neve's when they forced me off the road."

The mention of Neve again brought a lump to her throat, but she pressed ahead. "You're a fucking liar!"

"What does it matter?" said Crockett in surrender. "The idea was to get the scroll into Cessair's hands."

"And what then? How did you plan to kill her if you got yourself caught?"

"See, that wasn't part of the plan. They outmaneuvered me."

"Yeah, I'll bet *that* was tough. I've got to get you out of here."

"Hold on," said Crockett. "The head witch is planning a big

ceremony tonight. Going to use the scroll to turn her fifty most loyal toadies immortal."

"She's got the bogus scroll, right?"

"Exactly," retorted Crockett, trying to keep his eyes forward.

"Then let her send her lackeys to hell."

"There's a problem," said Crockett. "Something we didn't think of. You see, if a tomb robber had stolen the bogus scroll, he would go through the life ceremony, mix the poison, and turn toward the west. Game over. But Cessair has done this before. We can probably count on her mixing the poison. But when she gets to the turn west part, she'll know that's wrong."

"And that's when she'll come up here and light a fire under your nuts until you tell her where the legit scroll is," said Ricky. "Where is it, by the way?"

"Sittin' in the glove box of Neve's Volvo on some backstreet in Dublin," said Crockett. "Now get out of sight."

"Just sitting there? Unguarded?"

"There's nothing we can do about it right now," said Crockett.

"Is it even locked?"

"Look, first things first," said Crockett, his eyes darting back and forth, trying to watch the movements of all the people down on the floor. "What I was trying to tell you is that we need to get Cessair to turn to the west."

"I suppose you have a plan?"

"I didn't until you showed up. Get back by the wall on this side and stay hidden in the shadows. When it gets to the part in the ceremony where Cessair is supposed to turn, fire the shotgun!"

"How do you know she'll turn?"

"Everyone will turn! It's human nature. You hear something that loud, that you're not expecting, you turn towards it."

Ricky nodded. "Okay, that might work."

"I'm sure of it. Then you can come and untie me. We don't want Cessair to become suspicious or change her plans because I happen to go missing. When she looks up here, I want her to see my smiling face, right where it's supposed to be. Now git! Lay low for a few hours!" As she tensed to slide away, he stopped her. "Hold on a sec!"

"What?"

"How did you find me? Did they leave some sort of trail of breadcrumbs, or are you just an amazing guesser?"

"I'm a freaking mind reader," said Ricky. "Wait. If this plan of yours works, what about the guards?"

"*When* this works, we tie up the loose ends."

"But—"

The clicking sounds of safeties being flicked off gave Ricky a sick feeling, and she whirled around to see Cessair flanked by four large men brandishing handguns.

"Speaking of tying up loose ends," said Cessair jovially. "This could not have worked out better. Since you have been such a big part of this right from the beginning, Miss Crowe, it would have been a shame if you would have had to miss it!"

Ricky held the shotgun at waist level, not certain who to shoot if shooting became necessary.

"Why don't you drop that?" asked Cessair. "You know it won't have any effect on me. And if you shoot any of my men, one of the others will shoot Mr. Crockett and, well, there goes half my audience for tonight's big show!" One of the thugs pointed a Glock directly at Crockett's head. "And I know Mason is so looking forward to it!"

Ricky dropped the shotgun. One of the thugs rushed forward and kicked it along the floor until it hit the back wall.

"Now empty your pockets!" commanded Cessair.

411

The shotgun shells and a wad of bills tumbled onto the stone.

"Raul, get another chair for Miss Crowe. And some rope. Let's move them both over to the *east* balcony. That way I'll be able to enjoy the delicious look in their eyes at the exact moment of my victory!"

CHAPTER 51

They sat tied to the heavy wooden chairs that had been left behind after the failed renovation, positioned a foot or two from the edge of the balcony. The stone railing had crumbled away in this spot, affording them an unobstructed view of the hall.

Behind them had once risen the great tower—the Eye of God-- but it too had collapsed, taking part of the wall with it to the sea. Yet, the interior beams were dry and solid, leaving the structure as sturdy as any fortress. The breeze that had tugged at Ricky on the cliff blew gentler, now that the sun was nearing the horizon, and the air had begun to cool as well.

Cessair's thugs had lit torches in sconces on the ground floor and had brought in some modern battery-powered area lamps to fill in the gaps. As a result, the chapel floor of the abbey was lit up like a hockey rink. Markings chiseled into some of the stones indicated the burial location of the favored monks. In the middle of it all, the eye formed by the paving stones stared up at them. *An Tsuil.*

The eye of God, thought Ricky. *A God who sits by and does nothing.*

The lights also illuminated Crockett and Ricky and threw railing shadows that blended with the deeper darkness at the perimeter of the balcony.

So fucking close. Cessair had the fake scroll. In minutes, she would mix the poison and drink it or dab it. But when the scroll instructed her to face west, it would dawn on her that she had been tricked. When she realized this, she would examine the bogus scroll more closely, discover the switch. She would seethe with anger, probably torture them both until she learned the location of the genuine scroll. She would send her men for it and then it would be a simple matter to prepare the proper elixir and repeat the ceremony.

Ricky loathed herself for her carelessness. If she had hidden more quickly, their plan would have worked perfectly. She would have fired the shotgun at the appropriate moment, and Cessair and her minions would have been finished—the minions, immediately, and their twisted leader at sunup, suffering her last few hours as a pathetic mortal. Or, more likely, Ricky would have reloaded and finished the job immediately.

Instead, the shotgun and shells lay on the floor of the far balcony, useless to them. Ricky had come to the very summit of victory only to stumble.

If I'd been more careful, stayed in the shadows.

Or perhaps it would not have mattered. Perhaps Cessair had been watching the whole time, knowing that Ricky would come for Crockett.

"You can tell the thugs and foot soldiers from the about-to-be-anointed," said Crockett. "All of those who are going through the ceremony are dressed like they're going to a five-star restaurant. There are some Armani suits down there! And the thugs, of course, are dressed like thugs."

Ricky tried counting those who were dressed like vintage Streeps and DiCaprios. Although she always lost count as bodies weaved in and out of sight, it seemed to her that all fifty might now have arrived. Most were smiling, laughing, engaged in animated conversations. They behaved as if they had just dropped in for the office Christmas party. There were even bottles of champagne circulating, accentuating the upbeat and festive mood.

Ricky guessed it would be hard for most people to believe that these smiling, well-dressed professionals—probably lawyers, doctors, politicians among them—were killers, or that, at the very least, they supported the killings that had already occurred and the genocide to come. But she had seen their disingenuous smiles before. Drew. Her Aunt. Leo Brenner. Rio Armstrong—soulless narcissists who concealed their ugliness and evil behind masks of brittle empathy or charity.

"We can't just sit here like fucking rocks!" she said and then, without waiting for a response, asked, "Do you think we could move the backs of our chairs together and one of us could untie the other's ropes?"

"We're right out here in the open," said Crockett. "They just might notice us doing that."

"It's worth the risk. We might get loose before anyone looks our way. They're all so caught up in themselves and what's going to happen. They're like fifteen-year-olds who think they're going to get laid."

"After we get loose, then what?" countered Crockett. "Run away? No, this is our chance to destroy Cessair. If she gets halfway through that ritual and then realizes she's been had, it's going to be real bad for us. Unless we get her to turn to the west. That's still our best chance!"

"Which means we've got to get to that shotgun."

"Well, I'm all ears," said Crockett. "Tell me your plan. Right now, we're over here, tied up like junkyard dogs, and your shotgun is lying way over on the other side next to whatever's left of your delicates."

"If only one of us can get the ropes loose, maybe they'll be so caught up in the ceremony that they won't notice," said Ricky.

"Easier said than done," said Crockett. "They did a nice job on these knots. Damn it."

Just then, Cessair glided into the chapel. She had changed into a flowing white gown with a matching handbag, sleek and day-after-tomorrow fashionable, the sort of thing an Oscar hopeful might wear to the Academy Awards.

"My friends," she said, her voice echoing off the abbey walls, bringing all other conversation to a stop, "I hope you all appreciate what a watershed moment in human history this is, the opportunity to create a new race—a better race, and in doing so, to bring unity and harmony to the planet for the first time in its history!"

Applause broke out.

"She's got them convinced they're heroes," said Crockett, his voice thick with revulsion.

Cessair waited until the applause faded before she continued.

"The scroll offers a warning. It says that if you choose to walk in the footsteps of the gods, don't trip. For thousands of years, humans have been prevented from reaching their full potential by the threat of being crushed beneath the heel of a vindictive deity. Tonight, this group will no longer have to worry about such a fear. Tonight marks the first step toward an unprecedented golden age of peace and achievement, eradicating the forces that would wage war and create disunity. "

"She's talking about exterminating those who disagree with her."

Crockett nodded. "Whole races of people, if necessary."

"It's like Hitler!"

416

"Yeah. Only Hitler could be killed. Immortality is a pretty powerful carrot to dangle in front of people. And when people get frightened, they often side with power. That's another Hitler lesson."

In the intervals between Cessair's pronouncements, they could hear the waves washing back and forth over the rocks in back of them and far below.

Cessair moved to a table erected at the north end of the room, upon which a clay tablet rested.

"I'm going to move my chair so our hands can touch," said Crockett quietly. "You're right. They're so focused on Cessair that no one will notice. For a while, anyway."

He pushed with his toes and shifted his weight several times to lurch the chair into a position where their hands could touch, and as Crockett predicted, all eyes remained on Cessair, who was enjoying the spotlight, mixing ingredients from several containers that had been placed upon the table. Video equipment had been set up to capture every detail. Crockett's fingers began to work on Ricky's ropes.

"When I get you loose, stay in your chair," he said. "Pretend you're still tied up. Right before Cessair tells her army of fanatics to follow the light, make a run for it. It'll be the height of the ceremony and chances are they'll be so into it that you could do naked cartwheels across the balcony and they wouldn't notice!"

"I'm not interested in your little fantasies," said Ricky, who tried to flex, but still felt no give in her bindings.

"Get to the shotgun and give 'er a blast!" Crockett grunted, swore. "I don't think I'm making any progress. Too tight. Too many knots. And I can't move my fingers in the right direction."

Below, Cessair finished mixing the elixir. She recited some lines in Egyptian and then repeated them in English so as to cue her candidates. As Luja had explained, Cessair then proceeded to the next step, bringing the chalice containing the mixture to each follower. Ricky found it ironic that this evil entity who hated religion so vehemently had imitated its fondness for rituals.

"Look at their eyes," whispered Crockett, glancing back over his shoulder. "It's like they can already see the gates of Olympus! Damn! I'm not having any luck! Maybe if I had a couple hours!"

"We've got about five minutes!"

Ricky looked around for a solution. Tied to the chair, she could not reach the shotgun or fire it. The balcony was empty except for the two of them. Behind them, only the ruined wall and the sound of the waves.

She looked again at the scene below, Cessair moving slowly between the chosen ones. The Eye of God on the floor stared back at her, accusingly.

Or *was* it accusing?

Perhaps it might provide an answer. The wall behind them was gone. But at one time, there had been a great circular opening in it through which the sun would, at a certain time of day, and on certain days of the year, illuminate the eye on the floor.

Through the eye of God!

Ricky let out a gasp that choked back a sob. Then she gathered herself. "Turn your chair!"

"What?"

"Just shut up and do it! Face forward, toward the zealots! We don't have much time!"

Crockett threw his weight against his ropes a few times, turning the chair a bit in each instance until he had returned it to its original position. "Did you think of something else?"

"Yeah," she said, her mouth suddenly dry, her voice trembling slightly. "No matter what happens, keep facing forward! And don't yell!"

"Don't yell?"

"Don't say anything! Just keep your damn mouth shut!"

With that, she began to push with her toes, sliding backwards a few inches, then a few inches more, until she quickly moved out of Crockett's field of vision.

"What are you doing?"

"I told you to shut up!" Her chair screeched across the stone, but no one in the chapel below could hear. "Don't say anything! Not a sound!"

Screech, pause. Screech, pause.

He craned his neck, tried to see her. "Why would I yell?"

Screech, and then a long pause. Crockett's throat tightened.

"Ricky?"

No answer.

He started to call out, but then he remembered her instructions. After a glance toward the ceremony, he threw his weight against the ropes, turned himself partway around. Then he saw the crumbled wall and clenched his teeth desperately to keep from screaming. The legs of Ricky's chair had left marks in the dust that led to the opening created by the collapsed wall. Beyond this, there was nothing except the cliff, the unforgiving rocks, and the dusky remains of the evening. Ricky and the chair were nowhere in sight.

The marks in the dust ended at the broken edge.

CHAPTER 52

It had quickly become obvious that their wrists were tied too tightly. And time was growing short.

But a plan had occurred to Ricky. A terrifying, perhaps insane plan. Yet, there was nothing else. No cavalry was coming to rescue them. No lightning bolt from the blue would strike, burning away their bindings. If Ricky did not act, Cessair would discover their ruse, torture them until they would betray the world to stop the pain, and despite a modest delay, would still have her immortal army. And then she would turn the awful power of the scroll upon the world.

Ricky had scooted her chair backwards toward the gap in the back wall. Behind her was a chilling drop of one hundred feet to the crashing tides. Yet, it was not a sheer drop, at least not at first. Stone rubble and broken slabs from the tower floors clung to the top of the cliff, falling quickly away to a dizzying plunge. But one could stand on the narrow rubble ridge at the top, as Ricky had done when she had climbed to the abbey. And if one could stand there, perhaps it offered a landing area if one leaped down from above.

Or fell.

She had shivered as she neared the edge, not because the breeze was cool, but because of the horror of a plunge into the sea. Her heart hammered wildly at the thought, and she tried to block it out by simply focusing on the physical actions she needed to complete. Just keep sliding backward. Think only of that. Nothing else.

Two things had needed to occur for Ricky's plan to work. First, she needed to fall as close to the abbey wall as possible. If the arc of her fall carried her more than four or five feet from the base, she would skip off the edge of the rubble and onto the smooth slabs, followed by a plunge into the sea far below while still hopelessly tied to the chair.

Second, Ricky needed the chair to hit the rubble first, not merely to cushion her fall somewhat, but also to break the wooden joints of the chair, freeing her.

In short, she needed a bit of luck.

And to her amazement, she had gotten it. As the chair tipped, she had stifled a scream, her mind a sick explosion of searing white fear. The chair had shattered upon impact. She lay there a few moments, letting the pain subside. Realizing that time was short, she flexed, checking for broken bones, and when she judged it safe, began freeing herself. She slipped the shattered wood from beneath her wrists, which left plenty of slack in the ropes for her to slip them off. She did the same with her ankles. Then, carefully choosing her handholds, she began to climb.

When she reached the balcony floor, she saw that Crockett's chair was half-turned and that his head hung forward, chin on his chest, a tremor shaking him every few seconds. Then he caught movement out of the corner of his eye, looked up, saw Ricky and gasped. She made angry signs with her hands that he immediately understood as *Shut-the-hell-up*. Then he horsed his chair around so he faced the chapel again.

Ricky faded back toward the shadows near the vertical beams. When her back contacted the stone wall in the deep darkness, she felt confident that no one on the main floor would see her even if they looked directly at her. Now she simply needed to move to the south wall, staying in the shadows the whole time, cross to the west side of the balcony, grab the shotgun and, when Cessair told her minions to "follow the light," let go with a blast.

If Crockett was correct, Cessair would turn towards the unexpected blast—to the west. If that happened, then Cessair's plans would be foiled, and all they would need to do was find a way to get out with the counterfeit scroll before Cessair's surviving thugs got them.

Piece of cake.

She reached the south wall quickly and began to move across this portion of the balcony, remaining in the shadows. She proceeded a bit more slowly, for now she was directly in Cessair's line of sight.

She can't see me from down on the floor. She's immortal; she doesn't have super night vision.

Still, being able to look directly into Cessair's face chilled her as if she were staring down the Grim Reaper.

Halfway to the west side, she heard movement. Quickly the sounds resolved themselves into footsteps. Ricky froze and pressed herself next to a support timber in the shadows. One of Cessair's thugs strolled in her direction from the west side, a pistol in his shoulder holster.

She slowed her breathing, tried to remain absolutely still. Below, Cessair began to speak again, and Ricky realized that, in a few moments, she would utter the final words of the enchantment. And if Ricky did not fire the shotgun on the west balcony at that time, they would fail.

Come on, keep moving!

The figure stopped, almost right in front of her. He was a big man, with short, curly, light-brown hair, wide shoulders, a rugby shirt and a thick neck. He turned, placed his palms on the old stone railing and looked out at the ritual occurring on the floor below.

No, don't stop here! Keep walking!

But it was clear that he was settled, absorbed now in the proceedings, perhaps wondering what he needed to do in order to become one of Cessair's super soldiers. If Ricky tried to continue to the left, there was a good chance that he would see her. Although the shadow and the angle provided sufficient cover from the eyes of those below, Thick Neck would have no trouble seeing movement in the dark only a few yards away.

Yet, she *had* to move. Everything depended on her getting to the shotgun in time. This was the one chance they would have against Cessair. If she discovered the ruse and succeeded in transforming her chosen ones, there was no hope.

The one positive was that Cessair seemed in no hurry to finish, drawing out every ritual and playing to the crowd, her eyes glowing feverishly.

Even so, the end of the ceremony was moments away. A lot depended on Thick Neck's peripheral vision and how vested he was in the ceremony. Ricky drew in a breath and edged around the vertical beam, then along the stone wall, picking up her feet carefully to avoid making any sound, moving slowly yet continuously.

She realized Thick Neck was not focused on the ritual. His body language betrayed him: scratching his head, occasionally looking toward the hole in the east wall where the sound of waves carried above the cliff, shifting his weight. None of it mattered.

She had to keep going. Thick Neck had to keep watching the ceremony. The world depended on it.

Ricky stopped suddenly. Thick Neck had straightened, taken his hands off the railing, the muscles in his neck and shoulders suddenly taut.

He sees something. But what?

His back was still to her, but his head was turned just slightly to the right. He took a step. And then she saw what he saw.

The empty space next to Crockett.

In a liquid motion, Thick Neck swept his pistol from the body holster into his hand and began to survey the balcony to his right. He moved quickly, and in seconds, he would swing around in Ricky's direction. She lurched behind the next vertical timber—a fraction of a second before Thick Neck's laser gaze arrived. Yet, something made him suspicious. Perhaps it was a gut feeling. Perhaps he had heard something—a hurried breath.

He took a step in her direction. She could hear him moving even though the width of the timber kept her from seeing.

No! No! If he sees me, it's all over!

And she could hear Cessair's voice rising from below. She was approaching the final part of the ritual.

Ricky was out of time.

CHAPTER 53

"Come out here," said Thick Neck evenly but quietly.

Ricky said nothing. She considered making a run for it. She was not so much afraid of being shot as she was of being chased down. Thick Neck was clearly stronger than she was, and she guessed guys in his line of work were not hired if they were slow. A shot would disrupt the ceremony, and he would not want to risk Cessair's wrath. However, he would most certainly catch her. And then it would be over.

But she had to try.

"I'm unarmed!"

She edged out from behind the timber. Thick Neck kept the gun level on her.

"I'm unarmed!" she repeated. Then, as he took a step toward her, she dashed off, trying to use the element of surprise to gain the half-second that she hoped might make the difference. Thick Neck burst into a sprint almost immediately, and he was even faster than she had feared. Ricky only reached the corner of the west balcony before she was roughly tackled, bouncing off the stone floor painfully and coming to rest face down. Thick Neck twisted an arm behind her and drove a knee into her back. Although she could not see the main floor, she could hear Cessair speaking the final words of the ceremony.

No!

"Let our lives follow the light!"

Ricky closed her eye, but only for an instant, for at the word "light," a shot boomed from the west balcony, and she felt Thick Neck's weight slide off her. She scrambled to her feet, trying to process what had happened. Halfway along the west balcony, a man stood partly in the shadows, holding Ricky's borrowed shotgun, its smoking muzzle now pointed at the floor. She looked through the balusters and saw that, as Crockett had predicted, every head on the lower floor had turned toward the noise, even Cessair, who seemed as shocked and confused as any of them.

Crockett must have gotten free! But when she looked across the space, he still sat tied to the chair. Her gaze swung back toward the man who had fired the gun, and when he stepped into the light, she found herself as amazed as Cessair and her minions.

It was Leo Brenner.

"Holy Mother of God!"

The exclamation from Crockett echoed throughout the hall as he stared across the expanse at Brenner. Ricky scooped Thick Neck's pistol and took a step toward Brenner before stopping, her attention arrested by what was happening down on the floor. Cessair's chosen ones seemed even more disoriented than the circumstances warranted. Their eyes traveled around the hall, not focusing on anything in particular, as if they had suddenly grown anxious or uncomfortable. The fifty seemed to grow paler as Ricky watched, and now some raised their hands toward their faces, fearful, confused.

Through it all, Cessair's gaze was fixed on Brenner, though Ricky could not tell whether the fire in her eyes was fueled by hatred or passion. Perhaps a smile even teased her lips.

The transformation of the minions continued, accelerating. Their hair fell to their shoulders and then the floor; skin became translucent so that a lacework of pink and blue shone through; the eyes sunk deep into each skull; blood began to trickle from noses, ears, fingernails.

And then, one by one, each collapsed onto the stone tiles, eyes open, motionless.

Ricky ran to Brenner. "My God, Leo, I thought you were dead!"

"Nothing that some minor surgery, a few bandages, and a boatload of opioids couldn't fix," said Brenner. Ricky could now see that his entire torso was thickly wrapped beneath a loose-fitting shirt only partially buttoned, and he appeared more wan and winded than usual. "Lots of stitches, mostly. Had to put me out to pull out a couple bullets. They kept me two days and then I bolted. Tracking down you two was the hard part. Been in Ireland a day and a half. Come on, let's get Crockett!"

They headed back around the balcony, moving slowly. Brenner grimaced with each step, favoring his left leg.

"You okay?"

"Fit as a fiddle," replied Brenner, gritting his teeth through part of the response. "Just a little stiff from the tussle we had with Cessair's guards at the front door."

"We?"

"Brought some hired men with me," said Brenner. "We quietly took out the watchmen. But I wanted to see what we were up against before we charged inside. And I wanted to make sure we wouldn't be putting you two in greater danger. Told them to wait until they heard shooting, so our guys should be taking out the rest of Cessair's goons about now. What the hell is going on down there?" He gestured toward the floor.

"Immortality ritual. You just sent fifty of Cessair's devils straight to hell! Come on!"

She skirted the corner and led Brenner toward the east balcony where Crockett still sat tied to his chair. Gunfire echoed in other parts of the abbey and from outside.

"Let's hope my guys are good shots," said Brenner, struggling to keep up. "I'd hate to let you two down a second time."

"Leo, I—"

"Don't say anything," he said breathlessly with a wave of his hand. "I don't have any excuses. And I don't deserve your forgiveness."

"You saved our lives," protested Ricky. "First back in the tunnels beneath the train station. And now here!"

Brenner shook his head. "And left you to die in a desert grave before that. I can never fully earn back what I lost with that betrayal, but you're both here because of the HARP Foundation. I need to get you home!"

They rounded the last corner and moved toward Crockett, who fidgeted in his chair as if it were on fire.

"Come on! Hurry! What the hell, Leo!"

They arrived at the chair, Brenner sweating with the exertion. "You'd better undo his ropes. I'm not so good at bending right now."

"What the hell, Leo!" repeated Crockett as Ricky knelt to the task.

"It's good to see you, too."

"You're not dead!"

"Not yet."

"How's Doc?" asked Crockett.

"Believe it or not, sitting outside near a rented van a few

hundred meters down the dirt road," said Brenner, smiling. "He's all busted up but said he wasn't going to miss this for anything. Right now he's learning all about the Eye of God from a friend of yours we ran into on our way in, Ricky, a Brian McIntyre. I don't think Tom's ever had an adventure like this before. And Brian is quite a character."

"I don't think *anybody* has had an adventure like this before," said Crockett as the last of the ropes fell away and he bounced up from the chair. "How did you find us?"

"I don't know if we would have ever found you," said Leo. "But then, around sunrise this morning, Tom received a text message from Ricky telling him that Cessair was at An Tsuil."

Ricky almost laughed. "I thought Dr. Campion was probably in a hospital in Germany."

Leo nodded in understanding. "Once we went online and learned what An Tsuil was and where it was located, we rallied the troops."

"Thank God for Wikipedia." Crockett let his gaze wander to the grim scene on the floor below. "Looks like all of the disciples have found their way to hell. If we hurry, maybe we can still find Cessair!"

"Oh, I don't think there'll be any need to hurry," said a voice from the direction in which they had come. They spun around and saw that Cessair had turned the corner and was now approaching them along the east balcony, a pistol trained on them. "Drop your weapons."

"You're beaten Cessair!" said Crockett as she drew to within a dozen feet. "Your army is gone. You're mortal now, and we outnumber you."

"Mr. Crockett," said Cessair, shaking her head ruefully. "So many false assumptions, so little time. Five thousand years from now, I'll smile at this quaint memory."

"Five thousand years from now, you'll be dust," said Crockett. "At sunrise, you'll be following your minions to hell."

Cessair uttered a deliciously mischievous chuckle. "Did you really think you could defeat me so easily?"

"Shoot her, Leo, or I will," said Ricky bitterly.

"Yes, Leo. Shoot me!"

Ricky turned to Crockett. "What's going on here? She should be mortal."

"Unless…" Crockett stopped himself, thinking it through.

"Unless what?" asked Brenner.

Crockett's eyes met Cessair's. "Unless Cessair's name wasn't on the clay tablet."

Ricky shook her head, addressed Cessair. "That doesn't make any sense. The correct ritual would have made your immortality permanent."

Brenner's mouth dropped open as an idea occurred to him. "As someone who's felt Cessair's betrayal twice already, I think I'm getting the idea. Maybe Cessair never intended to make the fifty chosen ones immortal."

Ricky felt her hatred growing again as the realization hit home. "That's it, isn't it? Killing them was your plan all along. Leo didn't have to fire that shot! You knew what you were doing. You were going to turn to the west all along!"

Cessair smiled bitterly. "Bravo, to all of you. Did you really think your scroll trick fooled me? A clever forgery, however it was done. Nonetheless, it served its purpose."

"Purpose?" echoed Ricky. "What purpose is there in killing fifty of your own people?"

Brenner was ready with an answer. "Let me guess. To send a message. These fifty were Cessair's best and brightest, her most ambitious. And consequently, her most dangerous. The fifty most likely to set their eyes on the crown once *they* had achieved immortality. Oh, Cessair will eventually create her army of immortals, but first she needed to send the message to remind her followers who was in charge, and just how far she was willing to go to drive that point home."

Ricky's face contorted in disgust. "All captured on video, ready to go viral on social media, the ultimate incentive to remain loyal stooges."

"*My* ceremony will come in a few minutes," noted Cessair. But then glancing at the chaos below between her men and Brenner's, added, "or perhaps a little longer. The proper ceremony, of course. It's why I moved the two of you to the east side of the balcony. After witnessing the end that was in store for you, then you would be able to see *my* moment of eternal triumph!"

Crockett stared at her coldly, rubbing his wrists. "Sorry to rain on your parade, but you need the real deal to complete your immortality ritual. All you've got is the bogus scroll."

"Wrong again, Mr. Crockett," said Cessair almost gleefully. "Once I realized that the scroll you had been carrying was a decoy, I sent my men back to your car to search it. The real scroll is right here!" She patted the smooth, white fashion bag resting against her side.

Brenner shook his head. "So in the end, you stab your faithful in the back. Their sacrifices betrayed. No one gets immortality except Cessair."

"Not so, Leo. Once I've used the scroll to move beyond the grasp of God, then I *will* confer immortality upon a carefully chosen group—a group chosen for its single-minded loyalty rather than its ambition. Of course, your little intervention here has posed a temporary setback. I'll need to regroup, but that should take no more than a few days. So all of your efforts really have had very little effect on the overall. I am not beaten. I am not mortal. Of course, it is true that you outnumber me, so I suppose I should do something about that."

In a smooth, rapid motion, Cessair leveled her gun at Ricky and fired. Ricky lurched violently backward, over the stone railing and fell. Blackness enveloped her even before she slammed into the chapel floor below.

CHAPTER 54

Cessair swung her gun around to Brenner.

The echoes of the gunshot and Crockett's cry of startle reverberated off the walls.

"You crazy bitch!"

"Move an inch toward me and I'll put a bullet in your boss," said Cessair with a cruel smirk. "Even though he traded your life away once, I know you still feel a sort of loyalty toward him— however misguided."

"My God, Cessair!" said Brenner, stunned by what had happened, his eyes moving back and forth between the gun and the railing over which Ricky had disappeared—as if hoping that it was all a mistake, that she would come climbing back over it again.

"Yes," said Cessair coolly. "*Your* God. Not mine. Now, Leo, use the rope to re-tie Mr. Crockett's hands. Behind him, if you will. And Mr. Crockett, if you don't let him, I'll shoot him and then you."

Crockett could hardly speak, his face a mask of unbridled rage. "You're going to kill us both anyway!"

"Perhaps not," said Cessair as Brenner struggled to retrieve the rope and began to bind Crockett's wrists. "As I mentioned before,

I'm in need of new soldiers. I doubt that you'll be running to enlist, Mr. Crockett. But Leo, I think you might have some potential."

"Go to hell, Cessair!" barked Brenner.

Cessair made a face pretending to be insulted. "Really, now, Leo, weren't we good together? We can be again, for all eternity! I need an army, but I need a general, too! Someone who is strong, intelligent! Someone to bring order to a broken world! You won't be destroying the world, Leo! You'll be saving it! Hasn't that been your passion with the HARP Foundation all these years?"

"Don't listen to that crap!" spat Crockett.

"And the rewards, Leo, the rewards will be immense! To live like a king! And to *play* like one!" She narrowed her eyes at him conspiratorially. "How long does passion last, Leo? The intense heat of physical love? A handful of decades? Yes. Only as long as the body lasts, until men and women crumble back into the dust from whence they sprang. But for us, Leo...a fire that burns brighter, hotter, forever!"

Brenner finished off the knot, and Crockett could see his eyes darting askance as if he were considering his options.

"Leo!"

After a moment, he addressed Cessair. "There would have to be some conditions. There are certain people whose safety I would want guaranteed."

Cessair's eyes widened and seemed to burn with increased intensity, partly, it seemed, out of physical desire, and partly because she could sense the victory of her will over Brenner's.

"Of course." Then her expression hardened. "But not Mr. Crockett! He has proven himself an enemy, and his fate will be the same as Miss Crowe's!"

"Cessair, no!" cried Brenner.

"You have your conditions, and I have mine! Bring our friend over to the edge! Let him admire the view!"

Crockett's face drained of color. "Leo, no! You can't do this!"

Avoiding Crockett's frantic gaze, Brenner latched onto his left arm and dragged him roughly toward the spot where the wall had fallen away. The space was at least a dozen feet wide, and below, a rim of rubble after which the steep cliff dropped away to the rocky inlet far below.

"Jesus, Leo!"

"Do you think I want to do this?" Brenner said suddenly, his voice gruff, hoarse. "Do you think I'd choose this if there was another way? At least this way, I can make sure some are saved. And maybe I can have some influence in Cessair's new world."

Cessair laughed. "You're going to be a general, Leo, not a politician."

"God, Leo, no!"

The view from the edge was dizzying.

"I've got to do what I've got to do," said Leo, suddenly swinging Crockett toward him and looking directly into his eyes. This time, his voice was a whisper. "When you get a chance, you've got to take it!"

CHAPTER 55

Ricky's right eye fluttered open and the world began to return to her. At first, she felt confused. Then the pain helped her remember. And the distant shouting and gunshots.

She recalled the flash of the gun, and then falling.

Lying on her back, she tried to focus on the balcony, perhaps a dozen feet above. Her back and shoulders ached, but this was nothing compared to the pain on the left side of her rib cage.

That must be where the bullet hit.

But it had not killed her. Contemplating this would have to wait. Leo and Crockett were in danger.

Cessair.

They had to stop her. But guns would not do it. Cessair was immortal, had lived for five thousand years. And now it looked like she would live for five thousand more, terrorizing the world. Her Chosen Ones were all dead. But Ricky knew that Cessair would have no trouble attracting legions of unquestioning, ruthless followers. Pity, she thought, that Cessair's own name had not been on the clay tablet.

As she struggled to sit up, voices from above caught her attention. Cessair, her voice rising in excitement, trying to persuade Leo.

"I need an army, but I need a general, too! Someone who is strong, intelligent! Someone to bring order to a broken world! You won't be destroying the world, Leo! You'll be saving it!"

Leo had been weak once. Would Cessair win him over a second time?

Ricky had difficulty getting her legs under her. Finally, she rolled over onto her stomach, pushed herself onto her hands and knees. Bringing her left hand up to her ribcage, she found the bullet hole in her shirt, probed the skin beneath and found the entrance hole. When she drew forth her fingers, there was blood on her fingertips, yet it did not seem to be flowing from the wound.

That's good, right?

As she brought one leg up, she spotted the clay tablet on the makeshift altar at the front of the room only a few feet away, where Cessair had left it. Suddenly, Ricky pawed her pocket, brought out the paper upon which Luja had written the English translation of the ritual. She glanced toward the balcony and then stumbled against the altar, picking up the stiletto that Cessair had used to cross off names. Ricky first used it to scratch Cessair's name into the clay. Then she scraped a line through the name.

Earth.

"God, Leo, no!" Crockett's voice, and he sounded terrified. She had to hurry.

The small vessel containing the poison also sat on the altar.

Water.

She still needed to get Cessair to drink the poison. Or to inhale it. Or even to splash it on her so that it was absorbed through her skin. But how? Then she noticed the nearly full champagne bottle sitting next to a fallen minion just a few feet away. She scrambled to it, looked to the balcony again, and cried out, "Cessair!"

CHAPTER 56

"Are you afraid, Mr. Crockett?" asked Cessair. "I was hoping you would be. An awful way to die, don't you think? First, the terror inspired by the awful height, like looking your death in the face! Then, the heart-freezing fear that accompanies the knowledge that this is really happening, that there is nothing that you can do to forestall it, that in mere moments, you will truly and forever cease to exist! And finally, the horror of actually falling, a four-second plunge that, for you, will seem to transpire in slow motion, terminating in a moment of exquisite pain!"

Crockett slowly brought his eyes around to take in the full view. Though dusk, the sight was no less thrilling and terrible. After a moment, however, he broke into a laugh, loud and maniacal.

"You think you've won?" cried Crockett shrilly. "You've lost! Everything! At least I'll die human!"

"The point is, Mr. Crockett, you *will* die."

"But you'll always be a monster!" cried Crockett hoarsely. "You lost your humanity five thousand years ago! You're no longer one of us! You can fight us, try to enslave us, but you'll always be the monster, isolated by the ugliness of your power! I'd tell you to

438

burn in hell, but your hell will be right here, surrounded by the burning hatred of the billions who will resent every breath you draw!"

Cessair smiled grimly. "Your words might have stung five thousand years ago, Mr. Crockett. But after fifty centuries, I've discovered that I don't need the love or approval of people anymore. I love the power. As you say, I love *being* the monster!"

Crockett returned her grim smile. "I think it stings more than you'll ever admit!"

Cessair stepped forward, still smiling and slapped Crockett across the face with her pistol. As he recoiled from the pain and shock, she grabbed his hair, leaned in and kissed him on the mouth, slid to his right ear and bit. Crockett screamed and twisted his head, but Cessair gripped even tighter, twisting her neck deftly, and came away with part of the earlobe in her mouth, a trickle of blood curling down her own chin.

"Goddamn!" cried Crockett who, despite his pain, seemed to detect a tightening of Brenner's grip during the event, as if he had been afraid that Crockett might fall.

Cessair chewed for a few moments as if savoring it, and then swallowed. "I think that stings more than *you'll* ever admit!" she said, her eyes now more wickedly feverish than ever. Then, a cry from the hall below echoed off the walls.

"Cessair!"

Cessair turned toward the sound. Brenner's eyes widened, and he pulled Crockett back an inch or two from the brink.

"Ricky?" cried Crockett, his breath coming in short gasps. "Ricky!"

Cessair's face darkened as she looked over the railing. "You *can't* be—" Then she stopped, as a spray of champagne splattered across her face and down the front of her dress. When she opened her eyes, her first sight was Ricky holding the now gently foaming bottle, shouting, "Let our lives follow the light!"

Wind.

Then she spun to the west.

Fire.

Instantly, Cessair needed to steady herself. "What—?" Her face seemed to lose its warm coloring and grow pale. "What—?" she repeated.

Akash. Spirit. Magic. The power of the eternal.

Ricky's voice called out from below. "She's mortal! I did the ritual! I mixed the poison into the champagne, shook it up! She's mortal!"

Brenner pulled Crockett back from the edge another step. "It's over, Cessair!" said Brenner. "All of it! Put down the gun and stop this!"

Cessair appeared stricken, the enormity of it all crashing down upon her. Five thousand years of searching and planning, all of it for nothing. And by sunrise, she would be dead—no longer separated from God, face-to-face with her Maker to answer for fifty centuries of unapologetic sin.

She lowered the pistol. Crockett took another careful step away from the abyss. Brenner reached out toward Cessair to take the pistol. Then, from her right came the sound of footsteps and Ricky appeared through the shadows, running toward them. Cessair's features hardened again and she raised the gun toward Brenner, who stopped and backed away a step.

"You took everything from me!" hissed Cessair, her eyes burning holes in Ricky, who had skidded to a stop. "Allow me to return the favor!"

She fired, and Brenner went down to his hands and knees heavily. Ricky cried out but remained rooted to the spot, stunned into inaction. "But you," said Cessair, turning her attention on Crockett, "you, my friend are not going to get an easy bullet!" She rushed forward, hands out, her face afire with hatred. The motion was so quick that Crockett could not move to either side to avoid her, nor could he use his hands to stop her, since they were still tied behind him. In an instant, she would send him hurtling over the edge. Yet, as quick as Cessair was, something else was quicker. Ricky merely saw a dark blur and realized that Brenner had lurched up from the floor, intercepting Cessair inches before she reached Crockett. The two bodies that had once greedily clutched each other in ecstasy thudded heavily off the stone floor and then plunged over the broken edge.

"Leo!" screamed Crockett.

Ricky rushed forward, put a steadying arm on Crockett's shoulder as they stared fearfully down the terrible cliffs. In the dimming light they could see the two figures, clinging to irregularities in a severely angled stone slab about fifteen feet below, Brenner a few feet beneath Cessair.

"Leo!" called Crockett. "Hold on!" Then to Ricky: "Untie these!" He turned to expose the ropes, and in a few moments, Ricky had them undone.

"I—I think my back is broken," said Brenner. "I can move my arms, but I can't feel my legs. Nothing!"

"Shit!" said Crockett. "We've got to find a rope." He started gathering the short lengths used to tie up himself and Ricky.

"I've—I've lost a lot of blood," said Brenner. "I—"

Cessair laughed. "Poor Leo!" she said with a bitter smile. "This is what happens when you choose the wrong team! My legs work just fine, and it appears that I just might be able to reach that ledge above that will allow me to climb to the abbey's north lawn. I've got both scrolls, so I'll repeat the immortality ritual on myself, gather more Alchemy sheep, and in a few days, it will be as if you had never interfered."

Ricky could see that she was right. No one stood in her way on the north lawn. She could easily slip into the dusky woods, disappear, regroup. They had won a meaningless battle. Cessair would win the war for the soul of the planet now that she had both scrolls.

"How awful it must be, knowing that you will die, Leo! Knowing that nothing you did mattered at all! Knowing that you could have changed the world, but let it instead slip through your fingers because you were weak and afraid!"

With another wild laugh, she found a higher foothold and began to pull herself up. However, Brenner thrust one hand upward desperately and latched onto her left ankle.

"Let go you fool!" cried Cessair hoarsely.

Brenner responded by letting go of his handhold on the stone slab and grabbing Cessair's left ankle with his other hand as well, so that his entire weight was now supported by her.

"Let go!" cried Cessair, frantic now.

"I'm going to take your advice, Cessair," said Brenner wearily. "I'm no longer afraid! This time, I'm not going to let it slip through my fingers."

Cessair cried out, her face twisted and horrible. "Let go! I can't hold us both!"

"Are you afraid, Cessair?" asked Brenner, calmly. "I was hoping you would be. First, the terror of the awful height, like looking death in the face! Then, the heart-freezing fear that there is nothing you can do! And finally, the horror of actually falling, a four-second plunge in slow motion, terminating in a moment of exquisite pain!"

Cessair screamed, her face ugly with a kind of terror she had never known through fifty centuries. And then her fingers lost their grip, scrabbled for purchase on the smooth rock, found none, and they slid, picking up speed, disappearing over the edge in a horrifying shriek.

Ricky looked away and wept, clinging to Crockett, and she felt him shake too. She wept for Leo, for Bash, for her sister, for Neve. And she wept in relief. The tears flowed and she shook, great wracking sobs. They stood like that for several minutes. Finally she turned back, looked up into Crockett's face, and frowned through her tears.

"What the hell happened to your ear?"

CHAPTER 57

No college brochure he had ever seen had promised excitement, world travel, derring-do, and near-death adventures to those who pursued the study of climate science, and Mason Crockett reflected that, in light of what he had been through the past few weeks, he was glad that his chosen vocation was usually quite dull. In fact, he thought it might be appropriate to make a celebration of the dullness of his life, now that things were starting to quiet down.

Naturally, they would never be altogether the same. With Leo's death, the board of directors had chosen Sanderson to head the HARP Foundation. Sanderson was all right, though perhaps the most boring speaker Crockett had ever listened to. A thirty-minute meeting with Sanderson would seem to take two hours.

And Bash was gone. So was Sasha. They might never know for certain what had happened to her, but it was widely believed that she had been on the plane that had gone down near Zackenberg.

Who knows? thought Crockett with a bittersweet smile. Sasha had been feisty enough that she just might have had something to do with bringing down the plane. He liked to think that.

The FBI had seized control of Cessair's—or Rio Armstrong's

—assets. Both they and Interpol now classified Alchemy as a terrorist organization. The newspapers had mentioned the group's interest in the occult, the desecration of tombs in Memphis and at Newgrange, plus the bizarre ritual at the abbey. Coverage largely brushed the rituals off as the beliefs of extremist nutjobs who had chemically mutilated the corpses of those they had murdered at the abbey. No one gave any credence to the notion that a person could really live forever.

He had not returned to work at HARP yet. That would come on Monday, in two more days. Tonight, he would sit at home, drink a beer or two, and watch *Casablanca*. A quiet night with Bogie, Bergie and brew. Did it get any better?

The buzzer rang and he was surprised to find Ricky at the entrance carrying a canvas book bag. It had been two weeks since he had seen her, after their last interview with the feds. She wore dark jeans and a dark-green kaftan with a silver Celtic design around the neck. A black patch covered her damaged eye.

Stepping inside, she pointed to her own ear, but her meaning was clear. "How's it healing?" An irregular scar marked the place where Cessair had mutilated Crockett.

"Not bad. They said they could do some grafts, make it look almost as good as new, but I told them I'd have to think about it. This way, I can tell people I lost it in a knife fight. Chicks dig that sort of thing."

Ricky shook her head. "Still an asshole."

"What about you?" asked Crockett.

"Yeah, I'm still an asshole, too."

"No, I mean, how are you doing?" He gestured vaguely toward her left side.

"Fine. I guess the bullet must have missed all the important shit. Lucky, I guess. But I wanted to say thanks."

"For?"

"What the hell do you think? I wouldn't be here right now if not for you."

"Are you kidding?" said Crockett, offering her a seat at the kitchen counter. "I think you saved my life at least twice. I should be thanking you! I should be *worshipping* you!"

She smiled. "To be honest, neither of us would be here if not for Leo. He was hard to figure, I think. I mean, in the end, he was on our side, right?"

Crockett did not answer for a few moments. Then he said, "I think he was trying to buy time, to make Cessair think he was considering her offer. When we were standing on the edge of that cliff, he said something to me. Looked me right in the eye and said it in a way that sounded kind of odd at the time. He said, 'I've got to do what I've got to do. When you get a chance, you've got to take it!' I thought at the time that he was talking about selling his soul to Cessair. As it turns out, he was letting me know that, when the time was right to move against Cessair, he *would* do something. And he did. He took Cessair off the cliff. Saved my life. Probably saved us all."

Neither said anything for a minute. Then Ricky spoke. "The scrolls went with them."

They were silent again for a bit before Crockett spoke.

"I'm still not saying I believe all of this Noah's Ark stuff, but it sure does make you wonder what the look on Cessair's face would be if she has to stand and explain this to the Almighty! I'd kind of like to be there for that." Then he added quickly, "Figuratively speaking of course."

Ricky nodded. "She got what she deserved."

"Maybe," said Crockett. "Maybe the worst punishment of all for Cessair would have been success."

"I don't follow."

"Have you ever thought about it? Real immortality? Forever? Watching everyone around you die. Over and over again, for centuries. Millennia. Cessair was here for only five thousand years. What would one hundred thousand be like? Could the human mind withstand it? Or a million? Ten million? And in a hundred million years, when the planet is swallowed by the expanding sun, what then? Still alive! But there's nothing? After a trillion years, the last star burns out. But you're alive. Your mind still working for another trillion. And a trillion after that. Levels of madness and suffering that we can't even begin to imagine. One might argue that God was merciful to Cessair and her followers by setting them on a path that led to failure. How awful it would be to be truly immortal."

Crockett was surprised to see that a tear had trickled down Ricky's cheek.

"You okay?" asked Crockett.

Ricky nodded.

Crockett moved to the refrigerator, removed a bottle. "That's about as philosophical as anybody has ever gotten in this kitchen, and way too philosophical for a Saturday night in July. That's more like January talk, you know? The sort of thing people do in front of a fire when it's too cold to move."

Ricky nodded.

"But there's a cure for that," Crockett continued, placing a Coca-Cola in front of her.

"Thanks," she said, popping the top of the can and taking a sip. "By the way, I brought a present for you." She reached down into the book bag and brought out something wrapped in red, metallic paper.

"A present?" He accepted the gift, placed it on the counter.

"Should I open it now?"

Ricky nodded. He ripped into it, deftly slid out a black Lynyrd Skynyrd Free Bird t-shirt.

"It was Sasha's," said Ricky.

Crockett seemed momentarily stunned, "I don't know what to say. I guess I made more of an impression than I thought. His eyes traveled from the t-shirt to Ricky. "You know, this might be the right time for you to give *Casablanca* a whirl."

Ricky shrugged.

Crockett smiled, grabbed the remote. "Miss Crowe, this may be the start of a beautiful friendship."

Ricky grimaced. "I should have let you die."

"You'd never have done that," said Crockett. "Besides, I was pretty sure I was going to be all right."

"What do you mean?"

"Well, you mentioned that the legend said Fintan Mac turned himself into a salmon to escape from Cessair."

"So?"

Crockett grinned. "I'm a Pisces. Coincidence? I think not."

She curled her lip in faux revulsion. "I *definitely* should have let you die."

CHAPTER 58

After *Casablanca*, Crockett had put on *Notorious*. "I've always been a sucker for Ingrid Bergman," he had confessed. However, during the second feature, he had fallen asleep before the halfway point. Crockett sat slumped against the plump end cushions of the sofa, breathing deeply, while Ricky reclined against him, her head resting against his midsection.

She was wide awake. Thinking.

Thinking about what a mistake this was. She could not get involved in a relationship. Not a romantic one.

It was true that she was attracted to Crockett. That had not been the case at first, but what she had seen in him during their time together had changed everything. Every time she had thought of him in the past two weeks, she had wanted to call or hop on the bus, just to be with him, to see his smile, hear his voice.

Yes, his voice, hick accent and all.

She wanted to be close to him, closer than she had ever allowed herself to be with anyone, emotionally, physically, spiritually.

And she could tell that Crockett felt the same. Something in his eyes, every time he looked at her.

Every time.

The way he had held her on the ledge at the abbey. His arm around her shoulder in the van. How he had never left her side the entire trip home.

Her protector.

She smiled at the irony. She had hardly needed his protection when they traveled to Egypt. And she definitely did not need it anymore. If only she could go back in time and change what she had done. But that was impossible.

Luja had sensed it when Ricky had walked into her shop that afternoon, just a day after the talented spiritualist had interpreted the scroll for them. Luja had sensed the change—and the unnaturalness of it.

Is there any way to undo this? And survive?

None that I can see.

Ricky listened to Crockett's steady breathing for a few minutes, the room's only light supplied by the frozen movie menu on the TV screen.

If only she had trusted Luja. But Ricky was a skeptic. She had needed to know. Going after Cessair had, at the time, sounded like a suicide mission. The only way such a risk might be justified, was if the scroll was genuine. If it could truly make someone immortal. Both she and Crockett had entertained the notion that Leo might have somehow been tricked into believing that Rio was Cessair. And so that morning in Ireland, while Crockett had slept, she had performed the immortality ritual on herself.

Perhaps it had been the right thing. Would she have been brave enough to climb the cliffs otherwise? And she certainly would not have survived being shot by Cessair.

"I don't know how, but the bullet must have missed everything," the doctor examining her had said. "Looks like it went right through," he had added, marveling at how little blood she seemed to have lost and how well the entrance and exit wounds appeared to be healing already.

And if she had not survived the gunshot and the fall, Cessair would still be immortal and poised to take over the world, while she, Leo and Crockett would all be dead.

Yet, Ricky knew she had paid a dear price for the knowledge that they were not merely pursuing crackpots on some wild goose chase. The eternity scenario Crockett had described earlier in the evening had frightened her to the bone, though she had already imagined it a dozen times. Yet, so did the alternative: If she went through the death ritual, she would become mortal once again, but would die horribly when the sun rose.

How much courage would it take for someone in perfect health to take that step, to perform a ritual that would lead to their own death? She did not know whether she would ever be able to. Or perhaps it would take centuries before she would find her life to be... so unbearable.

It terrified her. All of it. But most of all, the thought of losing more people she really cared for. Or having to suddenly disappear from their lives when they reached the age of forty, fifty, sixty, while Ricky remained forever in her twenties. Disappearing over and over again. She would shred their hearts as well as her own. It might not have mattered to Cessair, but it mattered to her.

And so she would have to avoid intimate friendships, romantic entanglements. Tonight had been wonderful, just *being* with someone, but it had also been a moment of weakness, something she knew she should have avoided. No matter how she longed for something more with Crockett, to feel his arms around her, to stare into his eyes, knowing that she and he were connected in a way that transcended the mere physical, she knew that despite all of these things, it would be cruel to yield to any of these temptations.

Cruel to both of them.

Where I'm going, you can't follow. What I've got to do, you can't be any part of. Bogie's farewell speech in *Casablanca* haunted her. *Someday you'll understand that. Here's looking at you, kid.*

And so she carefully sat up. Crockett still breathed deeply, lost in slumber. Stealthily, she moved into the kitchen where she retrieved her bag. Then, with a final look at the beautiful sleeping soul on the sofa with whom she had shared so much, she slipped noiselessly out the door, down the stairs, and into the warm Chicago night.

THE END

AUTHOR NOTES

While a few of the locales in *The Book of Invasions* may seem right out of some game programmer's imagination, most of them really do exist. First on the list is ZERO Station. Yup, a real place, where students and researchers gather to study the climate and the fragile ecosystem in northeastern Greenland. It was great fun chatting with the actual staff in order to get a feel for the place. Yeah, I would have loved to visit in person, but a trip to Greenland was not exactly in the budget. What struck me as particularly interesting was the fact that in this frigid and hostile environment, the buildings were constructed so that they stood on supports a foot or two off the ground in order to provide the constant air movement that kept mold and rot at bay. That also gave me a perfect temporary hiding (and listening) place for Sasha, the ill-fated hero of chapter one.

I was also struck by ZERO Station's isolation. In many TV shows and films set in contemporary times, the protagonist is kept from summoning help because he can't get cell service. This often strikes me as a bit too convenient and even unlikely, unless the protagonist is hiking deep in the Bob Marshall Wilderness in Montana. However, at Zackenberg, communication really is limited in the ways described. To be at a remote outpost farther north than almost any other humans on the planet is a daunting circumstance in itself. To be virtually unable to communicate with the rest of the world adds another element of unease that would frighten the hell out of a lot of people.

Moving on to warmer climes, we come to Egypt, where the Pyramid of Djoser is a real place, as are the Hotel Sofitel and the

Swiss Inn. The Hollow Tomb is an invention. However, mastabas similar to it exist.

Newgrange is also a real place, and one of the most visited tourist sites in all of Ireland. The description of it in the book is pretty accurate, except that, as far as anyone knows, there is no maze of passages beneath the mound. Then again, has anyone checked?

One significant location that does not exist is An Tsuil, the Eye of God. While there are abandoned castles, churches and monasteries in Ireland, An Tsuil is a work of fiction—but, because of its location at the edge of a cliff above the Irish Sea, a great place to have a climactic good v. evil confrontation.

Lebor Gabála Érenn, also known as The Book of Invasions, exists, an attempt to create a rollicking and entertaining mythology for Ireland similar to what the Greeks and Romans created for themselves. The tales, originating a millennium ago or longer, were the work of many storytellers, and created an enormous family tree of Celtic deities. The myth of Cessair is among them, a myth that I massaged and embellished in bringing it to the pages of this book.

While I am not a scholar of Egyptian languages, I tried to give a reasonable depiction of the difficulties associated with the translation of Archaic Egyptian glyphs. I may have taken a few liberties in order to move the story along or smooth out the narrative, and I hope these will be forgiven.

ABOUT THE AUTHOR

ROD VICK

Author Rod Vick has led an unexpectedly interesting life, winning awards in national short story writing contests, climbing a mountain in bad shoes, running the Boston Marathon, battling a Coca-cola addiction, being chosen Wisconsin State Teacher of the Year, sinking a 40-foot putt for bogey, and meeting the President of the United States in the Oval Office. However, it wasn't until 2006 that he made a modest mark as a novelist, after deciding to try something outside his usual adult sci-fi wheelhouse. He wrote *Kaylee's Choice*, primarily aimed at middle readers. Hoping that the self-published book about a struggling ten-year-old dancer would find an audience, he was pleasantly (and, of course, unexpectedly) surprised when it sold thousands of copies and spawned a seven-book series. It also led to several serialized novels in national magazines that were later developed into the *Dance of Time* and *Irish Witch* book series. Recently, Mr. Vick has written historical non-fiction and an adult murder whodunit series as well.

The success of his novels has led to signings across the country in cities as inviting and lovely as Orlando, Nashville, Kansas City and Minneapolis, as well as cities somewhat less inviting and lovely. When he's not writing, he runs, dotes upon his Lovely Wife Marsha, wishes for benevolent fairies to come during the night to mow the lawn, and pitches a pretty mean horseshoe. More info on his books is available at www.rodvick.com.

If You Enjoyed This Book
Visit

PENMORE PRESS
www.penmorepress.com

All Penmore Press books are available directly
through our website

The King's Corpse

By

M J Jones

Medieval Saint relics stealing.

MJ Jones brings a hilarious detective story from the Dark Ages into the light of day. Our disreputable hero following his grubby profession leads us on a merry chase around the English and Welsh countryside.

His name's Tryff, he comes from Wales, and he steals saints for a living. Used to, anyhow. But everybody in England's got to have a lord, so Tryff's become radman, mounted protection (and general dogs-body) for the abbess of a little country convent. She sends him to find the missing body of her cousin Edward, the probably murdered king of England. It's a nigh on impossible job, but he takes it because he needs the money to buy his mother out of slavery.

Tryff's confronted with a vicious royal court, a double-crossing bard, and a revolting waker-of-the-dead. They rout him completely. Now he must look for the king's body in Wales. With but three English nuns for help, Tryff sets off to track down not only the king's body but also his mother, the Great Harp of King Arthur, and love besides. island.

PENMORE PRESS
www.penmorepress.com

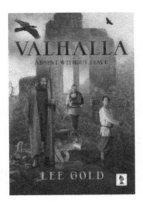

VALHALLA

Absent Without Leave
By
Lee Gold

The Age of Heroes is not done...

"An axe age, a sword age," Bookwyrm chanted. "A wind age, a wolf age."
"Brothers shall fight and slay each other," sang Knut. "Garm howls in Hel, and the wolf runs free."

Robin Johnson died a hero's death, rescuing people from a hospital during a California earthquake. So how is a hero rewarded? Robin finds herself not in Christian Heaven but in Valhalla of Norse myths, welcomed by heroes and the guardians of Asgard. But Robin had been something of an oddity in life and continues to be so in the afterlife. She's not content to spend the better part of eternity feasting and fighting and... drinking to Odin's honor. Accompanied by two fellow-heroes, a wolf, a telepathic sword and a chatty red squirrel, the renamed Robin Grima sets out to prevent Ragnarok, the doom in which nearly all the Asgardians die.

Their first quest: slay the dragon Nidhog, who gnaws away at the root of Yggdrasil, The World Tree. If they succeed in that, they can confront sea giants, hill giants, mist elves, Fenris Wolf, the Midgard Serpent, and Hel, corpsequeen of the dead. But the only way to really stop Ragnarok is to deal, once and for all, with the mastermind of plots and Odin's foster-brother — Loki himself.

PENMORE PRESS
www.penmorepress.com

Close to the Sun
by
Donald Michael Platt

WWII Fighter pilots, Air war over Europe. German Fighter aces, American Fighter Aces, War in Europe . Air War over Russia. German politics during WWII.

Close to the Sun follows the lives of fighter pilots during the Second World War. As a boy, Hank Milroy from Wyoming idealized the gallant exploits of WWI fighter aces. Karl, Fürst von Pfalz-Teuffelreich, aspires to surpass his father's 49 Luftsiegen. Seth Braham falls in love with flying during an air show at San Francisco's Chrissy Field.
The young men encounter friends, rivals, and exceptional women. Braxton Mobley, the hotshot, wants to outscore every man in the air force. Texas tomboy Catherine "Winty" McCabe is as good a flyer as any man. Princess Maria-Xenia, a stateless White Russian, works for the Abwehr, German Intelligence. Elfriede Wohlman is a frontline nurse with a dangerous secret. Miriam Keramopoulos is the girl from Brooklyn with a voice that will take her places.

Once the United States enter the war, Hank, Brax, and Seth experience the exhilaration of aerial combat and acedom during the unromantic reality of combat losses, tedious bomber escort, strafing runs, and the firebombing of entire cities. As one of the hated aristocrats, Karl is in as much danger from Nazis as he is from enemy fighter pilots, as he and his colleagues desperately try to stem the overwhelming tide as the war turns against Germany. Callous political decisions, disastrous mistakes, and horrific atrocities they witness at the end of WWII put a dark spin on all their dreams of glory.

PENMORE PRESS
www.penmorepress.com

Historical fiction and nonfiction
Paperback available for order on line
and as Ebook with all major distributers

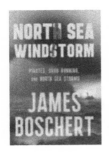

North Sea Wind Storm
by
James Boschert

Considering that oil and gas have been flowing from under the North Sea for the best part of half a century, it is perhaps surprising that more writers have not taken the uncompromising conditions that are experienced in this area – which extends from the north of Scotland to the coasts of Norway and Germany – for the setting of a novel. James Boschert's latest redresses the balance.

The book takes its title from the name of an area regularly referred to in the legendary BBC Shipping Forecast, one which experiences some of the worst weather conditions around the British Isles. It is a fast-paced story which smacks of authenticity in every line. A world of hard men, hard liquor, hard drugs and cold-blooded murder. The reality of the setting and the characters, ex-military men from both sides of the Atlantic, crooked wheeler-dealers, and Danish detectives, male and female, are all in on the action.

This is not story telling akin to a latter day Bulldog Drummond, nor a James Bond, but simply a snortingly good yarn which will jangle the nerve ends, fill your nose with the smell of salt and diesel oil, your ears with the deafening sound of machinery aboard a monster pipe-dredging ship and, above all, make you remember never to underestimate the power of the sea.

–Roger Paine, former Commander, Royal Navy .

PENMORE PRESS
www.penmorepress.com

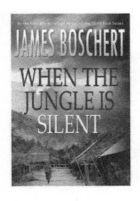

When the Jungle Is Silent

by

James Boschert

Set in Borneo during a little known war known as "the Confrontation," this story tells of the British soldiers who fought in one of the densest jungles in the world.

Jason, a young soldier of the Light Infantry who is good with guns, is stationed in Penang, an idyllic island off the coast of Malaysia. He is living aimlessly in paradise until he meets Megan, a bright and intelligent young American from the Peace Corps. Megan challenges his complacent existence and a romance develops, but then the regiment is sent off to Borneo.

After a dismal shipping upriver, the regiment arrives in Kuching, the capital of Sarawak. Jason is moved up to Padawan, close to local populations of Ibans and Dyak headhunters, and right in the path of the Indonesian offensive. Fighting erupts along the border of Sarawak and a small fort is turned into a muddy hell from which Jason is an unlikely survivor.

An SAS Sergeant and his trackers have been drawn to the vicinity by the battle, but who will find Jason first: rescuers or hostiles? Jason is forced to wake up to the cruel harshness of real soldiering while he endeavors stay one step ahead of the Indonesians who are combing the Jungle. And the jungle itself, although neutral, is deadly enough.

PENMORE PRESS
www.penmorepress.com

Penmore Press

Challenging, Intriguing, Adventurous, Historical and Imaginative

www.penmorepress.com

CPSIA information can be obtained
at www.ICGtesting.com
Printed in the USA
LVHW110749130622
721105LV00001B/12